An Alternative History of Britain

An Alternative History of Britain

The English Civil War

Timothy Venning

Pen & Sword
MILITARY

First published in Great Britain in 2015 by
Pen & Sword Military
an imprint of
Pen & Sword Books Ltd
47 Church Street
Barnsley
South Yorkshire
S70 2AS

ISBN 978-1-47382-782-0

A CIP catalogue record for this book is available from the British Library.

Typeset in 11pt Ehrhardt by
Mac Style Ltd, Bridlington, E. Yorkshire

Printed and bound in the UK by CPI Group (UK) Ltd, Croydon, CRO 4YY

Pen & Sword Books Ltd incorporates the imprints of Pen & Sword
Archaeology, Atlas, Aviation, Battleground, Discovery, Family History,
History, Maritime, Military, Naval, Politics, Railways, Select, Transport,
True Crime, and Fiction, Frontline Books, Leo Cooper, Praetorian Press,
Seaforth Publishing and Wharncliffe.

For a complete list of Pen & Sword titles please contact
PEN & SWORD BOOKS LIMITED
47 Church Street, Barnsley, South Yorkshire, S70 2AS, England
E-mail: enquiries@pen-and-sword.co.uk
Website: www.pen-and-sword.co.uk

Contents

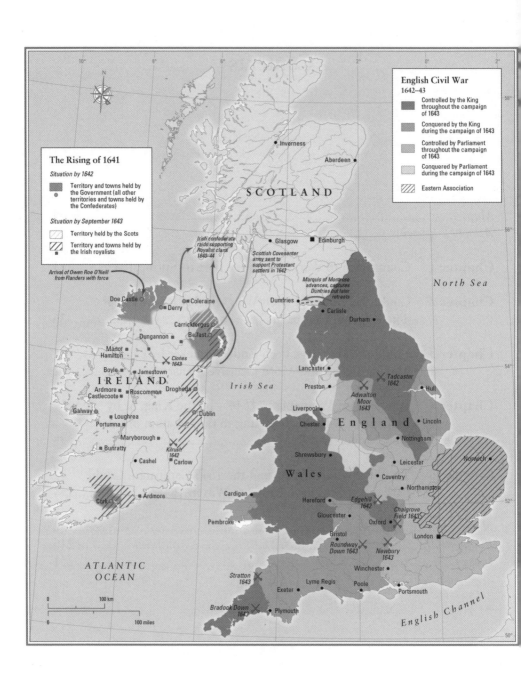

The Rising of 1641

Situation by 1642

▪ Territory and towns held by
the Government (all other
territories and towns held by
the Confederates)

Situation by September 1643

▨ Territory held by the Scots

▨ Territory and towns held by
the Irish royalists

Arrival of Owen Roe O'Neill
from Flanders with force

English Civil War
1642–43

■ Controlled by the King
throughout the campaign
of 1643

■ Conquered by the King
during the campaign of 1643

■ Controlled by Parliament
throughout the campaign
of 1643

■ Conquered by Parliament
during the campaign of 1643

▨ Eastern Association

North Sea

Irish Sea

Irish confederate
raids supporting
Royalist clans
1640–44

Scottish Covenanter
army sent to
support Protestant
settlers in 1642

Marquis of Montrose
advances, captures
Dumfries but later
retreats

Inverness ●

Aberdeen ●

S C O T L A N D

● Glasgow   ■ Edinburgh

Dumfries ●

● Carlisle

Durham ●

Lancaster ●

Preston ●   Tadcaster
                  1642
          Adwalton   ● Hull
          Moor
          1643

Liverpool ●

Chester ●   E n g l a n d   ● Lincoln

                              ● Nottingham

Shrewsbury ●

                ● Leicester   Norwich

W a l e s   ● Coventry

                ● Northampton

Cardigan ●

Hereford ●   Edgehill
               1642
          Gloucester ●   Chalgrove
                         Field 1643
Pembroke ●   Oxford ●
                              London ■
          Bristol
       Roundway   Newbury
       Down 1643   1643

                Winchester ●

Stratton
1643   Lyme Regis
      Exeter ●   ● Poole
                          ● Portsmouth

Bradock Down   English Channel
   1643   ● Plymouth

IRELAND

Doe Castle ○

■● Derry   ● Coleraine

Carrickfergus ○
Dungannon ●   Belfast ○

Manor ■
Hamilton   × Clones
              1643
Boyle ■ ● Jamestown
Ardmore ■
Castlecoote ■ Roscommon ● Drogheda ■

Galway ●
    ● Loughrea   ● Dublin
Portumna ■

Maryborough ■

Bunratty ■   Kilrush
             1642
    ● Cashel   Carlow

Cork ○   ● Ardmore

ATLANTIC
OCEAN

0   100 km

0   100 miles

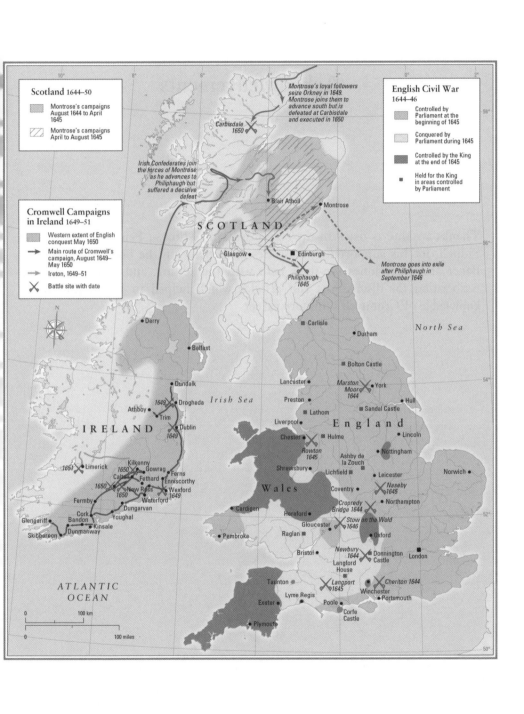

Scotland 1644–50

- Montrose's campaigns August 1644 to April 1645
- Montrose's campaigns April to August 1645

Cromwell Campaigns in Ireland 1649–51

- Western extent of English conquest May 1650
- Main route of Cromwell's campaign, August 1649– May 1650
- Ireton, 1649–51
- ✗ Battle site with date

English Civil War 1644–46

- Controlled by Parliament at the beginning of 1645
- Conquered by Parliament during 1645
- Controlled by the King at the end of 1645
- Held for the King in areas controlled by Parliament

Montrose's loyal followers seize Orkney in 1649. Montrose joins them to advance south but is defeated at Carbisdale and executed in 1650

Carbisdale 1650

Irish Confederates join the forces of Montrose as he advances to Philiphaugh but suffered a decisive defeat

Blair Atholl
Montrose

SCOTLAND

Glasgow
Edinburgh
Philiphaugh 1645

Montrose goes into exile after Philiphaugh in September 1646

Derry
Belfast

Carlisle
Durham

North Sea

Dundalk
1649 Drogheda
Athboy Trim
Dublin
1649

Irish Sea

Bolton Castle

Lancaster
Marston Moor 1644 York
Preston
Hull
Lathom
Sandal Castle
Liverpool

England

Chester
Hulme
Lincoln
Rowton 1645
Ashby de la Zouch
Nottingham

IRELAND

1651 Limerick
Kilkenny
Gowrag
Ferns
1650 Callan Fethard Enniscorthy
1650 New Ross Wexford
Waterford 1649
Fermby
Dungarvan
Cork Youghal
Glengariff Bandon Kinsale
Skibbereen Dunmanway

Shrewsbury
Lichfield
Leicester
Norwich

Wales

Coventry
Naseby 1645
Cropredy Bridge 1644
Northampton

Cardigan
Hereford
Stow on the Wold 1646
Gloucester
Oxford
Pembroke
Raglan

Bristol
Newbury 1644
Donnington Castle
London
Langford House
Taunton
Langport 1645
Cheriton 1644
Lyme Regis
Winchester
Poole Portsmouth
Exeter
Corfe Castle
Plymouth

ATLANTIC OCEAN

0   100 km

0   100 miles

Acknowledgements

Thanks are due as usual to my commissioning editor at Pen and Sword, Phil Sidnell, for his support for this series and advice on the book. Also to Ting Baker and Matt Jones for their help with the editing, and to the Cromwell Association for discussions and articles which helped to add depth to my knowledge of Cromwell's military career.

Chapter One

Countdown to War: December 1641 to Spring 1642

Forcing a confrontation in the New Year – who was most to blame? Did the 'Junto' deliberately try to panic Charles into over-reacting?

The main work of the early months of the 'Long Parliament' from November 1640 had been the demolition of Charles I's prerogative powers and ability to raise money without resort to a Parliament, plus the prosecution of his most 'dangerous' ministers Thomas Wentworth, Earl of Strafford (Lord Lieutenant of Ireland) and Archbishop William Laud. These measures were generally non-controversial among the majority of 'opposition' MPs determined to enforce reform on the King, led by John Pym, plus the 'opposition' peers led by the Earl of Warwick and his allies the Earls of Essex (future Parliamentarian Army commander) and Bedford. Notably, the elections to the Parliament – the second one in a year, so the regime was not 'rusty' regarding getting the local office-holders (Lord and Deputy Lords Lieutenant) to organize candidates where possible – had seen very few backers of the King's recent policies elected, and some who were evicted from the Commons 'on appeal' by the latter's elections committee. The initiative thus passed to the 'opposition' as the Commons set to work – and one overlooked 'what if' question is the potential for Charles making more of an effort to rally support, possible if a determined organizer (e.g. Strafford, absent in Ireland) had been called upon. As opponents of the 'Arminian' forms of ceremonial and doctrine (seen as 'popish', semi-Catholic, by mainstream Calvinist Protestants) and rigid centralist discipline enforced on the Anglican Church by Laud's faction, the 'opposition' also wanted reform of the Church. But the form that should take was less easy to agree – indicting Laud and returning the Church to 'purer' Elizabethan practices free of a supposedly Catholic taint was accompanied in the minds of hard-line Calvinist zealots by a need for 'Root and Branch' reform that might even involve abolishing the bishops and replacing them with control by the 'grass roots' boards of local 'presbyters' that existed in some Calvinist communities. Some of the MPs elected in autumn 1640 who had resented Laud's 'Arminian' Church ceremonial and centralized interference in local Church appointments – or the King's dubiously legal ways of raising non-Parliamentary finance – were to break from the radicals during 1641 over the attacks on the bishops. But the radicals were also resorting to an unusual degree of populist pressure via large 'spontaneous' demonstrations of Londoners for 'Root and Branch', huge petitions for reform to the House of Commons, and aggressive pamphleteering as the strict 1630s restrictions on the press lapsed. Rowdy and menacing scenes occurred during Strafford's trial as Londoners fearing his anti-Parliamentary potential converged on Parliament demanding that he be executed, and the 'politics of the street' began to emerge as a political force (as seen also in France in 1789, Russia in 1917 and Iran in 1979). The King dithered over whether to accept the demands for execution, and apparently regretted giving in to the extent that it hardened his resolve not to compromise thereafter.

The non-episcopal form of 'Presbyterian' Church, plus hard-line Calvinist doctrine enforced by strict discipline, had been in existence in Scotland from the time of John Knox until pro-episcopal innovations under James VI and I, which Charles had sought to build on for an 'Anglicanized' Church. As seen by its defenders, it was the 'original' form of Christian Church in the Apostolic age, before bishops with their discipline and 'Romish ceremonial' had emerged; restoring this was a godly duty in England as in Scotland. The survival of most of the administrative forms (and some of the ceremonial practices) of the Catholic Church in the post-1559 Elizabethan Church in England thus had to be ended to install a 'true', 'pure' Church. The revival of episcopal authority and 'Romish' doctrine (exaggerated by its critics) by Charles, Laud, and the Scots bishops in the 1630s in Scotland had been forcibly rejected by outright defiance and armed rebellion in Scotland in 1637–9, to which the King had sought to reply with invasion to face defeat and bankruptcy. Local pro-Church Highland clansmen (many of them Catholic) had been defeated and an invasion from Ireland promised by Strafford had failed to materialize, and in summer 1640 the new, Calvinist Scots army (staffed by many veterans of the Continental 'Thirty Years' War' led by their commander, Alexander Leslie) had invaded England and defeated the advance-force of Charles' less-experienced, badly led army at Newburn on the Tyne. Lackadaisical Charles, slow to collect the main army to march north using an outdated medieval mechanism of feudal summons, had still been en route to York. Facing a virtual 'strike' by part of the English nobility instead of them loyally assembling troops for him as required, Charles had had to agree to a truce with the Scots. This disaster in 1640 had forced him to call Parliament and agree to listen to his subjects' demands, and indeed the Calvinist faction of peers led by Warwick had seen the Presbyterian struggle in Scotland as their own and egged on the rebels – which arguably amounted to treason (and was seen as such by the King). While he was marching north to York, they had held a mutinous rally in London and been seen as threatening armed revolt; around a third of the nobility failed to join the King at York as required. Defeated and virtually bankrupt – though a potential loan of money and troops from Spain could have averted this had the Catalan and Portuguese rebellions not occurred in 1640 – Charles had had to summon the 'Long Parliament' and agree to the demolition of his administrative and financial powers, closure of his prerogative courts, reform of the Church, removal of his most disliked ministers, arrest of Laud, and impeachment of Strafford – who had urged him to use Irish troops to put down sedition in Scotland and possibly in England too. Strafford's execution rather than banishment (the latter was more usual for an impeached minister) was, however, more controversial, and was forced in May 1641 on a reluctant King who was thereafter more alienated from his critics – among whom until this point he had been seen as willing to offer senior posts and partial control of policy to Warwick, Bedford, Essex, and even Pym. Arguably he committed a major mistake in appointing a key Warwick ally, radical lawyer Oliver St John (Oliver Cromwell's cousin) who had led the 'defence' in the 'Ship-Money' case, as solicitor-general early in 1641. St John acted as an 'opposition' prosecutor, leading the indictment of Strafford and implicitly threatening similar vengeance on other centralizing royal ministers (e.g. Secretary of State Windebank) who fled the country. This heightened threat of judicial proceedings weakened Charles by unnerving his supporters – though the 'opposition' would have done their best to pursue it via Parliament's judicial role anyway.

The possibilities of political compromise and the 'opposition' working for the King would have averted war, and it has been argued that the sudden death of the moderate reformist leader Bedford – less intent on abolishing the bishops and opposed to killing Strafford – in May prevented a settlement. This is unclear, as other senior peers such as Warwick (not to mention the rabidly anti-'Arminian' Pym) would still have been insisting on a Presbyterian form of Church reform, which the King was to resist as late as 1648, and the Scots commissioners in London also urged this on the English (partly to protect their newly freed Church from an English episcopal backlash later). The outbreak of Catholic rebellion in Ireland in October–November 1641 heightened anti-Catholic hysteria in England due to the accompanying atrocities, with the English crisis having removed Strafford (whose firmness would have discouraged moderate rebels risking all on a revolt) from power there in favour of weak governance. Control of the army sent to put down the rebels and the extent of the confiscations of lands from 'disloyal' Catholics thereafter would probably have split the putative reconciliation of 'King and moderate opposition' – indeed, many of the Catholic rebels saw themselves as loyal to the King and seeking to save their lands and faith from a vengeful and confiscatory Protestant Parliament in London. There were links between Irish Catholic rebel officers and ultra-royalist courtiers in London, both of whom hated Parliament, and the position and future of Charles' Catholic Queen Henrietta Maria was also a potential source of tension. Her court loyalists, such as George Goring and Sir Henry Jermyn, and loud-mouthed, swashbuckling officers – the future 'Cavaliers' – were at the heart of (usually incompetent) plans to curtail Parliament. The issue of whether or not to abolish episcopacy in England – at the votes for which a majority of MPs could not be mustered in 1641– would have continued to divide radical and moderate critics of the King into 1642 even if a surviving Bedford and a reluctant Warwick and Pym had taken office under Charles in mid-1641. Also, Charles' attitude to further 'reform' was unlikely to be conciliatory, and he was already showing that he was untrustworthy and could go back on his word. He had considered an 'ultra' royalist courtier/army plot to seize London by a military coup, free Strafford from the Tower, and close down Parliament in May 1641, though the (over-optimistic) arrangements had failed and it had been abandoned.

Charles had agreed to go to Scotland in summer 1641 to sign up to the abolition of episcopacy, the restoration of a full Presbyterian Church, and the loss of virtually all his executive powers as the triumphant rebels demanded. But once he arrived Charles was involved in a dubious plot to arrest their leaders and install the more moderate Calvinist leader Montrose as his 'strongman' by a coup. This plan backfired too, leaving him feebly denying all involvement. But his main intention in either winning over or overthrowing the 'rebel' regime in Edinburgh seems to have been to gain the use of the Scots army to use in England, and on his return to London in late 1641 the question of agreement with or coercion of Parliament resumed. The Warwick-Pym faction was now facing a rising 'backlash' of local provincial sentiment in favour of the King, with the most disliked elements of his 'Personal Rule' of 1629–40 abolished, a rebellion in Ireland needing crushing, and further reform of the Church unacceptable to many people. There were petitions in favour of as well as against the bishops as their local supporters mobilized. An embryo 'royalist' faction opposed to further reform was emerging in the Commons, led by former critics of the King such as Sir Edward Hyde, and the radicals' demands for further reform and restraint of the untrustworthy King in the 'Grand Remonstrance' of

November 1640 was barely passed. Arguably, now that the unpopular elements of prerogative rule had been abolished – and future Parliaments every three years guaranteed by statute, whether the King wanted them or not – patriots should rally around not criticize their sovereign. Pym and his group were undaunted, evidently regarding compromise on the crucial question of the Church as dangerous, and now sought to throw all the bishops out of the Lords (which would improve their chances of winning votes there) and to continue to use noisy and threatening demonstrations by anti-episcopal radicals in London (e.g. the apprentices) to intimidate Parliament. Now the question arose of whether the latter could be used by the King to argue that he had to act against disorder and to rally alarmed moderate opinion to his side. For the first time since May, 'ultra' royalist officers and troops from the regiments stationed at York (immobilized there since the end of the Scots war) were brought in to London ready to strike.

In the event, bolstered in December by a firm move to take control of the Tower of London arsenal and the first mustering of armed troops in the capital to prepare to overawe or take on the City crowds and urged to a determined course of action by the Queen and her allies,[1] the King endeavoured to strike against the radical leaders. Technically, it was not an attempt to close down Parliament as in May 1641; he was staying within the constitution and not defying the Act which kept this Parliament in session as long as it so desired this. The Scots precedent should be remembered; he had attempted to have the 'rebel' leaders Argyll, Hamilton, and Lanark arrested (if not killed) by his loyalists in Edinburgh in mid-October in a similarly bold 'strike' at his critics. It should be noted that Charles issued a proclamation on 12 December requiring all MPs and peers absent from Parliament to return to Westminster as of 12 January; Venetian ambassador Giustinian reckoned that around 210 were currently absent.[2] Most of these men could be assumed to be boycotting the sittings out of frustration at the 'seditious' actions of the Warwick-Pym group, so their return should give Charles a majority in each House; and already he had nearly won the vote on the 'Grand Remonstrance'. On the 16th, the French ambassador (the Marquis de la Ferte-Imbault) reported that a court decision had been taken on the 12th to prepare for impeaching and beheading 'several of the leading Parliament-men'[3] – presumably by this means creating a majority in Parliament for it. Other spectators such as papal agent Rosetti believed a military coup to seize the Tower was being planned; possibly both were in Charles' mind, the military option being backed by the Goring-Jermyn court 'hotheads'. The often-overlooked order of 12 December raises a major issue – why did Charles not wait until 12 January before acting against his enemies? Had he initiated the planned arrests for impeachment only after enough 'loyal' MPs and peers returned, he could have expected to win the votes on these matters. Was he forced into premature aggression before 12 January by the pressure being put on him by the 'Junto' – who wanted to trap him in this way? Or was it a case of Goring's group winning him over? In either case, the King's inconstancy and wavering were disastrous for his reputation.

The return of an 'opposition' majority to the Common Council in the City despite the election of Gurney as lord mayor led to renewed mob intimidation of Parliament by anti-episcopal demonstrators, with a crowd led by militant Alderman Fowke delivering a huge petition against episcopacy to the Commons on 11 December.[4] On the 15th the militants in the Commons secured the vote to print the 'Grand Remonstrance' – which Charles furiously opposed – by the simple expedient of waiting until most MPs opposing them had gone home and rushing a motion into action; the effect of this was to remind the London public of the full list of Charles' misdemeanours and whip up opposition to him. Certainly some spectators such as the Earl of Hertford's steward Edward Kirton believed that the current menacing anti-episcopal demonstrations were being co-ordinated by the future Earl of Manchester and other opposition 'Junto' agents.[5] It is impossible to prove directly, but the 'cui bono' argument indicates the likelihood that 'hard-liners' were piling the pressure on Charles by manufacturing riots as at the time of the Strafford trial. Certainly Denzel Holles threatened the Lords with an appeal to the people if they continued to hold up the Commons' proposals on who should control the Irish campaign, implying openly that the Pym faction would unleash a mob on them;[6] this speech (21 December) went further than any threats back in May. The 'opposition' had just triumphed at the City's Common Council elections, which would have given them confidence about assembling such a crowd; and in reply the King dismissed Deputy Lieutenant of the Tower William Balfour, still in 'place' since his involvement in the May plot to free Strafford but now taking orders from his 'opposition' superior Lord Newport. His replacement was to be the fiery officer Colonel Thomas Lunsford, a hot-headed 'ultra' among the 'Reformadoes' who had been in the Army at York until November and was now at court; he was known for his hatred of the 'Junto'.[7] The appointment of Lunsford threatened another royal coup to seize the Tower and turn its guns on the City; but such a provocative security measure was only a logical reaction to Holles' threats. In a sign of the radicals' 'mindset', their favourite preacher Stephen Marshall spoke in a sermon to the Commons of them as 'Daniel' facing 'Nebuchadnezzar', i.e. royal persecution.

The crisis now turned into a series of mutual escalations, increasingly turning to the use of blatant force – in which the 'Junto' had led the way by the City demonstrations. Charles surprisingly backed down over Parliamentary anger against Lunsford and replaced him with Sir John Byron, but sacked Newport as the Governor of the Tower; the Christmas recess (25–6 December) saw more rioting and on the 27th bishops arriving for the sitting of the Lords were jostled by an angry mob. Surprisingly, the anti-Laudian 'hero' John Williams was booed, presumably for accepting the Archbishopric of York and so 'betraying' his cause. The suspicion arises that the 'Junto' Calvinist peers and/or Pym were backing the riots to drive these staunch pro-King voters out of the Lords. Most bishops now declared that they dared not come to the Lords any longer so they did not recognize Parliament,[8] and they were duly arrested for an alleged insult to the latter. The arrests could be couched in legalistic language as reacting to an insult to Parliament, but it was a blatant political act by the Warwick faction to remove them from their rights to vote in the Lords for whatever the King wanted.

The threat to impeach the bishops was a clear sign from the pro-Calvinist faction that they intended to force the issue of the episcopate on Charles, and the 'opposition' control of the City Common Council elections enabled easier mustering of a zealous City mob at a trial in Westminster Hall to secure conviction (as with Strafford). There was a rumour that the Catholic Queen would be impeached next – possibly played up by Pym in the hope of inflaming the King into a confrontation.[9] But the threat of new prosecutions could also be used as evidence that the Commons radicals were going too far in infringing the King's powers, provided that it was handled properly. Such radical proposals would not necessarily win enough Commons votes to succeed, unless the City apprentices besieged Parliament again to intimidate opposition. It was suspicious that Warwick now proposed that 600 of the troops being raised for the Irish war should be assembled immediately in London; they would be available until they sailed for use by the Lords-nominated Irish commanders (e.g. Essex) for use against the King. In fairness to Warwick, the King was undeniably concentrating troops at Whitehall (and building a temporary barracks) around the New Year.[10]

One of the main dangers to the royal cause lay in Parliament using its legal powers to arraign people for contempt of its authority, which could frighten off royal supporters from raising troops without Commons approval. (Pro-royalist MP George Digby was charged with this in January and had to flee abroad.) The King needed to be able to prove that it was Parliament abusing authority rather than him – which was not helped by evidence of wild talk at court about arresting MPs or by leaks about his attempts to hire troops from Irish Catholic peers. The dismantling of the royal prerogative, and the flight of the sternest royal 'prerogative' judges who had implemented Charles' will in the 1630s but now feared Parliamentary vengeance, made it difficult for Charles to be able to put out legal opinions that Parliament was abusing its powers. The Attorney-General, Sir Edward Herbert, was more loyal than his deputy, Oliver St John, but seems to have been intimidated into inaction until the impeachment attempt of 3 January.

Before the impeachment went ahead, as soon as Parliament reassembled after Christmas the royalist Lord Digby put forward a motion on 28 December that it was not able to operate freely – due to intimidation by the crowds – and legislation was thus now invalid. This was probably an attempt to lay the legal basis for cancelling any forthcoming Commons or Lords votes that defied the King, as on impeaching or abolishing the bishops or on 'Root and Branch'. Had it succeeded, the result would have been deadlock but no more embarrassing anti-Anglican votes however many MPs or peers were won over or pressurized into following Pym and Warwick. But the vote was lost by four, and the Lords voted to suspend and arrest those bishops who had voted for it – which indicates that the majority of peers still had faith in the right of this Parliament to decide on future governance, not that all who voted thus were totally won over to 'Root and Branch'.[11] Had the vote been won, the King would have been able to produce a legal basis for the closure of Parliament or – if 'moderate' MPs objected to that and he needed it to raise money – its removal to somewhere outside London. There were plenty of precedents for that, as lately as 1625, though then due to plague not disorder; and in 1644 Charles was to use this argument about intimidation invalidating a 'free' Parliament in summoning MPs to Oxford. Probably the hand of Hyde can be seen behind this idea.

When Herbert finally announced that Charles wished to impeach the 'Five Members' on 3 January – and that disloyal peers such as Warwick, Saye and Sele, Brooke, and Holland should not be appointed to the Lords committee investigating the charges – the failure to act quickly lay with Lord Digby, who did not as planned call for an immediate Lords vote. The announcement of the impeachment had been sudden and pre-empted 'opposition' organization of votes; if a vote had been taken immediately the motion could have succeeded and then the accused would be liable to immediate arrest. Possibly Digby had reckoned (accurately?) that the Lords vote would be lost, given that House's attitude to the bishops' actions on 28–30 December and the absence of the bishops' votes, and wanted more time to win peers over. The Commons rallying to the five despite a Lords vote for impeachment would have led to a useful charge of them defying the will of their fellow-House, which could be manipulated to the King's advantage. Instead, the Lords did not act and the accused could co-ordinate their reaction. When the command for impeachment was brought to the

Commons, in a non-provocative way by a respectful sergeant-at-arms, it was not drawn up in precise legal terms and so enabled its targets' faction to argue that it was not written in definitive enough terms for a formal reply. But what if the document had been undeniably correct in form, and the Commons had been forced to vote on it? Would the suddenness of the move have meant that the Pym faction could not intimidate their enemies into resisting the King? What if 'moderate' MPs had backed Digby's lead and voted to accept the impeachment?

The King's 'party' were not necessarily sure of enough votes in either House to push through an impeachment, but the delays while the attempt was debated should have caused a useful halt to other contentious (religious) measures. Whatever their strategy, the initiation of proceedings would enable the legal authorities – the King's men – to impound the accused's papers. Hopefully, evidence would be found of their treasonous dealings with the Scots in 1639–40, and/or enough evidence be amassed against their peer allies to arrest or blackmail the latter. Hyde apparently wanted more peers named as the accused – which would have decapitated their faction in the Lords during the investigation and been more likely to produce evidence in their homes but would have increased votes against their prosecution by adding to outrage.[12] The Warwick group had sought to add to their voting strength in the Lords by removing the bishops; now the King's supporters sought to reverse this by removing the leading Calvinist peers.

The attempt to arrest the 'Five Members' on 4 January was a major blunder, not least by the King leading the armed incursion into the Commons in person. The moment when Charles decided to resort to a personal raid is unknown; possibly the Commons proposal to remove the Queen's attendant Capuchin Friars from Somerset House on 3 January made her determined on quick action. The introduction of expert cannoneers to the Tower on the evening of 3 January, which caused panic in the City, implied that the King believed they could be needed to confront rioters – in reaction to his intended arrests? The accused MPs' homes had been raided by men of the King's new Guard at Whitehall, sealing up their papers ready for a search for evidence, on the 3rd, and rumours of imminent military action next morning led to the Commons sending Nathaniel Fiennes to Whitehall to investigate. The men of the new Guard who were hanging around the Guard/Great Chamber in the Palace were apparently waiting in readiness for orders, and after Fiennes' return action followed. In mid-afternoon the King emerged from his apartments and called on them to follow him, and a royal armed descent on Parliament followed. The fact that he carefully avoided taking his troops into the Commons chamber[13] (a courtesy that Cromwell did not follow in 1653) did not alter the dramatic nature of the 'insult' to the Commons, which his detractors could play up enthusiastically. By personally resorting to open force he placed himself in the role in which Pym had been portraying him by implication, as the ally of the violent, pro-Catholic clique around the Queen associated with the 'Army Plot' in May 1641 and the instigator of the treacherous 'Incident' plot in Edinburgh in October. Having recently sought to turn the weapon of legality against the radicals – by showing that they were coercing Parliament – he now firmly placed himself as its enemy, causing anyone who clung to the supremacy of 'Parliamentary privilege' to rally to Pym. Presumably he hoped that the majority of MPs would be relieved at a chance to be rid of the 'troublemakers' and reach a settlement, or that radical MPs' defiance of his proposed impeachment would be a useful political tool in another attempt to argue that Parliament was under constraint (and thus its measures should be invalidated).

But the Commons' sense of corporate unity caused a revival in Pym's group's support when Charles sent orders for their impeachment and then arrived himself. The Commons had asserted its right to be consulted before accepting such a demand on the 3rd, though they promised to consider it if it was properly legal. Refusing to wait for five days for a reply as they requested and considering that he had failed to dispose of them constitutionally, he made the fatal error of leading his troops to arrest them in person – once again, a reversal of his original policy. Was this due to nagging by 'hard-liners' (the Queen?)? This caused a massive rallying of Commons opinion to men who had been haemorrhaging support only weeks previously, along with the City sheltering them in defiance of the King as they slipped out of the Commons to take a boat down-river to safety. The royal participation and use of troops was evidently an attempt to overawe the MPs; last time the King had forced confrontation with the Commons, over its sudden dissolution in 1629, radicals had slammed the door in his messenger's face and held the Speaker prisoner to legitimize their condemnatory votes. Presumably the use of a body of soldiers was not merely to give him the necessary 'dignified' attendant escort but to deal with any lingering rioters or to prevent MPs slamming the door on his messenger again, and his presence should be guaranteed to dissuade all mannerly MPs from disorderly conduct. Arguably, sending a posse to arrest the MPs and allowing a repeat of their disorderly defiance in 1629 would have done more good to his cause in placing the 'Five Members' in the legal wrong for coercing Parliament. According to Ambassador Giustinian's despatch on 7/17 January the trigger for Charles' action was the Lords' order reversing his sealing up the papers of the 'Five Members' for investigation; but this (or the insult to the Queen in expelling her friars) did not need his personal attention. Perhaps the presence at his side during the 'raid' of Lord Roxburgh is significant, given that the latter had been involved in the 'Incident' – the attempted coup during Charles' visit to Edinburgh – as proposed supplier of the troops to take Argyll and Hamilton into custody.[14]

If it is more than rumour that Pym was tipped off by allies at court, namely the arch-intriguer Lucy, Lady Carlisle (according to a 1650s report Pym's mistress), it is apparent that the King did not observe enough secrecy about his plans in advance. Some less naïve courtier, aware of the danger of gossip leading to a 'leak' if not that Lady Carlisle was unreliable, would have been well-advised to ask the King to place armed guards in a barge on the Thames off Whitehall Stairs to intercept any boat heading downstream from Westminster to the City. The escaping MPs would have been caught and taken into custody – and not on Parliamentary premises. But the King lacked such shrewd advisers, not having a cynical 'eminence grise' to hand as Elizabeth had had William Cecil and Walsingham or James I had had Robert Cecil. Probably if Strafford had been alive and not in exile he would have been aware of the need to guard all exits from the Commons in case of a 'leak'.

At least the advance on Parliament was properly organized, with the more reliable Westminster militia being told to take over guarding the House from the pro-Pym City guards[15] and the Inns of Court volunteers being told to stand ready. Showing more leadership than he had done in Edinburgh where he had left the proposed action to Captain Cochrane and Lord Roxburgh and remained in a position to deny involvement if it failed, Charles also cleverly made his nephew, the Elector Palatine, accompany him to the Commons and so seem to endorse his action. The ambitious young Elector Charles Louis, elder brother of Prince Rupert and son of the highly popular 'Winter Queen' Elizabeth of Bohemia, had been on friendly terms with leading 'opposition' peers such as Essex since his arrival in London to seek aid in the summer, though they were of political use to him as ralliers of a Lords vote to give him aid and of military use as potential generals of an expeditionary force. Rumour had it that the Elector was less loyal to his uncle and was fishing for the chance of a crown if Parliament broke with and deposed Charles, though this was never proved.[16] But if he had had the nerve or ambition to absent himself from Whitehall during the crisis and so present himself as a potential rival to the King, the latter's flight in January could have enabled the more aggressive Calvinist peers to consider him as a possible military and political figurehead for their cause against a distrusted and treacherous King. The idea of setting up the Elector, a Stuart and a Calvinist, as the head of the 'Parliamentarian' cause in 1642 is one of the more intriguing 'What If?' scenarios of the crisis, but his uncle's co-option of him in January – and his acceptance of it – made him less attractive to the 'Junto'.

The targets fled in time due to a warning that the King was coming to arrest them – Lady Carlisle, later accused, was simultaneously an agent for Cardinal Richelieu and was supposed to be having an affair with Pym. (It is possible that Lady Carlisle, who could have cost Charles his best chance of decapitating the opposition, was the original behind Alexandre Dumas' 'Milady De Winter' in the Three Musketeers books.) The most defiant MP, William Strode the younger, had to be forcibly removed by his colleagues – and if he had stayed to face the King his arrest by the royal guards would have been another propaganda coup for Pym who knew exactly how to exploit such evidence of the royal threat to subjects' liberties. With the Commons forgetting its recent divisions and reunited against his violation of constitutional norms by leading troops into the House, wavering peers and MPs were shown that the King could not be trusted to support the national assembly of his subjects against the influence of sinister pro-Catholic 'plotters'. The unruly City was in a tumult again so Whitehall was unsafe, and the King received a hostile reception as he attempted to persuade the Common Council to do its duty at the Guildhall on the 5th.[17]

The implacable hostility to an untrustworthy King shown in the Remonstrance seemed justified, and the King's defiers turned to open resistance – the tactic that the Calvinist peers had planned in summer 1640 and once again physically centred on the City. Charles was able to enter the City physically, but seems to have been baffled as to what to do next when he failed to secure co-operation or submission. He had more troops at his back than he had possessed during the crisis over executing Strafford, but not enough for a prolonged search of or intimidation of London. As with the warning that the 'Five Members' had had, the court was inferior in terms of intelligence; a bribe to some City figure to find out the location of the fugitives and a quick descent (at night?) by armed 'Cavaliers' on their hideout could still have secured their persons while leaving Warwick's peers at large to condemn it in the Lords in retrospect.

After the attempted arrests – physical confrontation between King and opposition. Charles' flight
The Parliamentary 'Committee for Privileges', in contact with the fugitives, met in the City daily under the protection of the Trained Bands. The combined Commons and Lords 'Committee for Irish Affairs' – run by the 'Junto' – was empowered to sit during a short, self-declared Parliamentary recess to organize defence, and duly issued weapons from the Tower to two regiments en route to Ireland, which were conveniently assembling in

London. The regiments' commanders, Pym's brother-in-law Clotworthy (an Ulster 'planter' so a legitimate person to take control on military grounds) and Lord Conway, were loyal to the 'opposition'. On the 10th, the new City 'Common Council' met and gave command of the Trained Bands to the 'Junto' loyalist Philip Skippon – putting these 10,000 men under 'opposition' leadership. The royalist Lord Mayor was now a cipher, and the City lost. That day, with the fugitive MPs expected to return to Westminster soon under City protection and large crowds passing through Whitehall to assist them, Charles chose to take the course of personal safety over military confrontation and fled his capital to Hampton Court.[18] As a symbol of his disarray, the beds were not ready. On 13 January he went on to Windsor Castle. The initiative passed to the radical leaders who now had physical control of London and a majority in the Commons to pass further measures consolidating their position; peers and MPs who doubted the wisdom of their confrontational policy had no alternative source of power to rally to. The removal of Charles from London saw a return to the situation that Warwick's group had been planning in summer 1640, with the 'opposition' in control of the capital with its militia and the King in retreat without an army to call on immediately. This time, however, the King's critics had no need to seek the calling of a Parliament to back them legally; one was already in being. The King had also breached 'privilege' in entering the Commons with armed men, albeit technically only to enforce arrests for a legal charge of impeachment, and the defiant faction in control of London could be claimed to be defending the constitution as they would not have been able to do in an armed 'stand-off' in 1640. Their propaganda notably continued to present their cause as being 'for King and Parliament', open rebellion being likely to detract from their support; the fiction was maintained that Charles was a puppet of 'evil councillors' in need of rescue.

With the two 'camps' physically separated the chances of moderates on either side negotiating a settlement were drastically reduced. Luckily for the King, his peace treaty with the Scots of August 1641 was holding as long as he did not meddle with Argyll's ascendancy and the Covenanters were preoccupied raising troops to save their co-religionists in Ulster. (The first detachments of Leslie's army sailed there in April.) The English 'opposition' could not expect the Covenanters to come to their rescue as in summer-autumn 1640, giving Charles time to raise his own forces in the north of England. Had the Irish crisis not been a distraction, Argyll and his allies would have been more of a threat to the King and more useful to the latter's enemies in London. But even without the existence of two opposing armies as yet, only a royal surrender to the radicals' terms – a temporary handover of political control of the administration and army to them and abolition of the episcopal Church, as seen in the 'Newcastle Propositions' – could have avoided ultimate war. The King was now seen as provably treacherous, and the 'Parliamentary' leadership would only accept his complete political and military neutralization – the terms forced on him in Scotland in August 1641. John Adamson sees this as a coherent and long-term political objective of the 'Warwick group' from 1640, with the untrustworthy and 'pro-Catholic' King made a powerless 'Doge' subject to his counsellors as in Venice. The Venetian parallel may have been played up in 'opposition' figures' talks with that state's ambassador to flatter him; classically educated nobles and gentry had other Greek parallels for a limited monarchy to use as precedents.

Religion had been the main issue for a breach, but was not the only one – Parliament asserting control of appointments showed that the 'Junto' would not trust Charles to keep to any terms, and the armed descent on the Commons seemed to prove their point. Possibly Warwick, Essex, Brooke, and other Calvinist enthusiasts, regarding religious reform as paramount and the King unwilling to deliver this, had never expected Charles to do their bidding without coercion and the events of January 1642 just enabled them to carry their point with less enthusiastic MPs and peers. In that case, the attempted 'coup' in arresting the 'Five Members' gave the more radical 'opposition' leaders the physical backing and the legal excuse to rally support for a programme of legislative long-term coercion of the King. Had Charles not shown his seeming treacherousness, would they have retained enough votes from MPs and peers to carry such measures in a continuing confrontation with him over religion in spring 1642? Crucially, what would have been the effect if large numbers of peers and MPs who were absent from the Houses had obeyed the King's summons to turn up on 12 January? They could also have been intimidated by the City crowds, as those present in Westminster had been in May and late December 1641; but if Charles had had their support someone such as Digby might well have won a vote alleging that Parliament could not now meet safely. The 'constitutional' path to withdrawal of the royalist party from Westminster in January 1642 would have been a wiser one than the real-life withdrawal after a botched armed raid on the Commons.

On 20 January Hampden introduced a Bill to secure the forts and ports in the hands of people that Parliament could trust, a direct challenge to the King's rights as commander-in-chief, and on the 31st Sir John Hotham carried out the first act of pro-Parliamentary military defiance in securing Hull without waiting for the Bill to pass. Parliament also introduced a Bill to take over control of the militia from royally appointed Lords Lieutenant, which was sent to the King for signing on 5 February, and as he delayed doing so sent a threatening Declaration to him proposing to take such measures by their own authority. By now their relations with the King had degenerated into mutual mistrust and insults, with the Parliamentary delegation that caught the King on his northwards journey (at Newmarket) accusing him of complicity with wicked courtiers in planning a foreign invasion.[19]

Review of the January 1642 crisis
The crucial point in avoiding a breakdown of relations with a majority in Parliament and a physical confrontation was thus December 1641. The King's visit to Scotland in autumn 1641 and consultations with the local royal loyalists, Montrose's group, certainly saw him willing to go along with the reassertion of Presbyterianism that the triumphant Covenanters had carried out in Scotland in 1638–40 and promise to carry out their political and religious wishes, however much he was playing for time. He did not have a strong enough party or troops to challenge the apparent Covenanter unanimity and politico-military strength, so co-operation was wise and that policy added to the potential of rallying support to himself and isolating the extremists in due course.

But, having adopted that course in Scotland – significantly, in the absence of the belligerent Queen and some of his other 'hard-line' court allies – he could have resorted to the same prudent course in England on his return. The King could have relied on Hyde's advice on how to handle wavering MPs, and the outstanding issue of the Church been handed over to a clerical assembly for leisurely consideration during 1642. But how long would a determined group of Calvinist peers determined on 'Root and Branch' reform of the Church have been able to stay in office if their policies were frustrated? Given the King's rigid pursuit of his rights and dignity, it is probable that his anger at being lectured by men he already regarded as treasonous allies of the Scots would have limited his ability to put up with them. Warwick's group would have insisted that Parliament stayed in being to add to their ability to coerce Charles over the Church, and so delayed a final resolution of the King's finances for an Irish expedition well into 1642 – probably until a Church assembly was safely in existence and enacting reform. The chances of a breach between King and aristocratic ministers would have been high.

The repeated appearance in the speeches and written remonstrations of Parliamentary leaders of allegations of plots to bring in troops to suppress them by courtiers with foreign help show that the King would have had to avoid any possible indication of bad faith to his critics. Given the belligerent and loose-tongued hotheads milling about court, the nucleus of the

'Cavalier' leadership around Lord Digby – who was attending a levy of troops in Kingston-upon-Thames within days of the King's flight from London – some misunderstanding was highly likely. The 'opposition' constantly had the example of the 'Incident' to warn them of what Charles could do without warning. Even if the King had not panicked and attempted to seize the 'Five Members', it is possible that Pym's group (with Warwick behind them?) would have been seeking to take over the militia or a veto on Lords Lieutenant's appointments to combat the 'courtier plot' – which they feared well before 5/6 January 1642. The 'Army Plot' of April/May 1641 had shown what certain confrontational courtiers intended to do about Parliament.

(i) What if Charles had not confronted the Commons on 6 January 1642?

Charles could have been more amenable to maintaining a 'low profile' not a confrontation in London late in 1641 and into 1642, with Hyde and moderate peers rallying alarmed or impatient MPs against the excessive demands for further legislative action made in the 'Remonstrance'. Bedford (if still alive), Pembroke (if not dismissed), and Hertford – in a politically crucial role for the future as 'governor' of the Prince of Wales – would have been crucial. They could present the King – as was done by his supporters with less success in reality, particularly after the attempt on 4 January on the 'Five Members' – as the voice of responsible constitutional government against a rabid Puritan faction who wanted to overturn the established order and infringe the royal prerogative. The Irish Revolt would still have inflamed Protestant opinion among MPs and in London against compromise with 'pro-papist' High Churchmen and in favour of further Church reform. But with the King now needing an army to tackle Ireland as well he could have let Hyde's group lead his decision-making (with Bedford if alive, Pembroke, & co. bought off with more prestigious offices and promises of future influence) and done nothing to inflame MPs. Many would now be alarmed at the radicals' attempt to take over control of the Irish insurgency fighting army and the delay threatened to the prospective campaign with such insults to the King's authority. Nor could the radicals threaten the King with the Scots army, given that he had reached a political settlement with the Covenanters (August 1641) that was precariously holding and the latter had to divert their main forces to Ulster that spring. Possibly a second vote could be called on the issue of Parliament acting under constraint, though more peers and MPs would have had to be lobbied successfully than had been done in December. If enough currently absent MPs and peers had returned to London on 12 January as ordered, Charles would have been in a better position to win such a vote. The probability of rowdy City demonstrations outside Parliament in favour of 'Root and Branch', or impeaching the bishops, should have rallied votes to such a cause.

The threat to abolish the episcopate and impeach bishops could be used to rally moderate religious opinion, as it was in the more conservative counties during 1642 – and Archbishop Williams was available to be used as evidence for the King's willingness to trust non-'Arminians' as bishops. (However, the fact that Williams was jostled outside Parliament on 28 December shows that the radicals regarded his acceptance of the archbishopric as a 'sell-out' to 'popery'.) If there could be trustable 'Church Puritans' appointed to the episcopate to carry out a purge of 'Romish' influence within the limits of the 1559 settlement, why go beyond it in alliance with rebel Scots? As was argued by moderates in the Commons in early 1641, the Triennial Act should ensure closer supervision of the Church by Parliament from now on and prevent any pro-'Arminian' bishops operating without check. Colepeper's motion in September for acting within the Church as by established law– i.e. the settlement of 1559, without Laudian ceremonies – was the obvious solution, though even that was voted down by a majority of militant MPs. Nor could the Scots army be used by Warwick's faction to pressurize Charles into giving way, as it had left England as per the August 1641 treaty and now had to consider the Irish revolt.

In any event, even without the crisis over the 'Five Members' the radicals would have had two bonuses in winter 1641–2 to help keep up pressure – 'opposition' control of the City's Common Council and renewed demonstrations by Londoners outside Parliament from December 1641. If the King had been prepared to listen to calmer counsels than those of his wife and her supporters, these problems would have had to be tolerated and appropriate promises made about Church reform. The King would have needed to have majority Commons opinion on his side to be able to risk a vote on impeaching his leading critics, even if they had seemed to be holding up a resolution of the issue of an Irish expedition. A concerted effort to assert his legal rights by sympathetic office-holding lawyers and show that he was acting within the constitution would have been invaluable, particularly as the most vehement judicial defenders of royal prerogative on the 'bench' had been removed by Parliament in spring 1641 over 'Ship-Money' and the rest seem to have been intimidated or pro-Pym. (Significantly, there was no judicial exodus to the King's refugee administration in Oxford in 1642–3.) As the current Attorney-General Edward Herbert was less politically 'well-connected' to the Commons majority – or active on his sovereign's behalf – the crucial role was that of the Solicitor-General, Oliver St John. An ally of

Pym, former defence counsel to Hampden (and Cromwell's cousin), and assailant on all forms of royal prerogative rights throughout 1641, he would have needed tact and practical evidence of the King's 'submission' to uphold the 1641 settlement and willingness to reform the Church. Even with one crucial pro-Pym nobleman who had shied away from the radical act of killing Strafford (Bedford) dead, others could be wooed with political and religious offers and temporarily allowed to determine some important policies. But this seeming 'reward' for their near-treason in 1639–40 was unlikely from a monarch never known for his political flexibility or his willingness to make concessions at the right moment.

The defeat of the 'Remonstrance' by a few more votes in November 1641, or a rise in pro-royalist feeling in the Commons against radical attempts to take over leadership of the Irish campaign for a Parliamentary nominee, the unruly and intimidatory demonstrations by City apprentices, and a 'Root and Branch' Church reform in early 1642, could have rallied dozens more MPs against anarchy despite the rumours of court plots – if the King had given no further cause for mistrust. The return of absentees would have helped too. Aided by a judicious distribution of jobs to less implacable 'opposition' aristocrats, a need to rally the nation to reach a settlement quickly and fight the rampant Irish revolt, and royal assurances as in Scotland the previous autumn, the King would have seemed a source of national unity if an impasse had continued at Westminster through January to spring 1642. Pym would have been isolated and liable to lose crucial Commons votes with the Lords more pro-King, assuming that Charles had made enough concessions to isolate the implacable Calvinist lords (especially Warwick and Brooke) had they refused or soon walked out of office. A confrontation with these peers' Calvinist principles over the future of the Church was inevitable – but it could have taken place in more favourable circumstances for the King.

Physical control of Westminster was also vital, as the Queen's supporters had realized back in May 1641. If the 'Root and Branch' faction continued to organize demonstrations, could the regiments now based at the Tower disperse the militant crowds of Londoners intimidating Parliament without too much counter-productive brutality? Any such firm military action would lose the adherence of Calvinist peers to the King's government – but would free intimidated 'moderates' in both Houses to vote against Church reform. In this respect, the loss of the vote in December 1641 to propose that Parliament could not function effectively due to intimidation was a major blow; winning it would have given peers and MPs who were afraid of the raucous London crowds a legal basis to resist intimidation. Charles had more men in London in December 1641 than he had had in May and deliberately brought loyal (and hot-headed) soldiers back from York, so he was evidently considering physical confrontation. Time was on the King's side, as the longer the Irish crisis dragged on without an army being sent to quell it the more Pym's group would have seemed to be holding up a resolution. The excuse for not voting money for an army or letting the King appoint the commander (or senior officers?), that the matter of religion had to be settled, was less likely to satisfy the majority of the provincial gentry in conservative areas than the concerned congregations who were petitioning Parliament for radical religious reform. Nor would any threats by the Scots or their army commanders – the interference of either would have won little support and much criticism, and would have reduced the Scots' pre-eminent need to protect their co-religionists in Ulster. Warwick and Essex could not have used Leslie's army as a weapon as effectively in 1642 as in 1641 – and in spring 1642 Leslie himself sailed to Ulster.

The danger to the King lay in the emergence of evidence that he could not be trusted, in which respect the activities of the courtiers around his wife had to be controlled. Pym, using Lady Carlisle to gain access to this group, was capable of stealing written evidence of their plans to bring in Irish troops and displaying it to the Commons to undermine the King's cause – and the appointment of a senior 'opposition' figure to control the army intended for Ireland would have been vital proof that the King had no sinister intentions even if his wife did. Giving full confidence to Essex or his ally Leicester was an obvious solution. There was always a danger that some blunder in royal policy, or evidence that Charles was dealing secretly with the militant young 'Cavalier' courtiers or the Irish Catholic lords for troops, would cause any 'opposition' peers who had taken office since spring 1641 to resign in disgust and turn back to the course of Parliamentary coercion. This could have unravelled any uneasy 'opposition' participation in government that a still-alive Bedford had managed to arrange with the court in May or June 1641, even if Hampden (or Pym?) had been lured into office. The court links of Irish plotter Colonel Daniel O'Neill, a close relative of rebel leader Phelim O'Neill, were one obvious threat to 'opposition' figures entering or continuing in office had these been exposed.

Charles was never known for showing his undiluted confidence to any one minister or faction, or political course of action, once he had lost Buckingham. Only his Queen and his Church were non-negotiable. He would have been suspicious of men such as Essex and Warwick for forcing their way into office, while court enemies such as the Gorings and Digby sought to undermine them. Crucially, he never gave the invaluable (but socially inferior) Hyde the full direction of political affairs before or during the wars. The Irish crisis and royal over-confidence could have caused a breakdown in relations during 1642 and the King resorting to attempted intimidation or closure of Parliament. A comparison could be made with events in 1679, when Shaftesbury, Essex (Capel), and other 'Whig' peers had pushed their way onto the Privy Council through Parliamentary pressure during the similarly fevered 'Popish Plot' crisis – again centring on murderous plots by the 'papist' national enemy. That did not resolve the crisis, as the King resented the newcomers and the latter continued to push for their own policies (on 'exclusion' of the Duke of York from the succession). Dismissals and renewed conflict followed, as it could have in 1642 once Charles I had regained his nerve and put an army – and funds for it – together.

As in France in 1789, Russia in 1917, or Beijing in 1989, a show of force that the government was in physical control of the capital was essential at some point. The King had to remain in his capital not flee, but also to show that he was not hostile to Church reform as such. In that case, early 1642 could have been used to raise more troops to add to the Tower garrison and bring them to Whitehall ready for use – provided that the Commons did not get wind of the actions of loyal courtiers in doing so and try to arrest them, which the King would then have to countermand. (He could claim the troops were going to Ireland.) If the 'Junto' could bring in troops to London alleging that they were en route to Ireland (Clotworthy's command), so could the King – with more authority. The King would have to counteract Parliament's crucial legal ability to issue orders to military garrisons, either by subterfuge or by enough religious concessions to win a majority of MPs and peers to his side. Having had his pro-'prerogative' judges removed in 1641, he would have needed to show those remaining in office that he was acting legally – which meant using a more skilful and trusted attorney-general than the ineffective Herbert. (St John was unlikely to have supported removing Parliament's powerful politico-military weapon of issuing orders to commanders.) The senior judges remaining after the eviction of the men seen as the 'Ship-Money' villains in 1640–1 were either so timorous or so affronted by the threat posed by royal prerogative powers that they failed to flee London after the King left, even when he had a functioning Parliament in Oxford in 1644. They could not be looked on for legal support; the King needed to appoint new judges who were loyal to the Episcopal Church order and saw Pym and the City mob as a greater threat than royal powers.

If necessary a proper legal case could be constructed for impeaching Pym, probably Strode as well – abuse of legal process in the Strafford trial or contacts with the Scots in time of war would be a start – and attempts made to detach Hampden and/or Holles with office and assurances about a Church assembly. Alternatively, Holles could be impeached for his threats to the Lords. Opening impeachment proceedings would have led to seizure of their papers. Given the importance of faction and intrigue at court, it would have been useful to employ the enthusiastic young 'Cavaliers' in finding evidence of Warwick or Saye and Sele's dealings with the Scots in 1639–40 to blackmail them with a threat of trial into being co-operative. The real-life attempts to seal up the 'Five Members' papers in January 1642 were countermanded by Parliamentary orders – but this was technically interference with the judicial process and so open to legal challenge. If the leading implacable MPs had been impeached by due legal process – without botched arrests – in January 1642, logically trying one or more of their Lords allies '*pour encourager les autres*' was next. Could Lady Carlisle have been 'turned' into betraying Pym and securing his secret correspondence in return for a large payment? Unfortunately, the court 'hot-heads' most loyal to the King lacked the subtlety for that sort of useful and unobtrusive espionage and, as the 'Army Plot' had showed, preferred loud talk and vague plans that were easily discovered. Conceivably, as the secret agents employed by Cardinal Richelieu against his enemies in the 1630s and early 1640s were more competent the Queen should have asked her brother Louis XIII for their assistance in exposing Pym or blackmailing the errant English nobles.

Any Commons resistance to properly drawn-up charges against some royal critics could be used as evidence of their destructive behaviour in rallying 'moderate' support. If the Commons voted to refuse to consider a proper legally documented case for a trial, publicizing this would be to Pym's detriment and the Lords were more likely to back the King. If Pym called in the City apprentices to intimidate MPs into voting against an impeachment, the King only had to wait for the crowds to disperse for a new vote – and if the demonstrations continued to resort to force. Assuming that troops from Portsmouth could add to those available at the Tower and the King's own young officers, the outcome would not be in doubt. Military courtiers such as Goring would have taken on the task of dispersing the crowds with gusto, and illegal printing-presses could then be raided. The municipal government in the City – led by merchants fearful of anarchy damaging their property – would have responded to royal orders had the King showed firmness, with his troops on the streets and pro-Pym common councillors under arrest. But this scenario would have required the King to be consistent in rejecting the influence of his impatient wife and courtiers and playing a 'waiting game' for some weeks into spring 1642, stressing his legality and desire to meet all reasonable demands in the meantime. He would have needed to be more open to the advice of Hyde or ex-'opposition' peers (people who were marginal at court) and less to Goring's young enthusiasts than in reality.

(ii) What if Charles had arrested the 'Five Members'?

Ironically, if he had managed to capture Pym's leadership clique by surprise in January and put them on trial for treason the Commons would have been deprived of co-ordination to resist, however outraged and unwilling to pass pro-royal votes for weeks. The omens would have been better if the process had been carried out legally after a majority vote for it in the two Houses, but even an inflammatory arrest would have put these men out of action. With Pym and his allies incommunicado in the Tower, outrage in the Commons would have lacked leadership and the role of senior peers with groups of Commons clients been vital. Charles would have been wise to make more concessions to Warwick's 'party', though their Calvinist leaders would have remained implacable even with the Scots treaty of August 1641 depriving them of the certainty of Scots military aid to pressurize Charles. They would have been calling a Lords vote condemning the King and demanding the MPs' release.

It would have been vital for Charles to present a legal offensive, with Herbert producing evidence that the accused were guilty as charged and claiming that they had only been 'snatched' by force to pre-empt violent resistance. A delay in further action while tempers cooled, and/or the dispersal of any intimidatory demonstrations by outraged City crowds by the Tower garrison, should have reduced the chances of a majority of MPs or peers rallying to Warwick's implacable Calvinists more than temporarily. But the precedents of how arrested religious pamphleteers like Prynne had been able to continue smuggling out inflammatory literature while in custody in the 1630s suggested that similar manifestoes could have escaped any new censorship. Laud could not silence 'Puritans' in the 1630s, and Cromwell and the 'Rump' were to fail to silence John Lilburne in the late 1640s. London had a venerable tradition of 'underground' printing-presses, even if their influence was marginal in marshalling opinion outside the region.

Stalemate over Church policy would have continued and the King seemed untrustworthy and so unsafe to put his own choice in charge of a large army for the Irish campaign unless he had made a choice such as Essex, but provided that the riotous Londoners could be dispersed the King would have regained the initiative. He would not have had the ability to restore the apparatus of royal rule over provinces and Church that had been demolished in 1641 or had the determined and effective men to lead this sort of policy, and would have needed a Parliament to vote supply for his administration and navy as well as the Irish war. As the Triennal Act was in force it could be argued that the 'political nation' was assured that any attempt to return to past abuses would be dealt with by the next Parliament, and there were no pro-prerogative' judges left in high office to declare any non-Parliamentary taxation legal.

The Scots Calvinist leadership would have had to be bought off with promises of surrender to their demands for an English clerical assembly in 1642/3 to investigate the future of the national Church, with the hint that the King would accept a majority vote for a Presbyterian experiment. The latter promise could also have encouraged enough MPs to make them accept that the Irish war must be the priority and vote the supply necessary to fund the army, provided that an 'opposition' figure had been named as the commander so the force would not be used to turn on English 'rebels'. The promised Church assembly, and acceptance of the Triennial Act to reassure people that Parliament would meet again in 1645, would be necessary to counter allegations from those radical MPs not arrested and their Lords allies that the King intended to bring in military rule with foreign Catholic help. But once the Scots were militarily preoccupied in Ulster their ability to coerce the King would have been neutralized, and at home the ascendancy of Argyll was still at risk of a revolt from the pro-royalist Montrose.

At worst, a dissolution of this Parliament for refusing supply would have followed and then a prolonged impasse before the King could assemble a more tractable body – after due assurances and political gestures of his support for Church reform? – to resume the attempt to gain finance. Warwick's group of peers would have been likely to resume the threat of an illegal armed assembly to pressurize the King, as in 1640, but would have had no unpreoccupied Scots army ready to march south to aid them. Their potential to rally support would have been less than earlier, as the King had now allowed his subjects to have their way in Parliament over prerogative rule, 'Black Tom Tyrant' (Strafford), and Laudian Church reforms in 1641 and the Triennial Act was in place to assure people of no more 'Personal Rule'. The King was not now threatening the constitution; indeed, the 'lynch-mob' mentality of the Strafford trial in May 1641 and the threat of 'Root and Branch' to the Anglican Church were being exploited by royal propaganda to encourage a pro-King reaction in real-life 1642. Without a substantial provincial reaction against Parliament for challenging King and Church in 1642 Charles would have had no army. The amount of support that rebel peers could count on to coerce Charles in 1642–4 would thus have been less than in 1640, and if they had been denied a base in London (their 1640 headquarters) by a royal garrison their threat would have been further diminished.

With Scotland bought off by legislative surrender to a Presbyterian Church in 1641, Charles would have been attempting to recruit a Scottish army to fight for him in Ulster – whether led by Covenanter peers and generals like Leslie to get them out of Scotland, or led by moderates like Montrose to add to their military power for a later confrontation with the Argyll faction. The alarm caused across England by the lurid stories of massacres in Ireland would have been invaluable in assisting recruitment had the royal tenants-in-chief and County Lords Lieutenant been put in charge of raising an army for Ireland in 1642, even if the King had to auction some royal estates or plate to encourage 'patriots' to lend him money without Parliamentary sanction. Had he not dared to call a new Parliament to pay for war, his regime's fondness for dredging up ancient precedents for raising money in the 1630s meant that he could have tried calling the Lords without the Commons – in the form of a traditional 'Great Council' of the nobility. This would have been more reliable if Charles had granted more important posts to key 'moderate' figures than he did in real life, e.g. to Pembroke, Hertford, and Newport. The winning over of any firmly anti-Laudian Calvinists (Essex? Brooke?) would have required calling a Church Assembly to reform the ecclesiastical settlement; Charles had made promises of a return to the Elizabethan settlement of 1559 (which had comprehended moderate Calvinists) but was unlikely to have been flexible about the episcopate unless in extreme need of political allies. Many peers, including any former critics of the King now in royal employ in place of the disgraced ministers removed in 1641, would have needed strong assurances on matters of religion in order to avoid a repeat of the near-mutiny of Warwick's group in 1640. The role of Essex, possibly won over with the command in Ireland, would have been crucial; Warwick himself was probably irreconcilable even if spared a trial for 'treason' concerning documentary evidence of his links to the Scots.

The widespread resistance of nobles and gentry alike to raising an army without Parliamentary sanction in 1639–40 had been for a dubious war against *Protestant* rebels – men who were fighting the same sort of 'innovations' that Laud had launched in the English Church. Fighting a war against 'barbarous papists' who were massacring English settlers would have been a more congenial duty to the 'political nation', and as the apparatus of royal and Church 'misrule' had been destroyed and its leading personnel prosecuted in 1641 the current English government would have been less controversial. If the breach with Parliament had been over such demands as the abolition of the episcopate in alliance with the rebel Scots, the King should not have appeared as the mistrusted enemy of his subjects' rights that his attempt on the 'Five Members' made him appear in real-life 1642. Even if he had gone ahead and seized them, their allies in the counties would not have been powerful enough to hold up the moves by royally appointed lords lieutenant, deputy lieutenants, and JPs to raise an army. Unlike in real-life

1642, they would not have had possession of London and its resources – or of printing-presses to issue justificatory propaganda. The law courts, the Navy, and central direction of provincial officials would all have remained with the King. Provided that there was no evident threat to the legally obligatory calling of the next Parliament in 1645, there was no obvious ground for mass-support for a 'radical' move to coerce the King even had he dissolved the previous Parliament in contentious circumstances and put a few leading MPs in the Tower.

A meeting of convocation and tax on the clergy to raise money were possible, although the King would have had to be desperate to accept the need to sell off some Church lands (as the indebted post-Civil War regimes did) to raise money despite the fact that this dismantling of episcopal resources would have pleased 'Puritan' nobles and the Scots leadership.

What if Charles had delayed a confrontation?

Alternatively, the King might not have forced a showdown with the Commons leadership as early as January 1642. He could have waited longer before trying to impeach or forcibly arrest Pym's group, letting them seem to be holding up a solution and an agreement on the leadership and financing of the Irish army for their own irresponsible political ends and thus reducing their support further. This is assuming that Charles could have held his nerve and relied on political 'lobbying' to secure enough votes in the Lords and Commons to defeat an attempted impeachment of the bishops. The latter's enemies would have been using the weapon of popular protest to intimidate waverers, as with the Strafford trial in May 1641. But now the King had more armed men in London, the York troops who had escorted him into his capital in November and the reinforced Tower garrison. The measures that the 'opposition' were now pressing were more contentious than punishing the perceived 'tyrant' and 'coup-plotter' Strafford, whose death was seen as essential for national peace by normally moderate men like Falkland. Would the Warwick/Pym factions have been able to secure enough votes to impeach the bishops (for no clear crime) or abolish episcopacy? If the crowds had been held back by the King's troops in Westminster, the chances of defeating the 'Root and Branch' faction in open votes would have been hopeful. If enough 'loyal' MPs and peers had showed up in Westminster on 12 January 1642 as ordered, it would have improved Charles' chances of winning votes – but this is to assume that all the absentees would have dared to come to the turbulent capital and risk their political futures by openly taking sides in an evenly balanced conflict.

By early spring 1642 votes would have been ebbing from Pym, with the fear of disorder playing into the King's hands. Without the boost to their popularity of the attempted arrests, could they have been impeached successfully by spring 1642 if the King had 'stalled' and let them seem to be holding up dealing with Ireland? He would have needed to use Lunsford at the Tower and his troops to deal with the London mobs that Pym could summon to his aid for intimidatory demonstrations, perhaps with some fighting around Parliament as the troops broke up a riot by apprentices. With the radical MPs seeming to be supporting rioters and encouraging chaos, deft propaganda in the country would have rallied provincial support to the King's side and turned him into the voice of stability. Pym's printing-presses would need to have been seized to silence his cause, and the pro-royalist aldermen assisted in regaining control of the City.

The radicals could have lost the votes to control the leadership of the Irish army – or a compromise been reached with a majority of the Commons and a powerful group of 'opposition' Lords, putting Essex in charge – and enabled the King to start recruiting it in spring 1642. Some commissions to senior 'Puritan' aristocrats would have reassured moderate MPs that it would not be put in the hands of hotheads and used against Parliament; perhaps a more personally congenial royal general (Rupert?) could have recruited separately for a force to fight in one particular Irish province. Leading Protestant zealot nobles such as Warwick and Brooke could hardly have refused a royal request to raise troops in their neighbourhoods and proceed to Ireland to save their co-religionists – but once they were out of England they would be politically neutralized. Provided that the King temporized about the Church and held open the prospect of major reform like he did in Scotland in 1638–9, his arch-critics could have been isolated within Parliament. They would be outvoted on raising subsidies for the Irish war, with a promise of a religious assembly to review the Church to secure the votes of religiously zealous MPs and keep the Scots from breaking camp to advance further. Any motion by Warwick's group to keep a committee of peers or MPs in being during the vacancy between Parliaments (a possible threat given that one existed in Scotland) was unlikely to have secured enough votes to pass.

Once Parliament broke up with a promise of an early new meeting (via the Triennial Act), Pym's group could have been arrested on some excuse and left to rot in the Tower like Eliot in 1629. The same applies to Warwick's peers, as seen by the arrests after the 'Short Parliament' in spring 1640. There was nothing to prevent the King carrying out legal arrests once Parliament had dispersed, as Charles II was to do in 1681–2, or to turn loyal regiments raised for the Irish war on London street-demonstrations. The links that Pym's faction had built up with the Scots in a time of war in 1639–40 were an adequate excuse for charges of treason.

The horror of the Irish massacres being felt all over the country and Protestant opinion inflamed, the King could have raised a larger-than-usual army to deal with it that spring and summer – something on the lines of the real-life royalist army, with Lords Lieutenant raising regiments in each county. The local leadership would have had no alternative 'power-centre' in Westminster to support once Parliament had passed its tax- and army-raising measures and been dissolved, even if they disbelieved the King's promises about the future. Pym & co. would have stayed isolated in the Tower awaiting trial or even without a trial like Eliot in 1629, with no ability to raise support except by sympathetic but illegal pamphleteering. They would have been powerless and could have been left to rot, with the sort of Puritan peers that had led the 'opposition' to the royal rule without Parliament in the 1630s now bought off with satisfactory measures in Parliament and the nation rallying around an Irish war against 'popery', which would have presented the King as a national leader rather than a crypto-Catholic.

The dangers would come later, particularly if the King followed the terms of the 'Triennial Act' to summon Parliament in 1644/5, which finance for a continuing and costly war would have made advisable anyway. In the meantime there would have had to be a religious conference in London on the same sort of lines as the real-life 'Westminster Assembly' to placate 'Puritan' peers and the Scots, as the Commons would probably have insisted on being called before they voted supplies in 1642. But as episcopacy had not been suspended or abolished the bishops, in charge of what remained of the Church disciplinary powers in their sees, would logically have had the lead in selecting the English members of the Assembly. The 'Puritan' peers and MPs might well have forced Charles to accept that local congregations should also elect delegates, in order to boost the 'reforming' part of the membership, and anti-Laudian bishops led by Williams made a selection of more Calvinist clergymen from their areas. Both these groups had their own agendas in reforming the Church and coercing the King to keep any 'Arminian' revival at bay, and Laud's possible release from the Tower once Parliament was dissolved would have stimulated anger. But the Anglicans should have retained the majority, putting the supporters of abolishing episcopacy at a numerical disadvantage and putting the Scots in a dilemma as to whether to walk out in disgust.

Henderson, Johnson of Warriston, and like-minded zealots would have lacked their real-life power in such an Assembly, as the government in London did not desperately need Scots help against a military foe within England – and if the King had kept regiments in London the English and Scots Presbyterians would have been unable to use the weapon of the 'street' as Pym had done to press his cause in 1641–2. But this 'long-term' royal strategy argues for a greater political realism and cunning than Charles was to show in real life. He offered this sort of major short-term concession to the Scots in 1641 as he had no serious alternative at the time, with Montrose neutralized, but time and time again delayed too long in entering into similar actions in England as late as 1648.

Further developments during and after fighting the Irish revolt

The scale of the Irish revolt would have meant no quick resolution, even if the King had used officers who had fought in Europe and perhaps demanded that the anti-Catholic Scots leadership send troops there too. General Leslie, as a veteran of Continental warfare, was a logical choice to campaign in Ulster to aid his fellow-Presbyterians and had he refused to vacate Newcastle (on the Covenanter-run Scots Parliament's orders?) a pro-royal noble would have had the chance to assemble an army to take the task on. The Scots leadership under Argyll would have had a dilemma whether to carry out royal orders over the Irish war, thus aiding their fellow-Protestants, or to assume all direction of the Scots campaign in Ulster themselves autonomously in what could later be charged as acts of rebellion. They would have been uneasy at co-ordinating the war with the King's generals, men who they had fought in 1639 and 1640 and whose troops could later be turned on Scotland. Any loyal nobles given military commands in Ireland would gain experience for their men that the King could use for his next war against Scotland, although sending such men – Huntly? Hamilton? – to Ireland would neutralize their power at home for the moment. A logical choice for Argyll, as the leading 'political' radical Covenanter warlord, to send out of the way to command in Ireland was his junior rival Montrose, not yet known as a royal ally in 1642–4 and the victor over Huntly at Aberdeen in 1639 so acceptable to the Covenanter clerical assembly for a command. Once in Ireland, such enemies of Argyll's predominance in Covenanter governance would have been likely targets for royalist intrigue to induce them to turn against the Campbell chief.

Aristocratic royal generals' leisurely way of making war, a lack of an overall plan, and administrative inefficiency and lack of military experience would have held up even a large English army in Ireland. It would have been able to co-ordinate strategy with Ormonde and the royalist forces based in Dublin, but an early victory was unlikely. As with the royalist and Parliamentary armies in England in 1642–3, large and unwieldy forces of inexperienced men with inadequate weaponry would have lumbered around the country. Numbers and artillery had been useless for previous attempts to catch mobile forces of lightly armed guerrillas with local knowledge, as Essex's father had found when he tackled the last serious Irish revolt in 1599.

This campaign was likely to be just as frustrating, except perhaps in retaking occupied towns and castles, and to have dragged on into 1643 and then 1644. The Scots in particular would have been keen to solve the problem of the local Catholics, all potential future rebels, by mass-expropriations to complete the work their nationals had started earlier that century in Ulster. Militant English 'Puritan' peers with a taste for colonial ventures, such as Warwick and Saye and Sele who had funded a private colonial war against Catholic Spain in the Caribbean and settled Providence Island as a privateering base in the 1630s, were likely enthusiasts for expropriation too. The 'civilization' of the disaffected Catholic areas by English colonists had a long history among Protestant zealots, as seen by the involvement of Raleigh and Spenser in the 1570s 'plantations', and the probable Anglo-Irish commander Ormonde would have had problems with such men as subordinate commanders. Even if the King was not strongly opposed to such proposals for mass-evictions the Queen would have been speaking up for her co-religionists, and if the alarmed Catholic rebel gentry had used their clerical links with Rome to have a papal plea sent to London for less harsh measures this would have been disastrous to the Queen's reputation among her husband's countrymen.

There would have been dark hints among MPs in 1644/5 that crypto-Catholic court officers did not want to impose a firm hand on the Catholic Irish, particularly if there were local truces and arrangements for some ex-rebels to join the royal army. The King's generals may well have had an ultimate war against the 'rebels' in Scotland in mind, following the alleged plans of Strafford to use an Irish army to attack Scotland, and the King too have considered this as a useful idea – he sought to use the 'moderate' Irish on the mainland as his cause faltered in the Civil War in real life. This could have leaked out, and the recruitment of loyal pro-royalist 'Old Irish' to the King's army alarmed Protestant officers and opinion back at home. A 'Catholic' army in Ireland as an agent of autocracy and a potential intimidator of Parliament would have seemed a threat to xenophobic Protestants in the mid-1640s just as it did in 1687–8. A reassertion of the power of the Queen's faction at court could have assisted the alienation of some Protestant peers who could co-ordinate opposition, and moves been made in Parliament to force the appointment of 'patriotic' and trustable senior commanders in Ireland – such as the Earl of Essex, though if he had been entrusted with the 1642 army he would have been no more successful than he was as a sluggish Parliamentarian commander-in- chief in real life.

The army in Ireland could have seen Rupert as a successful cavalry-commander in battle and a capable leader of conventional sieges, but no use against guerrillas and too rash to withstand ambushes. Real-life capable and adaptable royalist and Parliamentarian commanders, e.g. Hopton and Waller, could have emerged as 'meritocrats' to lead subsidiary expeditions while the King kept the senior posts with aristocrats as in keeping with tradition, e.g. the Earl of Newcastle. Perhaps the raisers and leaders of new English regimental levies for the war, e.g. Bevil Grenville for Cornwall, would also have achieved success and been promoted. An army with some resemblance to the King's real-life forces of 1643–5, fairly 'professional' and learning by experience, would have been needed for a long war if the situation in Ireland had had six months or so from the outbreak of revolt in autumn 1641 to get out of hand before the political delays in England allowed an English army to arrive. A three- or four-year war was quite possible, on the lines of the Late Tudor experience of Irish revolts, with a 'plantation' of the main areas of rebel land following. Would some of the more zealous but impoverished junior provincial Protestant officers – in real life, Parliamentarian New Model successes – been keen to settle the lands of the papists and secure more estates and social status for themselves and a role as 'front-line' soldiers of the faith against a Catholic revanche? Was this the sort of opportunity that would appeal to a zealous and successful junior cavalry-officer with no major prospects at home like Cromwell (assuming that he had not emigrated to Massachusetts in disgust as he supposedly threatened to do if the Grand Remonstrance was not passed)?

With Parliament impatient for success against the rebels and radical hints that certain crypto-Catholic senior officers were not zealous enough about achieving victory, the Army leadership would have had to start providing results by the time the next Parliament met or they would be as obstructive as in 1641/2. Hence, a move to promote some new senior commanders on merit not birth would have been as vital as in the Civil War armies – and Protestant zeal should have encouraged some of the real-life 'meritocratic' Parliamentarian officers of 1642–4 to take part in the war. But the retention of Royal and aristocratic control of promotion would have meant no New Model Protestant army, however slow the Army was to reduce the rebel provinces. The difficulties of Irish warfare would have been such as to hand the best chances of promotion in the King's army to the sort of officers who exercised initiative and skill in the royalist and Parliamentarian armies in England in real life.

Would the need to have victories that could reassure public opinion and Parliament lead to a wise commander-in-chief promoting successful junior officers to command quicker than normal? Would an ineffective aristocratic commander like Essex, lumbering around the country being eluded by the Irish, have to be replaced due to popular discontent at the slow rate of military progress – or would royal favourites like Goring undermine him?

(The Queen would want a more loyal commander-in-chief with links to her court faction, so that he could turn his troops on Parliament on his return if needed?) Rupert might eventually get the overall command, with a secret royal agenda of building up his reputation and military expertise so that he could be turned on the Scots. The overall political leadership in Ireland would obviously be Ormonde's, as Lord Lieutenant and as the new governor once peace had been restored.

Having overcome the Irish, apart from a few isolated provincial guerrilla forces, the large and now well-trained royal army would have been available c. 1646 to be turned on the Scots – though quite a few zealous Puritan officers would have resigned their commissions sooner than do so. Would there have been an effective royalist political leadership in London capable of managing a Parliament into funding a Scots expedition on the excuse of rebellion if the Covenanters rejected all attempts at a political/religious compromise in talks with the King during 1642–5? The Covenanters, their military strength on the Border diminished by the need to send troops (and Leslie?) to Ulster to save the local Protestants, would still have insisted on no bishops anywhere in Scotland or even a Presbyterian reform of the English Church. If an English ecclesiastical Assembly had met in 1643/4 as per the royal promises of early 1642, the Covenanters were likely to have overplayed their hand as they did with the Westminster Assembly in real life. Also, the 'recruitment drive' for the English army in Ireland could have led to zealous Protestant MPs who in real life led the Parliamentarian Presbyterian faction in 1642–7, being away fighting for their faith, and so not available for the 1644/5 Parliament.

There was strong provincial antagonism to the established English Church in some areas in the 1640s, e.g. East Anglia, and the machinery of Church discipline had been destroyed in 1641 so agitating pro-Presbyterians could take over local congregations in the chaos. Thus, they would have had a strong presence in the Assembly unless the King and those 'High Anglican' bishops not arrested in 1641 had had the time to restore discipline. But there would have been royal local authorities in control of all English counties not Parliamentary allies, so probably the Anglicans could retain control of the parish and episcopal structure and secure a majority of votes in the Assembly to retain bishoprics. The Scots would have been defeated, but now facing a King with troops at his disposal – by 1644/5, including experienced returning veterans of the Irish war.

In the next Parliament of 1644/5, would most of the sort of provincial gentry and City merchants elected as MPs have been reassured by the King's actions since 1642? There should have been no royal attempts in 1642–5 to reverse the constitutional measures of 1641, and the King's leadership of the defeat of the Catholic Irish revolt and attempts to be reasonable with the Covenanters would show that he was not under the Queen's control. Or would the 'Root and Branch' militant enthusiasm for further Church reform in 'Puritan' communities have been revived by the elections for a new Parliament and stories of Catholic atrocities in Ireland, and led to a new confrontation in Parliament at any idea of using the army against Scotland? If the militants had the majority of MPs, would the King have ordered a dissolution and funded the Scots war out of the sale of confiscated estates in Ireland, or used returned troops from Ireland to assist with a 'Pride's Purge'-style eviction of opposition MPs? Or would the King have decided not to risk relying on Parliament to fund a Scottish expedition? Control of Parliament would have depended on the election of reliable pro-royal candidates, which was easier for lords lieutenant and loyal gentry to arrange in the counties than in the boroughs.

Would the King have had to wait for the conclusion of the Irish war to attack Scotland, or been impatient enough to encourage a rising against the Covenanters before then? How about Montrose, the leader of the moderate Covenanters – would he have been alienated enough by the Argyll faction and the clerics to start that rising in the Highlands which he did in reality in 1644? More radical Irish Catholics favouring total independence may have seized the initiative in that rebellion and received papal aid – though when this happened in real life it was assisted by the lack of English troops there. This would have split the rebel army, and Ormonde would have been encouraged to open secret talks with some rebel commanders, promising them pardon and exemption from the threat of seizure and settlement of defeated rebels' lands. (Parliament in both 1642 and 1644/5 would have been vocal in calls to 'cleanse' Ireland of Catholicism.) Could pro-royalist Catholic forces in Ulster alienated from the main rebel leadership over their refusal of peace-terms, or pardoned rebels required to leave the country, have been secretly sent to the Highlands by the King to start an uprising?

Irish Ulster Catholics were prominent in Montrose's army in real life, and Randall Macdonnell of Antrim would have been a crucial royal ally in rallying the royalist Catholics. Similarly, any Scots nobles who had led troops to Ulster to aid the Protestants there in 1642–3 (Hamilton?) would have had troops on hand to use for the King against their Covenanter countrymen. The uneasy royal/Covenanter truce after 1640 would have been 'cover' for the King to encourage the Scots nobility to raise levies to fight for his cause in Ireland, with the ultimate aim of turning them on Argyll's extremists. The most able commander available was Montrose, who as a firm Presbyterian could show the wavering Scots that the King was fighting not their Church but a monopoly of power by Argyll and a few politically minded clerics.

If there had been a revolt in Scotland against the Covenanter regime, rumours of royal encouragement and royal use of Catholics in it could have leaked out to MPs in London and caused suspicion of the King's intentions. But if the King was prepared to publicly tolerate a Presbyterian Church running Scotland for the moment, the pro-royal forces operating for Charles in Ulster could have formed the nucleus of an armed royal coalition to turn on Argyll's extremists even without a Highlands revolt. Hamilton would have been a crucial figure in persuading majority opinion among the Scots nobility to trust the King, and Montrose provided the crucial initial military victories with his tactical ability. But revelations of Charles' deals with Irish Catholic rebels to obtain their surrender would have hardened Presbyterian unity in resisting any accommodation with him short of total surrender of control over Church and senior offices. Control of Scotland was likelier to have been determined by a military clash than by a political compromise.

Ultimately a large and successful royalist armed force in Ireland would have provided the unquestioningly loyal backing the King needed and the military expertise that would make a victory against Covenanter forces easier than in 1639 and 1641, when the King's troops in the north were small in numbers, ill-funded, and inexperienced. Even with some troops still needed to garrison the newly regained rebel areas of Ireland, enough would have been available for success in an attack on the Lowlands – perhaps in co-ordination with Montrose's revolt, if that had followed the same trajectory as it did in real life, in 1645. More royal troops would have crossed from Ulster to assist them, and if Argyll and the Lowlands clerical militants had been holding up a settlement with the King more nobles could have joined Hamilton in throwing in their lot with the King if he seemed less dangerous than power-hungry Argyll.

A victorious king?
1646 could thus have seen the King with his experienced army in full control of all three kingdoms, even if his methods to achieve this had not been popular with a substantial section of the moderate but zealously Protestant MPs who had rallied to his cause for an Irish war in 1642. He might have had to shut down Parliament again in 1645/6 if they refused to fund his Scottish campaign, but had the Irish confiscations to rely on for an income for a few years. Some of the real-life Parliament's special tax-raising revenue measures of the mid-1640s (e.g. the assessments and new customs-duties) could have been set up in England to help royal finances on the excuse of a national emergency i.e. the Scottish war. The tax-raising and administrative innovations of the real-life Parliamentary cause would have been carried out by the King's men – an equivalent of the recent use of 'intendants' by

Richelieu in France, which could have provided a model to follow. This would have served to keep royal government going when there was no Parliament sitting easier than the government managed in 1629–40, and the result borne some similarities to the administrative situation of the Commonwealth. Special measures taken for the 'emergency' of double rebellion in the 1640s would then become permanent, with or without Parliament. But to do without the latter the legal justifications for 'prerogative' rule that had been roundly destroyed in 1641 would have had to be revived by a new generation of subservient judges, and it is doubtful if the King would have had the necessary experts and organizers available in the England of the 1640s. England lacked the long tradition of legally unquestioned royal legal authority in a Continental monarchy such as France.

Assuming that the need to conciliate domestic opinion had dissuaded the King from the political folly of reversing any of the religious measures of 1640–41 while he needed Parliamentary and provincial support for raising taxes and men to fight the Irish rebellion, there might have been an abortive religious commission of English and Scots clerics in 1644–5 to discuss the future of the Church like the Westminster Assembly. Laud would have had to stay in the Tower if he had still been there when the Assembly met, and perhaps a number of known 'Puritan' clerics been offered bishoprics via Williams. But the King would only have been playing for time, perhaps to calm the suspicions of militant Protestants in the 1644/5 Parliament while he needed their votes for taxes. The obduracy of the Presbyterians about bishops, vestments, the altar, the Prayer Book etc. would have enabled them to be portrayed as the cause of an inevitable deadlock. With his new large army enabling him to bring crack troops to London, the King could have kept popular demonstrations in favour of the Puritans under control and in due course closed the meeting down – perhaps as war with Scotland loomed or the King's encouragement to Montrose caused the Scots commissioners to walk out.

The personnel that would have come to prominence in a saved Anglican Church after 1645/6 would have been more moderate and less 'Arminian' than Laud and his contemporaries, a generation that was now passing, except for a few anomalies like Matthew Wren. Archbishop Williams of York would have been in the ascendant along with other Calvinists, and the machinery of ecclesiastical discipline of the 1630s would have had some years in abeyance and was unlikely to have been revived. Similarly, the royal government would have been unable to return to the 'feudal' machinery of pre-1640 despite an abeyance of political opposition and the potential for extra-parliamentary sources of revenue set up in the 1640s enabling the King to call Parliament less frequently. The likely timetables of Irish and Scottish wars would, however, have been such that the conflict on the Continent was coming to a conclusion with the pre-Westphalia peace-conferences by the time that order had been restored to Ireland and Scotland by c.1646, so the victorious army and a prestigious and experienced commander (Rupert, as Ormonde's chief of cavalry?) could not be effectively used to secure more of the Palatinate for Rupert's family than the Habsburgs were prepared to offer.

The 1650s could thus have seen a second period of 'Personal Rule' without Parliaments, or with heavily 'managed' and brief meetings with a 'blacklist' of undesirable candidates banned from membership such as opponents of the King's Scottish campaign. If Charles I had lived to a similar age as his father, he would have died at the age of c.58 in c.1659 and Charles II would then have succeeded – a monarch without the assorted traumas of the Civil War period and so possibly less cynical and alienated from politics, but still with memories of the Strafford impeachment of 1641 and so deeply suspicious of an out-of-control Parliament?

Chapter Two

Could the War have been Won Quickly by the King? The Edgehill Campaign

Could the King have been too weak to fight in 1642?

The initiative seemed to lie with Parliament in the summer of 1642, with the King having difficulty in raising troops in the north but a 'rebel' army starting to assemble around Northampton and Coventry. Indeed, the leading royal supporter Sir Jacob Astley initially feared that the King would be unable to resist a Parliamentary attack as his smaller army started to gather at Nottingham in August. He even had to disarm the local Trained Bands at Nottingham itself (mostly townsmen, a category usually pro-Parliament) for fear they would join Parliament. He made one legal slip in referring to his war in official documents as being with Parliament, rather than with a militant minority of the latter, his technical position – but did this reflect his real attitude? In his first speech to his army on the road from Nottingham on 19 August, he claimed their enemies were mostly radical sectaries, e.g. the much-feared Anabaptists, and were intent on overthrowing Church and State whereas he was the guarantor of the laws of the land – 'spin' at odds with the way he had bent some laws for State advantage in recent years. But the King's commissioners had achieved little success across large areas as they attempted to read out his 'Commissions of Array' and recruit troops, with successful armed resistance to them from pro-Parliamentary gentry including the Fairfaxes in Yorkshire.[1] The backing of the urban centres of the cloth trade in Yorkshire and Lancashire for the 'rebels' and the resistance of the garrison of Hull meant that the King's position was precarious even in the north-east, where he had to rely on inconvenient Newcastle as his major port. His aristocratic allies in the mostly rural areas had a major advantage as the principal landlords who could thus call up their tenants, but the success of the Earl of Newcastle and his fellow-Cavendishes in their areas (e.g. Northumberland and the Peaks) was not replicated by the Earl of Derby in Lancashire where the townsmen were mainly antagonistic to the King.[2]

Newcastle, an immensely rich landed peer and master of courtly manners with a set of huge mansions and a passion for horse-training, was trustable but a dilettante who failed to secure Hull quickly. It was fortunate that Charles' settlement with the Covenanter regime in Edinburgh in August 1641 and their need to send troops to Ireland meant that his precarious position in the north was not threatened by attack from the rear by Parliament's allies. Leslie had returned to Scotland and sailed to Ulster in spring 1642, and was now reconquering the province as far as his small-scale force permitted.

The Irish dimension

The Catholic rebels had been able to assume a dominant position over most of Ireland outside the Dublin area (held by a weak pro-Parliamentary regime, still technically loyal to Charles), areas in the south-centre (held by more unequivocal royalists, particularly the troops of the Marquis of Ormonde) and the small pro-Scots, pro-Parliamentary Protestant area in eastern Ulster. Having overrun most of the countryside in areas not held by major pro-royalist magnates such as Ormonde and Inchiquin, their disparate and initially haphazard local forces were able to gain the adherence of or overrun the remaining non-rebel towns in these areas – including strategic ports such as Wexford and Waterford. The lack of any resistance to them forced those landowners, 'tribal' Gaelic or 'Old English' by descent, who had not been involved in the initial plot to join with them for their security and the militant resolve of the English Parliament to expropriate all Catholics left the latter with no alternative. The initial rebel leaders had been men based in Ireland, mainly in Ulster; but in summer 1642 the first significant group of exiled Catholic officers in Spanish service returned to aid the rebel army, men with more military experience (in the Thirty Years' War) and so likely to demand and take a lead. The most notable of them was Tyrone's nephew Owen Roe O'Neill, a glamorous and charismatic commander with many Continental contacts but a potential rival to his cousin Sir Phelim O'Neill as the rebels' Ulster leader. Owen Roe, like many Continentally trained officers, was a more 'activist' Catholic than the majority of the 'native Irish' rebel leaders, and more inclined to seek aid from Spain and the papacy. The orientation of the Catholic clergy, the only 'national' organization able to spearhead policy and organization across Ireland (who thus took the lead as the rebels set up a government at Kilkenny), was also crucial. In a position of power as the leaders of their parish flocks, the clergy were vital to any consideration of a political approach to the King – and had a vested interest in securing their complete freedom from harassment or political control in any future government. Had the secular lords had more control over the council and later assembly at Kilkenny, it would have been easier for a 'moderate' Protestant royalist Irish magnate like Ormonde – used to social dealings with Catholic landowners – to come to an accommodation with them and hire troops for the King.

To add to the complications of the situation in 1642, the Dublin administration was led by largely pro-Parliamentary and anti-Catholic 'Lords Justices' still technically loyal to Charles. They were dominated by the 'planter' Sir William Parsons from Co. Offaly, a man with a vested interest in keeping the Protestantized lands of his Irish Midlands district free from Catholic claims and so naturally cleaving to the English Parliamentary cause. They ruled in the absence of the Lord Lieutenant, the Earl of Leicester – an English aristocrat appointed by Charles as a concession to his critics in 1641, not trusted by him, and not yet in Ireland. The main commander 'in the field' for the embattled government was Ormonde, who was trusted by Charles and when it came to a choice would favour him not Parliament or its nominee Leicester – as the lords justices were aware. That time for choice between Charles and Parliament had not yet come, and in the meantime the 'government' forces opposed to the Catholic rebels were small, under-funded, and hesitant in campaigns.

This aided the rebels' chances, though they lacked a centralized organization and political 'direction' until a governing council was set up at Kilkenny in May. Some rebel commanders distrusted each other too. But their rebellion had been nominally loyal to Charles in its initial declarations, provided that he would recognize the rebels' effective legislative and religious autonomy with a Catholic regime ruling Ireland. There were links between the leading dynasty involved in organizing the revolt, the O'Neills of Ulster, and personnel in the Royal Household where a fervently Catholic Queen with a multi-national staff could be expected to show their desire for Catholic rights some sympathy. Indeed the Ulster rebel commander Sir Phelim O'Neill's cousin Colonel Daniel O'Neill, an officer at court, may have alerted the Queen or senior courtiers to the planned rebellion – which was aimed at the expected confiscatory policies of the zealously Protestant Parliament in London. This opened up the possibility of co-operation between the hard-pressed King and the Irish rebels, provided that he granted them that politico-religious autonomy that he had already granted the Scots Covenanter regime in Edinburgh in August 1641. There was a logical argument for royal efforts to grant very liberal terms to the rebel regimes in both 'Celtic' nations – one Catholic, one Presbyterian – to use their armies against Parliament, a constant factor of the complex politics of the 'War of Three Kingdoms' from 1641 to 1648. This was certainly feared in Westminster, where rumours constantly circulated of Charles' equivocal attitude to the Irish rebellion and intentions of using the Irish rebels against Parliament. His possession of a French Catholic Queen, sister to Louis XIII, made a hunt for French and other European – Catholic – troops logical, as illustrated by his despatch of her abroad early that year to seek assistance, so why not Irish Catholic troops too? Acquiring proof of Charles' 'popish' links and intention to use the perpetrators of the October 1641 massacres against his Protestant subjects would be invaluable propaganda for the King's most trenchant critics at Westminster, and should bring in a stream of alarmed Protestant English recruits for the Parliamentary cause.

The 'royalist' Irish Catholic gentry of the 'Pale', facing an unsympathetic Protestant regime in Dublin which mistrusted them as potential rebels, despatched a Major Reade to Charles in March 1642 to assure him of their loyalty. Unfortunately, he was caught en route by the Dublin regime and racked in an effort to secure a confession that he was working for the King and Queen[3] – and of their involvement with the Catholic rebels. Another, more open Catholic 'Palesmen' attempt to contact the King was made in a petition forwarded to Ormonde, but he recognized it as potential political dynamite and saw that the 'Lords Justices' sat on it (May).[4] In the meantime the Dublin Parliament evicted all its Catholic MPs and broke off relations with the Catholics, probably inevitable given the mixture of fear of all Catholics as rebels and the undoubted pressure from Parliament in London (on which they relied) that would follow any attempt to put out feelers to the 'papist mass-murderers'. The extent of the October massacres was bound to polarize opinion, making any attempt by a senior 'moderate' royalist figure (such as Ormonde, the major landholder in Tipperary) or elements in the Dublin government to achieve partial reconciliation futile. The lurid stories circulating in England of thousands being slaughtered in Ulster had added to the perennial post-'Gunpowder Plot' English Protestant fear of Catholic plots and atrocities, and Parliament had now voted to confiscate all Irish Catholic lands when reconquered. Land in all four provinces was to be handed over to subscribers, 'Adventurers', who would put funds forward for a proposed Parliamentary loan of £1 million to pay for the cost of an army of reconquest – a dramatic extension of the early seventeenth century policy of confiscation of untrustworthy Catholics' land for loyal Protestants seen in Ulster. Indeed, the King gave his assent to this bill when it was sent to him for ratification during the ongoing and unsuccessful royal-Parliamentary negotiations that spring.[5] At the time he had little choice if he was to avoid accusations of pro-Catholic sympathies from radical 'Puritans' like Warwick and Pym, who were no doubt ready to use any evidence of his sinister intentions towards Parliament and Protestantism. The London merchants and others who were to fund the Parliamentary army of reconquest would have a powerful reason to oppose him unless he gave in. But his public anti-Catholic stance was in direct opposition to his real attitude to the usefulness of Irish Catholic troops, and showed him as cynical and devious – he was prepared to allow loyal Irish Catholics not implicated in the massacres to be dispossessed if this would win over his English Parliament.

Raising the armies

The most crucial issue in England was to be which set of orders to enlist troops – from the King or from the Parliamentary leadership in London – would be obeyed in the localities. Given the rudimentary nature of local administration and the usual deference showed by the gentry in each area to the leading landowners, much would depend on who the latter backed. The leading local aristocrats were crucial as holders of the lord lieutenancies of each county, the supreme office in local government – particularly in raising the militia for defence. (In some counties there was one dominant family, who usually held that office without interruption; in others there was competition between several families.) The deputy lieutenants, selected from the gentry, would probably follow their lead in choosing to obey the commissioners sent to collect troops either by Charles or by Parliament. Technically, Parliament had control of London and the judicial machinery, and thus could issue the usual orders given to mobilize the militia at the outbreak of war. The King was forced to resort to more antiquated 'Commissions of Array'. Legally, therefore, the local lords and deputy lieutenants had a 'safer' argument for recognizing Parliament's orders; and to complicate matters the King proceeded to dismiss some of these officials for refusing to carry out his orders, appointing new ones who would do so. In that case, which set of officials were the – usually politically divided – local gentry to obey? Indeed, the situation of having to make such a choice was unprecedented, and loyalty to either side could not be guaranteed; much would depend on individual consciences or calculations of best advantages. The latter would indicate that the aristocratic and gentry leadership of those counties furthest from London had the most at risk if they backed Parliament, as being furthest from help if Charles' supporters attacked them. But religion and attitudes towards the King's actions in 1640–42 would be crucial too, and the concerted action of a determined clique of local gentry opposed to 'popery' or to heavy-handed actions by the Government in the 1630s could be decisive in an initial decision to back Parliament. In all the counties in the south-west of England, far from London so at greater risk if they relied on the government in that city, the initial decision was taken nevertheless to back Parliament not the King. The authority of the local royalist military commissioner, the Marquis of

Hertford, was ignored; he ended up blockaded in Sherborne Castle. Having fought off an attack by the new Earl of Bedford at the start of September, he then bolted for Minehead to sail to safer South Wales; his deputy Sir Ralph Hopton chose to stay in England (which he might not have done had he had room on board for his horses) and headed for Cornwall. In Buckinghamshire, the loyalist Earl of Berkshire was stopped from reading the 'Commission of Array' by popular local MP John Hampden, hero of the 'Ship-Money' case, at Whatlington in the Chilterns and the latter's faction took over the area.

Charles' mostly aristocratic commissioners had more luck in isolated rural areas of the north and west where 'feudal' ties were strong and the tenantry would rally to their lords, e.g. in Wales (Sir Richard Lloyd in the north and the Marquis of Worcester's heir in the south). In Cheshire, the Parliamentarian commissioner Brereton was stymied by a posse of armed royalists. The prosperous and independent-minded citizenry of the towns were broadly speaking pro-Parliamentarian, even in these areas, e.g. Plymouth and Barnstaple in Devon, Taunton in Somerset, Lyme Regis and Weymouth in Dorset, Southampton and Portsmouth in Hampshire, and Gloucester in the south-west Midlands. Even the King's eventual headquarters, Oxford, had a strong pro-Parliamentary element among the townsfolk. The seaports of Tenby and Haverfordwest in remote Pembrokeshire held out for Parliament against the overwhelming royalism of most of south-west Wales, though backed by a section of the local gentry too. The clothing towns of Lancashire and the West Riding were pro-Parliament, and again were to face attack from their pro-royalist rural hinterland. Manchester and Bradford stand out as two geographically isolated but resolute examples. But it was not a simple case of the 'backward' rural areas remote from London supporting the King, with tenants obediently following their lords. The Earl of Hertford and Sir Ralph Hopton had less success in Somerset and Dorset than the Earl of Newcastle did in the north-east or the Earl of Derby did in rural Lancashire; the royalist Earl of Arundel, lord of the eponymous town and castle, was defied by the majority of th local gentry (led by strong 'Puritans' such as Sir Anthony Stapley) in West Sussex.

The gentry leadership of some counties – mostly in the Midlands, where neither side was clearly dominant – preferred to avoid becoming deeply involved and formed pacts for neutrality. Some counties were divided, as most notoriously in Leicestershire where one 'party' was dominant in the south and its rivals won over the north; the family of the royalist Lord Lieutenant and greatest landowner, the Earl of Huntingdon, could not overawe the local gentry. In Cheshire and Staffordshire, the complex pattern of divided local allegiances saw a breakdown of any central direction into effectively autonomous royalist and Parliamentarian 'statelets', dominated by hastily fortified manor-houses; the allegiance of a district was determined by that of its most dominant gentry family or group of families. Given strong enough beliefs, one well-resourced family with a castle could defy the majority opinion of the entire district – e.g. the Parliamentarian Harleys of Brampton Bryan in north-western Herefordshire, led by 'Puritan' MP Sir Edward and his wife Lady Brilliana. How soon and how violently the war began depended on the aggression of individual local groupings rather than on orders from the King or Parliament. Even towns were divided, as in Cambridge where the University declared for the King and tried to send him their plate but were stopped by Oliver Cromwell. The successful party in each locality depended on a mixture of luck and the question of which had the most armed backing immediately to hand.[6]

Worryingly, the King had failed to secure more than two ships from the regular navy, as their titular commander, the Earl of Northumberland, was unreliable and his royalist deputy, Sir John Pennington, was too slow to act when given royal authority to take over. He was swiftly removed by Parliament's nominee, the Earl of Warwick, a 'Puritan' enthusiast, organizer of private colonial ventures and piracy to harass the Spanish empire in the 1630s, and co-leader of the pro-Parliament peers in 1640–42. The sailors notably supported Parliament, as did most naval ports; possibly anti-Catholicism was a factor, as in Essex they joined in lynch mobs hunting down 'papists'. One notorious incident was the sacking of Lady Rivers' house in Colchester; and the sight of violent disorder was a bonus for royalist propaganda among the uncommitted. The loss of control of the sea meant that Warwick's captains could secure isolated pro-Parliament towns in the south-west such as Plymouth, reinforce the Hothams at Hull, cut off the nearest route for Continental invasion by backing rebel-held Dover, and counter the royalist control of Portsmouth by seizing the Isle of Wight and blockading Lord Goring's garrison into surrender.[7]

Quite apart from the strategic results, this Parliamentary success gave the worst possible indication of the King's position to abroad. He failed to secure the crucial backing of the major foreign Catholic states who might send troops on account of Parliament's militant Protestantism, with the loss of his capital indicating his weak position to observers. France was hostile due to his friendship with Spain; the latter was preoccupied with the Portuguese revolt, and Sir Thomas Roe in Vienna could not interest the Emperor in assistance. The Protestant Dutch 'United Provinces' were closely allied to the Stuarts due to the recent marriage of the King's daughter Mary to the son of their stadtholder, but the dominant commercial oligarchs of Amsterdam preferred Parliament and obstructed the Queen's efforts to win support. She could sell the Crown Jewels in Holland to provide money for the cause, but the merchant-dominated states-general stood in the way of any formal aid to Charles. The only military aid came from small groups of volunteers – most notably the family of Charles' exiled sister the Electress Palatine, whose second son Prince Rupert led a force to England and soon proved his capabilities as a dashing but somewhat light-fingered cavalry commander who conducted war by ruthless Continental standards.[8] In this respect, the Parliamentarian gentry of Kent dealt a serious blow to the King's overseas reputation by taking Dover Castle by surprise on 21 August. The vast fortifications would have prevented any siege from succeeding without a major effort that was at the moment beyond Parliament's resources, and Charles should have been more careful to secure a vigilant and determined garrison there. His lack of a navy would, however, have made reinforcement difficult, as with the equally vital but overrun Edinburgh and Dumbarton Castles in Scotland in 1639. Given that he had been in Dover in January to see his Queen off to France to raise funds for an army, his failure to ensure an adequate local military position then is a sign of his strategic carelessness though he did not have many troops to spare anyway.

The formal breakdown of government into two opposing authorities, each claiming sole legitimacy, continued apace as the raising of troops began. Charles had secured the adherence of the officers of the Mint from the Tower with their bullion, but the law-courts refused an order to leave the capital though Lord Keeper Littleton joined him with the Great Seal.[9] The Parliamentary reaction to royal orders to the courts led to their resolution on 27 May that the King was making war on Parliament and nobody should accept any orders that did not come from the latter, thus definitively usurping the royal authority. The King's reply to this was to issue 'Commissions of Array', leading to the rounds of visits to county towns and local gentry by rival recruiters from both sides. As a result of the initial levies, the advantage seemed to lie with Parliament in terms of numbers. They also had a geographically central military headquarters in Northampton, sitting on the main roads from London to the north, where up to 15,000 men assembled during July and August.[10]

The King also failed to secure Hull, as he responded to an offer of betrayal from the governor, Sir John Hotham. The incident of his pre-arranged arrival with a demand for surrender on 23 April was mismanaged, as his 'advance party' who had been allowed in (including Prince James) were having dinner when he arrived, the pro-royalist Lord Mayor failed to throw the city gates' keys down from the walls to Charles, and the King and

Hotham quarrelled at the gates over how many bodyguards Charles could bring inside. The King had to ride away empty-handed, and the artillery stored inside Hull – originally intended for the Scots and then the Irish campaigns – passed to Parliamentary control.[11] Thanks to the Parliamentary loyalties of the fleet, they could move it out of harm's way to London and bring in Parliamentary troops under Sir John Meldrum to keep an eye on Hotham. The incident was not decisive, but it gave the King's already sceptical potential allies like the Elector Palatine a bad impression of his effectiveness. To make matters worse in the strategically vital area of Yorkshire, a large rally of the local freeholders who had been summoned to meet Charles on Heyworth Moor on 3 June was anticlimactic (not helped by Charles' stutter) and he brusquely ignored a petition from the Fairfaxes.[12] This father and son duly became mainstays of the Parliamentary cause, with the younger, Sir Thomas, becoming commander-in-chief of the New Model. Then a second attempt to take Hull failed, though on this occasion it was due to the Parliamentary troops inside the town fighting off the royalists when they arrived to besiege Hull (at Hotham's request) in July. The King had responded to Hotham's suggestion that he bring a large enough force to give him an honourable excuse to surrender, but the effectiveness of Meldrum's men in combat rallied the defence and Hotham lost his nerve.[13]

Having appointed the ineffective Earl of Cumberland as his commander in the north, Charles advanced into the north Midlands to find a poor response. Meanwhile the pro-Parliamentary town of Manchester was defying his forces in Lancashire, serving to rally the urban areas of that county against the royalists, and the Fairfaxes held out in West Yorkshire. When he withdrew to Nottingham to rally loyalist enthusiasm by raising his standard on 22 August, the bad weather dampened the show. The fact that the flag was blown down could be seen as a bad omen, though largely in retrospect; careless soldiers had failed to dig it deeply into the ground. He had already failed to secure Coventry due to the townsmen's hostility. The response to his raising his standard was so poor that Sir Jacob Astley, an ultra-loyalist who was to command the last resisting royalist army in 1646, grumbled that the enemy could easily capture the King in his bed if they raided his headquarters.[14] Such a surprise raid was luckily beyond the mental capabilities of the Parliamentary commander, the Earl of Essex, who did not leave London until 9 September[15] and then proceeded to prepare for his first expedition without undue haste. The armies of both sides, moreover, were hampered by the inevitable fact that their amateur soldiers were unused to military discipline as well as being untrained. Incidents of insulting and looting the property of powerless supporters of the other side while heading for the general rendezvous were rife, with officers unable or unwilling to intervene. The pillaging of Bulstrode Whitelocke's mansion near Fawley in Buckinghamshire by passing royalist troops was a typical instance of this,[16] and already the rival armies showed enthusiasm for abusing each other's civilian supporters as 'papists' or 'traitors'. The nervousness of untrained ex-civilian officers, unsure if their men would obey them, was added to the usual problems with a disorderly seventeenth century army; and bitterness was bound to increase as the conflict spread and incidents multiplied. Nothing like this extent of armed anarchy had been seen in England for centuries.

As Essex marched north on Nottingham with a far larger army, Charles withdrew to Shrewsbury in the more supportive Welsh Marches rather than remain in the north-east within reach of the Queen who was expected to return soon by sea. He left Nottingham on 13 September; Essex was still in Northampton reviewing his army next day, and did not leave until the 19th. On the 20th Charles arrived at Shrewsbury; the chance to catch him before he reached his Welsh reinforcements was missed but the nature of the large Parliamentary army was such that it was unlikely to move quickly. The baggage-train had to negotiate the poor roads, and only the cavalry might have moved faster – and would then have left their inexperienced colleagues unprotected and exposed. The Parliamentary army seriously outnumbered Charles, though it was smaller than the 15,000 men claimed by its own propagandists.[17] The Welsh were more enthusiastic than the northerners for the King, as reflected by the fearful anti-Welsh propaganda of the London pamphleteers, and the 'feudal' bonds of their society and religious conservatism helped the gentry to raise substantial numbers of men. (A large number of Welsh royalists were to be wounded at Edgehill.) Should he have made his first stand in that area? But it would have been strategically less useful for Charles to have commenced his recruitment there rather than in the north-east Midlands; he needed to be in York and Nottingham in the summer to keep open links to the Continent and to seek to take over the arms depot in Hull. York had also been his headquarters when dealing with the Scots, whose army was close at hand in Durham – their command was not keen on the English crisis escalating to war and duly sent Lord Loudoun to mediate, but Charles rejected this.[18]

The loss of Hull and its arms depot was less vital than the defection of the fleet, in which matter deputy commander Sir John Pennington proved as unwilling to take the initiative as Hotham had been at Hull. He delayed taking action and was sidelined as the new Parliamentary Lord Admiral, Charles' foe Warwick, arrived to take over; feeling among officers and men in the fleet was against the King anyway. Possibly the Lord Admiral, Northumberland, could have swung some opinion in the King's favour had he been loyal, but he took Parliament's side. As the sudden mutiny by the fleet was to show in 1648, the officers and men were independent by nature and reluctant to follow their commanders – and most seaports in England were to be strongly pro-Parliament, as shown by the dogged resistance of Plymouth to the King in 1643 and of Lyme Regis in 1644.

The impressive size of the Parliamentary army was to some degree offset by two factors – the amount of forcible impressment, which seems to have been larger than for Charles' army and thus produced more men who were unwilling to fight, and the sluggishness of their commander Essex. Experienced in the Thirty Years' War but not in command, he showed no vigour in training his large – and thus potentially awkward to co-ordinate – army who only contained a small number of officers used to firearms and military manoeuvres. Neither factor could be evident at the time and so be useful to royal morale, though in the event the Earl's dilatoriness was to give Charles a (missed) opportunity to outmarch him in the advance on London after Edgehill in October. The Parliamentarians also possessed more ordnance, not least from having control of London with the Tower artillery as well as Hull;[19] but unless this advantage could be brought to bear on a battlefield it meant that their larger artillery-train would be slowed down on the muddy and rutted English roads. The poorness of training and lack of experience of the artillery's handlers in action meant that although it was normally a vital weapon for its possessors (as in the well-trained Swedish army) it was unlikely to be decisive. A quick and well-trained cavalry charge – as by Rupert's men – could overrun it on the battlefield, provided that it was not tackled 'head-on'. It was more decisive in a defensive position, as in the Tower artillery protecting London in November 1642.

The Royal Council advised another attempt to negotiate, and on 25 August envoys (the Earl of Southampton and Sir John Culpeper) were sent to London. Charles declared his support for the Protestant religion and the law of the land. Luckily for the King, the hostile Parliamentary reaction aided his cause. The Houses received the pair brusquely and demanded that he take down his standard and withdraw his formal accusations of their treason, but militants led by Strode had attempted to deny the pair a hearing and for once Pym was on the side of moderation in securing them a reception. On 5 September the King sent a second pair of envoys, Lords Spencer and Falkland, proposing that both parties withdraw their accusations of treason against the other and – according to the memories of Sir Simonds D'Ewes – privately promising a 'thorough reformation in religion'. The uncompromising Parliamentary reply aided royalist recruitment, by insisting that Charles abandon all his followers for prosecution as delinquents, causing any potential royalists who were uncertain about the wisdom of entering the war to fear their arrest should the King lose and thus join him with determination.[20] This threat to prosecute anyone who had aided the King stiffened the resolve of waverers and those who had made but not implemented promises, and outweighed the counter-effect of 'Prince Robber' (as Parliament nicknamed Rupert) showing his use of methods of war more common on the Continent by attempting to blackmail the town of Leicester into paying up £5,000 to the King with a threat of sacking.

Parliament had every reason to distrust Charles' offers as a tactic to divide them, but their harsh attitude to all who defied their power showed an arrogant belief in their legal rights that did great political damage – and was to continue to be a major asset for Charles. His propaganda was already reminding the uncommitted that 'Parliament' consisted of only around eighty of the MPs and a fraction of the Lords,[21] and as late as January 1649 he was able to claim that he was acting for the true liberties of the subject against the tyranny of a faction. But for this Parliamentary blunder, the army that Essex assembled could have outnumbered the royal forces even more heavily. The latter would have been lucky to be able to challenge them to battle, and could have ended up melting away apart from the young court cavalry and a few retinues of various northern aristocrats and Welsh magnates. The resulting mixture of aristocratic cavalry and unprepared rural infantry would have been at a serious disadvantage on a battlefield against the City militia, who were used to training with muskets, and the superior Parliamentary artillery. The infantry clash at Edgehill would thus have gone more decisively in the favour of Essex's men. The Civil War could have been over speedily, with the King forced to come to terms or take shelter with Ormonde in Ireland.

Instead, the numbers of royalist recruits rose during September while Essex made no quick advance to counter the threat. As the King raised troops at Shrewsbury from 20 September, Essex moved on Worcester where Sir John Byron had retreated after an abortive advance to Oxford to collect volunteers and money. Oxford had proved indefensible against the advancing Parliamentarian army, not least due to the pro-Essex sympathies of most of the townsmen; Worcester, later known as the ultra-royalist 'Faithful City', may have had a more reliable population but had useless tumbledown walls. Byron and Prince Rupert had to take the sensible course and retreat from there as well, but not before Rupert had used his cavalry in an unexpected and dashing assault on a Parliamentarian advance-force that had moved west of the Severn. As the latter, led by radical MP Nathaniel Fiennes, had heard that Byron was retreating from Worcester northwards they were caught unawares; and Essex with the main army was some miles to the rear, advancing up the Oxford–Worcester road on the city east of the Severn. The resulting clash in a meadow at Powick Bridge, the crossing of the River Teme south-west of Worcester, on the 23rd saw a clear victory for Rupert, further aiding royalist morale.[22] Fiennes was no match for him, and indeed was to come under serious Parliamentarian military criticism for having the 'cowardice' to surrender Bristol to Rupert at their next clash in 1643;[23] a politician not a soldier, he ended up as a respected councillor to Oliver Cromwell in 1653–8.

Essex secured temporary control of the Midlands, including the future royalist capital of Oxford, due to weight of numbers, and was able to occupy Worcester after Rupert withdrew and then go on to Hereford. The general trend of events across the country continued to be in Parliament's favour, with Hertford forced to abandon his lonely stand at Sherborne and head across country to the Bristol Channel to sail to South Wales. His colleague in the south-west, Hopton, took refuge in Pendennis Castle amidst a Cornwall initially secured for Parliament by the local magnate Lord Robartes, owner of Lanhydrock. The King had not yet left Shrewsbury, and showed his naïve faith in foreign aid by commissioning envoys to ask his uncle King Christian IV of Denmark for 3,000 German mercenaries plus money.[24] But the main royalist 'field-army' of around 5,000 infantry and 1,500 dragoons at Shrewsbury, plus Rupert's cavalry countered the numbers of their opponents with greater élan in battle. Parliament continued its aggressive and counter-productive legal orders with those of 15 October for the arrest of all persons who refused to contribute to their cause and the sequestration of the lands of bishops, deans, and chapters plus those of leading 'delinquents'. A planned Assembly of Divines to remodel the Church was voted for on the 19th;[25] as with the 1638 Scots Church assembly in Glasgow, the outcome could be expected to be rigged against the bishops by the careful selection of its members. But Charles at last began his march on London from Shrewsbury on the 12th, and contemptuously refused a petition from Parliament that he return to London and abandon his followers to their just deserts.[26] Recruits were being brought in across northern England by his politically defiant, though militarily logical, decision to allow the untapped loyalist minority of Catholics in northern England to contribute to his defence by joining the Earl of Newcastle's army. He wrote to Newcastle announcing this change of plan on 23 September.[27] Recruits were also starting to flow in for Hopton in Cornwall, though the military effect of either army would take months to become important.

Typically, Essex failed to anticipate his move from Shrewsbury and make a quick advance to cut him off. His delay at Worcester served no useful strategic purpose and made his lines of communication as dangerously extended as they were to be in Cornwall in 1644. While he dallied, panic in London at the King's orders to admit Catholics to the Earl of Newcastle's army and local royalist riots helped to persuade Parliament to vote for the creation of a second army in the region, 16,000 men, to be commanded by Warwick and assist the Trained Bands to defend the capital (21 October).[28] In the meantime, it was up to Essex to intercept Charles as the latter marched on London – directly, avoiding any delay to attack Parliamentarian towns in his path like Coventry. Once Essex's army, recalled from the Marches by Parliament, caught his forces up near Banbury on 22 October the political struggle was put to the test on a major battlefield. But Charles was caught by surprise at Edgecott on the 22nd to learn from Rupert that Essex was close behind him at Kineton, and had to fight an unexpected battle at only a few hours' notice.

Edgehill

The battle of Edgehill, as might have been expected for the first major encounter between two well-matched armies on English soil since 1487, was characterized by muddle and missed opportunities. The King had around 2,800 horse and 1,000 dragoons, outnumbering the Parliamentary cavalry of 2,150 horse and 720 dragoons; Parliament, however, had the larger infantry forces, around 12,000 to 10,500. Neither commander – Charles, operating through the ageing veteran Earl of Forth, and the Earl of Essex – was an experienced general, though Forth and Essex had served on the Continent. Forth was around seventy, and Essex nearly sixty. The advantage in offensive cavalry action lay with the King, not least as his cavalry had the moral advantage of one past victory at Powick Bridge and an inspiring commander in Rupert. But as so often in Charles' disastrous career, he showed indecisiveness and stubbornness at the wrong moments. If he had continued with the Earl of Lindsey, his original commander-in-chief, in command and ordered Prince Rupert, as commander of the cavalry, to submit to his orders, the royal forces would have been properly co-ordinated in their attack that day. But muddle and indiscipline in the royalist ranks reduced the effect of their best weapon. Also, Lindsey had advised against the King's army being drawn up in the tightly packed infantry squares, with cavalry on the flanks, as used by the Dutch against Spain and as recommended by Rupert. Lindsey preferred the slightly different order of battle adopted by the generation's greatest Continental soldier, Gustavus Adolphus of Sweden. But was this choice of following Rupert's advice a mistake? This formation had helped Gustavus to win vital battles over the less well-ordered imperial troops in Germany (though he had been killed in a cavalry charge at Lutzen). Its advantage lay in the infantry being well-trained in firing and re-loading their cumbersome muskets, and thus launching a devastating fusillade of gunfire into the enemy; the royal infantry at Edgehill lacked the Swedish infantry's training and so were less effective. Indeed, in the infantry clash there the royal troops were not able to deliver that sort of barrage; the larger numbers of the Parliamentarian infantry gave the latter the advantage in any case. Rupert was not infallible, and indeed his bold move to seize the strategic advantage for the battlefield by occupying the heights of Edgehill had its problems too. The steep incline of the slope up from Essex's lines to the royalist position meant that only a very bold or suicidal commander would attack up that incline, and Essex was neither. The royalists had to abandon their position and move downhill in order to get to grips with the enemy.

As events turned out, Rupert's success on the right wing in sweeping away the opposing cavalry was aided by the defection of an enemy regiment under Sir Faithful Fortescue, a South Devon landowner. The royalist cavalry, joined by Fortescue's men, swept away the panicking Parliamentary cavalry and trampled four regiments of infantry underfoot. This destroyed the 'left' of Essex's line. The charge was followed by similar success by Lord Wilmot on the royalist left wing, and the Parliamentarian cavalry on Essex's 'right' crumbled. The fact that it was the first major battle of the war, indeed, meant that both sides were inexperienced and the psychological impact of the first large cavalry charge on English soil since Bosworth would be great; whoever lost their nerve first could easily lose the entire battle. The advantage of 'élan' lay with the royalist cavalry, which was packed with enthusiastic young landed gentry under a charismatic leader. But they did not turn inwards on the Parliamentary centre once they had routed the opposition, which strategic logic and usual tactics would have dictated – and evidently the worst offenders, Rupert's men, had not had it drilled into them to do this. The King had no strategic expertise to order Rupert's tactics for him; the Prince might well not have taken notice of an order by the more experienced Lindsey or the Earl of Forth (his social inferiors) backed by the King, but then would have incurred the public odium of disobedience.

One bloc of Parliamentary cavalry under Sir William Balfour survived the twin attacks on right and left, retreated out of range behind some hedges, and was able to advance unhindered to support their own infantry in attacking the royalist infantry in the centre. This then silenced the royalist guns. Sir Philip Stapleton's cavalry regiment also held firm, and these two cavalry groupings now outnumbered the royalist horse left on the field. This duly gave confidence to Essex's infantry, musketeers being nervous of exposure to cavalry attack – if more royalist horse had still been engaged the Parliamentary infantry were likely to have been more cautious if not panicking The most determined and disciplined Parliamentary infantry regiments were those from 'Puritan' areas – Essex's from his eponymous county and MP Denzel Holles' from London. Rupert's men had charged off downhill northwards into Kineton village to loot the enemy baggage-train, leaving a crucial gap on the battlefield, and the King and/or Forth failed to send messengers after them quickly. The King might have been inexperienced, but Forth had enough knowledge of war to know the importance of constant and quick communication with subordinate commanders to cope with changing events in the field. When the two opposing blocs of infantry clashed neither side appeared to have much direction. The smaller royalist infantry force lacked their cavalry support, and although Balfour's Parliamentary cavalry charge was too small to do much damage – it reached but lacked pikes to spike Charles' artillery – the attack appears to have unnerved Charles' right wing. The confrontation petered out through exhaustion before Rupert belatedly managed to bring his disorderly cavalry back up the hill.[29] By that time the Prince could not retrieve the situation. Indeed, royalist witness Sir Philip Warwick wrote that the day of battle could have been Essex's last had the royalist cavalry 'done their parts' and stayed on the battlefield;[30] instead Essex had a chance of victory and missed it.

If there had been more co-ordination, even if Rupert had still gone charging off down the hill after the fleeing Parliamentarians and left the immediate vicinity there were other (smaller) royal cavalry forces on the field who their commander Lord Byron could have ordered into the attack. Instead, he allowed their pleas to reinforce Rupert. Using Byron would have been risky as he had less experience (and less men) than Rupert, but it could easily have unnerved the Parliamentarian infantry and caused flight. Instead, Charles – also under fire for the first time, and bravely refusing suggestions to stay out of range of the guns – chose caution. If Rupert had received and obeyed a recall-message, he could have returned to the battlefield with at least some of his more orderly men and taken on the Parliamentarians' undefeated wing. Nor did Charles show any realization of the need to co-ordinate the infantry, or allow Lindsey to take charge when the Earl of Forth proved too passive. The battle ended in a muddle, with the undefeated wing of Essex's army holding their ground until darkness made both sides draw off. The main reaction by Charles seems to have been shock at the unpleasant reality of war, with Lindsey and his standard-bearer Sir Edmund Verney among the most notable casualties.[31] Arguably, this shock added to his caution and his desire to avoid more bloodshed in the coming days – and thus may have lost him his best chance of a quick victory.

After Edgehill – could a quick royalist advance have ended the war?
With or without this victory, Charles held the better position after the battle
with the road to Oxford and thence London open. Essex was behind him,
and would have to march round ahead to block his route or at least attack
him heavily in the rear to halt his march. As the King's forces blocked the
main road south-east to Oxford and then London, Essex would have had to
manoeuvre around him on side-roads – in winter mud, and with
cumbersome artillery to protect – to get ahead of him. Moreover, Essex had
marched off northwards to Warwick Castle not towards London so the King
had a head start if he wished to advance on his capital. It was a strategic
mistake that could be exploited, though Essex had had little choice – if he
had stayed put at Kineton he was at risk of Charles attacking and if he moved
awkwardly round the royalist flanks (on open ground or muddy lanes) to get
ahead of him on the London road Rupert could have swooped down on his
straggling columns of men. Essex was also hampered by desertions and the
loss of his baggage-train; the fact that he did not move south-east on the
London road within a day or two to outpace Charles was an indication of his
lack of ability to 'second-guess' his opponents.

In reality, Charles allowed Essex to advance round his flanks and make up
for this mistake as he delayed at Oxford. The fact that Charles chose to move
on Oxford and rest there for a few days rather than head straight for London
was to be expected. Given his current lack of important garrisons in the
south, the place would be a valuable base if he was unable to bring the war
to a quick conclusion. Having reached the town on 29 October, he enabled
Essex – further from London – to take a flanking march across
Buckinghamshire to the Eastern Chilterns. Essex was able to reach London,
which had only around 6,000 men of the Trained Bands (under the
Continental veteran Sir Philip Skippon) and a gradually mustering force of
volunteers, on 7 November. Once Essex arrived, the Londoners had around
24,000 men and easily outnumbered the royalists. After panic before Essex's
arrival, their confidence revived to the extent that a 'sight-seeing' crowd of
families accompanied their troops out to the defences. Indeed, both Rupert
and Forth unsuccessfully urged Charles to greater haste – or to let the
cavalry (c. 3,000 men) race for London,[32] which would have had a
psychological impact on the poorly defended City at a crucial moment and
encouraged the 'pro-peace' party. In retrospect, Hyde reckoned that this
vital delay in Oxford may have cost Charles his best chance of a quick
victory.[33]

Would this have worked? Did Charles lose his best chance of success
through his slowness? The cavalry probably would not have been able to enter
the City, given the advantages that the defenders would have had from even a

few strategic barricades; feeling was strong in the City despite the presence of a group of pro-royalist merchants and horsemen were notoriously at risk from missiles when fighting in narrow streets. The last concerted attempt to invade London's streets by well-armed men marching in from the neighbouring countryside – Sir Thomas Wyatt's in 1554 – had been driven off. Skippon was a Low Countries veteran of the Dutch-Spanish war, and had the ability to use his artillery effectively from behind defensive positions; the Trained Bands were used to handling guns, though not on the battlefield. But unwalled Whitehall was difficult to defend from determined attack, provided that the Parliamentarians had not had the time they had in reality to dig trenches in Hyde Park. It had nearly fallen to the previous determined attack on it, by Sir Thomas Wyatt's men in February 1554, as some of Queen Mary's guards turned tail in a clash at Charing Cross.

The delay was vital, enabling better defences to be put up. Without that, a large royal force within a few miles of London (at Turnham Green and Hammersmith?) and Essex nowhere near should have caused panic in Parliament. Royalist merchants in the City would have had the argument of averting a catastrophic sack of the City to use in urging negotiations. Even if the royal cavalry proved inadequate a threat to force peace-talks, or the latter were a delaying-tactic (as they were at Reading in real life), the advantage would lie with the King. His strategic and psychological position would have seemed stronger in November 1642 had he been able to base himself at his palace of Hampton Court, a regular royal residence, not been forced back to Oxford. It would have been equally useful if Windsor Castle, the last bastion of Parliamentary power west of London, had surrendered; it did not. With possession of Windsor Castle and the vital bridge at Kingston-upon-Thames, Charles could have left a defensible force to protect his 'advanced' positions when he had to move back to a safer base for the winter. The strong walls of Windsor would have been able to hold out against the London artillery of the Tower for long enough to send a message to Charles about a relief-force, assuming that Essex would have left the capital without much of its artillery in order to mount a proper siege that winter.

In the first days of November there were strong representations for opening negotiations in both the Lords (led by the Earls of Northumberland, Holland, and Pembroke[34]) and, to a lesser extent, the Commons (led by Edmund Waller). The first two of these peers were former royal courtiers alienated during the winter of 1641–2 after losing ground to the Queen's faction, and the third had been notoriously snubbed by the King over court appointments and was a victim of royal personal mistrust rather than a committed ideological 'oppositionist'. Northumberland had been dismissed as lord admiral by Charles as unreliable. Accordingly on 3 November Sir

Peter Killigrew was sent to Charles to secure a safe-conduct for negotiators; Charles received him at Reading on the 4th and waited for two days before replying that one of those named, Sir John Evelyn, was unacceptable to him. This was suspected as an excuse, and Parliament was emboldened to ask the Scots for help to resist on the 7th, in which the less militant Lords concurred. Essex arrived back in London that day, and the Houses were emboldened to make a successful appeal to the City for financial contributions at the Guildhall on the 8th; 6,000 Londoners now volunteered for military service.[35] Both factors helped to tip the balance of force and morale in favour of the defence by the time that Charles arrived at Colnbrook on the 11th. As Pym told the citizenry at the Guildhall on the 10th, the Parliamentary delegation sent to the King at Colnbrook were empowered to accept any terms that guaranteed religion and liberty – but these had to be 'printed' not just promised by word of mouth.[36]

Without Essex arriving back in time to bolster morale and encourage waverers to stand firm more moderates would have been emboldened to join in appeals for a quick negotiated peace on any 'face-saving' terms. The loss of Windsor, which in the event held out against an attack by Rupert, would have been an extra blow. Even in the City there was a strengthening party of royalist merchants keen to avoid the City being sacked. The King would have been in a stronger position if he had been advancing rapidly, rather than halting first at Oxford and then again at Reading on 4–6 November to receive the first Parliamentary deputation, and had been ahead of Essex. Given the need to rest and find accommodation for the wounded at Oxford, the delay at Reading was more inexcusable – though the speed of an infantry march would at best have given him a slightly earlier arrival in the Hammersmith area by 6 or 7 November not the 11th. Blocking Essex's route back to London would have been more productive than hurrying on himself, given that the Earl could get back to the City unhindered on the 7th.

It was unrealistic to expect Charles to miss the opportunity of occupying Oxford en route to London and his troops needed rest, but he could still have decided to send out a faster-moving force of cavalry to block Essex's path – or, given his military inexperience and hopes of an enemy surrender, been persuaded that it was advisable by the more experienced Continental veteran Rupert. If it was judged too risky to advance directly on London, Rupert and his horsemen could have been sent up the Bicester road from Oxford to block Essex's routes south-east to London from Banbury and Brackley. This would have been enough to keep Essex back and the City without aid. If Rupert had been reported ahead of the Parliamentarian army the latter – recently routed by Rupert – are unlikely to have dared to attempt an encounter to test their strength. With Rupert's and/or Byron's cavalry at large in Buckinghamshire around 29 October – 4 November, the cautious Essex would have been halted and London left open to the advance of the King's slower main force with its cannon.

The King could still have halted at Oxford on the 29th for a few days to rest his men, provided that his cavalry were holding up the enemy – and news that Essex could not reach London would have encouraged panic there. The decisive actions for resistance in London, as seen above, occurred after, not before, Essex's arrival on 7 November. Nor were the amateurish defences of ditches and barriers that were being set up around the approaches to London able to withstand a determined attack, even granted that the royal cannoneers were inexperienced and the effect of a barrage from their guns on the defences would have been more psychological than physical. The longer Essex remained trapped in the Midlands, the greater the chances of the enthusiastic citizenry of London – who followed his men out to Turnham Green to challenge the King in real life – losing heart for a siege.

Charles had shown no ability to appreciate the advantages of speed or co-ordination before or at Edgehill, and delayed his advance on London. Quite probably he was hoping that the success he had achieved on the battlefield and his unopposed advance on his capital would reinforce disinclination for resistance and cause his opponents to listen to reason from the pacifist peers. A better use of scouts, to report on where Essex was and hopefully enable the royal army to intercept his line of march, and a refusal to halt while the Parliamentary commissioners were received would have added to his ability to dictate terms from a better standpoint or to storm the City if they were refused. Charles' army was no more hampered by the roads and battle-weariness than Essex's, and he could have arrived near Brentford a week or so earlier than he did if he had shown more urgency. If he had headed off Essex en route or if Rupert's cavalry had held the enemy up and forced them to move north into Bedfordshire to reach an unguarded road to London, Charles would have outnumbered the forces drawn up to oppose him even with around 6,000 volunteers now raised within the capital. Even without seasoned generals to command an attack, the threat of a catastrophic sack of London or a successful and impressively bloody skirmish with the enemy like Rupert's real-life attack on Brentford would have sapped the enemy's unity and will to resist.

The resolution of the 'hard-line' Commons faction that Pym led would have been opposed by the Northumberland/Holland group in the Lords with Waller receiving more support in the Commons, particularly if the King sent out conciliatory messages providing for an amnesty for all but the Parliamentary leadership. A resulting successful vote to send a Parliamentary delegation sent to the King, probably by now at Windsor or Hampton Court with his men at Hammersmith, could have enabled Essex to have time to march back into London and stiffen resistance – and Pym could have agreed to the delegation precisely to obtain this 'breathing-space'. Nor was the King likely to have agreed to ratify the terms that the Parliamentary majority had been insisting on as the basis for peace earlier in 1642, and would have been trying to secure again – acceptance of their 'illegal' Parliamentary legislation passed since he had left London in January, particularly over control of the militia, raising and funding of Parliamentary troops, and seizure of Church lands. But if the King had held the strategic advantage and been blocking Essex from London his refusal of these terms should have induced the 'moderates' in the Lords and, to a smaller extent, the Commons to insist that better terms be offered in order to save themselves and the City and the royalist party in the latter would have been able to take the initiative in demonstrating for peace. A temporary truce would have meant the two armies maintaining their current positions, which would mean that Essex (in Hertfordshire or Buckinghamshire, north of the King?) was unable to reach London and had to camp out in the countryside or crowd into a small town, no aid to morale. With the King nearer London, Parliament reduced to negotiating, and a royal triumph being in prospect Essex's army could have started to disintegrate as soldiers slipped away for their self-preservation.

If the King had had the (uncharacteristic) determination to march speedily on London while his cavalry blocked the roads to Essex's army, beaten Essex to the city, and then launched an immediate attack on the outworks around Hyde Park (perhaps on or near 8 November) the defenders would have been in a poor state to resist. Without Essex's men and their artillery they would have had fewer armed volunteers than mustered in reality, and had to depend on the Trained Bands and those cannons that had not left the Tower with Essex's army. Once the Trained Bands had been routed few reserves would have been available. Nor were their defences adequate to withstand a sustained bombardment or a determined infantry-charge, even given the inadequacies of the inexperienced royalist troops in 1642. The radicals in the City and the apprentices would have had no chance of stopping them once the Trained Bands ran out of ammunition. The experienced Parliamentarian commander on the scene, Continental veteran Philip Skippon, would have been helpless without adequate troops and he had a long line of defences to hold across Hyde Park and Pimlico. At the least, Charles should have been able to breach the defensive ditches and reoccupy Whitehall without daring to enter the warren of easily defensible streets in the City – a psychological success.

The leading rebels in Parliament and the City would have fled downriver as the royal army entered Westminster, and effective resistance would have been over. The City would have suffered swingeing fines, and the Parliamentary army in the field would have been likely to break up as many officers gave up and sought to make terms – their commander Essex was not known for his recklessness either. The current Parliamentary successes elsewhere in the country – e.g. in Yorkshire, where Archbishop Williams had to flee to Cheshire – and their control of the navy would have been little use had the capital been lost. The remaining Parliamentary militiamen in the counties of the south-east and Midlands and defiant garrisons such as Portsmouth and Hull would have known that they stood no chance against the royal army and would have had to make terms as best they could, probably sending delegations assuring their loyalty to the concept of 'King in Parliament', which royal propaganda claimed the King was defending against a minority of extremists. The only alternative was to wait for a series of sieges, which could have only one outcome; even the garrisons of well-armed rebel ports would have been open to voices urging surrender and a plummeting of morale. Provided that the voices of advisers such as Hyde and Falkland rather than the Queen were in the ascendant at the restored court at Whitehall that winter, the need to avoid the cost and time spent on more campaigns to mop up resistance in early 1643 would have been a prime consideration. A policy of clemency to all but leading participants in the 'rebellion' would have induced junior officers of outlying garrisons to take over control and surrender as soon as royal emissaries arrived, or even before then, and their proscribed seniors to flee to the Continent.

Long-term results

Once the immediate retaliation was over the King would still have needed to maintain a strong army for the Irish campaign, and in due course to tackle Scotland if he wished to avoid a humiliating acceptance of an autonomous Presbyterian Church and a minimal royal influence in government. Having won in England, he would have been encouraged to regain his other two kingdoms by force; but his victory would have saved the established Anglican Church in England and thus prevented even the moderate Covenanters from believing that any promises he made about their Church would be adhered to in the long term.

War with the Covenanters?

Even before Charles had reconquered Ireland he would have been endeavouring to restore royal rule to Scotland, and end the humiliation of losing control even of Privy Council appointments in August 1641. Given Montrose's insistence on Charles maintaining the non-episcopal settlement of 1638–9 as the basis for his adherence in 1641, Charles would have been unlikely to muster adequate support from the armed nobility to overthrow Argyll's 'hard-liners' without this sort of concession. The Covenanter Scots army would have been weakened by its campaign in Ulster, but Charles would also have needed to send troops to Ireland in 1643 to back up his weakened local commander, Ormonde, and so would have been unlikely to use his full forces against Argyll at once. If the Covenanters had lost their Parliamentary allies and faced invasion in 1643, they were still unlikely to settle for any peace-terms short of cast-iron guarantees about the future of their Church and a 'guardian' political role in the government for their noble leadership to watch over the King's actions. Argyll, who Charles had tried to have arrested in October 1641, would have insisted on this to save his own security from trial as a rebel – and he would have needed an amnesty for his killing royal loyalists in the Airlie campaign of 1640. This would have been unacceptable to the King, even if he had had to open negotiations about a possible compromise in 1643 to keep the Scots army from invading before he was ready to meet them. It is possible that Montrose, Huntly, and the devious Hamilton would have been encouraged to start an anti-Argyll rebellion to save Charles the problem of having to invade, though royal over-confidence in the aftermath of English victory would have reduced the chances that Charles would be capable of wisely conceding the abolition of the Scottish episcopate to maximize the rebels' support among Covenanters fearful of Argyll's military and the clerics' religious primacy.

If unbreakable Covenanter unity (strong-armed by Argyll) led to the outbreak of war with Charles in 1643, he would have needed to create a stronger force than he had had at Edgehill to be sure of defeating the Scots under their Continental campaign-veteran commanders, remembering his humiliations in 1639 and 1640, and at the same time he would have had to send reinforcements to Ireland to aid the hard-pressed Ormonde. There would thus have been a delay for raising men and funds, probably with an extension of the system of raising royalist regiments in those areas of the country which he controlled in 1642 (and in 1643 in reality) across England; former Parliamentarian regimental commanders who had not fled the country might well have had to prove their loyalty by joining the army to be sent to Ireland. (As zealous opponents of Catholicism they could be trusted against the Catholic Irish, but they could not be trusted against the Presbyterian Scots due to potential religious sympathies.) The systems of tax-raising and conscription in real-life royalist counties would have been extensive across the country while the Irish and Scots emergencies lasted, probably with loyal royalists as lords lieutenant of each county that had contributed troops to the Parliamentarians at Edgehill to ensure against disturbances (particularly if there was a Scottish war.) Given the need for money, it is probable that the chastised City would have had to contribute a large sum to the royal army and another to the civil administration and court by way of punishment. Charles was not likely to be short of money once he had sold off the estates of leading Parliamentarians and allowed others to pay a fine to retain all or part of their land – a royalist version of the real-life Parliamentarian 'compounding' process for ex-foes would have been a financial necessity whatever the political wisdom of restricting the number of people punished.

Royal rule in England – punishment or compromise?
The MPs who had argued in favour of the King in 1642 and left rebel-held London and those who had voted (decisively?) to accept his terms in December would have been the nucleus of a Commons obedient to his will however many others had fled or been punished with fines and disqualification from sitting. Charles might have accepted the advice of moderate civilian advisers to retain this truncated Commons with the mostly loyal Lords into 1643 to show that he was not opposed to Parliament on principle and could work with all but a few power-hungry rebels and religious fanatics. In due course the royal government, short of money, would have needed to call another Parliament if the Scots and/or Irish wars dragged on and troops had to be funded, although it is likely that there would have been a careful 'vetting-procedure' for elections by local royal officers in each county and borough to secure an obedient majority.

Even after a military victory the King would not have had the will to restore all the prerogative courts and ecclesiastical apparatus of coercion that had been broken up in 1641 – the wars would have been his priority and he would not have been able to afford more outbreaks of discontent. The administrative situation of 1641 would have been retained, though with a probability of an added layer of royal officials based on the royalist fund- and troop-raisers of 1642 – in each county to aid the collection of revenue and suppression of subversion. These would have been more like French royal 'intendants' than the Parliamentarian local committees that the real-life Civil War victors used to raise money and maintain local control, given that their nucleus would have been the lords lieutenants and trusted local nobles, men such as Newcastle in the north-east and Derby in Lancashire (or, where none such existed, gentry and royal estates-officials). It is a debateable point whether a carefully selected Parliament co-ordinated by men such as Hyde, centring around the 'loyalist' MPs of 1641–2 in the Commons, would have obediently raised whatever money the King needed for his wars without question and not been liable to some objections if the King pursued policies against Scotland and Ireland that gave the lie to his claims to be a loyal Protestant.

Charles could well have chosen to come to an agreement with nationally hated 'papists' in Ireland to secure the surrender of substantial bodies of resisters and detach the 'Old English' in Ireland – Catholic, but still loyal to the sovereign provided that they were not offended by his laws – from those 'native Irish', led by Gaelic tribal commanders, who were now involved with the papal nuncio and seeking independence from Stuart rule. Prominent leaders of Anglo-Norman origin would have been as alarmed by that prospect as in real life, and even more willing to come to terms with the King if he had already won in England. Their adherence would have been a decisive blow in the King's favour, but was unlikely without a guarantee of religious toleration that the King was capable of agreeing if he had nothing to fear from his Protestant critics in England. But doing so would have been controversial for his reputation even if it shortened the war. Equally, a substantial number of royalist MPs and peers would have been equally uneasy if Charles followed up a victory in Ireland by launching his army on the Covenanters (around 1646?). The latter would have been very unlikely to accept his preferred terms for peace while he was busy with Ireland in c.1643–6, which for the sake of his dignity would involve restoring his effective authority if not yet abandoning Presbyterianism. A war was accordingly likely and the battle-hardened royalist commanders fresh from Ireland the inevitable victors, with or without a 'moderate' Covenant lords' rising in the King's support, which Montrose was the most likely to lead given his feud with Argyll and his real-life willingness to use Catholic Irish and Highlander troops for the King's cause. The completeness and terms of victory would determine whether the King, forced to give binding assurances to defecting nobles to shorten the war with Ireland still an expensive drain on his troops and money, would dare to restore episcopacy. If he had had to mount a full-scale invasion and win a major battle, with or without armed assistance from Hamilton's moderate 'Engagers' or Montrose, he was less likely to be generous about the ecclesiastical settlement. In the latter case, Scotland could have suffered a military occupation like that of the 1650s – but by an army including Irish Catholics and possibly European mercenaries brought in by Rupert. The resulting repression of Presbyterians would have been as vigorous, and ultimately counter-productive, as that in real life after 1679, with either Hamilton or Montrose playing the real-life role of the King's 'manager' in Scotland that Rothes did in the 1660s and Lauderdale did in the 1670s.

Chapter Three

Could the War have been Ended Quicker by Charles Making Better and More Decisive Plans?

The situation as of early 1643. The likelihood of early stalemate due to the nature of the war

The abortive scenario of November 1642 – the King moving in on London from Oxford – was the best chance of the war ending quickly in 1643, with the fall of the capital as decisive. There was, however, a difference from the situation at the time of Edgehill, when the only serious 'theatre of war' had been the clash between the main armies – the King versus the Earl of Essex. The war had now become entrenched in the localities with independent armies acting in each district under the discretion of their local commanders and at most a few general orders for engagement from London and Oxford. As of autumn 1642 there had been some significant clashes in the regions, but none of decisive national import. These clashes, e.g. in the south-west (particularly northern Dorset), the Midlands, and Lancashire, were more of a matter of the rival 'royalist' and 'Parliamentarian' magnates in each county separately issuing 'legal' orders from their leadership to raise armies and then fighting over who took control. There had also been a strategic 'side-show' to the royalist advance on London as the 'rebels' in control in London sought to seize the vital harbour of Portsmouth in Hampshire and keep the King from using it to bring in French or Dutch troops, in parallel to the (less centrally directed) declaration of governor Sir John Hotham of Hull for Parliament not the King. But the retention of Portsmouth for the King by its royalist commander Goring or the King's securing of Hull in autumn 1642 would not have made much difference to the outcome of the war. It was the 'main actions' at Edgehill and Turnham Green that were decisive late in 1642; after that one battle could not sway the course of the war (at least quickly) for most of 1643 and well into 1644 except arguably 'First Newbury'.

The provincial commands' independence of action also arose from the fact that the men in charge usually had strong local connections, particularly in holding the county sheriffdoms and deputy lieutenancies. These (usually) loosely run local offices were the Government's mechanism for supervising local affairs, raising money, managing elections, and raising troops; their holders were thus the key to maintaining local control and providing troops for both rival authorities in London and Oxford in 1642–3. In those counties where particular families had powerful – sometimes overwhelming – resources and influence their adherence to one particular side would often determine which party gained control in 1642, as with the Hastings family (Earls of Huntingdon) for the King in Leicestershire. But in most cases there was no dominant family or group of allied families, and a struggle between rival groups adhering to different sides followed – as with the royalist Grenville-Godolphin-Slanning 'bloc' and the Parliamentarian Robartes dynasty in Cornwall, with the Earl of Cumberland (royalist) versus the Fairfaxes in Yorkshire, and with the rival factions in the long-fought-over Cheshire. In some areas the towns, dominated by mercantile families with a strong 'Puritan' religious tradition, backed Parliament and most of the gentry backed the King. This was the case in Dorset and Devon, for example. Isolated pro-Parliamentarian towns or rural areas in the north and west duly faced the threat of blockade or temporary and reluctant submission, as with Taunton in Somerset, Lyme Regis in Dorset, and the small 'triangle' of Parliamentarian land and towns in South Pembrokeshire. In Lancashire, the Parliamentarian townsmen of Manchester defied the strong grip on the nearby countryside of the Earl of Derby, based at Lathom House. A mixture of townsmen (e.g. at Tenby and Haverfordwest) and gentry (e.g. the Laugharne family) kept southern Pembrokeshire in the Parliamentary camp despite geographical isolation in a royalist area. There was pro-Parliamentarian sentiment even in the royalist 'capital', Oxford, and a pro-royalist faction of merchants (led by Sir Nicholas Crispe) in the City of London. In the less agriculturally developed, more 'pastoral' areas of north and west the landed aristocracy had more of a dominant position, could raise large armies of tenants, and could usually bring in their counties on the King's side – as with the area of south-east Wales dominated by the Herberts of Raglan, Marquesses of Worcester, and the Cavendishes' area of Derbyshire and Nottinghamshire. There were even some royalist gentry, though outnumbered, in 'Parliamentarian strongholds' such as Norfolk and Kent – and these could have revolted had they been adequately supported by an arriving royalist army.

Local rivalries duly led to private struggles independent of military strategy in London and Oxford, where rival groups of gentry, who usually fought it out politically at the hustings, now raised small armies and fought over control. The north was particularly autonomous, with a royalist grandee with massive resources and court links, the Earl of Newcastle (William Cavendish), granted sweeping powers from Tees to Tweed by the King and authorized by him to bring in the Catholic community as soldiers (the first time they had been trusted since the 1569 revolt). His immense wealth aided him in paying for equipping his troops at a time of poor 'central' royalist funding (winter 1642–3), and thus in raising morale as well as in practical benefits. His four regiments of infantry, kitted out in woollen jackets made from the sheep on his lands, were known as the 'Lambs', and as the 'Whitecoats' (though only one regiment was actually wearing the colour white). His lack of military experience was made up for by his deputy, the Scot Lord Gethin. Once he had moved south from his governorship of his titular town to add Yorkshire to his 'domain', superseding the ineffective Earl of Cumberland – who had signed a local truce with Lord Fairfax in September 1642 – and defeated the Fairfaxes at Tadcaster (16 December) he commanded all the north except some of the pro-Parliamentarian 'wool towns' of the West Riding. Leeds and Halifax were temporarily overrun, but Lord Fairfax's son Sir Thomas (who had had military service in the Netherlands) held Bradford. Questions must be asked about the reliability and/or competence of Newcastle's subordinate Mountjoy Blount, Lord Newport, a Warwick-Pym ally in 1641 who failed to come to Newcastle's aid when summoned at Tadcaster (allegedly due to a forged letter) but was not removed by his easy-going commander. Was it a deliberate delay? Newcastle was a specialist on equestrian matters, one of the best horsemen in the country, and so useful in commanding cavalry as well as having the social 'clout' to command obedience from the local gentry and was married into the Durham family of Ogle, but he was not directly experienced in war. For the moment, his ability to use more experienced subordinates showed that he could win a battle, as at Adwalton Moor in summer 1643. His attitude to campaigning was later regarded as too 'laid-back', as symbolized by his relaxed attitude at the crucial battle of Marston Moor in 1644 when he was caught unawares smoking in his carriage by the Parliamentarian advance.

The royalist Stanleys (Earls of Derby) faced similar trouble from towns in Lancashire; the north Hampshire Paget dynasty, Marquises of Winchester (based at Basing House, a fortified royalist district headquarters like the Stanleys' Lathom House) were isolated by being Catholic. Even where the local dominance of one party was overwhelming enough to snuff out military resistance early, as with Parliamentarians in East Anglia, Lincolnshire, and the south-east, there were still dissenters who might be able to bring in an army from outside to redress the balance. The Parliamentarian Eastern

Association faced this threat as the royalists moved south over the Trent in 1643, with Newark the key to the defence. Initially the Eastern Association, co-ordinating the resources of the staunchly Parliamentarian counties north-east of London, was placed under the aristocratic Lord Grey of Groby rather than a more experienced 'professional'. Grey, the son of the inadequate south-western commander-in-chief Lord Stamford, was probably appointed for nepotistic and also local reasons – he could command obedience in the area as a major landowner in Leicestershire. Lord Fairfax, head of his family, rather than his more experienced son Sir Thomas commanded in Yorkshire; and it is possible that a similar deference to the 'natural' leadership of the nobility even affected the appointment of Sir William Waller (a veteran of the Queen of Bohemia's army) to command the 'Western Association' as he was married to Lady Anne Finch, an aristocratic 'Puritan' patroness associate of the Warwick circle. In Sussex, however, the local landed power of the royalist Fitzalan-Howards (Earls of Arundel) could not prevent Parliamentarian predominance from 1642; a brief royalist incursion in that year was halted at Haywards Heath and a more serious one by Sir Ralph Hopton was halted at Arundel in winter 1643–4. The Parliamentarians, possessing the advantage of the machinery of central government in Westminster, were the first to set up local associations to co-ordinate action while the royalists relied more on the personal initiatives of great magnates invited to act by the King. This gave them the advantage in mobilizing and co-ordinating resources, but the further a grouping of Parliamentarian gentry was from London the more it was at risk of being overwhelmed. Their south-western leadership, centred in Devon with an army under the local Chudleighs and the imported Earl of Stamford, was overwhelmed in late spring 1643; the similarly isolated West Yorkshire grouping under the Fairfaxes was reduced to a few towns but survived, as did the neighbouring Lancashire Parliamentarians. The loss of a battle and thus men, ammunition, and morale would bring in 'neutrals' to support the winners and could create a 'snowball' effect, as with royalists in the south-west in May–June 1643; it was less serious if the defeated side had a few fortified towns to fall back on and use to hold up the enemy. That factor saved the Parliamentarian cause in the Pennines in 1643. Arguably the royalist failure to take Taunton in 1643–5 tied down enough troops to watch its garrison to blunt the effect of the local royalist advances, albeit not decisively – as did the Parliamentarians at Lyme Regis in summer 1644. In this respect the war in England had elements of a 'people's war', in which a few hundred dauntless civilians (women as much as men) leavened by experienced soldiers could achieve major strategic impact. The Parliamentarian defence of Lyme Regis and Taunton was the equivalent of the Soviet defence of Stalingrad in the Second World War, holding up the 'flood-tide' of enemy advance until the defenders could be rescued.

In the meantime, the fissiparous nature of the 'power-balance' as created during the last months of 1642 and early 1643 argued against an easy victory in any region for one side, assisted by the sheer novelty of war and the lack of military experience and adequate weaponry of both sides. A massive 'sweep' across the countryside by a locally invincible army might well not secure the surrender of a strategically vital town (often a port that could bring in supplies by sea or river), and thus divert the victors from leaving their conquered region to assist their national leadership. This factor aided Parliament more than the King, as they had the adherence of the townsfolk of large and/or well-defended towns in royalist areas – though the loyalties of the majority of towns did not automatically lead to open support of Parliament if the royalists were the dominant local party. Plymouth, with its naval tradition and access to ships, ammunition, and artillery, held up a part of the royalist army that overran Devon in late spring 1643; isolated Hull defied the Earl of Newcastle in 1643; and Gloucester played the crucial role in 1643 by hindering a royalist advance from South Wales and then distracting the King from attacking London at an important moment. In 1644 it was to be the turn of Parliamentarian Lyme Regis to hold up the royalist advance of Prince Maurice's army through the south-west. The damage was probably worst at Lyme Regis, reflecting not only its smaller size but the determination (and brutality) of both sides.

Accordingly, one major victory by any local army would only clear one sphere of the war, and leave it open to the enemy to triumph in other areas and make up for this loss. But the largest forces remained those of the central 'field armies', those of the King based on Oxford and of the Earl of Essex based on London. Their manoeuvres centred on the south-central region of England in 1643, with their furthest moves west at Gloucester. They were both within striking-distance of Oxford and London, the cavalry more so than the artillery-encumbered infantry, though the state of the roads (particularly in bad weather) hampered quick advances and the leading generals on both sides proved unwilling to take risks. If either of those two armies destroyed the opposition the victors stood a chance of marching quickly on the enemy 'capital'. The fall of London or Oxford would not end the war, but it should demoralize the losing party to the extent that increasing numbers of their local commanders sought terms of truce and laid down their arms. Such a 'tipping-point' would lead to a momentum towards accepting the inevitable, as finally occurred in the autumn of 1645; only a few quixotic loyalists in difficult-to-attack outposts were likely to hold out to the end. (The last royalist strongholds early in 1646 were mostly in isolated parts of Cornwall and on islands; the even more isolated Channel Islands and the Isle of Man held out for even longer.) By this argument, the 'tipping point' could have occurred earlier than in reality if one side had suffered catastrophic losses to their main army – but the lack of professionalism in either side's 'command structure' early in the war made this less likely. Crucially, in spring 1643 Parliament had the advantage of possessing the reserves of artillery and ammunition that the King had owned at London and Portsmouth and the ammunition and artillery gathered at Hull in 1640–41 for the Scots war.[1] The King's main army at Oxford was seriously short of them until it could import or manufacture them and imports were difficult without possession of Bristol, Plymouth, or Hull. Oxford itself was at a disadvantage as a strategic base and arsenal compared with London in 1643, as it was a university town not an established military base and port; resources had to be brought in overland from West Country ports and Bristol was not in the King's hands for some months. A major convoy of weaponry and ammunition that the Queen had bought in Holland arrived with her by sea at Bridlington in Yorkshire on 23 February 1643 and she set up her headquarters in York, her presence inspiring the Parliamentarian governor of Scarborough Castle (Sir Hugh Cholmeley) to defect. After a delay her convoy was escorted to Oxford in June, redressing the balance in terms of ammunition. The Marquis of Hertford (driven out of Devon into South Wales) was able to bring Welsh reinforcements to Oxford early in 1643 before Waller's army cut the route from that region across the lower Severn valley. More imports of ammunition to the royalist area followed, and the local production of royalist 'arms-factories' also gathered pace through 1643. But the advantage for a quick offensive by the better-equipped army had lain with Parliament for a vital few months as the 1643 campaign season opened, during a period when the King's south-western offensive had not yet gathered pace and his reserves of Cornish pikemen were tied down defending their own county. The loss of the fleet in 1642 was also crucial, as it meant that the King's hired ships had to run the gauntlet of Parliamentary interception to bring in supplies – when the Queen arrived at Bridlington from the Continent she was harassed by Parliamentary ships, shelled in the town, and had to take refuge in a ditch.[2] Eighteen merchant and four naval ships fell into royalist hands when the port of Bristol was secured in summer 1643, redressing the balance somewhat.

The Earl of Essex failed to take advantage of this 'window of opportunity', except for a successful siege of Reading in May, which forced the King's outposts back closer to Oxford. Even at Reading, the strength of the defences could have held him up longer had the defenders been more determined. To be fair to him, his army needed to gain experience of fighting together and using its equipment and tactics successfully before clashing with the King's army – so his slowness in action in this expedition was wise. The most crucial 'what if' of this clash is not that of the actual siege, but of the fact that it was necessary at all. The town had been slackly defended in the late winter as an attack was not expected, and in January 1643 local Parliamentarian commander/MP John Hampden (dominant figure of Buckinghamshire) led a picked force down from the Chilterns to reconnoitre. Apparently he and his Scots deputy, Colonel Hurry, had been tipped off, presumably about disaffection or slack guards, but they had to give up as rain made the River Kennet too swollen to cross a bridge near the town. An attack had to wait for a methodical advance of Essex's main army, which left Windsor Castle on 13 April to link up with Lord Grey of Wark's reinforcements from the Eastern Association.

Essex's siege of Reading (15 April) was a 'textbook' blockade, with the attackers moving west round Reading to dig lines of fortifications that gradually moved in closer to the defenders' earthworks. It was aided by the Parliamentary success in securing Caversham Hill (overlooking the town from the north, across the Thames) on the 17th and then taking Caversham Bridge to cut off supplies from over the Thames. Even so things nearly went wrong; a royalist swam across the Kennet to blow up the attackers' arsenal and was caught in time, preventing an enfeebled bombardment that might well have led to the defence keeping its nerve better. The King's march from Oxford on the 24th to relieve the town ended in disaster as a half-hearted attempt to retake the bridge by Lord Ruthin on 25 April was beaten back, by an inferior body of Parliamentarians to their subsequent elation at this proof of Divine backing. Possibly Rupert's absence in the Midlands, where he had just taken Birmingham (3 April) and Lichfield (town 10 April, cathedral 21 April), hampered royalist enthusiasm. The garrison were denounced as useless by their Catholic commander, Sir Arthur Aston (whose religion may have hindered their willingness). Even so, Essex's success in securing quick surrender was down to luck; Aston was incapacitated by a blow on the head from a falling tile and the deputy commander John Feilding, brother of the Earl of Denbigh, was anxious to preserve lives. He had already opened negotiations under a flag of truce, and as he heard the relief-force approach he refused his officers' request to breach his promise and launch a break-out as this would be dishonourable (even if the King ordered him to do it). Once Charles had pulled back Feilding saw no point in fighting on, and surrendered two days later in return for his men being permitted to leave unmolested (26 April). The fact that his brother was a Parliamentarian commander, Lord Denbigh, did not pass unnoticed and he was court-martialled and sentenced to be shot but was reprieved on appeal. Essex had been lucky. A ponderous commander trained in detailed siege-warfare in the Thirty Years' War, Essex was to prove a major frustration to his subordinates over the coming year-and-a-half. His responsibility for the failures of Parliamentary strategy has been argued over, and was already an issue at the time as frustration built up. However, his conduct on the march to Gloucester later that year was to show that he was an able strategist, if less than dashing – the reverse of Prince Rupert. An element of anti-aristocratic 'class' spite was detected in the attacks on him after the failures of 1644, at least as seen by his fellow-aristocrat Manchester who blamed 'low-class' officers led by his main critic Cromwell.

It was alleged that an aristocratic commander like Essex could not take the political struggle seriously enough, and conversely that his critics were using his failures as an excuse to attack the aristocracy for radical political motives. Certainly Essex showed strategic misjudgement in the 1644 campaign, pressing ahead too far into Cornwall and not returning to safety quickly enough (see section on that campaign). This was more damning than his hesitancy in 1643, when he had a largely untried army made up of men from disparate areas who were neither experienced nor used to fighting together. Ultimately Essex's hesitancy and depressive character were to play a part in the reaction of winter 1644–5, which led to the establishment of the New Model, the first 'national' rather than regional force and a body staffed on merit not social background. The Parliamentary choice of supreme commander thus helped to hold up success in 1644 and to mould the means of creating a 'war-winning' army in 1645; a more successful aristocratic commander would have stood in the way of the emergence of Fairfax and Cromwell – and of the latter's agenda for a radical settlement in 1646–8. But the need for MPs to conciliate the Lords, and Essex's great prestige and Continental experience in an age of deference, meant that replacing him quickly by a more dynamic commander – necessarily another aristocrat – in 1643 was impractical unless he voluntarily stepped down.

Warwick, the leader of the Lords 'Calvinist' group in 1640–42 and the King's fiercest political opponent since 1639, was commanding the fleet and anyway lacked military experience. One of the great unanswered questions of the Parliamentary leadership in 1643–4 is how the senior peers who had dominated civilian resistance to the King and plotted coercion with the Scots in 1640–42 were eclipsed. One prominent pro-Presbyterian peer who was thus amenable to the Pym-Holles-Haselrig faction of Presbyterian MPs, Brooke, was soon killed (see below). But the equally Calvinist Warwick, a major figure in 1640–42 and patron of many 'godly' preachers, showed far less political dynamism in defending the aristocratic leadership of

Parliament in 1644 than earlier. Was he too preoccupied running the fleet, or did his lack of military experience mean that his reputation was waning among MPs? It is important to remember that Essex had no obvious – qualified – successor among the peers as commander-in-chief, were he to be dismissed for his poor performance on the battlefield.

Any new commander-in-chief in 1643 would have had to have the backing of the most coherent and radical group of MPs led by Pym, and thus to have shown his devotion to Calvinism and 'Root and Branch' principles – necessary for conciliating the Scots leadership. The only suitable radical (i.e. 'Puritan') aristocrat who had the social status and the military experience in 1643 to have been a viable supreme commander was Lord Brooke, commander of the associated counties of Warwickshire and Staffordshire. He may already have been considered as a suitable successor for Essex, but unfortunately he was killed by a sniper on 2 March while besieging Lichfield Cathedral.[3] Had he been available in winter 1643–4, would he have had the seniority and the reassuring anti-Laudian reputation to have been chosen as Essex's successor? And could his favourable views on toleration within the Church[4] have given him the support of rising Independents such as Cromwell against the disciplinarian Presbyterians in the main religious controversy among the Parliamentary leadership in 1644–6? At the best, Brooke could have been an aristocratic religious 'counter-weight' to the pro-Presbyterian Essex and Warwick – and if peers and socially deferential MPs cavilled at appointing a socially junior commander-in-chief he could have been chosen to succeed Essex. Would this have placated impatient MPs determined on a more aggressive military strategy without their real-life expedient of creating a new (New Model) army? Would some of the critics of Essex, such as Cromwell, have accepted the aristocratic but less sluggish Brooke as a replacement commander-in-chief for the crucial campaigns of 1644 or 1645?

As it was, the death of Brooke helped to drive the West Midlands Parliamentarians into a cautious posture, which the arrival of Prince Rupert's quick-moving and devastating cavalry force made even more logical. Without Brooke, their garrisons were even more at risk of sudden attack; and on 2–3 April Rupert launched a massive and unexpected attack on the major local Parliamentary weapons-supply centre, Birmingham. The town was quickly overwhelmed and was systematically looted, in a brutal manner that added to Parliamentary hatred and fear of 'Prince Robber'. There had been looting by both sides of overrun towns already, more by a lack of officers' control over greedy and undisciplined soldiers than by policy – the strict and honourable Parliamentarian William Waller had been unable to stop his men looting Winchester in December. But this sack of

Birmingham was a deliberate act intended to terrorize other towns into surrendering, common practice in Continental warfare where Rupert had been trained; and the King reprimanded Rupert for it.

Before the main campaign: rising desire for peace, but not where it mattered?

The anti-royal and anti-Anglican belligerency in the City had arguably been the main political weapon that Pym and his allies had used in intimidating their moderate rivals during 1641. Rowdy crowds from the capital had surrounded Parliament shouting demands for the death of Strafford and the abolition of episcopacy, which had an effect in causing prudent or cowardly MPs and peers to fail to vote as the King wished on such matters. The City's defiance of Charles after he failed to capture the 'Five Members' in January 1642 led to him withdrawing from Whitehall to the north, and thus showing foreign observers that he had lost control of his capital. The populace had rallied to join Essex's army and Skippon's Trained Bands in marching out to Turnham Green to defy the advancing King in November 1642, as recalled by participant Bulstrode Whitelocke.[5]

But now in January 1643 there was a significant demonstration and petition by the apprentices for opening negotiations, and the City's Common Council sent a delegation to Oxford to ask for the King's terms. Other petitions to the Commons came from the most solidly pro-Parliamentary counties of Bedfordshire, Hertfordshire, and Essex. Arguably their recent discovery of the unwelcome high cost of a war in taxation was the main cause of this. Meanwhile Pym's proposal for a defensive Protestant covenant with the Scots (against the supposed new pro-royalist Catholic league being agreed among the Irish rebels) was voted down. More importantly for the Parliamentary ability to fight, the trade-slump in London caused by war was hindering their finances. The existing customs-farmers refused to loan them any money, probably fearing that after the 'close call' of the King's advance in November they were a losing cause. In retaliation Parliament resorted to forced loans – the King's highly unpopular method of raising money in similar difficulties in the 1620s – and arrested any wealthy citizens who would not pay. The leading royalist merchant in the City, Sir Nicholas Crispe, escaped in time to Oxford but his wealth was impounded. There was a useful political potential for the King from this, and demonstrations against the war (mainly its economic cost on trade and unemployment) in December had forced the Commons to vote to negotiate on the 16th. But typically Charles' current stance was too implacable to rally support, despite the latent possibilities of anxious MPs and peers defying Pym (whose plan for a military alliance with the 'rebel' Covenanter Scots had been voted down). His immediate reply to the Common Council petition, delivered to them on 13 January, was to denounce the recent treason of his ungrateful subjects and demand that named pro-Parliamentary leaders in the City be arrested before he would return – at the head of an army. Pym was duly able to rally support to reject the terms.[6] In fact the Venetian ambassador Agostini heard from Charles' envoy that the King intended to be in the field by May at the head of 40,000 men, and would advance down the Thames to cut off trade and blockade London into surrender.[7] Given the current royalist shortage of ammunition and the multiplicity of local armies being raised against him, this was wildly optimistic.

The official Parliamentary terms for negotiations, which the City petition had anticipated, were based on those made in the Lords on 20 December by Northumberland's group of moderate peers. They were requesting formal royal approval of all bills that the Houses and the immanent Assembly of Divines should agree – i.e. including a reform of the Church agreed with clerical participation from the pro-'Root and Branch' divines selected by Parliament. Charles was to agree to pay off the debts that Parliament had run up, allow Digby (seen as the mastermind behind the court 'offensive' to arrest the Commons leaders in January 1642) and all those impeached before 1 January 1642 to stand trial, and exclude Bristol and Hertford (two senior royalist provincial commanders), the Queen's friend Sir Henry Jermyn, and a few other 'ultra' courtiers from office and court. The privileges of Parliament were to be guaranteed; there was to be a new Militia Bill so Parliament could control the local armed forces, and Northumberland was to be reinstated as Lord High Admiral to control the navy.[8] This served to secure political control of the agenda, personnel, and armed forces of government and a reform of religion as devised by the Warwick-Pym 'party' in 1641, an English counterpart of the neutralization of the King's power in Scotland, which he had accepted in August 1641. The unwelcome experience of the reality of war led to the Commons voting to proceed on that basis on 26 December, though Vane had warned in the heated debate on the 22nd that it was unworkable as the King would never agree and his critics would lose negotiating strength by letting their guard down. More support was given to the moderate Sir Symonds D'Ewes, who warned that the chances of success in the field against the King's armies were minimal; rising chaos in England and the refusal of tenants to pay their rents meant that poverty and famine would ruin their cause.[9]

The King received the delegates of Parliament at Oxford on 1 February; they included the pro-royalist MP Edmund Waller who had remained in London to rally support for him and who was shortly to use the negotiations' failure to start a plot to seize the City. His own views on the terms were dismissive; he wrote to Ormonde on the 2nd that no force but God could make him accept them. In his formal reply on the 3rd, he required the return of all his seized revenue, forts, and ships, the withdrawal of all anti-royal printed declarations, abandonment of the Parliamentary claim to tax or imprison his subjects, and agreement of a Church settlement that would preserve the (Anglican) Book of Common Prayer. At most there would be a declaration in it to 'satisfy tender consciences' – whatever that meant in practice. All persons exempted from pardon were to be tried by their peers. In the meantime, there was to be a military truce and free trade between the areas occupied by both factions but no military disbandment – meaning that the assembly of local royalist armies, which was gathering pace that winter, would continue.[10]

The gap between the rival sets of terms was unbridgeable, with each demanding recognition of their own sovereign rights to dominate the post-war political and military scene. The delay had served more to satisfy the opponents of open war on both sides that armed struggle was the only option than to commence serious talks. Given that the terms of both sides were hardly altered from those of spring 1642, if either had been serious enough to contemplate a workable resolution they knew where they would have to make concessions. The military initiative now lay with the King, despite his weaker military position at present in terms of poorer armaments and the loss of the south-east, the capital, and the most convenient major ports.

The royalist advances of spring–summer 1643: potentially decisive?

The triple royalist advances from the west, south-west, and north in spring brought the King's cause close to success. Crucial Parliamentary strongpoints defied each advancing royalist army – Plymouth in the south-west, Gloucester in the west, and Hull in the north. The major royalist advances in three areas (south-west, South Wales, and the north) in spring 1643 were slow and were marred by serious reverses. It is sometimes assumed that there was a 'grand strategy' by the King in bringing his forces from each extremity of the kingdom to move inwards towards London, and certainly the Earl of Newcastle at York and Sir Ralph Hopton in Cornwall were required to head away from their heartlands towards the south-east. The triple advance was in any case logical, as each 'provincial' army was going to assemble in a 'safe' area – Cornwall, eastern Yorkshire based on York, and Wales – and then move forward to aid the King's main army. The King would have had a safe port to bring in military supplies had a plot to surrender Bristol to Rupert in March succeeded, but – like the Hotham plots at Hull in 1642 – the personnel involved were caught in time.[11]

In the south-west the initial advantage had lain with the Parliamentarian commander in Devon, the Earl of Stamford, who had the larger army and a charismatic and successful deputy in local James Chudleigh (whose success was played up by Parliamentary propaganda as the 'Western Wonder'[12]). Unluckily Stamford, appointed to higher rank as socially superior, lacked Chudleigh's flair and was not a 'professional' by training or in his approach. His past failures had been excusable – his withdrawal from Hereford, where Essex had left him as governor at the time of Edgehill, in December was strategically necessary (also his plundering had enraged the local population). His advance into the far west necessarily left the Severn valley defenceless, enabling the Marquis of Hertford to cross it with Welsh reinforcements for Oxford. But in his advance into Cornwall – a fiercely parochial region – Stamford, a lackadaisical commander, lost touch with the more experienced Scots commander of Plymouth, Ruthven, who was defeated on 19 January at Braddock Down. Ironically, it had been the Parliamentarian crossing of the Tamar into Cornwall that was the greatest fillip to royalist recruitment – an unnecessary provocation that created a new threat from indignant but until now uncommitted locals? The enthusiastic but badly armed and untrained Cornishmen were not invincible, as shown when their first 'thrust' over the Tamar into South Devon was routed at Modbury (21 February). But the main new royalist army came together as an effective force quickly, and on 23 April Chudleigh failed in his attempt to drive Hopton's men off Beacon Hill overlooking Launceston in an attack into north-central Cornwall.

It should be remarked that there had been no great enthusiasm to fight for the King in Cornwall in late 1642, as the royalist recruiter Lord Hopton had found – the alleged 'provincial' and 'conservative semi-Catholic' Cornish hatred of 'London rebel Puritans' was not in evidence then. The local JPs had objected to Hopton as a disturber of the peace, and the tide had only turned when Hopton's ally Nicholas Slanning seized four Parliamentary ships that had been blown into Falmouth harbour by bad weather to provide weapons and ammunition. John Arundell then seized nearby Pendennis Castle to ensure royalist recruits' safety as they prepared for action. Without these two actions (one down to luck), would Hopton have had a viable army? Would Stamford have been able to secure Cornwall in January 1643 and so prevent the royalist overrunning of the south-west that followed his defeat? This is not just a minor matter – the 'chain reaction' of events that followed the Parliamentarian failure in Cornwall ended with thousands of Cornishmen and Devonians marching as far as Bath to defeat and neutralize the so far successful Parliamentarian general William Waller later that spring. Miscalculations and inefficiency in Stamford's campaign played their part in meaning that there was no major Parliamentarian army active in the Southern Cotswolds in June–September 1643 ready to relieve the siege of Gloucester, and so Essex had to be called in from London.

Stamford's next 'push' later that spring, to confront Hopton's new Cornish army in the north of that county, was equally muddled. Establishing himself on a defensible hill top at Stratton to threaten the royalists at Launceston, he sent his cavalry off to secure Bodmin and so threw away one of his best advantages until such time as they returned. His force still outnumbered the enemy by around 4,500 to 2,400 and had more artillery, but – as later with Waller at Lansdown – the Parliamentarians seem to have been over-confident that numbers and artillery would deter a 'head-on' attack by less-well-armed but enthusiastic pikemen. Lofty contempt for the untrained Cornish peasantry may have played a part. On 16 May the royalists attacked up the steep hill above Stratton, aided by the local knowledge of Sir Bevil Grenville whose family home was nearby, and by sheer determination smashed the well-prepared defences. The dogged Cornish pikemen trained by Sir Bevil Grenville overwhelmed a superior defensive position despite running short of ammunition, and Stamford lost his nerve and led his cavalry off the field rather than risking a counter-charge. The abandoned infantry under Chudleigh had their captured cannons turned on them and were routed. Stamford, the first notable example of half-hearted aristocratic Parliamentary commanders whose failings led to their eclipse by professionals in 1644–5, lost the battle, his reputation, and most of his army (300 killed and 1,700 prisoners), and Chudleigh defected.[13]

The first royalist attempt on Bristol by Rupert in March failed, and Sir William Waller (commander of the army of the 'Western Association' from 11 February) used Gloucester as a base for an offensive into Monmouthshire against the Herberts, reaching as far as Chepstow and Hereford. Had this been sustained, it would have neutralized the royalist ironworks in the Forest of Dean. He successfully ambushed a second South Wales force of royalists en route to the King in Oxfordshire at Highnam, two miles from Gloucester – this showed what could have been done to Hertford's first expedition had a local Parliamentarian army been available in January. But while he was assisting Gloucester's governor William Massey to destroy the royalist bridge at Tewkesbury Prince Maurice arrived with cavalry from Oxford. The royalist superiority in cavalry gave them victory over Waller's smaller force at 'Ripple Field' between Tewkesbury and Upton-on-Severn on 13 April, but Maurice was unable to exploit his victory as Waller withdrew in good order. Once the majority of the Severn valley royalists were called off to assist with the King's siege of Reading in mid-April, Waller was able to extend his control of the area by marching on Hereford, which fell to a surprise attack on 25 April. This cut off the King's South Welsh recruiting-ground from Oxford, forcing royalists to march even further north to evade Parliamentarian-controlled territory, but the collapse of the Parliamentarian position in Devon following the battle of Stratton nullified Waller's gains. His attempt to take Worcester, with the next bridge on the Severn north of Tewkesbury and Upton, on 21 May, met a stiffer resistance (from local Colonel William Sandys) than Colonel Cave had put up at Hereford, and he had to retreat as news came that he was desperately needed back in Somerset.[14] Had the royalists not had this success in the south-west, the King's concentration of his Midlands forces at Oxford could have seen his supply-route west cut. The main responsibility for Parliament's eclipse in the south-west Midlands thus lay with Stamford.

In the north-east the Fairfaxes held the Earl of Newcastle back from the West Riding, though his subordinate Lord Goring defeated Sir Thomas at Seacroft Moor (30 March) with 200 dead and 800 captured. Tadcaster was recaptured but Newcastle failed to move in quickly to besiege Leeds, as urged by Goring; apparently he accepted his deputy Lord Eythin's advice that it was too risky. The younger Fairfax, an inspiring commander nicknamed 'the rider on the white horse', was able to regather his forces free from a royalist attack, and on 21 May emerged again to retake Wakefield in a surprise attack against superior forces. Goring was ill in bed at the time and was caught unprepared, and he and many of his men were captured and so could be exchanged for Parliamentarians taken at Seacroft Moor. But this confused melee in the streets of Wakefield provided another major 'near miss' of the war – Fairfax, future commander of the New Model, was cut off with a party of royalists who had surrendered to him by a surprise counter-attack and nearly killed or captured. Due to neither side wearing distinctive uniforms, he was lucky – the royalist attackers thought he must be a fellow-royalist too and did not attack him and his captives 'sportingly' did not betray him.

The presence of the Queen and her Continental reinforcements in York in February–March helped to swing the calculations of the undecided or timorous in the King's favour, though there was no quick resolution to the negotiations with the treacherous Parliamentarian Sir John Hotham about his handing over his father's garrison at Hull. Hotham now turned up at York to propose to the Queen that he receive a barony, his father a viscountcy, and the pair of them £20,000 for their trouble – one of the most blatant prices of opportunism during the war. In the north-west Sir William Brereton's Cheshire Parliamentarians held the Stanleys back in Lancashire. His deputy, Gell, defeated and killed the Earl of Northampton, royalist commander in the central Midlands (based at Banbury), at Hopton Heath on 19 March as the latter moved on Lichfield. The Earl, head of the local Spencer dynasty of Northamptonshire, lacked nothing in loyalty or enthusiasm and had poured his money into recruiting and equipping his army; he was shot down while riding ahead of his men in disregard of his safety and he memorably refused an offer of quarter from his enemies as 'base rogues'.[15]

Northampton, like Stamford on the opposite side, was essentially an amateur in a war that was to be taken over by professionals (and those who learnt quickly); but it is notable that the number of idealistic aristocrats who paid the price for a lack of prudence on the battlefield was greater among royalists than among Parliamentarians. Brooke, killed by a lucky shot by a sniper at Lichfield cathedral, was almost alone among such casualties on the 'insurgent' side.

The arrival of the Queen with a large collection of ammunition from the Continent was a useful bonus to the royalists in Yorkshire, and she duly proceeded south to Oxford to meet her husband on the battlefield of Edgehill in July. (Her dashing service to the cause was slightly marred in propaganda terms by her having to take refuge in a ditch from shelling by Parliamentarian ships as she landed at Bridlington on 22 February.) Her convoy's military potential induced the shameless Parliamentarian commander of Hull, Hotham, to turn up asking for a peerage and £20,000 in return for him defecting. The situation in the north/central Midlands was more evenly balanced, with towns such as Lichfield taken and re-taken; Northampton's death at Hopton Heath prevented the most hopeful effort to restore the royalist position in the region, by a well-known local figure who could thus command respect. In his absence the task fell on Prince Rupert and his cavalry – a fast-moving and increasingly feared force but under a leader increasingly criticized for not adhering to the expected rules of war on harassing civilians. Rupert's spectacular sack of Parliamentarian Birmingham on 3 April disrupted the latter's production of weaponry but had little strategic impact. Some districts, e.g. Staffordshire, were a complicated network of strongpoints (often country houses) held by rival garrisons with no overall control by one party. The lucky shot that killed the Parliamentarian commander of strategically vital Warwickshire and Staffordshire, Lord Brooke, at Lichfield on 2 March was a political as much as a military success given his potential role in the Lords as lieutenant to the Earl of Warwick.

'Waller's Plot', May 1643: a 'Peace Party' coup?
Nor were the royalist hopes of using the King's 'Commission of Array', smuggled into the City by Lady D'Aubigny, to raise a force of loyalists to

surprise the enemy leadership in their beds – 'Waller's Plot' – likely to succeed except with extreme luck, given the difficulty of co-ordination. As with the Gunpowder Plot in 1605, a written warning by a plotter warning his relatives to get out of London alerted the authorities to an imminent attack. One intercepted messenger was leading MP Hampden's cousin, an example of tangled family loyalties. At most the royalists were believed to have the passive support of a third of Londoners; even if the 'war party' leadership then in London (MPs Pym, Hampden, Stapleton, and Lords Saye and Sele and Wharton), militant Lord Mayor Isaac Penington, and his leading officers had been seized it was risky to assume that everyone else would passively fall into line and cease resistance. The City's commander, Sir Philip Skippon, would have needed to be neutralized and the Trained Bands to accept the leadership of City loyalists using the King's commission; local murmurings in the Bands against Pym (who was at first believed to have invented the plot as an excuse for anti-pacifist action) did not necessarily imply enthusiasm to support the King. Assuming the majority of the Bands had stayed loyal and had leadership, Skippon or (if he had been a prisoner) his deputies would have had time to retake any seized strongpoints before the King's main army could arrive from Oxford. Even a cavalry 'dash' by Rupert's men to aid a rising would have taken a few days.[16]

The King could probably have relied on sympathetic legislative action for peace in the event of a coup from some of the Lords remaining in London, led by Northumberland (soon to defect), Portland, and Conway. They had recently voted against negotiating on the basis of the terms brought by a royal emissary, ironically Hampden's cousin Alexander. (The latter's main purpose was to deliver instructions to Waller's plotters, and Pym's suspicions of his intentions led to the surveillance of his movements, which exposed the plot.) But it appears that one of the less belligerent Commons leaders, Denzel Holles, was at least aware of the plot's intentions and did nothing about it; he was under suspicion and threat of summary arrest later that spring and was noticeably excluded from the King's list of 'traitors' to be denied pardon. He was opposed to a long war and thus may have been prepared to countenance a sudden coup to bring it to an end by handing over London, if not to actively aid it. He and his Commons adherents (whether informed in advance or taken by surprise) could well have had the determination to act in bringing in a legislative resolution for talks had Waller and his plotters seized Pym and the leading belligerents and occupied City strongpoints. The political decapitation of the Parliamentary 'war party' and takeover of the Trained Bands by the King's loyalists would have freed the other MPs from intimidation. In real life, the details leaked out at the end of May and Pym was able to order arrests; in the reaction to this evidence of royal untrustworthiness the militants carried a vote for a mandatory 'Covenant', an oath for all to take to resist the King by force, and forced the Lords to accept the calling of an Assembly of Divines to reform the Church. The oath made the position of the 'peace party' weaker, as from now on any open calls for talks that Parliament had not voted for could be declared treacherous.[17] The quarrel between radical MP Henry Marten and the potential 'peace party' peer Northumberland in May (over Marten's opening the latter's mail to search for evidence of treachery)[18] was symbolic of a wider mistrust between the fully committed and the equivocal at Westminster.

In the meantime, the prospect arose of the King being able to open up a new 'front' in Scotland. There was considerable discontent among the Covenanter nobility against the virtual dictatorship of Argyll and his clerical allies, leading to the possibility that a faction of anti-Argyll nobles would either revolt or stage a coup (as the King had encouraged during his visit to Edinburgh in late summer 1641). There was, however, a crucial dilemma for the King – should he rely on those firmly Presbyterian nobles who had adhered to the 'rebel' cause in 1637–40, who insisted on a comprehensive abdication of royal political and religious power in Scotland while still accepting a monarchy? Or should he accept the offers of help from Catholic nobles such as the Gordons, based in the Highlands and unable to help him effectively in 1638–9, and their Catholic co-religionists in Ireland? The Marquis of Hamilton was the main supporter of the former cause at Oxford in early 1643, having adhered to Argyll and backed the King's reduction to a figurehead in the royal-Covenanter agreement of August 1641 – and Charles had then thought of having him and Argyll both arrested in the 'Incident'. Now Montrose, a firm Covenanter but a 'royalist Presbyterian' more receptive to retaining some powers for the monarch and driven by loathing of Argyll, arrived in York from Scotland to meet the Queen in March. He offered to raise a revolt in Scotland, including Catholics and bringing in the Gordons from Buchan and a force of expatriate Scots Catholic troops from Ulster under the swashbuckling mercenary captain Alistair Macdonald, 'Mac Colkitto'.[19]

The Macdonalds in Ulster had the advantage of being hereditary foes of Argyll. Any such Catholic revolt and invasion would by its nature diminish the chances of other Covenanter nobles joining in, as they were more wary of Catholics than was Montrose, so it would be unpopular in the Lowlands. But if successful its leaders would restore Charles' power in Scotland, which Hamilton's allies were unlikely to do. The Queen, as a Catholic, may well have favoured Montrose's plans; but for the moment Charles found Hamilton's plan safer and gave him his approval. Montrose's mission to

Oxford was unsuccessful and he left empty-handed, and the King empowered six Presbyterian Scots aristocrats leaving Oxford to plan a coup to depose Argyll.[20]

The royalist successes – with important limits to their strategic advantages

The major royalist successes in the south-west, from Braddock Down in January to Roundway Down on 13 July, saw the seeming triumph of the royalist gentry and the neutralization of their enemies. Once Stamford had been routed at Stratton in mid-May Devon lay open to attack. The pro-Parliamentarian coastal towns – Plymouth and Exeter in the south, Barnstaple and Bideford in the north – held out but Hopton was able to sweep east across Devon and in June meet up with Prince Maurice at Chard, and isolated inland Parliamentarian towns like Bridgewater and Taunton surrendered to them. So did isolated garrisons like Dunster Castle. Waller arrived in Somerset to stiffen resistance, and one of the intriguing 'what ifs' of the war saw his advance-parties briefly capture Maurice in a raid on his camp at Chewton Mendip. Maurice was not recognized and was soon rescued – but if he had not been, would he have still been prisoner in 1644 and so not been available to mismanage the royalist siege of Lyme Regis then? Maurice, Hopton, and Sir Bevil Grenville moved forward on Waller's Parliamentarian army at Bath, outnumbering him with about 4,000 royalist infantry, 2,000 cavalry, and 500 royalist dragoons to about 2,000 Parliamentarian cavalry and 1,500 infantry.[21] Waller had to fight alone as Essex failed to make any effort to speed up his campaign preparations and relieve them. The militarily talented Waller, already nicknamed 'William the Conqueror' (from his quick taking of Portsmouth in August 1642), was among their most flexible generals and had been a wise choice by Essex to command the west. He made the most of the steep hills north of Bath to defend his army, not facing a frontal attack from the south-east as he managed to hold onto Claverton Down above the city and the royalists kept their distance. Having taken Bradford-on-Avon to cut the road east to London, the royalists did not dare to try to attack up steep, wooded Claverton Down and moved off north onto the open downs north-east of Bath. Waller moved out of Bath onto the nearer part of the ridge to deny it to his enemies on 4 July; they halted for the night at Batheaston so he did not have to race them to it. He chose a position up on Lansdown that would have to be attacked 'head-on' across a valley. On 5 July the royalists riskily attempted just that, charging uphill to tackle superior Parliamentarian artillery (which luckily fired over their heads for much of the climb due to the steep incline).

The élan of the recently victorious Cornish infantry carried them across Waller's breastworks and the royalist cavalry followed, with the numerically superior Parliamentarian cavalry charging them five times – aided by the slope downhill – but failing to break them. As with the failure of Haselrig's cavalry regiment of 'Lobsters' to drive the royalists back the previous day on Tog Hill, the royalists' enthusiasm defeated a technically superior enemy albeit at large costs in terms of losses. Only 600 of the 2,000 royalist cavalry survived the charge up Lansdown, with their leader Grenville among the casualties,[22] and such losses were vital in the long term despite the inspiring effect of their sacrifice in raising morale and recruits. For the moment, Waller withdrew in good order into Bath and even claimed the battle as a victory. He was able to regain the initiative as Hopton was wounded in an accidental gunpowder-explosion on the 6th, and he retained control of the ridge of hills above Bath. Swooping down on Hopton's exhausted army and its incapacitated commander at Devizes, his expected success in storming their camp was prevented as royalist cavalry reinforcements were hastily collected from Oxfordshire by Prince Maurice.[23] They were able to collect three brigades under Lord Wilmot, a vital asset in the next battle, and relieve Hopton's army in Devizes from the demoralizing bombardment of Waller's artillery up on the ridge above. The resultant clash at Roundway Down (23 July) saw a complete royalist victory, although Hopton's officers were too nervous to dare to emerge from Devizes to take Waller in the rear as Maurice and Wilmot hoped. Haselrig was almost captured or killed in a scuffle as his crack regiment of 'Lobsters' was destroyed – his breastplate deflected several sword-strokes. Around 6,000 Parliamentarians were killed and 1,000 captured[24] – and if Haselrig had been killed it would have diminished the 'hard-line' Presbyterian republican leadership in the Commons in 1647–8 and 1659–60. The 'Western Association' army briefly ceased to function as an effective force, leaving the royalists in full control of the West Country, apart from a few isolated ports and other garrisons.

But although Waller's destroyed army had to abandon the western campaign their foes had received heavy losses. Further Cornish losses followed in endeavouring to storm the outworks of Bristol for Rupert on 26 July, including their regimental commanders Slanning and Trevanion, although enough of the defences were overrun to alarm governor Nathaniel Fiennes into surrendering. (The infuriated Parliament duly considered executing him for cowardice, and the act was still cited against him a decade later.[25]) The killing of all the four senior Cornish commanders, the 'four wheels of Charles' wain (i.e. the constellation of the Plough)' as in the royalist song – Grenville, Godolphin, Slanning, and Trevanion – reduced the number of competent commanders available in the south-west, particularly the dashing Sir Bevil Grenville who had raised the Cornish infantry. But the string of successes leading to the annihilation of Waller's army at Roundway Down, followed by Rupert's capture of Bristol on 26 July, secured a wide area of the south-west and its major port for the King.

The Fairfaxes were on the defensive in Yorkshire; the Scots had not yet come into action to take the advancing northern royalists in the rear, and the check that the latter received from Cromwell and the Eastern Association was not as vital as the royalist successes further south. The defection of one major Parliamentarian garrison-commander in the north, Sir Hugh Cholmeley at Scarborough,[26] could point the way for others – at least political moderates like him who lacked zeal for the cause despite distrusting the King and had not wanted a long war. Had Sir John Hotham succeeded in his secret contacts with the royalists at Newark in June he could have handed Hull over and enabled Newcastle's army to march on south in force, but luckily Cromwell and John Hutchinson warned Essex of their fears in time and Hotham was seized on 18 June. Nevertheless, Newcastle used his local military supremacy well and secured Sheffield with its ironworks to supply his army, keeping the Fairfaxes on the defensive. He sent 7,000 men south to escort the Queen to Oxford, 2,000 later returning, but had enough troops remaining to destroy the Fairfaxes' local force on Adwalton Moor at the end of June. Hopton's royalists were soon to rout the south-western Parliamentary army under Waller similarly. Following this he could overrun both Bradford and Leeds, the main Parliamentarian towns of the West Riding, although the fugitive Lord Fairfax's arrival in Hull enabled the Parliamentarian general to frustrate the machinations of the Hothams to hand it over.[27] Effectively Yorkshire was in royalist hands by early-mid July – and the gentlemanly Lord Newcastle refused to shoot a defiant enemy commander, Sir John Savile, for refusing to surrender an indefensible position (Howley House) and so holding him up for a day.[28]

On the southern flank, the royalists could operate from the strongly fortified base of Newark dominating the lower Trent valley and now threatened Lincolnshire. A pre-emptive attack by all the local Parliamentarians on Newark was urged by Oliver Cromwell, now a regimental cavalry commander in the Eastern Association operating to defend the area, but Lord Grey refused to act supposedly because of fears that his Leicestershire mansion would be sacked if he moved away from the locality to attack Newark.[29] A royalist cavalry 'probe' under Newcastle's young cousin Colonel Charles Cavendish reached as far south as Grantham and on 18 April defeated Lord Willoughby of Parham, one of the Eastern Association deputies to Grey of Groby, and the younger Hotham at Ancaster Heath near Boston. The surviving Parliamentarians retreated to Sleaford to join up with three of the Association's regimental commanders – Cromwell, Sir Miles Hobart, and Sir Anthony Irby. Cromwell, as events were to show, was despite his inexperience already picking up the ability to be an outstanding cavalry commander – and was an early target of the royalist press for his alleged 'Puritan' zeal in desecrating Peterborough Cathedral.[30] (This may have been exaggerated for political reasons.) On 11 May this force advanced to retake Grantham, from which Cavendish had withdrawn, and they followed their foe towards Belton where the two (largely cavalry) forces ran into each other. Initially Cavendish had the best of it, his attack overrunning three Parliamentarian regiments who were caught off-guard; but when Cromwell arrived to rescue the latter his cavalry defeated Cavendish's men, of whom around 100 were killed. Much was made of this first Parliamentarian cavalry defeat of the normally superior royalist horsemen, initially by the weekly 'Special Passages' newsletter, but its tactical significance – and that for the victor's role in the war[31] – was greater in retrospect. At this stage Cromwell's role was mainly in patient siege-work to reduce isolated royalist strongpoints, such as Crowland Abbey and Burghley House.

A second attack south by Charles Cavendish reached Gainsborough in late July. The town had just fallen to the Parliamentarian Lord Willoughby of Parham, and on the 28th Parliamentarian reinforcements under Sir John Meldrum (commander at Nottingham) and Cromwell moved in to protect it from Cavendish's attack. They surprised and routed the royalists near the town, killing their commander, and the emerging cavalry expert Cromwell avoided his future rival Rupert's mistake at Edgehill. Where Rupert had followed a successful cavalry charge at Edgehill in October by charging off after a fleeing enemy, leaving his infantry dangerously exposed, Cromwell reined his victorious cavalry in and set about attacking the untouched royalist wing to complete the victory. Unlike Rupert he could think strategically at the height of the action and his men were more disciplined, and Cavendish was surrounded and killed. (Royalist propaganda had him shot in cold blood by Cromwell's 'low-born' ex-brewer subordinate, Colonel Berry.[32]) The victory was quickly negated as Newcastle, marching up to support his cousin with a larger force, encountered the victorious Parliamentarians as they pursued the refugees; the outnumbered victors were forced to retreat and Cromwell skilfully extricated his men from Gainsborough without being intercepted. On the 30th the town fell to Newcastle, technically opening the way to the Fenland, although in the event the Earl chose not to advance further. Lincoln to his rear was still in Parliamentarian hands, and served to hold up a royalist 'sweep' on the enemy heartland as Gloucester was doing in the West Midlands and Plymouth was doing in the south-west. Plymouth, like Hull, was a well-defended 'Puritan' town with an artillery base, and the Devonian Parliamentarians had rallied to defeat the Cornish invaders at Modbury, in what amounted to a 'local' war.[33]

Assisted by the arrival of the Queen from Holland, the royalists in the north were now locally dominant. The King had also achieved militarily minor but psychologically important successes, such as the 'razzias' carried out by Prince Rupert's raiding cavalry across the western approaches to London (as far east as Wycombe) in late spring. One of the most respected and morally upright heroes of the Parliamentarian cause, Hampden, had been killed in the course of this campaign while trying to intercept Rupert at a minor action, Chalgrove Field (18 June).[34] The incident was an unlucky coincidence for him – Rupert had been intending to intercept a Parliamentarian convoy of funds as it lumbered across country from London to Thame and had missed his target and started to retreat when he was intercepted. Hampden, happening to be at the nearby town of Whatlington when news of Rupert's presence was received, hurried out to join the local levies and was killed in a skirmish as the reckless Prince charged the defensive Parliamentarian position rather than riding away. Hampden's force was outnumbered by around four to one, so he probably had no idea of the size of Rupert's cavalry when he decided to intercept it. Had he known, would he have declined battle and survived? Having sent his infantry on ahead towards the Thames, Rupert had no need to fight and could have just covered their march as they made their escape with their loot to Chiselhampton Bridge and safety. He had his men drawn up in a lane ready to ambush the Parliamentarians. But instead of waiting for them to take the bait (which they might not have done) he charged the Parliamentarians across an open field to teach them a lesson, and Hampden fell in the melee – shot from behind and so not identified and 'targeted' but unlucky.

In one of the many ironies of the war, Rupert's presence on the raid was due to a 'tip-off' about the convoy from the Scots Parliamentarian defector Colonel Hurry, a serial deserter who had previously betrayed Montrose's plans to Argyll's men at the time of the 'Incident' in October 1641. Hurry had helped to prevent a royalist coup in Edinburgh then; now he accidentally affected the Parliamentarian cause's future. Even more than Brooke, had Hampden been alive in 1644 the death of the Commons leader Pym would have raised his political potential. The grumbling at Essex's lack of vigour or ruthlessness was to mount during the next year-and-a-half, and he had already disheartenedly offered to resign his command over Rupert's guerrilla successes. Had Brooke been alive and successful in the Midlands in summer 1643, would enough belligerent peers as well as Pym's group of

MPs been prepared to replace Essex with him? And would Hampden have taken over Pym's role in the Commons that winter? But it should be remembered that, although Hampden had a prestigious reputation as a defender of 'English liberty' against unwarranted royal taxation, he was religiously a Presbyterian and a 'Root and Branch' supporter. Such a foe of the bishops in 1640–41 would have been unlikely to have taken a more moderate line than Pym on the form of religious 'purge' necessary to be included in any compromise peace-terms in 1643–5. His survival to lead the Commons in 1644 would not necessarily have caused greater flexibility, and he was likely to have been as insistent as Pym on doing whatever was necessary to keep the Covenanters 'on side' to secure victory.

All the royalist advances had their limits. The Fairfaxes were able to hold out and link up with Hull, where the Hothams were arrested and Lord Fairfax became governor, and in the south-west Waller escaped the destruction of his army at Roundway Down. Returning to London, he accused Essex of dilatoriness. But both in the north, with Hull unsubdued, and in the south-west with the royalists facing the defiance of Plymouth, the locally recruited armies were unwilling to leave such a major garrison to threaten their home areas. They could neither transfer their main forces to the King's command, giving him military superiority over the new army that Essex raised during the first half of August among the defiant Londoners, nor advance into the East Midlands and Hampshire in strength to force all the Parliamentarians to withdraw towards London. In addition, at this point both of the King's headstrong nephews neutralized senior and successful royalist commanders, resulting in the latter's transfer out of the field of war. Prince Rupert quarrelled with the Marquis of Hertford, commander-in-chief in the south-west, over the governorship of Bristol and the King transferred the Marquis to Oxford. The King appointed his younger nephew Maurice to take senior rank over the Earl of Carnarvon in recently conquered Dorset – resulting in the latter complaining at his successor's counter-productive plundering and being recalled.[35] Even the 'Puritan' stronghold of Dorchester, with a strong 'godly' civic tradition, meekly surrendered.

The King's choice to besiege Gloucester. The 'defeatist' threat at Westminster of the Lords and Essex demanding negotiations. Two vital episodes?

At this point, early August, the King visited Bristol to sort out the dispute over the governorship and had to decide whether to take his main army east towards London or north to take the Parliamentary strongpoint of Gloucester. The garrison of the latter, under Edward Massey, was not strong enough to pose a serious threat to the local royalists, but (as with Plymouth and Hull but with less strategic sense) the royalists preferred to overrun the town rather than leave it defiant but contained by a small besieging-force. Massey himself sent a desperate plea to Parliament for help on 1 August warning of the possibility of betrayal and surrender, and may have been contemplating reaching terms – he was to turn royalist in 1648. He was apparently in touch with an old friend in the royalist army, William Legge, offering to desert if the King arrived.[36] If he was serious, it is possible that he might have surrendered as Charles deflected his march on London to turn to Gloucester, meaning that the King's attack was only held up briefly and Charles would still have time to march on London. If the King turned east towards London, the evidently worried Massey would not have been a major threat to the royalists' rear – though the latter were not to know this. But could Charles have reacted if he heard of Massey's message to London? Given the time it took to relay messages from London to the royal headquarters, it is not certain that any royalist spy would have been able to get a message to Charles about Massey's panic in time to persuade Charles to discount the need to turn against Gloucester (or, conversely, to persuade him to launch an attack on it quickly). On the other hand, too much can be made of the nebulous 'offer' by Massey ; it could have been an 'insurance policy' to cover Massey's future treatment by a victorious king if he had to surrender to overwhelming odds, or even a bluff to buy time so the King did not hurry to attack. The town's defences and morale were apparently poor, and did not improve until militant local MP and alderman Thomas Pury returned in early August.[37] At this juncture, 5 August, the town's leadership sent a letter to Parliament calling for a speedy march to their rescue – setting the scene for the first 'King vs Essex' confrontation since Turnham Green.[38]

As it turned out, royalist counsels at Charles' headquarters (Bristol) were divided over how to react. Local royalists preferred Charles to help their security by moving in on Gloucester, not on towards London; the 'hard-liner' Queen, absent in Oxford, preferred a march on London. According to Sir Philip Warwick's later account, the decision to attack Gloucester first was made on the advice of civilian adviser Sir John Colepeper, after the Queen's ally the Earl of Sunderland had left Bristol for Oxford expecting Charles to head for London.[39] Sunderland left Bristol on 7 August; within a day or two Massey's intermediary's oral message to William Legge at a 'prisoner-exchange' about Massey handing over Gloucester was given to Charles so this was probably the catalyst for a royalist attack.[40]

Crucially, Essex could not react quickly to the appeal sent from Gloucester to Parliament. His army had been demoralized by the clash at Chalgrove Field and the death of Hampden, supplies were not ready, many more recruits were needed, and he was so depressed that he sent in his resignation (which was not accepted).[41] When he did take the field to try to catch Rupert's army in Buckinghamshire, without success, he wrote to Parliament in favour of opening negotiations to end the seemingly endless stalemate.[42] But his hopes were not realistic; the King had just declared the present Parliament illegal again and the Parliament had arrested pro-peace peers Portland and Conway and shot two of Edmund Waller's 'Peace Party' plotters. Pym's latest call to continue the war was passed by Parliamentary vote.[43] Attention in London then shifted to the relief of Gloucester, with Essex encamped at Kingston-upon-Thames while Parliament voted him funds and measures to raise recruits. But the City radicals, distrustful of the defeatist Essex, organized a mass-petition to Parliament to set up a new army of 10,000 men to be kept and commanded separately from Essex's and assist him.[44] This showed a desire to tie him to a more vigorous and trustable commander, in which context William Waller's name was put forward, and was a substitute for dismissing Essex, which it was clearly realized (with disappointment?) was not yet possible. Radical Henry Marten chaired the committee to organize this new army, and Waller's appointment was approved by the Commons[45] despite complaints by Nathaniel Fiennes that Waller's taking troops from his command at Bristol had left him defenceless.

In the 6 August debate, Pym sought a compromise by keeping Essex as overall commander but having Waller protect the Home Counties, which was accepted.[46] If Waller had not lost his army at Lansdowne and Roundway Down he would have been in an even stronger position. But the Lords were still acting as a drag on the 'war party', voting to send moderate Lord Holland at the head of a delegation to Essex's camp to urge him to open negotiations with the King. This could build up a dangerous momentum for peace and risk the Lords and Essex combining to thwart the 'war party' in the mood of pessimism after Chalgrove Field, but the seriousness of the danger was lessened by the Lords' proffered terms – allowing the King to keep all the fortresses that he had held as of January 1642, restoring all expelled royalist MPs to Parliament, and closing down the anti-Anglican Assembly of Divines at Westminster. This was too much for even Essex to accept, and he refused; the Commons also voted against it.[47] Their choice was 'assisted' by a large and angry 'rejectionist' demonstration in Westminster before the vote, marshalled by Lord Mayor Isaac Penington, with rumours that if the vote had gone the other way Holland, his MP ally Denzel Holles and others would have been arrested to nullify any approach to the King. But would this have infuriated Essex into marching his men into Westminster to oppose the militants? Arguably Holland, Portland and their allies had overplayed their hand in trying to lure the King into talks with easy terms to meet. But less 'defeatist' terms could have swayed more MPs or Essex in favour of it – and thus caused a conflict between Lords and Commons and a 'showdown' between radicals and moderates? Unlike in 1647 and 1648, the Parliamentary 'hard-liners' (then Cromwell, in 1643 Pym) could not rely on a large, militant and united Army to stage a coup in London if the 'peace party' seemed to be about to betray the cause; they would have had to use the City's Trained Bands. There was a real risk of the Parliamentary political leadership turning on itself in August 1643, before the King had even taken Gloucester or marched on London. There was even a noisy demonstration at Westminster by women in favour of peace on 9 August, with threats to throw Pym in the Thames; Waller's cavalry had to disperse them. Because they failed, have these threats to Parliamentary unity been ignored by historians?

The Gloucester campaign. A fatal distraction from a quick royalist march on London?

When Charles arrived outside Gloucester and sent a summons to surrender on 10 August Massey refused. Parliament responded to his appeals by ordering Essex (currently inactive with very few troops available) to raise a new army of volunteers. The King put the cautious Earl of Forth, not Rupert, in charge of the siege of Gloucester and the royalist 'probes' of the defences were duly less effective. Apparently the King was wary of a quick assault in case of heavy losses as had occurred earlier at Bristol, but still thought the siege would only take ten days or so according to Hyde. It was hoped that if Essex had to march all the way to Gloucester his exhausted troops would be easy prey when they arrived[48] and meanwhile the Earl of Newcastle was ordered to bring his army south-west from Yorkshire to assist the attack. According to the King's envoy, Sir Philip Warwick, Newcastle refused to come and apologized that his officers were unwilling to march so far until local Hull had been taken. His militarily experienced deputy Colonel James King also advised staying put.[49] Clearly the Earl lacked the force of character to order his subordinates to obey and risk a refusal, or the flair to persuade them to follow him in taking a gamble. If he had turned up at Gloucester, this would probably have been too late to stop Essex arriving first as Essex moved reasonably fast – but the extra troops could have been vital to Charles in the subsequent battle.

If Rupert had assaulted the perimeter at Gloucester with the vigour he had showed at Bristol, the defence might well have crumbled before Essex's army arrived. But the King now reverted to a cautious approach of blockade – the classic Dutch (as opposed to the aggressive Swedish) tactics for siege in the Thirty Years' War. As it so happened, the defenders were down to two or three barrels of gunpowder by the time Essex arrived so a frontal attack could have succeeded. Essex left Colnbrook for Gloucester on 16 August; he reputedly had around 15,000 troops but many of the ideologically 'committed' Londoners were short of experience and his cavalry was under an inexperienced new commander (Sir Philip Stapleton MP). The intended cavalry commander, the new Earl of Bedford, defected to the King and his deputy, Sir William Balfour, was detained by illness.[50] The first crucial task was to keep the army intact until it reached Gloucester, which meant avoiding a cavalry ambush by Prince Rupert's feared and well-trained cavalry en route. In the meantime, seven of the small body of peers remaining in London – three of them, Portland, Conway, and Lovelace, known to be sympathetic to the King since 1642 but the others merely advocates of a negotiated peace – abandoned the capital for Oxford. Three of the 'peace party – Northumberland, Holland (Warwick's brother), and Bedford – were important figures, if only in terms of showing which way the war was perceived to be going. None had close connections to the militant Calvinist peers, the faction of Warwick and his ally Saye and Sele, who were leading the 'rebel' Lords. Probably the rowdy intimidation of the recent voting in Parliament by the Londoners, at Pym's faction's behest, was the last straw for them. They were duly 'welcomed' to Oxford by the King during a trip there as the siege of Gloucester got underway, as representing a propaganda coup, though they (Holland in particular) were treated with coldness for their past actions.[51]

While this drama was showing the collapse of the peers' 'peace party' in London, Rupert was missing out on an opportunity to hold up (if not worse) Essex's army when the latter's 'advance guard' infantry blundered into some royalist cavalry as they arrived at Oddington on the River Evenlode to camp for the night (3–4 September). The Parliamentarians were made aware that the enemy was close, but not in what strength; if Rupert had launched a cavalry raid this would have caused chaos as Essex's advance-troops were split up between two villages and so outnumbered. The main Parliamentary army was miles to the rear, at Chipping Norton, so a rescue would have been delayed – but for once Rupert was cautious, letting the enemy cross the Evenlode next morning without major action. From then on, Essex was able to move his men into the safety of the valleys with their criss-cross of hedges that impeded a royalist cavalry attack. Nor did Rupert interfere as they were approaching Gloucester and had to drag their wagons and artillery down steep Prestbury Hill, an ideal time for a raid on them.[52] Should Charles have moved in to assist Rupert and attempt to force a battle before Gloucester was relieved?

Gloucester and Newbury – potential turning-points

If the King had either headed east through Wiltshire towards London not north to Oxford in the first week of August, or had quickly received Gloucester's surrender on the 10th thanks to treachery within and headed across the Cotswolds, he would have had the advantage of time (and in the case of surrender, morale). It was 22 August before Essex's army of 8,000 men was ready for review on Hounslow Heath and the 26th before the full force of perhaps 15,000 set out. In those few weeks the King could have been closing in on London. Had Plymouth not held out that spring, he should have had extra men from the Cornish royalist regiments – with an inspiring commander had Sir Bevil Grenville not been killed at Roundway Down. Instead his army sat it out outside Gloucester to no effect and had to raise the siege on 5 September, moving back up Birdlip Hill en route to Sudeley Castle. Essex entered Gloucester safely on the 8th, but supplies there were so low that he had to encamp most of his army outside in the fields – where a royalist raid would at least have demoralized them but none occurred.[53]

As the King finally marched away from Gloucester to intercept Essex he still stood a chance of making up for his loss of time in August by achieving a decisive victory. But the size of the rival armies and the inadequacies of their commanders made this less likely than another drawn battle unless luck came to the aid of one side. According to royalist official Sir Edward Nicholas, at this point he had around 6,000 cavalry and 9,000 infantry; Essex had around 15,000 men.[54] No action was fought outside Gloucester, where the King had the advantage of the higher ground on the Cotswold escarpment around Painswick – though on the precedent of what had happened in October 1642 at Edgehill Essex would have refused to fight an enemy possessing the advantage of high ground. Following Essex's relief of Gloucester he marched north, and the King moved ahead of him to Pershore to block his route north-east towards Warwickshire. However, Essex doubled back to the south and took the main road south-east towards London from Cirencester (16 September) towards the Kennet valley, apparently left uncovered by Rupert's cavalry.[55] Had this not occurred Essex could have been trapped and forced to give battle on a site chosen by the King – he was in royalist territory in the Cotswolds and could not sit out a blockade with his men running short of food. Essex's combination of the feint via Tewkesbury towards Pershore and swift march south-east again shows that he did not lack strategic ability or energy in 1643 compared with what was to happen to him in summer 1644. By contrast, the King failed to listen when Rupert warned him of the implications of his men raiding a Parliamentary outpost near Tewkesbury in the middle of the night of the 14th–15th to find them ready to ride not in bed – i.e. that they were about to bolt for London.[56] He failed to launch a quick pursuit of Essex with Rupert's cavalry, drawn up ready on Broadway Hill on the 15th but not used until the enemy had a substantial 'lead' and time was wasted trying to find them. Nor did the artillery, needed in case of a battle, move off from Evesham to follow the main army until the 16th.

Whichever royalist commander was responsible for enabling Essex to have a head start (probably Charles himself), the result was that the King was forced to hurry after the main Parliamentary army and give battle wherever he managed to block their road – which turned out to be Newbury. Charles was still too far behind Rupert's cavalry vanguard to help when the Prince caught up and attacked Essex's rearguard near Aldington on the afternoon of the 18th so the latter escaped, but he managed to reach Newbury ahead of Essex. The Parliamentarians would now have to pass the King's army in order to continue towards London, with their supplies running out. The battle that followed on 20 September was bloody but indecisive, and made worse by the lack of open ground for Rupert's cavalry to operate on the fields and common to the south of Newbury. Battle in fields divided up by hedges gave an advantage to the army that had better infantry, as the musketeers could shelter behind hedges to fire without fear of a cavalry charge. A mixture of fields and ditches also aided a defensive formation of pikemen against cavalry. (In fact we cannot be certain how extensive the local fields and hedges were at the site in the 1640s as opposed to when later maps were drawn up.) A crucial strategic position on the battlefield in the path of Essex's route Eastwards to safety, the 'Round Hill', was left unoccupied as the royalists drew up their lines and was seized by Skippon and the Trained Bands – the most disciplined and experienced part of the Parliamentarian army. They thus had high ground to aid them, and all attempts to overrun them failed. An exhausting hand-to-hand infantry combat for control of lines of hedgerows under cannon-fire saw the royalists suffer heavy losses, most notably Lord Falkland, and have to leave the road to London open for Essex's army. Despite the arrival of the Queen's convoy of arms and other improvements in their position since April, they were too short of bullets to resume the battle on a second day. Essex, in contrast, had more ammunition thanks to the professionalism of artillery-train commander Sir John Meyrick. What if the positions had been reversed, though – would the King have been able to blockade the roads and starve Essex into fighting again on easier terms? The most vital 'what if' of the battle was the fact that Parliamentarian cavalry commander Stapleton had a clear shot at Rupert at close quarters, but his pistol misfired. Had Rupert been killed, would the blow to royalist morale have strengthened or weakened the King's determination to fight on? Or saved the royalists from taking on the enemy and thus defeat at Marston Moor?

As of the end of the 1643 campaign, three major figures had all nearly been killed – Fairfax (Wakefield), Haselrig (Roundway Down), and Rupert (Newbury). Two who had been killed – Brooke and Hampden – had fallen to fluke 'lucky shots' in minor actions.

The Parliamentarian army, short of supplies after their long march to relieve Gloucester and back, could have started to disintegrate through hunger and poor morale had the King at least secured a 'draw' and been able to hold his position for a few days, blocking their route to safety. Recriminations among their leadership were possible, given the rising dissatisfaction with Essex's ever-cautious strategy, which his unusually risky march to Gloucester had temporarily abated. But the royalist failure kept the Parliamentary army intact – arguably victorious – and enabled them to reach Reading. The war continued as a virtual stalemate between the two main armies, with the King holding Oxford and the Parliamentarians at Reading blocking his route to London.

If Charles had managed to destroy Essex's army decisively in a battle on favourable ground after the relief of Gloucester, his blunder in taking on the siege would not have mattered. (Essex was too experienced to have voluntarily offered battle on unfavourable ground, as at Painswick; he would have had to be blockaded into it.) His forces were dominant in Wales, the north, and the south-west, and the isolated rebel ports along the east and south coasts that Warwick's fleet could support were not a decisive factor apart from tying down royalist troops. Had the King been triumphant in the main theatre of war in August or September, he should have been able to move on towards London and force the main unbeaten Parliamentary regional army – that of the Eastern Association – to march to its rescue. Defended by substantial outworks, the capital stood a better chance than in November 1642 of holding out until relief arrived unless pro-royalist aldermen seized the City to avert a sack. There could still have been another major battle before the end of the war, this time outside London between Charles and the Earl of Manchester's Eastern army – including Cromwell. But the royalists would have stood their last main chance of a decisive victory ending the war in 1643. Indeed, if the attempted betrayal of Hull in June had succeeded the small Fairfax force in the West Riding was not dangerous enough to prevent the Earl of Newcastle moving south towards Lincoln and threatening the Association's heartland. The latter's leaders would then have been unable to spare their main army to save London. Their best cavalry commander, Cromwell, won his first successes that campaigning season against approximately equal numbers, and his strategic ability and disciplined units would have been hard-pressed against superior numbers. In the aftermath of the retreat from Gainsborough on 29 July, even

Cromwell believed that the local Parliamentarian cause was under imminent threat of being overrun by Newcastle unless assistance arrived.[57]

Effects of a bolder royalist strategy in summer 1643

What if the King had won in a direct clash with Essex, either during the Gloucester campaign or at Newbury? Assuming that the King's victorious army had defeated the Earl of Manchester – a cautious commander who drove Cromwell into a fury in 1644 – or Manchester, had been seriously outnumbered and had negotiated a truce, the main war could have been over by October or November. The Commons were without Hampden and Pym was dying, so leadership of the political resistance would have been denuded – though Warwick's Calvinist peers and the surviving Commons leaders would have tried to negotiate the best terms possible and the uncompromising stance that Parliament had shown in its potential terms in winter 1642–3 would have been difficult to abandon. Outlying Parliamentary garrisons and the fleet would have had no option but to surrender on the best terms available, and those moderate peers who had not fled to Charles already and City royalists would have been likely to take the lead in political offers as the King closed in on London. Those who had defied him since 1639 and been responsible for killing Strafford, especially Warwick, would have known that they could expect no mercy and would have fled to the Continent.

Having assured the public of his defence of the laws and the Protestant religion, Charles would have been in no position to prefer the harsher retribution demanded by the 'ultras' in his camp (e.g. Rupert, more used to Continental warfare and uninhibited about blackmailing defenceless towns into 'contributions') to those of Hyde's faction. If Falkland had not been killed in the 1643 campaign he, as a peer, would have had more influence with Charles than Hyde but either would have had to counter the Queen's demands. The King would have been short of money, so there would have been likely to be harsh fines on leading Parliamentarians (Pym and Hampden were dead) involving the royalist equivalent of Parliament's 'compounding'. The Earls of Essex, Warwick, and Manchester would have been lucky to escape without treason charges or at least the loss of most of their estates, and violently anti-royalist MPs such as Henry Marten would have been in the Tower or in exile. A general amnesty for most of the Commons remaining in London – as the terms of the City's surrender? – may have saved senior political figures who had attempted to coerce the King and alter religion but not to threaten the monarchy, particularly Denzel Holles (notably excluded from the King's 1643 'blacklist' of MPs to be denied pardon) and Philip Stapleton. Holles' 'peace party', who cavilled at the unexpected length of the war and/or the need to submit to strict Presbyterianism to bring in the Scots army that autumn, included other opponents of episcopacy like Sir John Maynard and John Glynne, and can be linked to that faction – broadly 'Presbyterian' in orientation – who attempted a negotiated settlement with the defeated King that preserved his throne in 1646–7. Hampden was dead and Pym was dying, and the most likely people to be excluded from any offers were the most irreconcilable survivors of the 'Five Members', Sir Arthur Haselrig and William Strode, and the Independent leader Sir Henry Vane junior. In real life Vane was leading the negotiations with the Scots in Edinburgh in late summer 1643, and if there at the time that the King's cause collapsed is likely to have stayed on to encourage armed resistance on Argyll.

If financial necessity – not least to pay for the Scottish and Irish campaigns – had led to the royalist exchequer launching 'compounding' as well as the continuation of Parliament's excise-taxes in 1644, the fines were likeliest to be levied on Parliamentarian officers rather than ordinary troops. Both armies were mainly led by regimental colonels from the gentry and junior ranks of the aristocracy in 1642–3, but the poorer officers would have been hard hit and some may have been forced to sell up and emigrate. Cromwell, in serious financial difficulties in the 1630s and reduced to a tenant-farmer (the malicious royalist propagandists called him a brewer), could have found it easier to carry out his alleged threat in autumn 1641 and emigrate to Massachusetts, particularly as the iconoclastic 'purge' of the East Anglian churches by local Puritan militants that he had supported would now be reversed by the restored Anglican Church under the 'ultra' Bishop of Norwich, Matthew Wren. The disciplinary mechanism of the pre-1641 Church had been destroyed and Laud broken by imprisonment in the Tower so a firm restoration of Anglican clergy and practice to Parliamentary areas should not have led to many prosecutions. But where there was a determined bishop to be restored – e.g. Matthew Wren in Norwich – all 'intruded' clergy of non-Anglican views could expect expulsion, and there is a probability of local disturbances and of vengeful reaction from royalist gentry anticipating that of 1661–4 in reality.

Scotland and Ireland: effects of a royalist victory in 1643
The Scots and the rebel Irish would have been undefeated in early 1644, facing a triumphant King and an exhausted but strong and experienced royal army. Once a subservient Parliament, either a 'recruiter' one led by the MPs who had backed the King in 1642 or a newly elected body, had voted supplies and the fining of 'rebel' Parliamentarians got underway the King would have needed to consider the crises in his other kingdoms. Dismayed at the loss of their ally and thus of the gamble that they had made since 1639 of backing

the King's enemies, the Scots Presbyterian nobility would have been divided over whether to come to terms. The clergy, led by Henderson and Johnston, would have mostly favoured resisting the forces of 'Antichrist' rather than allowing episcopacy to return, which the King would have demanded. It would have been a matter of political choice rather than religious fervour that determined the outcome, as the nobles had the greater say in Parliament and even in the Church Assembly had the power of patronage over the selection of local delegates.

It is unclear if moderates such as Montrose and those men who in real life were prepared to negotiate with the King in 1645 at Uxbridge, e.g. Loudoun and Lauderdale, would have joined up with the King's allies Hamilton and Huntly to force a compromise peace, probably involving the arrest of the uncompromising Argyll and the armed intimidation of the clerics. But Argyll would have been isolated and at risk of desertions had he decided to resist the King by force; the King could be expected to repudiate the terms of the Anglo-Scots political settlement of August 1641 as forced upon him and to demand the return of his ability to control the Edinburgh government. The return of the episcopate is less certain, at least if the King had chosen to avoid an immediate and costly invasion of Scotland in 1644 and to rely on Montrose and Hamilton to lead the majority of the Scots peers to his side by overthrowing Argyll. On the precedent of Montrose's terms for aiding Charles in 1641, he would have insisted that the Presbyterian Church settlement of 1638–40 be maintained – though a victorious King could have gone back on it once his power was restored and the leading Covenanter clerics been arrested for treason.

If the King had preferred to concentrate on Ireland, accepting the religious reforms of 1638–40 would be necessary for peace – until he had defeated the Irish and could use force on the Scots. If the majority of the Scots lords had held out against Montrose and Argyll had maintained his supremacy, it is probable that either a royal army would march on Edinburgh in 1644 or the King would (as in real life) give his commission to Montrose to raise a rebel force in the Highlands and attempt to defeat the Covenanters by force of arms. In either case, the Scots army under Leslie would have been fighting a royalist force – in the Highlands or on the Border – in 1644. They would have had a far more formidable foe than in 1639–40, as the invaders were now experienced on the battlefield.

In the meantime, the royalist victory in England would also give a fillip to those Catholic lords in Ireland who had risen against Parliament's intentions in autumn 1641 but were loyal to the King. They had claimed then to be loyal to Charles personally but to be hostile to the 'new order' in Westminster, and in September 1643 a temporary 'Cessation' was agreed between the rebel

Irish regime at Kilkenny and Ormonde's troops.[58] (The implication of this truce was that the rebels were at liberty to carry on attacking Parliament's Irish allies, particularly the Scots Presbyterian army in Ulster.) Now they would have to prove their loyal words and isolate those Catholic lords who preferred a papal alliance. (Ironically, like their religious foes the Covenanter lords their view of the ideal outcome for their cause was a greatly enhanced political autonomy and religious supremacy.) Unencumbered by the need to placate public opinion in a submissive England, the King would have been able to make lucrative offers to the 'Old English' lords in Ireland. But this would have been from a position of strength; in real–life in 1644-5 he made generous offers to the Catholic lords from weakness, promising pardon in return for support and even indicating official toleration of the Catholic Church. (Any revelation of this would have had a negative impact on the ability of moderate Presbyterian lords in Scotland to trust the King and have boosted Argyll's arguments for resistance.) The royalist army of the Marquis of Ormonde would have been reinforced by battle-hardened English royalists in 1644, giving them a major advantage. The fact that the King was in full control of England would have encouraged the rebel Catholics' regime at Kilkenny to face up to the alternatives of obtaining the best terms possible or defying the King outright. As with Argyll's regime in Edinburgh, a split between 'ultras' and moderates was possible – but unlike Argyll and his militant clerics they could call in aid from abroad, i.e. Spain (their traditional ally in late sixteenth century revolts).

The uneasy truce that Ormonde had negotiated with the Irish rebels in 1643 was not converted into a political settlement as the rebels endeavoured to secure Ormonde's support for a joint move to drive the Scots Presbyterians out of Ulster. Currently the King's forces held parts of the south-east of Ireland and the rebels the hinterland. If early 1644 had seen the King victorious with his troops pouring into Dublin the rebels would have been in a far weaker position than they were in reality. Protestant warlords such as the Earl of Inchiquin, royalist commander in Munster, were totally opposed to any royal agreement with the rebels involving religious toleration or an attack on Ulster; the royalist defeat at Marston Moor in 1644 coupled with Charles' flirtations with the rebels led to him defecting to Parliament. Not having this option in the case of royalist victory in England, he would have had to stand by impotently if the Ulster Protestants – allies of Argyll – supported their Edinburgh co-religionists in defying the King in 1644 and the King's troops attacked them. The latter campaign would have opened up the way for the Kilkenny 'Confederates' to come to terms with the King, now seen as pro-Catholic and likely to restore the latter's lands in Ulster. But the now strengthened Ormonde would have been insisting that those pro-royalist Protestants in the rebel-held parts of Southern Ireland who had been expropriated by the Kilkenny regime in 1642–3 regained their lands, and it is probable that the terms that the rebels demanded of the King would have been too high for him to concede. Thus unless Ormonde had been able to achieve a definitive victory over the rebels in 1644 they would still have been holding out in 1645 when the new Pope sent a Nuncio, Rinuccini, to lead their government as requested and to demand that the King accept full toleration of Catholicism as a State religion, a Catholic lord lieutenant, and the removal of the Ulster settlers.[59]

The disastrous papal policy was not affected in real life by the urgency of saving the King's declining cause in England by securing a quick alliance on easy terms, so it is unlikely to have been any more realistic if the King had been victorious – particularly if his forces were concentrating on a war in Scotland against Argyll in 1644–5. Thus, the King's victory in England in 1643 may well not have averted an eventual war of reconquest by the government in Dublin, this time probably in 1645 or 1646 and led by Ormonde – and Prince Rupert? – rather than Cromwell. There would still have been massacres and land-confiscations, given English bitterness at the 1641 revolt, but royalist commanders would have been less antagonistic to Catholics 'per se' than Cromwell's militants were and may have included some English Catholic nobles who had ventured their funds to raise men for the King and ended up as commanders. The resulting terms of defeat for the Irish Catholics would have been far easier than they were in real-life 1649–51, and the subsequent history of Ireland less polarized as a result.

In reality... : the Irish situation in 1643

In the way that events actually developed in England in 1643, the Irish war remained a 'side-show' for both parties with neither able to spend resources on it. The Catholic rebels had secured control of most of the country, apart from parts of Ulster (in Protestant hands and backed up by Munro's Scots Covenanter army), the 'Pale' around Dublin (run by the pro-London administration of the Lords Justices'), and some inland areas of central Ireland loyal to the King's general Ormonde. Charles had ordered Ormonde, Lord Clanricarde, and other pro-royalist 'Anglo-Irish' magnates to open negotiations with the Catholics in January 1643, despite the danger of any accommodation, which necessarily guaranteed the predominance of Catholicism in Ireland, being used as Parliamentarian propaganda. The pro-Parliamentarian 'Lords Justices' in Dublin had had the assistance of a small expeditionary force under Lord Lisle, eldest son of the new Lord Lieutenant Leicester, since 1642; it marched around the country ravaging rebel areas but achieving little and not taking major towns encountering any major rebel army. Leicester himself had obeyed a royal order to halt at Chester and return to him at Oxford in winter 1642–3, not go to Dublin.[60] Charles feared that as a 'godly' Protestant peer friendly to the Warwick-Essex faction he would aid the Parliamentarian cause rather than back him and Ormonde.

In military terms, Ormonde had had more success against the rebels than Lisle – and had more potential to win over rebel Catholic noblemen (Gaelic or 'Old English') as he was a major Irish magnate on social terms with them and Lisle was an English interloper of 'Puritan' leanings loyal to the pro-plantation authorities in London. The rebels' military position to coerce Charles had been strengthened during summer 1642 by the arrival of Owen Roe O'Neill, who took over command in Ulster, and other expatriate officers from Spanish service on the Continent; many of their leaders, such as the 'Old English' general Thomas Preston, claimed to be personally loyal to Charles as King provided he would guarantee their Catholic co-religionists' control of the country.[61] In civil affairs the clergy had secured a dominant position in their 'government's' Confederacy Council, set up at Kilkenny, and its local committees in each area; thus they could insist that any peace with the King secured the full rights to Church office and ecclesiastical lands of the Catholic, not the Protestant, clergy across Ireland.[62] Another crucial militant Catholic was the Confederation's 'Secretary' at Kilkenny, Richard Bellings, a frustrated Catholic lawyer with a probable grudge over his lack of promotion by the Protestant authorities in Dublin. As the envoy to Rome of the 'rebels' in 1644–5, he would encourage the Pope to send a new legate to stiffen Irish Catholic negotiators' terms for aiding Charles – thus denying vital aid to Ormonde. Accepting the 'hard-line' position and guaranteeing Catholic control of the country would damage Charles' reputation in England. Charles duly wrote to Ormonde on 12 January 1643 that he could not concede the abrogation of all anti-Catholic penal statutes that the Kilkenny government demanded, nor grant Irish parliament legislative independence; but he was prepared to exercise the statutes laxly.[63]

The strength of feeling in the army based in Dublin over winter 1642–3 was royalist enough to enable Charles' partisans to defeat attempts to suborn it by two Parliamentarian representatives, MPs Reynolds and Goodwin, who the Commons had sent to Dublin. They (and their £20,000 funds) had received a favourable reception from the 'Lords Justices', but now they had to return home to avoid the army arresting them on Charles' orders. The money was used to reinforce Ormonde's recruitment and supplies rather than that of the Parliamentarian army under Lisle, and with the extra troops Ormonde won an important victory over the Catholics' general Preston at Ross on 18 March.[64] There were not enough supplies to keep the campaign going, however, and as Ormonde had to return to Dublin the continued lack of funds worked in his favour with soldiers blaming Parliament for its miserliness. The King's negotiators met those of the Confederation at Trim in March, with the latter repeating their demands for complete restitution of the Catholic Church and legislative independence for their proposed Catholic-run Parliament. They offered the King an army of 10,000 men if he would give in to this. Their list of grievances against the current regime of the 'Lords Justices' for bad faith, tyranny, systematic religious oppression, and boasts of exterminating Irish Catholicism were probably more accurate than the lurid complaints that the pro-Parliamentarian section of his Council in Dublin sent Charles on 16 March, arguing that the ungrateful and treacherous Catholics had already killed 154,000 Protestants in the rebellion and had to be suppressed by the sword and forcibly Anglicized or expropriated for the Protestants' public safety.

The Dublin government would not consider accommodation with the rebels, understandably enough, but lacked the aid from London to enable them to break with Ormonde's royalists yet; accordingly Ormonde faced no immediate threat from them. But the best that Charles could hope for from the rebels was a truce, which Ormonde was duly empowered to arrange pending negotiations between the King and the rebel emissaries at Oxford. Ormonde could not have the Irish Catholic terms mollified by the reasonable argument which he made in a letter to rebel peer to Lord Barry on 1 June, that granting a 'free Parliament' dominated by Catholics was inconceivable to the embattled Protestant minority, which had no cause to trust them after October 1641.[65] He could not rely on the 'moderates' mostly 'Old English' Catholics – at Kilkenny, as the clergy and militant Catholics (backed by Owen Roe O'Neill) would not trust Charles' goodwill to ameliorate the penal laws voluntarily and they insisted on their co-religionists having the full legislative power to carry out their demands. The arrival of a papal envoy, Scarampi, in Ireland added to the strength of the 'hard-liners' and brought the hope of armed Continental assistance if needed. Ormonde did not have the troops or supplies to secure better terms by military effort, as when he scraped enough men and supplies together for a new campaign Preston avoided battle and he had to return to Dublin. He was forced to send envoys to Kilkenny from a position of weakness, and on 15 September a truce – the 'Cessation' – was agreed with the royalist/Dublin forces holding their current possessions around Dublin and Cork and other isolated garrisons. The Scots army in Ulster was not represented or included in the talks, and Ormonde had to agree to leave them to their fate should the rebels attack them[66] – which if it leaked out would assist Parliamentarian propaganda about Charles' pro-Catholic sympathies.

Chapter Four

Was the War Winnable in 1644 – by the King, or by Parliament without Resorting to the Creation of the New Model Army?

Strategy in spring–summer 1644: did the King throw away a strong position? Did the Parliamentarians fail to follow up major opportunities?

The situation after the Newbury campaign: military stalemate? Two royalist reverses, in the south and north
The effective stalemate produced by the King's failures at Gloucester and Newbury in 1643 was in danger of producing a long war. Neither of the two central armies – the King's at Oxford or Essex's at London – was able to defeat the other, with their comparatively equal sizes and fire-power matched by cautious generalship. In the other theatres of war, the situation was complicated by local allegiances at variance with the prevailing loyalties of an area and isolated garrisons, too strong to be stormed or starved out except by major effort, in towns and fortified houses. The royalists held almost all the west and south-west with Wales, apart from isolated towns – most on the coast (e.g. Plymouth and Lyme Regis) but a few inland (Gloucester being on a useable river, Taunton not so).

The Parliamentarians held the south-east from Hampshire to Kent, with East Anglia and most of the East Midlands, and had the most disciplined and coherent of the local armies in that of the Eastern Association whose control extended as far north as the Trent. They also had the most effective strategist produced by the war so far, Sir William Waller, in command of the local Parliamentarian army in the south and put in charge of a new South-Eastern Association in December; this bonus for Parliament, however, followed Essex haughtily insisting that Waller had to give up his recent independent commission and become his subordinate again. This led to Essex making another threat to resign, but Waller gave way with good grace.[1]

Commanding his new army as Essex's junior, Waller managed to halt Hopton's dangerous advance into Sussex in January. This incursion was carried out at Charles' rather than local royalist commander Hopton's own wishes, as the victor of the south-western advances of 1643 wished to deal with Parliamentarian strongholds to his rear first. He intended to clear Dorset and Hampshire then head for London. Charles was insistent on a move to rally the royalist gentry of Sussex and Kent, and Lord Ogle's capture of Winchester (independently of Hopton's plans) paved the way forward. Without this sign of local Parliamentarian weakness, would Hopton have been able to insist on the (safer?) taking of Wardour Castle and Poole to 'clear' the royalist rear before risking an attack on Sussex? Charles himself moved into the area briefly – but only to reprovision the massive fortified residence of the Marquis of Winchester at Basing House, a formidable collection of earthworks that Waller had failed to take on 7–13 November. Had the King added his force to Hopton's, their chances would have been greater. Sir Edward Ford, principal royalist adherent in West Sussex, captured Arundel town for Hopton on 2 December, and the general arrived to receive the surrender of the castle (home of the ineffective and ageing royalist Earl of Arundel) on the 9th.[2]

Crucially, Hopton had chosen not to press a direct attack on his old foe Waller (now based at Farnham Castle) when he confronted Waller's small force outside Farnham on 27 November but had wheeled away to head for Arundel. Waller wrote that Hopton heavily outnumbered him and could have won.[3] Once Hopton had headed into Sussex, the panicking Commons had the time to send reinforcements (led by Haselrig's regiment) to Waller who regained the offensive. The royalist force was too small to make much impact, particularly once Hopton had to put a garrison into Arundel; the plan relied on swift and continuing momentum, which did not take place, with a dash to seize Bramber bridge (the crossing of the next river beyond the Arun, the Adur) repulsed.[4] The campaign fell apart when the Earl of Crawford allowed himself to be surprised at Alton, east of Winchester and north-west of Arundel, by the reinforced Waller in a dawn attack on 13 December. The 'Night Owl' Waller's overnight march from Farnham and swift attack was spotted too late to mount an effective defence, while Crawford rode off to Winchester in a futile attempt to fetch rescuers; the royalists were overwhelmed in several hours' fighting around the church and 900 prisoners were taken.[5] On 21 December Waller besieged Ford's garrison in Arundel Castle, and sat down to starve them out. Hopton, at Petersfield, made an attempt to relieve Arundel and came within three miles of the town, but was apparently satisfied by a report from a refugee that it had enough stores to hold out until he could receive enough reinforcements to challenge

Waller. He withdrew to Petersfield to wait for them.[6] There was less food than he was told, the King sent a cavalry force under Lord Wilmot too late, and the garrison of Arundel surrendered to Waller on 6 January; 1,000 prisoners were taken. The most memorable casualty of the episode was the royalist poet and metaphysician Edmund Chillingworth, who died in the castle during the siege.[7] Had Hopton been given more troops or won a battle at Farnham on 27 November, or Waller reacted less decisively in his attack on Alton, the threat to Parliament's control of Sussex might have been more effective.

The Eastern Association army was now under the command of the Earl of Manchester (formerly Lord Mandeville), a competent but uninspiring Presbyterian aristocrat who was to come to symbolize the amateurish, lackadaisical approach to war and lack of zeal for victory with which men like Cromwell charged their social superiors in the year to come. Cromwell, the epitome of his own call for 'plain russet-coated captains' who might lack breeding but knew what they were fighting for and loved what they knew,[8] was so far only a regimental commander in rank, but was now to be put in charge of Manchester's cavalry. The coherence and motivation of his own regiment had served as an example for others and he had shown his skill in some minor clashes, and he was seen by his seniors as a useful cavalry-commander but was to prove increasingly at odds with his commander (not least over the latter's lack of willingness for quick action). The north of England was divided, with most of the prosperous towns of Lancashire and the West Riding held by Parliament (the latter by the Fairfaxes) and the isolated local royalist centre in Lancashire at the Earl of Derby's Lathom House. Most of the north-east was controlled by the commander of the northern royalist army, the Earl of Newcastle, from York. Control of the north-west Midlands was denied to either party, with the situation in Cheshire and Staffordshire evenly balanced. As far as overall command of resources went, the supremacy of Parliament in terms of weapons and ammunition in early 1643 was being eroded more as time went on by royalist production and imports.

The end of the campaigning season of 1643 saw similar frustrations for the royalists in the north-east as in the south-east, with their furthest 'probes' rebuffed. In this case, lack of men was not as decisive as it was for Hopton. With the Earl of Manchester's Eastern Association army held up in August by the siege of King's Lynn (surrendered 27 September), there was no large Parliamentary force available to relieve Hull from the siege that Newcastle (soon to be made a Marquis) launched on 2 September. The attack had been advocated by Newcastle's deputy Eythin, to secure the 'rear' before any advance into Lincolnshire, while the King preferred a straightforward advance south leaving Hull alone and made Newcastle his commander for the Fenland counties in anticipation of his arrival there; Newcastle, backed by the Queen, took Eythin's advice. The defence of Hull had been in secure hands under the new governor Lord Fairfax since 4 July, the Hothams having been deported to London. The younger Hotham evaded arrest at first and tried to ride to royalist lines but was captured at Beverley; their unreliability and shameless double-dealing made even royalist Secretary of State Nicholas pleased at their capture.[9] Under effective leadership from the expert Fairfaxes Hull's defences held out, with more ammunition and supplies being delivered across the Humber in mid-September by Cromwell from Lincolnshire. Sir Thomas Fairfax was able to use the Humber to flood the royalist siege-trenches. The Fairfaxes' cavalry being of no use in a siege, the latter under Sir Thomas then left the town by water to join the Parliamentarians in Lincolnshire. He joined Cromwell and Lord Willoughby at Boston to wait for the Earl of Manchester to bring reinforcements. In both these episodes, Parliamentarian control of the sea was vital – as it was to the equally successful defences of other Parliamentary ports from sieges by superior siege-armies, e.g. Plymouth in 1643 and Lyme Regis in 1644.

While Newcastle could not starve out or storm Hull, the escaped cavalry assisted Cromwell with operations in Lincolnshire and in due course the Earl of Manchester brought his infantry on from King's Lynn to join them. On 11 October an attempt by Sir John Henderson, royalist governor of Newark, to relieve Cromwell and Fairfax's siege of Bolingbroke Castle led to a clash at Winceby near Horncastle. As at Gainsborough earlier, the Eastern Association cavalry proved to be superior at 'Winceby Fight' and rallied despite being driven back in the initial royalist onrush; discipline held and when Cromwell himself was unhorsed he was quickly able to find a new mount without the setback panicking him or his men. Singing a psalm to uplift their spirits, the Parliamentarian cavalry drove Henderson's men back in disarray to flee to the safety of Newark,[10] whose garrison's offensive potential was significantly diminished by the reverse. Meanwhile Manchester was able to reinforce Hull on 5 October, and a sally by the confident defenders on the 11th overran part of the siege-works and carried off one of Newcastle's prize cannons 'Gog and Magog' (the only real hope that the Marquis had of battering his way into the town[11]). Given the lack of fighting-spirit or military experience among his men compared with those in Hull, who were carefully reprovisioned throughout the siege, a frontal assault was unlikely to work even if a breach had been opened in the walls earlier; his lack of control of the Humber had made the siege a dubious enterprise throughout. On the 12th he gave up and retreated, and once his army was away from the district Manchester could move on to force the surrender of Lincoln (20 October).[12] All Newcastle could do was to use his intimidatingly large army – risky for Parliamentary forces to meet in the open field – to 'warn off' Sir Thomas Fairfax from an attempt to overrun the Peak District by marching after him to Chesterfield, from which Fairfax prudently withdrew.

The threat of a royalist assault on the Fenland and East Anglia was effectively ended with the joint Parliamentary successes at Winceby and Hull – one showing their cavalry's superiority, the other their ability to withstand a siege by the north's main royalist army. Strategy, control of vital communications, better supplies, and morale all played their part. None of these were sufficient to control the open country should a massively superior royalist army appear, but it left the royalists on the defensive and as events in the north-east turned out it was Parliament that was to receive the decisive local advantage of outside help in 1644. The reputation of Newcastle also suffered a reverse by his failure at Hull, although the Parliamentary side also had commanders 'under fire' from their own side – as was shown by Cromwell's fierce criticism of Lord Willoughby of Parham in the Commons on 22 January. Typically with Cromwell, practical worries about Willoughby's lackadaisical attitude to the serious business of war and annoyance at his blunders in the Gainsborough campaign were combined with 'godly' disgust at his employing profane and immoral officers who would draw down Divine wrath. He accused Willoughby of procuring women, and the latter challenged Manchester to a duel.[13] For the moment, a combination of deference to the 'natural' social order and a desire not to undermine the current commanders saved Willoughby (though his Lincolnshire command was added to the more effective Manchester's); but such attacks on the 'unprofessional' and insufficiently zealous 'High Command' of 1642–3 were to multiply as the war failed to be won quickly in 1644. Unlike with the royalists, where appointments lay solely with the King, an effective remedy lay at hand if sufficient votes could be mustered to replace the accused.

New factors among the Parliamentarians – the deaths of Pym and Hampden and the 'Solemn League and Covenant'

In these circumstances, it could be assumed that if there was to be a breakthough in action it would come from the main armies as they manoeuvred against each other for a second full year in the field. Accordingly Parliament concentrated on giving Essex a strong force of 10,000 infantry and 4,000 foot in its plans for 1644, and the City's Trained Bands – a disciplined force used to fighting together which had been crucial at Turnham Green in 1642 and Newbury in 1643 – lost its autonomy from the main army.[14] The death of the Parliamentary civilian leader Pym, who had held the cause of the King's enemies together for three years, on 8 December 1643[15] did not alter his colleagues' unanimity to fight on. The only difference was that his successors as the most effective co-ordinators of policy, the younger Henry Vane and Cromwell's cousin Oliver St John, were not in favour of a disciplined Presbyterian State Church like him and more likely to become at odds with the predominant party among the divines in the new Westminster Assembly – and the Scots.

Vane, the leading lay negotiator, had done his best to moderate the Scots' demands for an English Presbyterian State Church in the 'Solemn League and Covenant' alliance, which his group of delegates had arranged with the Covenanter government in Edinburgh. Given the Parliamentarians' need of assistance, their delegation had had little room for manoeuvre – particularly since Argyll's regime had entrusted drawing up their terms to the zealous clerical disciplinarian Alexander Henderson, a man more likely than the lay aristocrats to insist on England following the Scots example into a fully Presbyterian Church with moral discipline enforced on the laity by religious courts. One perturbed English delegate, Lord Grey, had even refused to go to the talks in anticipation of the expected outcome. All the delegates and the majority of the MPs and peers remaining in London were 'Root and Branch' backers who had made a choice in 1642 to support the party of Pym and Warwick, a militantly 'Puritan' group whose victory would inevitably mean the abolition of bishops and a 'reformation' of the English Church that would enforce Calvinist theology and go beyond the religious settlement of 1559. But this was not the same as a Scots-style Presbyterian Church. Despite their similar theological outlook and mutual loathing of anything that savoured of 'popery' – a powerful common aim in the context of Catholic atrocities in Ireland and a deeply suspected King – the Scots system involved subordinating the laity to the moral supervision of Church courts and having clerical appointments 'decentralized' and de-laicised to boards of local 'presbyters' in each parish or district church. This would end the English system of patronage to parishes and religious lectureships by the local lay patrons, usually gentry and aristocracy – a system that had enabled 'godly' patrons like Warwick and Essex to put their 'Puritan' clerical allies into the local Church even in the 1630s except where harassed by indignant 'High Anglican' bishops. Accepting a Scots-style Church would end this, and the Scots' 'hard-line' approach to strict rules in censoring sermons and writings would restrict the increasingly heterodox theology being explored by pro-Parliamentary religious enthusiasts (particularly the 'Independents') since Laudian censorship collapsed in 1640–41.Was censorship by Laud's episcopal machinery to be replaced by an equally unwelcome 'tyranny' by ultra-Presbyterian Church courts, and were all local congregations to be forced to accept orthodox Calvinist disciplinarians as their new clergy?

Vane, an opponent of the Laudian Anglican Church but sympathetic to the 'Independent' congregations springing up in Parliamentarian areas, and Philip Nye, one of the four clerical delegates most open to allowing freedom of expression within non-episcopal Protestantism, had had their doubts about the Scots' proposed form of the 'Solemn League and Covenant'. In the end an ambiguous form of words had been arranged, whereby the English Church was to be reformed in line with the 'word of God' and the best current Continental practice. Both were open to interpretation, with the Covenanters and English adherents of a disciplinarian State Church (e.g. the preacher Stephen Marshall, Vane's main clerical colleague at the talks) interpreting them one way and the more 'liberal' wing of the Parliamentary leadership (Vane among the 'war party' and Holles with his 'peace party', and Philip Nye among the clerics) interpreting them another way. The phrase 'the nearest conjunction and uniformity', however, implied that the Scots example should be followed, and Scots delegate Robert Baillie noted that the English delegates were keen to keep a door open to admit the 'Independents' into the new Church.[16] Indeed, too forceful an insistence on a disciplinarian Presbyterian solution to the dilemma of the Church's future would encourage alarmed moderates to think of a truce with the King as the lesser evil. Baillie hoped that the arrival of the Scots army in England would help acceptance of the Covenant, though whether he meant by gratitude or moral blackmail is uncertain.[17]

The loss of Hampden
The main lieutenant of Pym in the political struggles of 1640–42, John Hampden, had been killed in a minor action at Chalgrove Field in Oxfordshire in June 1643 as he intercepted a local raid by Prince Rupert. He had had great political prestige among MPs at Westminster as the courageous Ship-Money 'martyr' of 1639, willing to stand up for principles against the King's 'illegal' taxes and bring a legal 'test case' at the risk of ruin. He had also been more prominent than Vane in organizing political strategy against the King even before Parliament met in 1640, and his eminence had been recognized by Charles naming him as one of the 'Five Members' in January 1642. Unlike Vane and St John but like his cousin Cromwell, he had been in command of raising troops in his own district (Buckinghamshire) and served as their colonel in 1642–3, albeit with less autonomy than Cromwell had in the Fenland as his home area was the site of Essex's concentration of the main army at the start of the 1643 campaign.

Had he still been alive his combined military and political role would have been crucial in 1643–4, as a man with a foot in both civilian and military camps like fellow–MPs Cromwell and Waller. His strategic military skills were never tested, though all paid tribute to his personal courage and the devotion of his men, and he would probably have played only a minor role in warfare as a colonel under Essex.

Being in his army in 1643 might well have resulted in Hampden being able to criticize Essex's mistakes from close quarters and so play a role in the Earl's gradual undermining in London, but he was too junior to have been accepted as his successor as commander-in-chief by the peers. In politics, Hampden would have had a difficult choice over whether to accept the strict disciplinarian form of Church government insisted on by the Scots and their Presbyterian allies; he had shown himself to be against episcopacy in 1640–42 but would probably have been alarmed at the Laud-like intentions of his allies. He would then have had to make a choice over whether to move over towards greater toleration of the Independent sects as Vane did, and may have been open to persuasion by Cromwell on this matter. Hampden's opposition to a negotiated solution to the war in winter 1642–3 placed him with Pym, Haselrig, Marten, and Vane against the 'moderates' like Holles, and showed that he did not trust the King. But the threat of imposing the rigours of the Scots Presbyterian model on England in 1644 would have presented him with a dilemma, and made his decision on future action crucial to the Parliamentary cause. Together, he and Holles – prestigious as two of the 'Five Members' – had the political influence on wavering Members to have argued against relying on the Scots for aid and for serious talks with the King.

Charles' offer to Vane

One indication of the King's ability and willingness to exploit unease in the Parliamentary camp with Pym and Hampden dead came that winter. Probably royal allies in Edinburgh (Hamilton?) had tipped the King off about the efforts Vane had made to water down the strict religious terms of the Anglo–Scots alliance. Recognizing Vane's new pre-eminence and his liberal attitude to the future of the Church, the King wrote secretly to him in December assuring his support for freedom of conscience. Vane did offer a reply, though his determination for continued war indicates that he was presumably hoping to draw out the King's hypocrisy in making such a gesture while he was also known to be encouraging the Irish papists to attack his Protestant subjects in England and Scotland.[18] Ironically, the 'Cessation' in Ireland served to undermine the King's chances of being trusted by leading Parliamentarians as it showed that he was prepared to order

Ormonde to accept turning a blind eye to rebel Catholic assaults on the (Scots) Protestants in Ulster. It led to tensions among Irish royalist Protestants, who were now supposed to make a common cause with the murderers of their kin from 1641, and trouble when Irish royalist troops appeared in England as these could be called 'murdering papist rebels' by Parliamentarians. This was not a major factor in tipping the balance of rural opinion against the King, but it showed the dangerous side-effects of Charles coming to rely more on non-English and non-Protestants. It was also a major piece of bad luck for Charles that those Catholic but not anti-royal peers sitting on the 'rebel' Confederation's ruling Council at Kilkenny, particularly the Earl of Castlehaven, were not more effective generals or political leaders – they were eclipsed by Continental war veterans (and pro-papal 'hardliners') such as Preston and O'Neill. None of them was prepared to stand up to the capable and 'focussed' O'Neill (nephew of the iconic 1590s rebel leader Tyrone), or to the clergy and the Pope.

Missed chances of strengthening the 'centre' and opening negotiations, winter 1643–4?

The agreement for the Scots Army to move into England and assist Parliament made co-ordination essential, added to which (four) Scots commissioners were now returning to Westminster. Accordingly a motion was introduced in the Commons on 30 January for a small committee to be set up to work with the latter and report their deliberations to Parliament, and this administrative initiative soon went further. For the first time the Parliamentarian leadership – now effectively led by Vane and St John in the Commons – set up a coherent decision-making executive to co-ordinate the war-effort (16 February 1644), the 'Committee of Both Kingdoms'. This was a body of seven peers and fourteen MPs for the 'better managing the affairs of both nations in the common cause'. The proposal was introduced in the Lords on 1 February by Lord Saye and Sele, Essex and Warwick's Calvinist ally (and Nathaniel Fiennes' father) but also close to Cromwell.[19] This proposal was an occasion for a serious clash between the 'war party', under Vane and Oliver St John, and those MPs and peers who were thought to be in favour of a negotiated settlement. Holles remained the most important Commons believer in peace, but he was already being sidelined as the 'Council of War' (which contained both MPs and generals) took more major decisions – and the fate of Northumberland and Portland in summer 1643 showed that the 'hardliners' could use the London crowds to intimidate the 'peace party' if driven to it. The measure presented an implicit threat of the 'war party' and their Scots allies hijacking the conduct of the war to rule out peace-initiatives and impose harsh terms for talks with Charles, and the mollifying statement was agreed that the committee would only deal with such matters as were agreed by both Houses. It would only deal with the King as directed by votes of both Houses. However, the committee's proposers secured its right to 'advise, consult and direct' the military operations and to deal with foreign states.[20]

In personal terms it should be noted that the issue was dealt with at the time that feelings were running high in London over the vote to remove the allegedly lacklustre Lincolnshire commander Lord Willoughby of Parham, as proposed successfully by Cromwell; Willoughby even challenged his successor Manchester to a duel, although he was eventually persuaded to settle for a subordinate command under him. The episode effectively placed the 'targeted' Willoughby as a victim of the aggressive 'war party', with Cromwell's harsh words about lukewarm generals making his position clear and the fact that he had attacked a peer raising resentment in the Lords. It was a forerunner of the large-scale clash over Cromwell's attack on Manchester that autumn, with the implicit criticism of ineffective aristocratic generals 'per se' pointing at Essex. Essex, a cautious strategist during the 1643 campaign who had showed no keenness to fight, was not free of suspicions by the 'war party' of preferring to talk peace to winning the war.

The religious issue also divided the members of the two Houses remaining in Westminster now that an Assembly of Divines was meeting in Westminster to consider the future shape of the Church of England, as demanded by the Parliamentarians' new Scots allies. Was it to set up a full Presbyterian Church on the Scots model, as implied by the terms of the Anglo-Scots alliance, and was this too great a price for Scots assistance? The Scots' insistence that the English take the Covenant, which the Presbyterians at Westminster were passing into legislation, added to the beleaguered status of both Anglican Parliamentarians and the 'Independents', the smaller number of politicians committed to a less disciplinarian and more liberal Church that would incorporate the growing number of unorthodox Protestant sects. The Assembly had a small body of Independent clerics led by Goodwin and Nye, but was overwhelmingly weighted in favour of a Presbyterian State Church. It did issue a conciliatory declaration on 23 December in which it assured that there would be room in the new religious order for congregations who could not submit to Church control on grounds of conscience,[21] in so far as the 'word of God' permitted it. But this was primarily a temporary tactical move; one of the Scots leaders in the Assembly, Baillie, wrote that his faction only intended to give way on toleration until the Scots army had won some great victories and put them in a stronger position. In reply the Independent clerics in the Assembly issued the 'Apologetical Narration' at the New Year – a call for complete freedom from State Church control for congregations and for no form of clerical discipline.[22] These positions were incompatible, though it took three years for the effects to work out into a physical struggle for control of Parliament and the country.

Meanwhile the possibility of a royalist/ Independent alliance against the disciplinarian Presbyterians – English and Scots – began to emerge. The King's 'moderate' adviser the Earl of Bristol, an ex-critic of his in the 1620s, dabbled in some secret contacts with moderate Presbyterians in London who were opposed to the alliance with Scots Covenanters and the implicit outcome of this in a rigidly Scots-style Church for England. This occurred during the Assembly of Divines' debates over the form of Church government to be adopted in England, a crucial 'fault-line' between the Presbyterian 'hardliners' and the advocates of toleration (the latter including the Independents such as Philip Nye). The latter feared a 'Pym faction'/ Covenanter alliance to create as harshly centralized Church under the Presbyterians as there had been under Laud's Anglicans. Accordingly Bristol sought to lure them over to the King, and an imprisoned pro-Independent divine called Thomas Ogle was able to write to Bristol claiming significant support for his position (including his own gaolers) and to slip out of his London prison to visit Oxford. But the Parliamentary 'Committee of Safety' was apparently aware of his activities, whether or not he was allowed to escape in order to draw in fellow-dissidents who could then be arrested. The 'Ogle Plot' was aimed at securing a mutiny in the Parliamentary garrison at Aylesbury as a sign of goodwill to the King, but this was scotched and Ogle's ally at the town, Colonel Morley, may have been 'turned' or been a double agent all along. When Rupert arrived at the gates in snow on 21 January 1644, expecting dissident officers to open them, he found them shut and had to return to Oxford.[23]

The religious issue was a potent source of discontent in London against the chosen strategy for 1644 of close alliance with the Scots – though the malcontents included both a pro-peace faction (mostly moderate Anglicans) and a more militant Independent group who were committed to success in war without giving too much to the Scots. The Parliamentarian military failure to win a decisive engagement with the King in 1643 – especially at Newbury – strengthened the hand of those English Calvinist MPs and peers who had sympathy with the version of Presbyterianism imposed on Scotland by the Covenanters and who were prepared to see it enforced on England too as the prerequisite for Scots military aid. Arguably this was the logical politico-military 'follow-up' to the alliance of the King's Calvinist detractors in both kingdoms in the Anglo-Scots treaty of August 1641, not a new initiative; the political terminology of the projected settlement then also had the King kept as a nominal sovereign but neutralized by his 'godly' subjects in both kingdoms. But now the English leadership of 1641 was altered, as Pym, Hampden, and Lord Brooke were dead and the Earls of Warwick, Essex, and Manchester (the latter formerly Lord Mandeville) were constrained by their naval and military commands; the latter two were to be politically undermined during 1643–4 by their military failures. A reaction to the threat of a disciplinarian Presbyterian State Church – potentially as autocratic as Laud's episcopal structure – was led in the Assembly by Philip Nye and the Cornish Independent preacher Hugh Peters, the latter increasingly close to Cromwell, with backing from the legal expert John Selden who argued that the changes to English Church practice that the Covenanter clerics required would breach current English law (which Parliament was supposed to be preserving against the tyrannical King). One common factor that bound together some of the most vociferous opponents of Presbyterian discipline was an involvement in the North American colonies in the 1630s, particularly sympathy for the less oppressive form of Church government instituted at Rhode Island by Roger Williams. Men like Peters had seen the practical effects of excessive disciplinarian control by boards of meddling 'elders' in Massachusetts and had no wish to see it in England too.

Late in 1643 the triumphalism of the dominant Presbyterians in the Assembly of Divines at Westminster, openly aiming for a disciplinarian Presbyterian State Church on the Scottish model, led to an overture to Oxford by alarmed Anglicans and Independents in London. The 'Ogle Plot', named after Thomas Ogle who took the proposals to the moderate royalist peer Bristol, was a call for the King to promise a reformed Anglican Church stripped of its current bishops (though not episcopacy 'per se') and with toleration for those sects who could not accept its disciplinary structure. This was in effect the form of settlement reached between Anglicans and sects in 1689, and its open royal support might have had valuable results in widening the breach between the Presbyterians and their critics in London. So far Parliament had seized the temporalities of some thirteen of the bishops, particularly Laudians, but the episcopal office itself was still recognized pending the proposals of the Westminster Assembly of Divines – whose decision, given their membership, was a foregone conclusion. The Commons (7 September 1642) and Lords (10 September) had both voted for a letter to the Scots regime assuring that episcopacy would be abolished, a clear statement of intent.

There was indeed a current move by an important group of pro-Independent intellectuals in London in favour of resolution of the religious issue by a wider degree of toleration than that envisaged by the dominant bloc of Presbyterian MPs and their (now militarily invaluable) Scots allies. March 1644 was to see publication of a call for liberty of conscience by Henry Robinson, making it the first condition for military demobilization and the abandonment of the demands for vengeance of both parties[24] – a coherent and well-thought-out plan for solving the current military 'stand-off' but one that required a degree of goodwill that was lacking. In July the eminent New England religious leader Roger Williams, now in London and an ally of the Independent Sir Henry Vane, brought out his 'Bloudy Tenent of Persecution', a rallying-call for religious freedom on principle for the Protestant sects no doubt based on a warning from what he had observed of intolerant Presbyterian triumphalism in Massachusetts.[25] Indeed Vane, who had gone along with the Covenant in the cause of military necessity as a leader of the Scots negotiations in 1643, regarded the latter as more of a civil than a religious compact and was clearly uneasy at the danger of a disciplinarian Church continuing (now Presbyterian not Anglican) with Scots backing.

The split between Presbyterians and their moderate Anglican and Independent critics, centred on this issue of Church discipline, was to widen and was to break up the Parliamentarian alliance when the form of a settlement was being debated in Parliament in 1647–8 – though by that time the Independents had the advantage of a large and successful army on their side. The King was to make much of his role as a better guarantor of religious and civil liberties than Presbyterian MPs in this period – but only once he had lost all military power to enforce victory on his terms. Perhaps inevitably, this early opportunity for the King to exploit his enemies' divergence on religion was missed. Despite Bristol's support for conciliatory gestures the King was confident of military success without needing such manoeuvres and he failed to make use of the opportunity offered by his summoning of all peers and MPs who could get to Oxford to attend his rival (i.e. solely legitimate) Parliament in January 1644.[26] He had been attacking the London Parliament for being under constraint and thus potentially illegal from winter 1641–2, when unsuccessful motions to that effect had been introduced into the Commons led by Digby; but it is noticeable that he had not used this political weapon in the war until now. The obvious people to argue for this course were Hyde and Sir John Colepeper, former 'opposition' MPs demanding reform in spring 1641 who had defected to the King to save the Church and law and order that autumn; were they ignored? The combination of summoning a 'legal' Parliament to Oxford and putting out 'feelers' to the Independents showed – belated – political sophistication by the King, but this was at odds with his current dealings with the Irish Catholic ex-rebels who both moderate Parliamentarian MPs and

Independents loathed. The King would seek aid from any quarter, including mutually contradictory ones at the same time – as shown more emphatically as he became more desperate in 1645–7.

The question has to be asked – why did he not summon as many loyal MPs and peers as could escape London to join him in York in summer 1642, or in Oxford that winter? Was this a result of the marginalization of Hyde and ex-Secretary of State Viscount Falkland by the more aggressive royal advisors and military men around the Queen? The leaders of the latter were Harry Percy and Sir Henry Jermyn. The comments to the Venetian ambassador by Charles' envoy to London in January indicate that Charles then anticipated a victory in the field,[27] in which case he was too confident to think that he needed to acquire the legal weapon of a Parliament of his own. But what would have happened if the defection of Northumberland, Holland, and other peers to Charles' side as his military position improved in 1643 had coincided with a prudent royal summons to all loyal members of both Houses to join them in Oxford?

The indecisive court correspondence with Vane only led to the Earl of Essex discovering it and complaining that it was his role (as commander-in-chief) not Vane's to handle such missives.[28] A secret royal letter to the Lord Mayor and Corporation in London, a place filling with enthusiastic Independent congregations and badly affected by the trade-slump, was revealed and led to hasty displays of loyalty to Parliament; no serious offers that might have been viable fodder for a negotiation were delivered to the French envoy Count Harcourt (who arrived at Oxford in December 1643). In return for Charles receiving Harcourt, his general George Goring's father, Lord Goring, went to Paris to negotiate for aid and secured armaments in the Spanish Netherlands – but the death of Queen Henrietta Maria's brother King Louis XIII the previous autumn meant that serious French aid was unlikely. Had Louis not died aged 42, leaving a 5-year-old son, the improving French military position 'vis-à-vis' Spain in their ongoing war could have helped Charles to secure troops in 1644 or 1645. As seen with retrospect, France was of negligible military assistance to the King – but had Louis XIII not died this might well have changed and the French armies under Louis' cousin the Prince of Condé were veterans of recent successes against Spain (e.g. Rocroi). Condé and Prince Rupert together on the battlefield would have made a formidable team. In real life, the new regency of winter 1643–4 used Harcourt to try to mediate with Parliament but were thwarted as the latter arrested the mission's exiled English Catholic adviser, Wat Montagu (an 'ultra' royalist but also cousin to the Parliamentary commander Edward Montagu, Earl of Manchester). Harcourt was not particularly sympathetic to Charles either, due to there being veterans of the Spanish army in the 1630s in Charles' service.[29]

The new royalist Parliament failed to adopt any reassuring legislation, such as reaffirming the penal laws against Catholics or promising pardon for most of the Parliamentary supporters, which could have reassured those MPs in Westminster and officers in the field who had doubts about the intentions of the clerical Assembly regarding toleration. Indeed, its existence implied that any negotiations between the rival Parliaments would be hampered by questions of which one was legitimate – as was proved in March when they both denounced each other. There was no sign of the King giving any public leadership to moves for conciliation, or of backing Bristol against the devious Secretary of State George Digby who preferred to concentrate his efforts on suborning Parliamentary garrisons (as at Aylesbury).

Effects of the Scottish invasion. Nantwich (and Monck), the Oxford Parliament, and fears for toleration in the English Church

The King was belatedly having serious thoughts about widening the war, and was finally considering the earlier offers by the disaffected Earl of Montrose to raise a Scots rebellion. Montrose (appointed to the Scots command in February under the titular leadership of Prince Maurice) was a Presbyterian, a commander of the 1638–9 revolt, and so could bring in Protestants alienated from Covenanter dictatorship. His offers to raise an army to fight Argyll in 1643 had been ignored despite the Queen' support, which he had secured at York in March, although he went as far south as Gloucester to appeal to Charles during the siege that summer. The main Scots royalist adviser who preferred to use the 'moderate' Covenanters rather than the Irish and Scots Catholics, Hamilton, was now arrested by the King and deported to distant Pendennis Castle in Cornwall in disgrace,[30] leaving the field clear for Montrose. (Evidently Charles was tired of waiting for Hamilton's promises to suborn Covenanter peers to bear fruit.)

But the planned invasion of Scotland would also involve the use of Irish Catholics, with an army being brought in from Ulster by the Earl of Antrim and hopefully more troops from the main rebel army in central Ireland once the latter had reached agreement with the King's lieutenant Ormonde. Conversely, the King's current negotiations with the Irish Catholics – perpetrators of notorious atrocities in 1641 – following the 'Cessation' served to alarm a substantial body of opinion among his own Parliament at Oxford. The Scots' crossing the Border at Berwick-on-Tweed on 19 January gave promise of the royalist army in the north being outnumbered and its lands having to be evacuated, with the Marquis of Newcastle having to abandon his midwinter sojourn in the Peaks and head north. Sir Thomas Glemham and around 5,000 mostly local (and inexperienced) royalists, about half of the numbers he was supposed to raise at Newcastle to stop them, stood in their way. In the now-common manner of a major move by one side's troops reverberating across the 'chessboard' of interlocking local wars, the Scots invasion was a major bonus to the embattled West Riding Parliamentarians under Sir Thomas Fairfax. It freed them from the threat of another descent by Newcastle's army, which remained formidable despite its rebuff at Hull in September.

The Scots army was a formidable new player on the English campaigning scene, consisting of some 18,000 infantry, 3,000 cavalry, 500 dragoons, and 120 guns and commanded by Alexander Leslie, Earl of Leven, as in 1639–40. His lieutenant-general of horse was David Leslie (no relation), and the various regiments were mostly under the command of the leading trusted Calvinist aristocrat in each recruiting-district. Their presence with the army was to encourage Charles to deal with them behind the high command's back later when he sought a Scots alliance in 1645–6, hoping they would be more amenable than Leven or his 'controllers', Argyll and the Kirk. Newcastle had to hurry to his titular town to lead the defence, sending Eythin ahead with an advance party, as his lieutenant Sir Thomas Glemham fell back from Alnwick, demolishing bridges ahead of the Scots. Luckily Leven had to halt at Morpeth for several days to wait for late-arriving Scots troops who had been held up by flooding, otherwise the town of Newcastle might have fallen unless Glemham's garrison had had the nerve to resist vastly superior numbers. On 2 February the Earl of Newcastle reached his titular town a few hours ahead of the attackers, and the latter sent the Earl of Argyll and MP Sir William Armyn to require its surrender on the 3rd unaware that the reinforcements had arrived. Surrender was refused, and the attackers proceeded to take an outlying defence work at the 'Shield-Field' and repel a sortie from the town but then had to wait for their artillery to arrive by sea. Leven was surprised to find the Earl had arrived (and committed the social solecism of addressing his demand for surrender to the Mayor and corporation rather than the military commander). The royalists sank ships in the mouth of the Tyne to obstruct the Scots and Parliamentary shipping and sent their cavalry out of the city south to Gateshead to launch useful 'hit-and-run' raids rather than keep the horses eating up supplies in the town. No early success could be expected for the Scots with the defence so strong, and their base at Corbridge was disastrously raided by Sir Marmaduke Langdale's and Sir John Fenwick's northern royalist cavalry on the 19th. On the 22nd Leven left the siege to a 'holding-force' and marched most of his army up the Tyne to find a bridge and continue the advance on York. Hampered by snowstorms, driving rain, and broken bridges, he was able to cross at several fords at Ossington on the 28th before the Earl of

Newcastle could catch him or the river became impassable; in both matters he was lucky by a few hours and had he failed the Scots could easily have been held up for weeks. Leven then headed on into County Durham as Langdale evacuated Hexham to race him south. The Earl of Newcastle followed Leven across the countryside, and a clash was avoided by both sides when they were close to each other on 3 March at Chester-le-Street. A clash did occur on 6 March near Sunderland, where the royalists probed the Scots position on Humbledon Hill in the afternoon after a delay caused by snow. The invaders' position was defended by the steep Barnes Burn ravine, and Newcastle fell back; next day the Scots made their own probe to his position on Hastings Hill and he set fire to houses to protect a withdrawal. The Scots then moved on to set up their base at Sunderland, for a series of 'cat-and-mouse' manoeuvres where Leven deliberately put his troops into positions where the formidable royalist cavalry could not charge them.[31] The most significant of these clashes followed the Scots' seizure of South Shields on 20 March, which blocked the mouth of the Tyne and made the fall of the town of Newcastle likely. The main royalist army moved north to try to retake it, but was blocked by Leven at the 'Whitburn Lizard' ridge; a clash followed as the Scots assaulted his positions around east and west Boldon and were beaten back. The royalists claimed the victory, as played up by their newsletter 'Mercurius Aulicus' – but they could not retake South Shields.

The Earl of Newcastle was too cautious to attack the Scots frontally and so avoided a major battle, and as there was no adequate geographical obstacle south of the Tyne to aid him and hold the Scots up the latter had the advantage. Only on 24 March could he engage the enemy, and when he drove them back into Sunderland their artillery in the town opened up on his men and prevented a pursuit. His urgent appeal to Rupert for help went unanswered, and when he heard on 12 April that his subordinate Sir John Belasyse had been defeated in Yorkshire by the Fairfaxes at Selby he headed back to York. Behind him, the Scots moved towards the city to link up with the Fairfaxes.[32] The main reason for his retreat was thus Belasyse's failure, but the latter was outnumbered two to one so would have needed more skill and training for his men to win. Given the Scots' numbers and artillery and Leven's skill, once Newcastle had lost command of the line of the Tyne the royalists only had a slender chance of preventing the Scots entering Yorkshire and upsetting the balance of forces in the north. Severe weather preventing a crossing of the Tyne would have been their best hope. As the royalists retreated to York, Fairfax was able to send his lieutenant Sir William Constable to retake Whitby.

The recent landing of royalist troops from Ormonde's Irish army at Chester in December 1643 – itself a result of the 'Cessation' – had put the

Parliamentarians in Cheshire under threat and lost them every remaining town except Nantwich, which was besieged. Lord Byron, the local royalist commander, was a ruthless character who butchered captured Parliamentarian troops and civilians trapped in Barthelmy church in cold blood, about which he boasted in a letter to Newcastle (captured and published to blacken his name[33]). On 29 December Fairfax duly set out from the West Riding to save the situation and reinforce the Cheshire Parliamentarian commander Brereton, though he was held up at Manchester by snow. On 25 January they destroyed Byron's army in a hard-fought encounter outside besieged Nantwich. A river swollen by rain in the thaw helped to keep the royalist army divided in two, but there was still a hand-to-hand struggle from hedge to hedge with the field-boundaries inhibiting the royalist cavalry that was Byron's main asset. Their infantry in the town were overwhelmed and Byron fled with the cavalry to Chester; 73 royalist officers and 600 men were captured.[34]

There was one long-term important long-term result for the nation as well as short-term Parliamentary revival in the district; among the many royalist prisoners who accepted an invitation to change sides was the future mastermind of the Restoration, Colonel George Monck. He was indeed in England due to Charles' Irish policy of allying with the Catholic ex-rebels, having asked his commander Ormonde for a transfer to England after that alliance dismayed him. He joined the Parliamentary army, after an interval in prison in London unlike many of his less scrupulous colleagues, and embarked on his rise to control of Scotland in 1652–9 and pivotal role in England in 1660; had he remained in the royalist army he was very unlikely ever to have joined the 'New Model' and won Cromwell's trust. In the short term, the fact that the King had relied on 'barbarous and bloody' papists imported from atrocity-afflicted Ireland to turn on his English subjects in Cheshire was made much of in the Parliamentary propaganda after Nantwich. The Parliamentary success in Cheshire, however, did not stop more Irish reinforcements landing in North Wales and moving on to Prince Rupert at Shrewsbury, and Fairfax was unable to secure Lancashire from the threat of their co-religionists at Lathom House, the Earls of Derby's fortified mansion. In the Earl's absence his wife – one of a distinguished quartet of formidable female defenders of besieged mansions with Ladies Bankes and Arundell (royalist) and Lady Harley (Parliamentarian) – refused Fairfax's order to surrender. He had to leave Alexander Rigby (MP for Wigan) to deal with her while he returned to Yorkshire on more pressing business.[35] As with the similar Catholic aristocratic stronghold at Basing House in Hampshire, Lathom continued to be a thorn in the local Parliamentarians' sides for a long time to come.

The Scots invasion focussed the minds of both royalists and Independents on the threat of the Scots imposing a Presbyterian religious settlement. On 27 January, 44 of the King's attendant peers and 118 MPs in Oxford – most of the Lords and about a third of the Commons as constituted before the war – signed a letter to the Earl of Essex requesting his help in effecting a negotiated settlement. The King would guarantee to receive advice for his subjects' religion and safety.[36] However the first major hurdle to opening any negotiations – the rival claims to legitimacy of the respective Parliaments at London and Oxford – were never overcome. Essex returned the request without comment except to promise pardon for those at Oxford who would come over to the Parliamentary side, subject to the possibility of fines, and the two rival bodies ended up with each voting defiantly in favour of its sole legitimacy. The trickle of MPs who did accept Essex's offer to defect seem to have been most affected by the King's current flirtation with Catholicism and the threat of his bringing in foreign Catholic troops. But the effect of this shift in royalist strategy on its civilian English supporters was not dramatic enough to seriously undermine the King. Meanwhile, the King agreed that Montrose should raise troops in north-western England and cross into Galloway to start a rebellion against the Covenanters, a plan that proved wildly optimistic, and that the Marquis of Antrim (Randal MacDonnell) should go to Kilkenny to secure Catholic mercenaries from the rebel Confederate Irish to send to Montrose. (He ended up having to send his own men from Ulster.[37]) The main conduit for the over-optimistic Irish schemes in Oxford was Lord Digby; Hyde complained that he was being excluded and would doubtless have been more cautious if he had been allowed to take part. The titular Lord Lieutenant of Ireland was still the Earl of Leicester, appointed in 1641 to mollify Parliament and now in Oxford; he would not have approved of Charles using Catholic troops so on 13 November 1643 he was replaced by Ormonde. Another snubbed Protestant with a claim to act for the King in Ireland, with more serious consequences, was the Munster 'Old English' peer Lord Inchiquin, whose claims to preferment were passed over as the Catholic Marquis of Antrim outmanoeuvred him. He went home in a sulk, and later defected to Parliament – a blow to any claim that the King could call on the loyalty of Anglo-Irish Protestant gentry despite his dealings with their Catholic foes. Inchiquin would have been a valuable ally for Charles for reasons of reassurance to Protestants in all three kingdoms.

The new Parliamentarian executive, the 'Committee of Both Kingdoms', brought a possibility of better central direction for the war-effort in 1644. Already the 'Council of War' organized in summer 1643 was taking on more administrative work from the Commons 'Committee of Safety' and, like the new Committee, it had generals as well as MPs on it; but the new Committee had more non-MPs and crucially included the Scots. It was significant that the most forceful of the Presbyterian MPs, Holles, was excluded – possibly due to suspicion of his ambiguous attitude to a 'win at all costs' war policy. It was in a sense the first all-British 'Cabinet', the first executive arm of government not to be headed by the Sovereign, and uniquely included representatives from both England and Scotland. Its English members included both peers like Essex, Warwick (commander of the fleet), Manchester, and Northumberland, and MPs committed to a forceful 'war effort' such as Cromwell and Waller (both serving in the field for most of the time as generals) and the 'civilians' Vane, Haselrig, and St John. But the opportunities for rising figures like Cromwell were potentially hampered by the terms of the Scots alliance that had engendered it; all of Parliament's military and civilian appointees were legally required to take the Covenant, by an ordinance coming into effect as of 5 February.[38] Cromwell duly signed up, as had Vane, despite his reservations about the implications of a Scots-style Presbyterian Church settlement to 'tender consciences' – the probable face-saving excuse to his conscience being the clause that the form of Church would be 'according to the Word of God', which was open to interpretation. He also took up the new rank of lieutenant-general and thus sole cavalry commander under the Earl of Manchester, i.e. his immediate deputy in the Eastern Association army, in which role he was able to show his ability on a wider battlefield when the Parliamentary armies joined together that summer. The command led to his success at Marston Moor and thus to his being chosen as deputy to Fairfax in the New Model in 1645, although it was not the only route to his emergence as a national military figure as Fairfax had already noted his ability on the Hull campaign in 1643.

At this juncture a new factor entered the scene on the Parliamentarians' side, as their alliance with the Scots in 1643 bore fruit with the invasion of Northumberland; by mid-April, as seen above, they were nearing York. Simultaneously, Lord Fairfax made the most of his opportunities in Yorkshire in January despite his son's absence in Cheshire to recover the East Riding for Parliament and Sir William Constable overran the North Riding, recovering Whitby. Outnumbered, the royalist forces were estimated by the Marquis of Newcastle in mid-February as only 5,000 infantry and 3,000 badly armed cavalry. Charles responded to his appeals by sending Prince Rupert to help, and the latter – now 'Lord President of the Council in the Marches' to command in Wales – raised recruits at Shrewsbury (21 February) and then proceeded to Chester. The potential arose for the royalist cavalry 'supremo' to use his brilliance at 'hit-and-run' tactics to hold up the Scots advance. But he was delayed in Lancashire by the need to assess the strength of the Earl of Derby's headquarters at the family mansion, Lathom House (commanded by the Countess), and was called south again by the King to relieve Newark. He left Chester on 12 March, reinforced by a mixture of Irish from Dublin and Midlands royalists,[39] and advanced so quickly (partly by night) that the Parliamentarian commander Sir John Meldrum discounted the rumours of his approach. His success in the relief on 21 March – by a typical cavalry charge against Sir John Meldrum's besiegers – netted him prestige, Meldrum's artillery train, and the security of the main royalist stronghold in the north-east Midlands for the crucial summer 1644 campaign.[40] Had Newark fallen, the royalist position in the area could have been 'rolled up' after their northern collapse in July; Rupert's success thus aided the King's ability to hold out in Oxford through the year.

But on the increasingly complex 'chessboard' of shifting military strengths across England, Rupert's march south-east to Newark left the Marquis of Newcastle and the royalist command of the north-east exposed to the Scots. The Marquis retired south from his position at Durham on 12 April. Luckily for the Parliamentarian and Scots strategy, the King and his advisers did not decide to challenge the Covenanters' control of Scotland with a royalist rising until the Scots were inside England. Only then did Charles commission Montrose to revolt within the Highlands in Scotland and Antrim to bring in assistance from Ulster – if such moves had been commenced in 1643 the main Scots army could not have intervened so decisively. Did Charles' delay in deciding to rely on Montrose doom his supporters' position in the north of England in spring 1644, putting York under threat and thus setting the scene for the confrontation at Marston Moor in July? It would not have mattered in the long term for him had he won at Marston Moor – but in retrospect his indecision over Montrose's offers in 1643 added to the risks posed by a large and well-trained Scots force being able to assist the Parliamentarians in the July 1644 confrontation.

Charles' main hopes of outside help to his cause in early spring 1644 were centred on two other developments. One was a possible long-term truce with the Catholic rebels in Ireland for a joint military effort against Parliament, negotiated by the royalist commander Ormonde to follow the 'Cessation'; it was clear that this would entail guarantees to the Irish Catholic Church and Parliament. The other was the over-optimistic belief that the Dutch could be lured into sending troops by the Prince of Wales' marriage to Stadtholder Frederick Henry's daughter. The previous autumn the death of Louis XIII of France had also raised the possibility of a more active policy towards the war by his successor, the regent Anne of Austria, under the anti-Spanish influence of her Italian chief minister Cardinal

Mazarin. The French had decisively defeated the Spanish at Rocroi so if their attempts at mediation failed they might be free to send troops to aid the King; their first mission that winter (under Count Harcourt) achieved no success either in London or in Oxford but a possible royalist alliance was still rumoured. Probably royalist possession of a major port like Hull and/or a viable fleet would have encouraged Anne and Mazarin to intervene, though French troops could still use Bristol; any intervention risked retaliation from the Parliamentary fleet. It could also alarm Spain and lead to an alliance of Spain and Parliament; Philip IV was still at war with the Dutch (and thus with Charles' son-in-law William and his father Stadtholder Frederick Henry).

At this point the Dutch themselves offered to mediate, but the Parliamentarian 'war party' under Vane prevented the Lords from securing control of the negotiations by a new mixed committee of peers and MPs. In March the Houses voted that talks be handed over to the 'Committee of Both Kingdoms',[41] on which the 'hard-liners' had a majority – thus making it impossible for war-weary moderates to 'bounce' the militants into a settlement if the King offered reasonable terms.

Disorder or bad luck in royalist military strategy, spring 1644? Cheriton and the defence of Oxford

The Scots advance necessitated a major royalist effort in the north to assist the beleaguered Lord Newcastle, with troops diverted to assist him. The logical commander of this force was Prince Rupert, who was active in the northern part of the battlefront, rather than a general such as Sir Ralph Hopton who was probably a better strategist at fighting battles (as seen in the 1643 south-western campaign, e.g. at Lansdown). As seen above, the first attempt to use Rupert for this in February–March had been aborted by the threat to Newark. Rupert was an effective and inspiring cavalry commander on the battlefield but lacked discipline or the ability to focus on the needs of several wings of troops across a whole battlefield, as seen at Edgehill. He was probably the wrong commander to send to confront the disciplined Scots infantry in a major battle, particularly as reinforcement to the uninspiring Newcastle who needed an ally with proven quick reactions in handling a large and separate army on the field rather than a cavalry commander. But his rank and the King's personal affection made his claims successful, and the brilliance of Rupert's defeat of the Parliamentarian Scots general Meldrum at Newark added to his reputation. It showed his abilities in forceful attack, but he lacked a coherent and disciplined army to press forward into the heartland of the Eastern Association that now lay open and thus prevent the Earl of Manchester's army linking up with the advancing

Scots. The victory had little effect apart from the overrunning of Lincoln, Gainsborough, and a few minor towns and the Earl of Manchester's army remained intact and out of reach. It was in any case a more coherent force than Rupert's medley (garrison troops unused to fighting together) and was likely to have won a major clash. The main thrust of the royalist war effort remained the Scots march south and Newcastle's gradual retreat towards York through March.

But the Scots advance was slow, and the royalists had time to achieve successes elsewhere before the need arose to save Newcastle's army. Instead, the familiar story of poor royalist tactics produced disaster in the south. This time it was a mixture of excessive caution and excessive zeal that ruined the chances of the army commanded by Hopton and the Earl of Forth (the aged veteran of the Swedish wars who had commanded the royal vanguard at Edgehill) in Hampshire. Hopton's advance east into Sussex in December had been halted by the need to take Arundel Castle, which Waller had quickly retaken in January. Waller's new south-eastern army of 5,000 foot, 3,000 horse, and 600 dragoons, reinforced by a Scots brigade under Sir William Balfour, was proposed by the Southern Association to Parliament on 12 February, and eventually passed by Parliament on 30 March after squabbles over funding and over Waller's reluctance to take orders from Essex (who he felt had left him to his fate at Roundway Down in 1643).[42] His deputy in charge of cavalry was Sir William Balfour, who had seen service in Holland and had prudently taken Parliament's rather than the King's side while Lieutenant of the Tower of London in the Strafford trial crisis in 1641.

This army was originally intended to take the main royalist stronghold in Hampshire, the heavily fortified Basing House (the Catholic Marquis of Winchester's main residence), with the aid of treachery by the owner's brother Lord Charles Paulet. (Waller had made one attempt on the house in November.) This was prevented when the turncoat Sir Richard Grenville fled to Oxford with details of the plot,[43] but Waller advanced westwards anyway from Arundel on 19 March, planning to meet Balfour's men at Petersfield. They then proceeded to East Meon on the 26th, ready to cross the Downs westwards on Winchester.

They faced an army of around 7,000 royalists from Winchester under the Earl of Forth, Charles' septuagenarian veteran commander from Edgehill in 1642 (sent from Oxford by the King), and Hopton – around 3,200 infantry and 3,800 cavalry. The royalists had emerged from Winchester to find Waller and had lined up on Old Winchester Hill close to East Meon, but Hopton decided to secure a better position that would give him easier connections to Winchester; as things stood the two armies were more or less equidistant so Waller might manage to cut Hopton off from his base. Their confrontation on 27 March near East Meon thus led to both sides moving off north-westwards – parallel to each other – rather than fighting, and the royalist cavalry managed to get ahead as they headed for Winchester.[44] Hopton's men managed to reach the Itchen valley first, upstream east of Winchester, and secured both the town of Alresford and a defensible position on nearby Tichborne Down. The Parliamentarians halted to their south up the Itchen valley at Hinton Ampner, with their right wing stretched uphill eastwards onto Cheriton East Down. The battle on 29 March was fought on even terms with neither side at a disadvantage of gradient. The royalists would be facing south-east, the Parliamentarians north-west. Apparently the Parliamentarians did consider moving off without a battle, but it was as well that they did not as an overnight noise of rumbling wagons persuaded royalist Colonel George Lisle that a retreat was imminent and the royalist cavalry were readied to ambush any such move.

In the resulting clash around Cheriton on 29 March, Forth, the over-cautious royalist commander at Edgehill, failed to advance to take Hopton's advice at a crucial moment. Hopton's men under Colonel Appleyard had driven Waller's men back from Cheriton Wood, securing the East Down, and while the Parliamentary forces were demoralized Hopton proposed a charge along the open downland by around 1,000 troops. The Earl refused to run the risk, the enemy was allowed time to recover, and the battle then hinged on a hand-to-hand struggle in the nearby valley over the village of Hinton Ampner, which the royalists were attacking. But this royalist advance up the Itchen valley into the village was risky, given that the Parliamentarians uphill to the east were still in a strong position. Even success in securing the village posed dangers for the royalists, as the village was exposed to attack from the Parliamentarians on the downs to the east; it could easily be cut off and surrounded if the enemy had possession of the higher ground. This duly happened.

Young and over-bold Sir Henry Bard with his regiment rashly charged the Parliamentarians in the valley in a superior defensive position in defiance of orders, pressing on southwards up the valley away from the main royalist line. His force was cut to pieces, as Sir Arthur Haselrig sent in several troops of horse to take advantage of the gap between Bard's men and the rest of their army. (The newsletter *The Scots Dove* gave the main credit for the victory at Cheriton to one of the troop-commanders, Colonel Richard Norton – a local man who thus knew the ground well.) Sir Edward Stawell was sent to Bard's rescue to save the embattled royalist infantry by taking on the enemy cavalry, and drove back the enemy cavalry across the Cheriton common but came up against artillery behind defended hedges and could not cross. As at Newbury in 1643, the defensive advantages of hedges for disciplined Parliamentarian regiments proved decisive, though the struggle was so close-fought that it could have gone either way. Waller was nearly captured at one point. But more royalist regiments hurrying up to the clash could not arrive in time as the lanes leading up to the common were too narrow to allow swift passage. They were constrained into a narrow enfilade and could be taken on and defeated by their interceptors one by one, and the battle was lost. The royalists lost around 300 soldiers and a number of officers, including two commanders (Lord John Stuart, the King's cousin, and General John Smith); the Parliamentarians lost around 60 men.[45] Fortunately for the royalists, Hopton was able to hold out long enough on Tichborne Down to enable their artillery to get away and reach Winchester; he then followed in reasonable order.

As Essex wrote of the battle, 'I tremble to think how near we were to the very Precipice of Destruction'[46] (Lords Journal, vol 6, p.25).

He wrote that with Newark untaken, Lincolnshire lost, Gloucester unsupplied, and the royalists roaming at large across the north and west the cause would have been lost and: 'there was but a step between us and death or (what is worse) slavery'.[47]

Typically, he played down his rival Waller's part in the victory, putting Balfour's contribution ahead of his, and then used the narrowness of their success to argue for giving himself not Waller more men. Had Waller lost, as he had done against Hopton in the western campaign of 1643, the royalists could have swept forward into Sussex as they did across the west after their previous success, and required Essex to abandon his planned advance on Oxford with the central army in order to stabilize the situation. The open countryside would have been overrun by a superior royalist army as Devon, Dorset, and Somerset had been after the destruction of Stamford's army in spring 1643, and the Parliamentarians would have been driven back on the 'Puritan' town of Lewes (which usefully had a castle) and the south-eastern ports. Arundel Castle would have been lost again, and the Parliamentarian Sussex ironworks come under threat. Kent had not yet shown the war-weariness that made it a royalist centre in 1648, but Waller would have had to attempt to raise a new army in London to stave off the capital's being encircled. Instead the defeat opened Winchester and Salisbury to attack. The royalists were without a coherent army south of the defensive forces around Oxford, unless the King came to their rescue, at a time when his main concern for the next few months would be saving the north. Hopton and Forth lost the initiative and control of central southern England apart from isolated garrisons; the next major action there was to be the long-drawn-out siege of the formidably fortified Basing House. The King's concentration of his field-army at Marlborough threw Waller onto the defensive after an initial 'surge' as far as Christchurch, and in mid–April Waller moved back to his headquarters at Farnham; the recall of Balfour's brigade undermined him further.[48] Parliamentary attention was now concentrated on their general rendezvous at Aylesbury for Essex's summer campaign.

The Parliamentary advance on Oxford and their missed chances; Cropredy Bridge

The royalists had now lost their main army in the south, but the outcome of the war that year would depend on the two larger confrontations – the King and Essex in central England, and the Scots and Newcastle in the north. Flushed with success, the 'Committee of Both Kingdoms' now intended all three of their armies in the south – Essex's, Waller's, and Manchester's – to concentrate on Oxford. The royalist capital was defended by an outlying group of garrisons, the most important being their most easterly position on the Thames at Reading. In the meantime the King had sent the Marquis of Antrim to the Irish Catholic rebel leadership at Kilkenny to request a speedy despatch of the 10,000 troops promised in 1643 plus another 2,000 to accompany Antrim to Scotland, and had despatched Montrose on an initial – unsuccessful – foray into Galloway. In the west of Wales, another potential route into England for royalist or Confederate Irish reinforcements for the King, a dominant position had been seized early in 1644 by Sir Henry Vaughan (sheriff of Carmarthen) and his ally Lord Carbery, with possession of Haverfordwest and Tenby. However, a young Parliamentary officer with experience in the Netherlands, Rowland Laugharne, upset this promising scenario by rallying the local resistance to blockade Tenby, which was later stormed, while at sea Captain Swanley drove the royalist shipping out of Milford Haven and then blockaded Tenby harbour. Both harbours were lost by the end of March, preventing any Irish shipping using them.[49] It has been argued by Mark Stoyle that the surprisingly resilient Parliamentarian force in Pembrokeshire ultimately undermined the King's potential for raising Welsh troops, as the local royalists had to be reinforced by Sir Charles Gerard's troops. The latter aroused indignation for 'living off the land' and robbing and ill-treating the locals, thus diminishing recruits, and possibly the haughty and uncomprehending attitude of the English aristocrat Gerard (and other officers), aroused racial antagonism. This can be compared with Charles – more excusably – relying on equally unpopular Irish Catholic troops in Protestant Scotland.

Newcastle, unable to spare more than a handful of men to aid Montrose, was faced with an advance by Fairfax from the West Riding to coincide with the Scots advance; after Selby fell on 11 April he retreated into York where the allies duly besieged him. The Scots (c. 17,000) were reinforced by Fairfax

(c. 5,000) so the royalists (c. 8,000 plus a small garrison) were outnumbered by over two to one and would need rescuing.[50] The walls of the northern capital would not hold indefinitely, making the despatch of a major royalist army to rescue him a matter of some urgency. In the meantime the royalists in the south-west were held down by Prince Maurice's long and unsuccessful siege of Lyme Regis (from March), though Waller was forced to stay inactive at his headquarters at Farnham. Parliament failed to send Waller major reinforcements, merely replacing Major-General Browne's departing brigade with a force the same size, and concentrated on Essex's army's rendezvous with its Midlands allies at Aylesbury (19 April). Waller's requests for more men to march west were ignored.[51] Free from a Parliamentary advance by Waller into Dorset, the royalists retook Wareham on 21 May to enable the import of munitions for their south-western forces by an easier route than through divided Weymouth where each side controlled one shore of the harbour. The royalist position in southern Dorset relied heavily on useful geography, in that their two main redoubts – Corfe Castle in Purbeck and the island of Portland – were extremely difficult to attack. Corfe, like Lathom House in Lancashire, was defended by a doughty female commander – Lady Bankes – when her husband Sir John, the King's former attorney-general, died in 1644.

The King was given a breathing space during April by the slowness of recruitment to Essex's army in London and the Earl's quarrels with the Parliamentarian 'war-party' over his allegedly suspicious dilatoriness. Essex failed to be ready to meet the intended rendezvous with Manchester's Eastern Association army at Aylesbury on 19 April; nor could Manchester leave Prince Rupert's army poised in his rear at Lincoln so he missed the rendezvous as well. On 6 May Manchester recaptured Lincoln, and so could march on to aid the Scots at York.[52] But the King had only around 10,000 men at his call in Oxford, 6,000 infantry and 4,000 cavalry, which he reviewed at Aldbourne on 11 April after the return of the troops beaten at Cheriton. He needed reinforcements, which he could not bring from Maurice's preoccupied army in the south-west so he called in Sir William Vavasour from the Severn valley.[53] Had Hopton won or at least avoided serious losses at Cheriton in March, extra men would have been available to send north from royalist-occupied Hampshire. Instead, Charles ordered Rupert to send 2,000 foot and a cavalry-regiment and to be ready to join him near Oxford in the first week of June.[54] Rupert was thus distracted from any immediate move to reinforce York.

This would mean Rupert leaving the relief of York perilously late, and he proceeded to Oxford himself to offer his uncle his own opinions on strategy. His proposals were that the King maintain a defensive posture in Oxford, keeping strong garrisons in Reading, Wallingford, Abingdon, and Banbury to tie down the Parliamentarians, and himself manoeuvring around the area with a mobile cavalry force. The enemy armies would be unable to take these garrisons without defeating the King and securing their own safety first, or to march after the King while leaving the garrisons holding out to their rear. Either attacking the mobilizing-process of troops in the field or settling down for a series of sieges would be dangerous for them. While they were thus held up, Rupert could concentrate on the north and relieve York; he would then be at liberty to manoeuvre quickly in the open countryside with his mobile cavalry and harass the enemy armies.[55]

Essex closes in on Oxford: a choice of tactics for the King

The King seemed to adopt this plan rather than the bellicose demands of other commanders for a march on Essex's headquarters at Aylesbury to wipe out the shame of defeat at Cheriton with a quick battle. He and Rupert left Oxford on 5 May, the pregnant Henrietta Maria having left for Bath on 17 April (Maundy Thursday[56]). Charles was never to see his wife again. Almost at once his plan was modified as Forth persuaded Charles to evacuate Reading (18 May). Next day Essex, from Aylesbury via Henley, and Waller, from Surrey, occupied the town. Waller moved off for a quick 'strike' at Basing House on 21 May,[57] but failed to surprise it and returned to the Thames valley (Abingdon, 26 May). By now the Earl of Manchester, allowed to proceed with a northern campaign instead of attacking Oxford, had retaken Lincoln in Rupert's absence (6 May) and was advancing over the Trent and Humber to join Fairfax and the Scots at the siege of York. Prince Maurice was still tied down (since mid-March) at the siege of Lyme Regis, and the Parliamentarians had relieved Gloucester (again); its commander Massey now advanced across the Cotswolds to threaten the links between Oxford and the West Country. In the north, Montrose crossed the border with a small force recruited in Cumberland to strike at Dumfries in mid-April but was forced to flee south again due to lack of support.[58] His arch-enemy Argyll had been with the Covenanters' Army in northern England but had returned quickly to the Lowlands on news of a Gordon attack on Aberdeen, and Argyll's well-armed troops at Perth blocked Montrose from making a dash to the Highlands.

On the 24th Massey's army from Gloucester entered Malmesbury. On 25 May the King's forces abandoned Abingdon to Essex, and at a council-of-war on the 27th it was decided that he should take the field to manoeuvre at large around Oxford and keep its communications with the west open.[59] This was a variation of Rupert's original idea, which had, however, envisaged himself and the King protecting the outlying garrisons not having to defend Oxford itself. The change reflected the King's lack of manpower to hold all the outlying garrisons safely, a situation made worse by the advance of Massey from Gloucestershire (which the royalist capture of Gloucester in 1643 would have avoided) and Maurice being tied down in West Dorset.

Charles was now in danger of encirclement in Oxford and a siege from the two combined Parliamentary armies before he could lead his men out to conduct the mobile campaign he and Rupert had envisaged. His dangerous situation was shown on 2 June, when Waller – having now crossed the Thames to the north bank at Newbridge, upstream from Oxford – nearly surprised him in person at Woodstock.[60] Essex, meanwhile, had crossed the Thames downstream from Oxford at Sandford on 28 May and advanced east of the city to the crossing of the Cherwell at Islip, where on 2 June he received an unsuccessful appeal from the Dutch ambassadors for peace-talks.[61] Charles was thus nearly trapped between two large armies, though Oxford was defensible by the marshy water-meadows and the Cherwell to the east, the Thames protected it to the south and west, and the city had a line of entrenchments dug across the northern approach on the peninsula between Thames and Cherwell. He decided to leave Oxford to lure the enemy away and link up with reinforcements in the West Midlands, and late in the evening of 3 June he set out westwards with around 3,000 infantry and 2,500 musketeers on horseback. Waller only heard the following afternoon, and his pursuit was vital hours behind the King; on the 4th they hurried as far as Burford while the King reached Evesham. By the time the Parliamentarians reached Evesham he was safe in Worcester and they had to give up the pursuit (6 June[62]).

But what if Charles had been captured on the 2nd at Woodstock? It would have been a shattering blow to his local forces and might well have caused his deputy Forth to surrender Oxford on demand, leaving only Rupert and Maurice at large with substantial armies and Newcastle besieged in York. The two impetuous Princes could well have refused to surrender, taking their orders instead from the (heavily pregnant) Queen who had left Oxford for the safer south-west and was at Exeter; but would most of their men have deserted? Luckily Charles was able to return to Oxford in time, and managed to lead his forces out of the city unchallenged at night and evade pursuit as he retired via Worcester to Bewdley. The King's weakness in Rupert's absence showed up the problems of operating from a royalist 'capital' so exposed to encirclement, and a headquarters further west into his own heartlands (at Worcester or Shrewsbury?) would have been strategically safer. But the use of Oxford, a larger city and containing one of the kingdom's two universities (and enough potential sites for the court and administration), had made sense in autumn 1642 when it had been Parliament in London on the defensive.

Essex's choice: the south-western campaign, not pursuing the King
The initiative and the advantage of numbers lay with Essex and Waller, who had Oxford virtually surrounded and the psychological advantage of having forced Charles into effective flight. The King's smaller army was not yet sufficient to meet their joint forces in battle, and would not have been able to raise many recruits in the West Midlands and Marches had they advanced quickly. A determined pursuit should have forced Charles either into battle on inferior terms or into demeaning further flight that would diminish his chances of raising an army large enough to win a clash. But at their vital council-of-war on 6 June at Stow-on-the-Wold Essex ignored his colleague's advice that the primary need was to catch Charles, who while he was free had the capacity to raise army after army. This comment, relayed by Waller and Haselrig to the Committee of Both Kingdoms in a letter of 7 June, touched the most essential point of the war – to gain control of the King.[63] Essex preferred to march off south-west to relieve Lyme Regis and attempt to take over the major source of royalist troops and food-supplies in the south-west, thus weakening the King's forces ahead of a final battle that could come later. The blame may lie with his adviser Lord Robartes, principal Parliamentarian commander in his own county of Cornwall until chased out by Hopton in 1643 and confident of his support there.

Essex now left the blockade of Oxford and pursuit of Charles to Waller and headed off into Dorset from Stow on 7 June. (In fact the Commons had sent MP John Crew to the generals on 3 June to inform them that Waller was to head for Lyme, not Essex; he did not arrive in time. As late as 11 June the Commons voted for Waller to command on the expedition, not Essex.[64]) Essex ignored the orders of the 'Committee of Both Kingdoms' sent after him on 12 June to despatch a sufficient force to Lyme and bring the rest back to Oxford himself,[65] which he received en route to Lyme at Blandford Forum. He argued that the passage in the Committee's letter to him on 30 May referring to the relief of Lyme as leading to an effort to recover the west gave him this discretion; the phrase was not so definitive in reality.[66] Thus Charles received the valuable time to raise more men safe from immediate pursuit, and the Committee (having clashed with the remnant of the Lords over their right to direct Essex as they saw fit) gave way and allowed Essex to remain in the west on 25 June.[67] As events had it, on the 15th – the day after Essex received and ignored the first letter at Blandford[68] – news of his approach made Prince Maurice lift the siege of Lyme. The main component of the campaign was thus achieved very quickly, but Essex persisted with his plan and moved on to retake Weymouth and then march on Exeter; before he heard that the Committee had given way he threatened to retire from military service if he was no longer thought fit to be trusted.

The one major advantage Essex could have achieved in the far west was to surprise and capture the Queen at Exeter while she was recovering from giving birth to Princess Henrietta. Capturing the Queen would have forced Charles to negotiate, and while she was held up at Exeter she asked Essex for a safe-conduct but was implacably told to surrender and accompany him to London. But she managed to escape in time and flee to Falmouth, whence she sailed for France in mid-July – not to return until the Restoration. Her ship was nearly captured and she had to hide from shells in the hold, but she ordered the captain to sink it rather than surrender to the pursuit and he managed to evade the enemy.[69] Warwick, who should have been patrolling the coast, did not have enough ships to watch every port and tackle the opportunistic Dunkirk privateers who were preying on Channel shipping. In the meantime, the need for Essex to garrison each port recovered for the King as he pursued the Queen west (e.g. Dartmouth) diminished the size of his army.

Lyme – the Parliamentarian 'Stalingrad'?

The siege of Lyme was a vital strategic bonus to the Parliamentarian cause, tying down Prince Maurice's army for weeks from March to June. As this siege affected the central issue of the summer 1644 campaign – the abandonment of the Parliamentarians' concentration on the Oxford region – it played a major role in the latter's disrupted strategy, quite apart from it leading to Essex's unnecessary march into Cornwall. A rapidly advancing and mobile royalist army was tied down in western Dorset for weeks at the 'high tide' of their advance, in the manner of the way in which Stalingrad was to hold up the German advance in southern Russia in 1942. The way that the 'minor' obstacle had to be fought for house by house and never fell was equally a boost to the embattled defence's morale, though it should be noted that other local towns (e.g. Taunton) played a similar role at other times. The small town of Lyme Regis was only one of a series of ports useful to the royalists for shipping in supplies, and its layout gave the advantage to the attackers who could either bombard or attack the town from above down steep slopes. The harbour, protected by the famous breakwater of the Cobb, was detached from the town, half a mile to the west, and could be cut off from it if the heights above were seized – which would make starving it out easier. But the existing line of defences held, and the Cobb was not isolated. Despite a fierce bombardment that damaged most of the houses the future Admiral Robert Blake, a local from Bridgewater, organized a successful defence to assist the Mayor, who was in command, and the 500 or so troops and 3,000 inhabitants had the luck that Maurice did not construct a battery capable of hitting ships docking at the Cobb until after Parliamentary ships from Portland had brought them more ammunition. The most perilous point of the two-month siege was when the defence was seriously short of ammunition after the first attack, but Maurice had been disheartened by his failure and kept his distance until after the new supplies had landed. His raiding-parties later managed to reach the Cobb and set fire to the ships there, but nothing vital was lost. The Earl of Warwick brought in fresh supplies by sea on 23 May, and with this help the defence fought back daily assaults that breached their earthworks on 27–9 May. On the 30th his gunners fired red-hot embers onto the town's roofs, but the fires were put out in time. The siege was abandoned on 15 June as Maurice withdrew to confront Essex, who had reached Weymouth, and the Parliamentarian control of western Dorset was resumed as the Earl marched on into Devon. At sea, Warwick's fleet of eight ships cruised along the coast and kept the supply-lines open to Parliamentarian Plymouth.[70]

Logically Essex should now have called a halt to his march, but he was now free of any requirement to consider returning to Oxford to link up quickly with Waller thanks to the Commons giving way to his insistence on being allowed to march westwards. His claims that his orders from the Committee had encompassed restoring Parliamentarian rule of the south-west seem to have distorted their intention, which had envisaged this as a follow-up the relief of Lyme but not so soon. He pursued an ultimately futile campaign across Devon and Cornwall, marching further and further away from his lines of supply, while Waller was hard-pressed in his confrontation with the King. Digby saw his decision as a blunder occasioned by hatred of Waller.[71] Logically, he was probably seeking a major strategic coup – the reconquest of Devon and Cornwall – that would show him as such a brilliant commander that he would be indispensable. In any event, his advance meant that he was no longer 'covering' Waller's southern flank, leaving the latter more exposed to the royalists. Waller had marched from Sudeley Castle near Cheltenham (taken on 9 June) into the middle Severn valley to back up the embattled Earl of Denbigh (who was forced by the King's approach to abandon the siege of Dudley Castle), and was prevented from crossing the Severn by the royalist breaking of Bewdley Bridge.[72] But for this setback, could he have broken up the King's efforts to recruit troops and return quickly to Oxford? While he waited in Stourbridge and Parliament was preoccupied with their dispute with Essex, Charles had the chance to decide what to do – tackle Waller and Essex separately in the south, or join Rupert in the north Midlands? His decision at the council-of-war at Bewdley on 13 June was to return to Oxford and tackle Waller before Essex returned. On the 16th he marched east from Worcester, while Waller was still waiting for him east of Bewdley; and his 'head-start' gave him the ability to reach Oxfordshire first. At Evesham, with Charles 20 miles ahead of him, Waller gave up the chase. And the letter that Lord Digby, in the King's entourage, wrote to Rupert on 17 June shows clearly that the royalists had been afraid that Oxford – with less than a fortnight's provisions in store – would have had to surrender before Charles arrived had Essex been on the scene. Alternatively, Digby had feared that Essex was about to reinforce Waller to press Charles hard in the Severn valley.[73] Instead the Earl was away in the west and the King had the initiative. Did the Lyme episode lead to an unexpected reprieve for Oxford that kept the King's headquarters safe into 1646?

The confrontation of King vs Waller in the East Midlands, June – July 1644

Around 9,500 royalists (with more than the usual proportion of cavalry) followed Charles's sudden sortie from Woodstock across to Buckingham (22 June) to threaten London, with Waller away to his west returning from a sortie to Gloucester. Waller was at Stow-on-the-Wold on the 24th–25th, several days behind the King at best, and the Parliamentarians were now on the defensive as they lacked a major army to defend the capital (the Eastern Association army was still in Yorkshire assisting the Scots at York). Taking an under-defended London in June/July was not so easy or so final a move as it had been in November 1642 for the King, as Essex and Manchester were at large with experienced and undefeated armies and the Scots would march south with the latter if he was recalled. But if Charles had judged the attack on London too risky for fear of Waller taking him in the rear, he could still have raided the East Midlands and East Anglia and done immense damage – or marched north to aid Rupert and forced Waller to follow him. (Rupert was now on his march to York, via Cheshire and Lancashire.)

But Charles' delay while he sent messages back to Oxford to consult his advisers lost him the advantage of surprise. The Trained Bands were mustered to defend London, and General Browne (veteran of Cheriton) was ordered to march out and link up with Waller. This gave Waller equal numbers with Charles,[74] though Browne's men had less experience of battle. In fact Browne was short of men and had to wait while he recruited more,[75] and sending Manchester's troops south would have been wiser. Waller's army, at Stow-on-the-Wold on 24 June and at Shipston-on-Stour on the night of the 25th–26th, was able to catch Charles up with their London reinforcements arriving too. On the 26th further Parliamentarian troops from garrisons at Warwick and Coventry joined Waller, now around Shipston-on-Stour, and on the 27th Waller advanced to within five miles of the royal army near Edgecott. A confrontation across the River Cherwell near Banbury followed, with the Parliamentarians keen for battle. Waller had probably 1,000 more infantry and Charles probably 1,500 more cavalry, giving each a chance of victory if a battle enabled them to fight on their terms. Waller's London troops, crucially, were inexperienced in battle. They marched parallel to each other along the river-bank, and on 29 June Waller took advantage to cross eastwards at Cropredy Bridge when he noticed a gap opening between the royalist vanguard and the main body of troops to the rear (around 1,500 cavalry and 1,000 foot) as the vanguard hurried ahead with the King to attack an isolated Parliamentarian position.

Waller threw his troops into the gap of about a mile between the two royalist divisions, and calculated that he could annihilate the enemy rearguard (around 1,500 cavalry and 1,000 infantry with the artillery train) before the rest returned to the rescue. Lieutenant-General John Middleton and Captain Butler led Haselrig's and Vandruske's regiments across the bridge while Waller himself took more cavalry over a ford, and Quartermaster-General Baines brought the infantry over the bridge behind the cavalry. The gamble failed; Middleton's cavalry broke through a body of royalist horse (under Lord Wilmot) sent back to assist the rearguard, but these then managed to make a stand at Hay's Bridge and those Parliamentarians who assaulted the royalist rearguard were repulsed by the five regiments in the Earl of Cleveland's brigade. Lacking adequate musketeer support, which was still on the west side of the Cherwell and rattled by the strength of resistance, the 1,200 or so Parliamentarians on the east bank were subjected to repeated charges and steady shooting and panic spread. Guns taken onto the east bank were overrun, but the Tower Hamlets and Kent regiments held the bridge for the Parliamentarians and Waller was able to hold out with the rest on the eastern bank in a strong position on Bourton hill. The battle petered out, and the King did not pursue his advantage and moved off next day. Waller recalled that he received a 'private' message from the King under flag of truce during the battle, which he sternly told the messenger to deliver to Parliament, and another invitation to defect from a former, now royalist lady-friend. His losses were not that great in numbers; the most damaging losses were the overrun artillery (eight pieces according to him, eleven according to royalist sources) plus their captured, Scots commander Colonel Wemyss.[76]

The campaign ended with more complex and wearying counter-marching across the south Midlands, with neither side having a decisive advantage. Charles was halted on an intended march north to join Rupert by the news of Marston Moor, while Waller reached Northampton (3 July) and halted too to collect reinforcements. His London troops under Major-General Browne were badly behaved and attacked their commander, having to be sent off to the discipline of a siege, and when reinforcements from London turned up at Northampton some of the existing London regiments declared that their term of service had expired and left the army.[77] Given this behaviour, even Waller could not have achieved much had he succeeded in breaking up the royal army at Cropredy Bridge. The blame for the even nature of the two opposing armies – and thus the stalemate – lay with Essex, who had thrown away the chance to pursue the retreating King after he left Oxford for Bewdley and was not present thereafter to assist his colleague in outmanoeuvring the royal army. Between them the two commanders, working together in pursuit of the King across the south Midlands, should have been able to shepherd him into a trap and force a battle – assuming that their personal relations had held up, which was dubious. It was lack of numbers that most hindered Waller at the decisive moment at Cropredy Bridge, but if the Earl been marching his army in parallel to Waller's to 'shadow' the King he might not have come up to assist his colleague in time. Essex lacked Waller's strategic abilities – above all the capacity to think quickly – and was shortly to be outmanoeuvred in an avoidable disaster in Cornwall. But if he had been willing to return quickly to the south Midlands once Lyme was relieved he would have been able to pin the King down between himself and Waller, and been available for any joint action with the victors of Marston Moor during later July or August. It should, however, be added that the King's army in this campaign appears to have had more professional soldiers, enlisted for the 'long term' and used to fighting together as a unit, than the Parliamentarian armies (the diverse forces of different county Associations and from London). The likelihood is against Essex and the superior in ability but socially inferior Waller being able to co-ordinate a battle-strategy adequately, or their men carrying it out.

Marston Moor: the decisive blow in the north. Rupert's fault?
The initiative in the campaign of early summer 1644 in the south Midlands had lain with the Parliamentary armies, until Essex marched away to Devon and left the King free to take on Waller on equal terms. The campaign of June 1644 saw Charles secure a modest victory at Cropredy Bridge out of an initially perilous position, which could have left him either captive or without an army. Rupert could have defeated the Scots, Eastern Association and Fairfaxes in Yorkshire and returned south to find Oxford lost. Even if Charles had managed to march on London from Buckingham at the end of June and defeated General Browne's Trained Bands he still had the

earthwork defences of London to storm and Waller, the victor of Cheriton, undefeated in his rear – which should have emboldened the government in Westminster to hold out. But now Rupert's campaign in the north to relieve York led to the largest royalist defeat yet, and the loss of all England north of the Humber except a few outposts. Having left Shrewsbury on 16 May, he headed into Lancashire to relieve the Earl of Derby's besieged family mansion, Lathom House, by destroying its besiegers at Bolton on the 28th.[78] The town, known as 'the Geneva of the north' from its proportion of earnest 'Puritans', unfortunately lacked walls and was stormed. Rallying the Lancashire Catholics and joined by Lord Goring with 5,000 more cavalry and 800 infantry, Prince Rupert took control of Liverpool after a five-day siege and then crossed the Pennines into Yorkshire at the end of June.[79] He could still have been too late to save York, as on 13 June Newcastle had been driven to treat for an honourable surrender, which would allow his army to leave with their baggage and enable Anglican services to continue at the Minster. This was refused, but his messengers sent to Rupert to warn that he could only hold out for six more days were captured.[80] The best chance for the emboldened besiegers to take the city by storm was on the 17th when a mine under the walls was set off, but owing to feuding among their commanders the engineer in charge, Manchester's deputy General Crawford, only informed his superior of the intention to set off the explosives – not Fairfax or the Scots commander Lord Leven.[81] Manchester's men stormed the breach alone and were repulsed, and the city was still holding out when Rupert arrived in the neighbourhood. As he advanced the siege was abandoned on 1 July, and the Parliamentarian generals moved off west onto Marston Moor to block the route to Rupert's last reported position at Knaresborough. Instead he marched round to their north to cross the Ure at Boroughbridge, putting that river between him and the enemy, and moved down to York from the north-west.[82] He had somewhere over 7,000 cavalry and 6,000 foot, i.e. the numbers estimated in a letter from the governor of Liverpool to Ormonde before the march plus some reinforcements from Lancashire royalists. The enemy had around 15,000 Scots plus around 4,000 men in Manchester's army.

Rupert was now encamped outside the north gate of York, but a battle was not certain. The question arises if it was his impetuosity that led to a battle that his foes did not want or expect. It would appear that he was encouraged (if not obliged) to fight by a letter from the King (dated 14 June), which spoke of Rupert helping him to hold out if he both relieved York and defeated the enemy. Colepeper certainly thought that this was enough to give Rupert the excuse to interpret it as an order to fight.[83] Next morning (2 July) the Parliamentarian army started to retreat south towards Tadcaster. Their intention to avoid battle was evident, despite still possessing the advantage of numbers. But when Rupert's cavalry started to move out onto the Moor to confront those Parliamentary troops still remaining there, the commanders (including Cromwell) concluded that the Prince intended battle and sent urgently to their colleagues to return. Newcastle, summoned out onto the Moor with his men to join Rupert by a message sent to him via Goring at 4 a.m., was late and according to his wife was dismayed at Rupert not accepting his invitation to join him in York and annoyed to be told what to do by Goring.[84]

When Newcastle arrived at the camp he found Rupert intending to fight and argued in vain against it on the grounds that the enemy commanders were on bad terms with one another so their army could be expected to break up soon. More royalist troops were on the way to York to make numbers more even. He was supported by Gethin, who had had experience of Rupert's rashness in cavalry charges in Germany in the late 1630s and had failed to rescue him from capture then – which could not have improved their personal relationship. In reply, Rupert insisted that the letter the King had sent him on 14 June gave him a positive order to fight, which he was going to obey, and Newcastle gave way to his social superior. In fact, the rambling terminology of the King's letter was more ambiguous, though it did refer at one point to relieving York and (or by?) beating the Scots.

Rupert had not been beaten in the field, though he had failed to act in co-ordination with the royalist infantry at Edgehill, and had more evident ability and a better record than at least one of the three commanders facing him (Manchester). Fairfax had won a number of minor victories in the north-east but not commanded in a major battle, and Leven was a veteran of European wars with plenty of experience but had not fought in England before. The trio had never had to co-ordinate a battle before, and to add to tensions during the siege of York Sir Henry Vane had recently arrived from London with a troubling political suggestion that the only way to secure a permanent settlement with a trustable partner was to depose the unreliable King.[85] It is possible that Vane's proposed candidate for the throne was, ironically, Rupert's brother the Elector Palatine, who was to arrive in London in August – Vane's brother and brother-in-law were in the Elector's mother Elizabeth's household in Holland. The only enemy commander who Rupert seems to have been wary of was Cromwell, about whose presence on the battlefield he enquired. Cromwell's reputation was for a mixture of discipline and flexibility, a combination that the royalists lacked, but he was not in a position to control the Parliamentarian strategy. A victory at York should break up the new Anglo-Scottish army into its component parts, and enable a subsequent invasion of the East Midlands in co-ordination with the King from Oxford – with the Scots unable to interfere.

Battle was therefore a worthwhile risk, provided that it could be co-ordinated properly. The danger was in the unequal numbers – the royalists had around 17,500 troops and the Parliamentarians and Scots around 24,000. As the armies formed up, Leven's Scots were in the Parliamentarian centre facing Newcastle's military lieutenant Lord Eythin; Fairfax and his father were on the right facing Goring's royalist cavalry; and Manchester's troops (including the cavalry under Cromwell) were on the left facing the other royalist cavalry regiments. Rupert may have intended to take command there, or else to lead as commander-in-chief in the centre. The actual outbreak of fighting, late in the afternoon of the 2nd, appears to have been unexpected to both sides. Already that day the royalists had had to deal with the problem of a mutiny by angry troops from the York garrison, disappointed of a supposed promise by Eythin that they would be paid before fighting, which Eythin later denied. They started looting the abandoned Scots siege-camp, and Newcastle had to round them up before hurrying out with his entourage to the Prince's lines – to be told off by him for arriving late. It was now around 9 a.m. Rupert had drawn up his front ranks close to the enemy, only separated from the Scots rearguard (under David Leslie) by a shallow ditch, as was criticized by Gethin when the latter joined him. This put them at risk of a sudden charge, although luckily Leslie sent messengers to Leven for urgent reinforcement rather than seizing the opportunity to attack. He was probably unsure how many men he faced.

Logically an experienced commander like the Prince would not have wanted to hold this dangerous position for long – certainly not overnight. He was therefore expecting to fight quickly when he drew up the initial positions, and the delay was due to Eythin's slowness to arrive with the main body of around 4,000 infantry. When Eythin arrived hours later he reportedly said of Rupert's carefully mapped plan of attack 'it is very fine in the paper but there is no such thing in the field'. The Prince offered to make changes to be told that it would take too long and was advised to wait and fight next day. He clashed with Eythin over his disastrous impulsiveness in Germany in 1638, and Newcastle withdrew to his carriage to rest (reportedly at Rupert's suggestion). Thus neither Rupert nor Newcastle was expecting the battle to begin when it did, well after 4 p.m.; Newcastle had lit his pipe and was smoking back in his carriage and Rupert had given his men permission to break ranks and had ridden to the rear when the Parliamentarians, led by Cromwell's Eastern Association cavalry, took advantage of the situation and charged across the ditch into his front ranks. An inopportune shower of rain showed up the problems of seventeenth century muskets, as it wet the matches that the royalist musketeers were holding ready to light their guns and held up their shooting into the advancing enemy lines. In addition, the action of Lord Byron in charging his cavalry out ahead of the infantry to tackle Cromwell meant that the royalist cavalry impeded the musketeers' line of fire for a crucial few minutes.

Cromwell's initial assault was repulsed and was not decisive, but it would have been avoided had Rupert – clearly careless, as at Edgehill – withdrawn his men to a better defensive position as soon as he decided to postpone an imminent clash. The armies' avoidance of a clash that day would have led to the Parliamentarians continuing to withdraw to Tadcaster, and a battle would have been unlikely until the royalists' reinforcements had arrived. The Parliamentarian attack crashed into the royalist infantry, but the latter held and were supported by a cavalry charge by Sir William Blakiston's brigade. Goring and Sir Charles Lucas held their royalists against the first cavalry charge by Sir Thomas Fairfax and then counter-attacked, supported by Rupert. According to an account of the battle in Sir Symonds D'Ewes' diary, the Eastern Association cavalry were at first repulsed in some disorder as Rupert's cavalry met them head-on and needed reinforcement. General Leslie's Scots cavalry came to the rescue, and Rupert was pushed back. In the Parliamentarian centre, Major-General Crawford pushed the royalists back from the ditch and then charged into the gap between the latter and Rupert's cavalry, taking the royalist centre on the right flank and driving them backwards; Baillie's Scots infantry was thus able to cross the ditch in force. But on the Parliamentarian right, the geography of the battlefield – thick furze hampering a charge, and a ditch and hedge protecting the defence of the one lane that could be used to attack – enabled royalist musketeers to hold up the advance of Fairfax's father's Yorkshiremen. His son's cavalry charge was repulsed by Goring's cavalry, and the retreating horsemen trampled the Yorkshiremen underfoot as they recoiled into the Parliamentarian ranks. Goring then exploited this reverse to push the disordered Fairfax troops back, though one Scots cavalry regiment with the latter stood firm.

As with the similar victory by the royalist cavalry at Edgehill, the flight of one wing of the enemy was followed by the royalists chasing them off the battlefield and then plundering the baggage-train rather than wheeling inwards to turn on the exposed Parliamentarian centre. Even without the help of Goring's cavalry, the exposed Scots infantry were hard-pressed and many fled the field – including eventually Leslie, their general, who would hardly have left had he considered the battle winnable. His deputy Baillie stood firm with three regiments, but it would have been hopeless had Fairfax not managed to fight his way over to Cromwell to reveal his wing's situation and Cromwell's disciplined troopers then moved back to take on Goring's cavalry. The latter belatedly returned from plundering the baggage to add to the assault on the Parliamentarian centre, but were caught and routed by Cromwell's cavalry. Had they arrived before Fairfax had fetched the Eastern Association troops, the crumbling Scots would probably have been overwhelmed and Cromwell's intervention would have come too late to save the battle from being at best a messy draw.

The destruction of the Scots army would have enabled Rupert and Newcastle to reconquer the north of England unopposed – and have produced equally beneficial results for Montrose in Scotland, as it was Leslie's well-organized infantry who finally halted his career of unbroken victories at Philiphaugh in 1645. The Eastern Association army would have been forced back to defend the East Midlands and East Anglia, and a combination of a more decisive result in Charles' favour over Waller at Cropredy Bridge and the (real-life) defeat of Essex in Cornwall would have left the Association's army to face the royalists alone that autumn. In this sense, even an indecisive result at Marston Moor could have doomed the Parliamentarians in the long term unless the Eastern Association had managed to hold the King's and Rupert's armies long enough for the creation of a more professional army in the Parliamentarian-governed counties.

Once Cromwell's cavalry had defeated Goring's, the moment of most danger passed for the Parliamentarians. The Scots rallied, and one force under David Leslie destroyed Newcastle's own regiment, the Yorkshire 'Whitecoats', while Baillie moved forward with Crawford's troops to push back the remainder of the royalist infantry. Rupert's cavalry on the royalist right, who had proved unable to secure their usual success against a more than usually coherent body of enemy cavalry, were overwhelmed by weight of numbers and forced into retreat. The Prince was separated from most of his men in the enemy onrush and took refuge in a beanfield – and was duly mocked for hiding among the tall crops by Parliamentary versifiers. The battle finally ended as darkness fell, though in such confusion that – in similar circumstances to the chaos at Barnet in March 1471 – false reports initially reached Oxford that the defeated side had in fact won.[86] (The rout of one wing of the victors' army was wrongly taken as decisive.)

Parliamentary failure to follow up Marston Moor. Was the military stalemate inevitable given the nature of the armies and their command?

Rupert, as commander of what royalists remained, had around 6,000 cavalry left intact after the battle, which saw around 4,000 royalists killed and 1,500 taken prisoner. This was inadequate to meet the victors with any hope of stemming their advance, and defence of the north was abandoned. While Rupert rode back into Lancashire, Newcastle gave up the conflict and fled to the Continent;[87] York surrendered on 16 July. Only a few isolated towns in Yorkshire, among them Scarborough, now held out for the King and the demoralized royalist survivors in the north-west (Rupert's men and around 3,000 under Clavering in Cumberland) could be handled by a fraction of the victorious army. Rupert had to retreat to Lathom House, where he found that Lord Derby had gone off to the Isle of Man; on 25 July he arrived at Chester. Yet the victors failed to march south and take on the King's intact army around Oxford at a time when they had the advantage of momentum and confidence, let alone to attempt to have Essex recalled urgently from Cornwall to join a joint advance on the enemy capital. With Warwick's fleet controlling the Channel, a message could have been sent from Parliament to Plymouth giving Essex orders with every hope of reaching him in a few days if the wind held – though not that he would obey it. Now that Parliament's troops had broken Rupert's army and had the Scots as reinforcements it would have been logical to resume the plan of late spring to move in on Oxford.

However, local priorities were put first at the final council-of-war held by the three commanders on 30 July. Leven and the Scots were to reduce the town of Newcastle, which was holding out to their rear (and was thus holding up their ability to operate far from home as Plymouth had held up the Cornish royalists in 1643). The Fairfaxes were to reduce Scarborough and the other royalist towns, thus completing their control of Yorkshire; and the Eastern Association army under Manchester was to return to their home territory to complete the task of reducing isolated local royalist garrisons. Undoubtedly their soldiers, raised by local gentry (by county committees in the Association territory) for defence of their region, preferred to fight closer to home while there were still local enemy forces at large; the expedition to York had been a 'one-off'. Among their commanders, Manchester made it clear that local matters were his priority – though he also believed in the ultimate desirability of a negotiated settlement and thus had reasons not to press for a decisive victory, as the impatient Cromwell was to protest. It is also possible that the unwillingness to move fast or to fight that came to infect Manchester's weakening army later that summer would have occurred even had they been more decisively on the offensive, and that their usefulness would have been limited. But it was symptomatic that Manchester, lingering for a month at Lincoln, expended more energy on denouncing his insubordinate junior officer John Lilburne (the democratic controversialist) as a 'base fellow', following his capture of Tickhill Castle,[88] than on preparing to attack the main local target, Newark. Lilburne was a strong Independent, and as such was anathema to the Presbyterian Earl. Manchester also secured Newcastle's family home, Welbeck Abbey (7 August).[89]

The priority shown by the council-of-war on 30 July was evidence that the Parliamentarian generals were not yet as single-minded about a winning strategy as in a similar situation after victory at Naseby in 1645. Then the New Model command – under one of the three commanders at Marston Moor, the younger Fairfax – was to press on with using their troops as a single force to systematically mop up resistance in the royalist heartlands, isolating and then closing in on Oxford. There was a difference in 1645 in that the King then did not have an unbeaten army in the field in the south, as he did after Marston Moor. (He had in fact defeated Waller at Cropredy Bridge a few days before.) But the latter could have been taken on next, leaving a portion of the Scots army to hold Rupert and Clavering in check, if the Parliamentarian leadership had been determined to finish the war quickly. Even if there had been resistance from the lower ranks, which was too powerful to ignore, the option could have been considered before being rejected. The Scots and the Yorkshiremen might well have resisted marching on towards Oxford to link up with Waller, but Manchester's Eastern troops would not be so far from their homes if they did so. But the chance was missed, and the King in Oxfordshire was allowed time to make the most of the respite and head off south-west into Devon to catch Essex. It was as if there was no adequate concept of overall strategy in the war, something enhanced by the presence of a trio of equally-ranking Parliamentary commanders rather than the single commander (Fairfax) who the London leadership belatedly decided to put in command that winter.

The failure to follow up Marston Moor increased tension between more determined and 'professional' officers such as Cromwell and their commanders, with the difference in social rank and religious aims between Cromwell and Manchester adding to the clash. The Earl's dilatoriness on campaign that summer and autumn added to the frustrations; he flatly refused to march hundreds of miles away from the Association's designated territory to rescue the trapped Earl of Essex.[90] The Committee of Both Kingdoms, who he asked for men, sent him 1,800 recruits originally intended for Essex's new (southern England) army. His excuse was his desperate shortage of men, which was genuine – but if he did leave his 'home area' there was no local royalist army in a position to attack it. Ultimately, it was to lead to the major political crisis in London that autumn over the aims and means of waging the war, the 'Self-Denying Ordinance', and the creation of a unified, professional, and more religiously coherent Parliamentary army. That in turn resulted in the new force, officers and men alike, having a greater sense of cohesion and purpose in religious and political matters – and thus the clash with the Presbyterian leadership of the Commons in 1647–8. The New Model was to overturn the Presbyterians' attempts at enforcing a settlement on King and country and physically occupy London in two political crises, leading to the purge of anti-Army MPs by Colonel Pride in December 1648 and the reduction of the legislature to a 'Rump' subject to the Army veto. This outcome would have been inconceivable from the divided Parliamentarian armies of 1644, a group of local forces raised in separate areas of the country for local campaigns and without a coherent and unified leadership. If the victors of Marston Moor had been able to bring most of their force to bear in the south Midlands later in July 1644 to link up with Waller, the outnumbered Charles would not have been able to bring his forces into action against Essex and drive the latter into a trap which broke up his army.

The 'caveat' to this possibility is the poor state of Waller's army after Cropredy Bridge. His forces, made up of local levies from the Parliamentarian-controlled south-east and including Londoners from the Trained Bands, were uneasy and mutinous at campaigning so far from home for so long. His letters make it clear that he had great difficulty with discipline and rising desertions during July,[91] a problem shared with General Browne's force (put together to defend London as Charles advanced to Buckingham in late June) nearby. Waller had around 2,500 cavalry and 1,500 infantry at the end of June, many of them Londoners anxious to go home – not much of an ally to assist Manchester's army and detachments of the Scots in taking on the King. Indeed, it was Waller who first suggested the idea of a permanent, professional Army in a letter to the 'Committee of Both Kingdoms' on 2 July:

> an army compounded of these men (the locally-raised troops) will never go through with your service, and until you have an army merely your own, that you may command, it is in a manner impossible to do anything of importance.[92]

The troops, as well as their commanders, were thus inadequate to the task of a prolonged and coherent campaign in summer 1644. Nor could the

Committee in London deliver leadership by letter and order Essex and the other commanders under its orders (i.e. excluding Leven's Scots) to combine to close in on the King. Essex had already defied them over the western campaign. That does not rule out the possibility that a major victory by one side in the south would have led to the break-up of the opposition armies as their soldiers judged the cause of fighting on to be hopeless. Bringing all the possible Parliamentarian troops to bear towards Oxford in the aftermath of Marston Moor would at least have halted Charles' march towards Essex's army (decided at a council-of-war at Evesham on 7 July, i.e. before he knew for certain what the victors of Marston Moor intended).

On 26 July Charles was in Exeter, linking up with Prince Maurice who had had to abandon the siege of Lyme but still had over 4,000 troops in the field. Essex, currently at Tavistock, knew that he was short of men and supplies as his message sent to Parliament (via Philip Stapleton) makes clear.[93] He had no real possibility of major reinforcements in marching into pro-royalist Cornwall as seen by the local enthusiasm for the King's cause in 1643, yet he chose to cross the Tamar westwards on the 27th and ended up trapped by the advancing King. His demands for Parliament to send aid could not be met, the new army that was due to have started mustering in London on 20 July being non-existent and Browne's (at Abingdon) being in little better condition than Waller's, and Waller was slowly putting together a new army at Farnham. The latter was not likely to move on time in the third week of August; about a third of his existing force was sick, the Kent recruits dallied at home through August (leaving Sevenoaks on 2 September) while Colonel Richard Norton had drawn off the Hampshire troops to attack Basing House. Waller's under-strength army did not reach Salisbury until the second week of September.[94]

In the far west, Essex faced a combination of the King's main army and local generals like Richard Grenville with expertise of the terrain. The march into southern Devon had had a strategic logic and had drawn the King away from the south Midlands, and even now the Queen had escaped encirclement in Exeter and capture Essex could keep the King tied down for weeks more. Arguably Essex was over-confident of Parliament sending him reinforcement in time to meet the King on equal terms and did not calculate his advancing foe's strength or resolution adequately – the mistake that Charles was to make in May–June 1645 when he stayed inactive in the face of the advancing New Model in Leicestershire, waiting for Goring's arrival. On 1 August Charles crossed the Tamar, destroying the bridges so if Essex did escape he would have had to ford it and probably to abandon his wagons and artillery.

Having the main road east blocked by the King's advance to Liskeard (2 August) and being unwilling to risk a forced march north in unfamiliar country round the north-west of Dartmoor, he had to retire on the Fowey peninsula. Based at Lostwithiel from 3 August, he optimistically asked Parliament to send Waller to fall on the King's rear.[95] There was a strategic logic to his move, though it left him trapped. Critics of Essex's 'incompetence' in being surrounded in Cornwall ignore the reality of the danger in marching away quickly inland to safety north of Dartmoor – it exposed the infantry to harassment from enemy cavalry. At Fowey, he was within reach of Warwick's fleet offshore who could evacuate at least part of his army in an emergency; and he was probably still expecting the delayed Parliamentary reinforcements to arrive. But he was over-optimistic about the latter. The King sent him a request for talks for a compromise peace that might save England from the Scots, possibly hoping that he could be tempted into deserting his cause now that his army was trapped (and encouraged by rumours of the dissensions between the 'war party' and 'peace party' in London?). Essex prudently replied that all such requests had to be addressed to his employers, Parliament.[96] Meanwhile there were equal problems over strategy and personal feuds in the royalist camp, with ambitious officers resenting Charles' elderly if experienced Scots commander-in-chief Lord Brentford and angling for his job. The dashing but brutal cavalry commander Lord Wilmot was thought to be less than totally loyal to Charles, who he was supposed to have hinted might be worth deposing to arrange a compromise peace with Parliament and a fresh start under an untainted new king (Prince Charles, aged 14). It was suggested that Wilmot, whose new bride had Parliamentary kinsfolk, sent Essex a private note to accompany Charles' letter, asking him to come to the King's camp so they could combine and arrest Charles' 'hard-line' adviser Lord Digby.[97]

The current arrival in London on 18 August of Rupert's elder brother, Charles Louis the Elector Palatine, from the Continent indeed opened up the possibility that the King's eldest nephew could be offering himself as an alternative king for a compromise peace-settlement. The Prince's friendly relations with the Essex-Warwick 'opposition' peers had been noted by the King in 1641–2 – and may well have led Charles to insist that his devious nephew accompany him on the attempt to arrest the 'Five Members'. The effect of the Elector's arrival in the 'enemy camp' may have been adverse to Rupert too, and current gossip that the King would make him commander-in-chief did not lead to anything. Was Charles persuaded not to do this in case Rupert linked up with his brother in London to coerce him into an unwanted peace? Was Wilmot suspected of links to the Elector? At all events, Rupert was too busy raising troops in the North Wales Marches to hasten to

Cornwall and reassure the King. When an alternative and experienced new candidate to lead the cavalry, Goring, arrived at the royal headquarters at Liskeard from Yorkshire on 7 August the King gave him Wilmot's post; Wilmot was arrested and forced to leave the country. Even if Wilmot had been untrustworthy Goring, a rash strategist and a drunkard, was no better – and was resented by Wilmot's officers. Charles' other appointment, of Hopton to take over the ordnance from Lord Percy (brother of the Earl of Northumberland), was more effective. Possibly Percy, a friend of Rupert's and centre of the 1641 'Army Plot' intrigues, was also suspected of disloyalty to the King. Did Charles face a real danger of a coup by Wilmot and Percy?

The royal army now closed in on Fowey, overrunning the 'strongpoint' mansions of Boconnoc (4 August) and Lanhydrock (12 August). Essex's defence was noticeably poor in strategy – particularly in allowing the royalists to seize the east bank of the River Fowey with Polruan to make the harbour of Fowey unusable. This, added to offshore winds that prevented Warwick's ships from docking, reduced the number of troops he could evacuate and on 26 August his main cavalry grazing fields at St Blazey to the west were overrun by Sir Richard Grenville. His cavalry (around 2,000 men under Sir William Balfour) escaped by road early in the morning of 31 August, but when he fled by boat from Fowey on 1 September he had to leave his infantry under Philip Skippon to surrender. Skippon urged his officers to fight on, but was overruled. Luckily the terms offered saw them only temporarily removed from the war as the royalists had no capacity to hold several thousand prisoners. They were disarmed of their heavy artillery and allowed to march away into Devon.[98]

The royalist victory in the south-west seemed to make up for their loss of all the north, at least so long as the Scots were preoccupied, and the military stalemate continued into1645. The upshot was the creation of the New Model and the emergence of a force able to challenge whatever peace-terms the Commons sought to impose on the defeated King after 1646.

The second battle of Newbury: a missed chance for a reinvigorated King?

The King's success in Cornwall left Essex at large and with the potential to restore most of his army, but added to Parliamentary despondency without leading to any noticeable determination to negotiate. The psychological and military advantages lay with Charles, who informed the French envoy Sabran during his advance eastwards that he did not need men or munitions but money.[99] The Parliamentary forces remained divided, quite apart from the problem of having local levies raised by county or Association area who were reluctant to move far beyond their region; the Earl of Manchester's troops refused to leave the east of England to march on Cheshire in the late summer to deal with the threat posed by Rupert's rebuilding his army there. The small army of Waller stood in Charles' way (Blandford Forum, 14 September), aided by Haselrig and by Middleton's cavalry, as did Essex's escaped cavalry from Cornwall – which had regrouped at Dorchester but was unlikely to accept anyone's orders but Essex's.[100] Essex himself sailed from Fowey to Plymouth and then sailed on to Portsmouth, and was thus out of the action for the moment as Waller stood in Charles' way at Shaftesbury. The Parliamentarians fell back before Charles' advance as he entered Sherborne on 8 October, to obey orders from London to wait until Essex and Manchester could join them and create a larger joint army to challenge the King.[101] The Earl of Manchester with the Eastern Association army – inactive at Reading for crucial weeks in September – was now belatedly marching to Waller's rescue and reached Basingstoke on 17 October. He had been trying to avoid having to move, complaining that his men did not want to abandon their own homes to a risk of royalist attack in order to help the south-west.[102] He finally moved forward to Basingstoke, arriving on 17 October. Nor was Essex any help, as he was insisting that Waller and Manchester must be told to accept his orders before he would help them.[103] Luckily Rupert was still held up in the north-west, where the careless Lord Herbert of Cherbury (having refused a royalist garrison offered by the Prince) had to admit a Parliamentary force to Montgomery Castle on 7 September and Rupert made a vain attempt to retake it. The strategic loss and disruption to the route that Irish reinforcements used to reach the King was reckoned as bad as the fall of York by Rupert. The presence of a large and rapacious royalist force in the district was disrupting the wool-trade and annoying the local Welsh farmers and drovers, with possible long-term threats to recruitment – as Archbishop John Williams vainly warned Rupert.[104] But the Prince was also under threat of internal royalist intrigues at this point, as the arrival of his elder brother Elector Charles Louis in London raised the possibility that his foes could tell the King that both brothers wanted to secure peace with Parliament (or the King's crown for Charles Louis?). Sir Henry Vane, after all, had already raised the idea of securing peace by acquiring a new and more trustworthy King.

There was a possibility that Charles might catch and destroy Waller's force before the latter met up with his colleague Manchester, which would have given the King the chance of beating the two armies one by one by force of numbers and then relieving the Parliamentary sieges of Donnington Castle and Basing House without hindrance. This would restore his position in the south to what it had been before Cheriton nearly seven months earlier, with the advantage that Manchester's army was now weakened by poor leadership, unwelcome absence from its home area which its general had no ability to overcome, and discontent among the officers (Cromwell and the other colonels had recently threatened to resign their commissions). The new Parliamentary allies, Leven's Scots army with their Presbyterian ministers and zeal for imposing the Covenant on England, were absent from the southern campaign and were not popular among the most effective – mostly Independent – officers in Manchester's army. This would inhibit effective co-operation in resisting the King if he secured victory in the south and it came to a decisive battle between him and the remnants of the defeated Parliamentarian forces plus the Scots.

But Waller had the strategic ability to evade Charles, and retired successfully through north Hampshire ahead of him to meet Manchester and restore the Parliamentarians' safety in numbers. He had a narrow escape from Charles' vanguard at Andover on the 18th, largely due to carelessness by Prince Maurice in the attack.[105] Next day he joined up with the advancing Manchester, now reinforced by four of the five City regiments, and on the 21st Essex with his surviving forces joined them near Basing House. The Parliamentary army now had around 19,000 men to the King's 10,000 or so; their main weakness lay in the divided command, which Parliament had made worse by creating a joint command for the triple army of a 'Council of War', including the three generals, their senior officers, and two civilian MPs from the 'Committee of Both Kingdoms'. The latter, like French Revolutionary government delegates or Soviet commissars, were entitled to interfere in the military process to the generals' irritation; no decision of the Council on action was to be valid without their agreement. The King now moved off to Newbury (22 October) rather than fight the triple army in relieving Basing House, and intended to remain on the defensive and wear his opponents down. But, inspired by news of the fall of Newcastle to the Scots, the Parliamentarians decided to fight and on the 26th caught up with the royalist army, which had set up a strong defensive position north of the Kennet, in front of Donnington Castle. Due to illness, Essex was absent from the battle.[106]

The royalist position was difficult to attack either directly, which the Parliamentarian generals judged impossible, or from the east due to the River Lambourn (running from north-west to south-east) protecting it. The attackers decided to send a part of their army under Balfour and Skippon round the royalist lines to the east and rear, avoiding Donnington Castle, to fall on the western end of the enemy line (Speen village, held by Prince Maurice) from the north and uphill. This force had the best Parliamentary strategists and most versatile commanders in action, Waller and Cromwell, assisting the two generals. In the meantime Manchester would launch a diversionary attack from the front on Shaw House. The plan was pursued on the 27th, though Manchester's men pressed too far forward and were nearly trapped; the royalists had anticipated it and from Digby's letter (written on the battlefield after Manchester's men retreated) it is apparent that he expected the attack on Speen and that it would be held.

If the attackers decided against a direct assault and resorted to blockading the King, who would be cut off from his northern route to his base in Oxford, they had fewer provisions and would be exposed to the elements in open country in October. Digby then expected the King to be able to break out, link up with Rupert who was raising more men in Bristol, and advance into the Eastern Association counties. Accordingly Prince Maurice prepared strong defensive earthworks on the hill on the outskirts of Speen, and early on the afternoon of the 27th Balfour and Skippon arrived as expected on Wickham Heath to his rear. The royalist position was covered by a strip of open ground commanded by Maurice's guns, with hedges breaking up the countryside to the sides, which thus hindered a Parliamentarian cavalry charge. The attackers, however, pressed on and stormed both Speen Hill, retaking the guns lost by Essex's men in Cornwall a few weeks earlier, and the village behind. But Manchester delayed to advance on Shaw House to divert the royalists once he heard the sound of gunfire as had been arranged, despite urgings from his senior officers led by the Scots General Crawford. The timing of the belated attack was later disputed as Cromwell made it part of his official complaints to Parliament about the Earl's incompetence and the latter's defenders disputed it, but it appears to have been about dusk (quarter to half-past four), an hour or so after the attack on Speen. Both Crawford and his colleague Scoutmaster-General Watson, though hostile to Cromwell, had to admit to a delay in the attack – and one on the Earl's orders. In the meantime the force that had taken Speen pressed on slowly across the lines of hedges towards the King's cavalry on the more open Newbury Field, but were beaten back and never launched the intended cavalry attack. Balfour reached the final hedge before the open field, but was repulsed by a royalist charge.

Cromwell's conduct was open to criticism for being more passive than usual and Waller admitted that he had not done much, but it was probably due to caution on a hard-fought field not a devious plan to embarrass Manchester; his part of the battlefield was open to gunfire from the royalists in Donnington Castle. After sunset Skippon's infantry reached the final hedge and continued the struggle into the moonlit dusk, at which time Manchester finally made his attack on Shaw House, but neither was successful. It has been suggested that if Manchester had left Shaw House alone and changed his line of attack to head straight for the King's main force he would have had time to take him in the flank while Balfour and Skippon were still on the offensive, which would have had a chance of routing the royalists. But this degree of flexibility was beyond him and 'Second Newbury' ended in a stalemate like the first encounter there a year before. Given that Parliament had had a decisive advantage in numbers and an adequate plan if carried out properly on time (or swiftly altered to divert the attack on Shaw House), the main strategic failure lay with Manchester. But the political authorities had laid their army open to this sort of muddle or hesitation by imposing an unwieldy 'Council of War' in command.[107]

The aftermath of the battle was equally marked by Parliamentarian failure to seize a strategic advantage. The King left the battlefield with the cavalry almost at once to ride to Bath and link up with Rupert and the artillery was placed in Donnington Castle, but the infantry (which left later in the night for Oxford) was still within reach of a swift pursuit and would be vulnerable to the enemy's cavalry. Manchester, advised late at night by Colonel Birch that the enemy was moving away, refused to move until daylight. Waller and Cromwell, sent in pursuit next morning with most of the Parliamentary cavalry, soon discovered the situation. The royalist infantry had reached the Thames at Wallingford and the pursuers would be at risk of ambush from the lanes and hedges if they pressed on that route so Waller and Cromwell rode back to Manchester to suggest moving their army on Woodstock. That would cut off Oxford from the King and Rupert in the Bath area, forcing the latter to attempt to relieve it – with a mostly cavalry army – and thus another battle. Alternatively, Waller proposed that they take the army after the King to force a battle in the Somerset Avon valley.

Manchester opposed it, apparently criticizing the more militant civilian Council member Haselrig for his eagerness for battle and saying that God did not favour their cause enough to give them victories, and his caution carried the resulting vote.[108] Arguably the poor morale, exhaustion, and weak leadership of the Parliamentary army would have made a long march to the Avon valley a risky strategy, and even Waller could not have inspired or forced men who did not normally fight in his army to the extra effort. The infantry could well have been at risk of royalist ambush and defeat from Rupert's fresh forces, and the cavalry would have had to bear the brunt of action. But the Parliamentary command did not even take that risk – Haselrig, usually more determined, is more likely to have weighed up the military risks than the evidently depressed Manchester. The latter's failure led to the final showdown between him and Cromwell, which was unlikely to have been avoided that winter in any case given their different approaches to making war.

The Parliamentary army moved on slowly towards Woodstock on 2 November but halted at Harwell, having covered only eleven miles in two days, and the end of the season's campaign dissolved into bickering and a retiral back on Newbury. The King returned unhindered to Oxford from the Avon valley, Rupert followed him with over 5,000 new troops, and when the royalists moved back on Newbury to relieve Donnington Castle (9 November) the Parliamentarian leadership resolved not to fight. The immediate strategy was reasonable as the King could defend his position with the nearby artillery in the Castle and there was fear that he would evade battle and slip round the enemy into Newbury, but no action was taken when he was moving away from this advantageous position back north either. At the decisive debate near Shaw House on the 10th, the usually warlike Haselrig said that their cavalry was too weak at around only 4,500 men (probably down by around 3,000 since the three armies' junction a month earlier at Basing); morale was generally low. Cromwell was for fighting anyway and spoke of the danger of a French army aiding the King in the spring, but Manchester's caution carried the day. It was at this juncture that the Earl made the famous and revealing remark that:

> If we beat the King ninety and nine times, yet he is King still, and so will his posterity be after him; but if the King beat us once, we shall all be hanged and our posterity made slaves.

As Cromwell replied, 'If this be so, why did we take up arms at first?'[109]

The Parliamentarian army moved back to Newbury and the King on to Marlborough. The former's leadership now transferred their quarrels to London, and on 23 November Waller and Cromwell were summoned before a Parliamentary committee.[110]

Montrose's gamble: an unexpected bonus for the King

The King's opponents now had to resolve their differences or face being worn down by a more unified and determined enemy, with the added problem that Montrose was having remarkable success in the Highlands. The latter had had no success in his first foray into the south-west earlier that year, and when he decided to try his luck in the Highlands and went to York it was just after Marston Moor so no troops could be spared. Lacking enough men to force his way across the Border, he had to cross it with two companions, disguised as a groom and hiding his royal standard in their luggage (August). Luckily for Montrose the Marquis of Antrim had managed to send a force of around 1,600 men under Alistair Macdonald, 'Mac Colkitto', across from Ulster during June, so he had a suitably battle-hardened and manoeuvrable force to add to his local levies. They were initially intended to operate in the lands of Lochaber, which the Macdonalds of Islay and Coll had long disputed with Argyll's Campbell clansmen; Alistair's father, 'Left-Handed Coll' Macdonald, had been the clan's leader in resistance to the Campbells in earlier decades and Alistair's men were mostly expatriate mercenaries, driven out of their ancestral lands to take service with their Macdonnell kin in Ulster. But the Macdonald army that landed in June had to move on east into the Highlands when the Campbells captured or burnt their ships.

Heading for Badenoch en route to join an anti-Covenanter revolt by the Gordons, their route was cut off by the pro-Covenanter Grants so they had to move south into Atholl. The Gordons' leader Huntly, as useless a commander as in 1639, had been pushed into seizing Aberdeen by the more active Sir George Gordon of Haddo (supposedly to co-ordinate with Montrose's arrival in Galloway in April) but had fled into the mountains as Argyll arrived. Thus the Irish levies were conveniently close to Montrose in Atholl as he arrived in the area to meet his Graham kinsmen in mid-August, and he arranged a rendezvous with them at Blair Atholl where both they and the local Stuarts and Robertsons – who were initially braced to attack these Irish intruders – accepted his leadership.[111]

With his mixed Scots-Irish force assembled and a combination of local Catholic resentment of the Covenant and Macdonald hatred of the Campbells acting in his favour, Montrose was able to launch a highly successful guerrilla war on the forces of the Edinburgh regime. His own genius for strategy would have been useless against the far more numerous and better-armed armies of the Covenant but for his having a highly mobile force of Highlanders and Ulstermen, used to long marches and quick retreats as well as being feared in battle for their ferocity in the charge by their Lowland victims. The long-standing antagonism between Highlanders and Lowlanders and the popular conception of the former as bloodthirsty 'papist' savages acted as a psychological weapon in Montrose's favour, and was magnified by his seemingly incredible successes, which masked his army's lack of numbers or heavy weapons. The 5,000 or so royalists moved down the Tay towards Perth, and made short work of around 7,000 well-armed Covenanter troops under Lord Elcho at Tippermuir outside Perth on 1 September. The Covenanters used 'Jesus and No Quarter' as their watchword, without any irony at its incongruity; for them the godly cause was equated with slaughtering Catholic Irishmen and Highlanders. The ferocity and speed of the royalist charge unnerved their largely untested Lowlander militia opponents who turned tail and fled after a brief encounter, with around 2,000 being slaughtered. But Montrose had had to string out his army on a broad front to pretend that he had more men than in reality, to restrict their shooting to one volley (which luckily did the trick), and to tell men who had no ammunition to throw stones.[112]

From then on the swift-moving royalist force proceeded to dart across the length and breadth of eastern Scotland, keeping ahead of its better-equipped but nervous pursuers. The multiple but inexperienced Covenanter forces in Scotland initially under-estimated the challenge, and were unable to catch the small army, besides lacking Montrose's genius for using the terrain when he chose or had to stand and fight an often exhausted enemy. The Covenanters were reduced to placing a price on Montrose's head 'dead or alive',[113] regarding him as having put himself beyond the normal courtesies of war by his using 'barbarian' Catholic Highlanders, and it seems that Argyll tried to have him assassinated by suborning his officers. (This is the probable explanation for a murky incident after Tippermuir involving the murder of his lieutenant Lord Kilpont, whose killer fled to Argyll.[114]) But the royalists were on more of a 'knife-edge' than their enemies, given that many of the local Highlanders – used to quick raids to steal cattle and plunder, not to a long campaign – returned home after Tippermuir and could not be ordered to obey military discipline and stay. Some Angus tenantry under pro-royalist gentry came in to replace them, but as long as Huntly and his more dynamic sons, maternal kin to Argyll, remained aloof the Gordons' manpower (the main source of warriors in Buchan) would follow suit. It did not help that Montrose had been attacking Aberdeen and coercing the Gordons on the Covenanters' behalf as recently as 1639, and Huntly's son Lord Lewis Gordon joined the Covenanter defence of Aberdeen as Montrose attacked in mid-September; a minor clan commander, Nathaniel Gordon, defied his chief and led several hundred cavalry to join Montrose.

The well-armed Covenanter army defending Aberdeen, some 2,500 men to Montrose's 1,500, was defeated outside the walls on 13 September. Its superior armaments and cavalry were not used to their best effect due to poor generalship by the inexperienced Lord Balfour of Burleigh, and a chance to overrun the royalists was missed by a cavalry brigade that had outflanked them. They stood still rather than pressing on, and Montrose had time to react. Unlike Rupert or Cromwell Montrose did not have enough cavalry to launch a disciplined and effective charge, and had to rely on the effect of a devastating infantry charge by Macdonald's Ulstermen followed by his men's superior ability in hand-to-hand combat. This could be countered by either cavalry or cannon, but the enemy command lacked the quick thinking to notice Montrose's dispositions and do that; when Sir William Forbes' Covenanter cavalry wing charged into Macdonald's massed ranks the latter dispersed to let them sweep past without effect and then took them in the rear. The royalist cavalry were interspersed with musketeers so that the latter could shoot down their opponents, thus demoralizing the larger cavalry force that faced – but did not charge – Nathaniel Gordon's small cavalry unit and softening them up ahead of an attack. Once the Covenanter cavalry had been driven back, the Macdonalds could deal with their infantry in close combat. The Covenanters were outgeneralled by ingenious tactics, and their precipitous retreat into Aberdeen was followed by the sack of the city – where the numerous atrocities committed by the excited Highlanders added to Lowland terror of Montrose. The sack was the first major massacre of the Civil War in either England or Scotland, and was hardly an act of deliberate policy as Montrose was unable to control his undisciplined levies who were not used to military discipline (though he made no effort to do so either). The defenders' shooting of a royalist drummer-boy sent with a message was the official pretext.[115]

In military terms, Tippermuir and Aberdeen were sufficient reason for Argyll and his lay and clerical allies to recall a substantial force from England (where Leven's main army was besieging the port of Newcastle). It would not have been easy for Leven or one of his more effective lieutenants to track down and catch Montrose's mobile force in the Highlands, but at least the Covenanters would have had adequate commanders and troops used to battle. That this was not done argues for a mixture of superior Lowlander and Covenanter contempt for the quality of their 'barbarian' opponents, written off as cattle-lifting clansmen, and Argyll's personal underestimation of Montrose. The Campbell chief made a personal effort with his clan troops to catch Montrose after the sack of Aberdeen, taking advantage of Alistair Macdonald's return to the west in search of reinforcements, and caught up with him at Fyvie Castle in October. But his force lacked adequate military skill (as opposed to numbers) to storm the defensive bank that protected the approach to the castle, which was surrounded on its other three sides by marshes, and Montrose and his Ulster Macdonald commander O'Cahan beat the Campbells back and then slipped away.[116] Argyll lost another chance as Montrose outmarched him in the wilderness and was then rejoined by Alistair Macdonald with a large new contingent of men from the Macdonald clans of Lochaber, keen to settle old scores with the Campbells; from now on the armies were better-matched and each successive royalist success added to Montrose's reputation.

The key to defeating the highly motivated and manoeuvrable royalist force lay in a mixture of firepower, cavalry, and generalship, and even then any Lowland army with a large artillery train or cavalry force was at a disadvantage lumbering around the Highlands after fast-moving clansmen.

Lacking a force of experienced troops to pursue him, the mission was delegated to those poor-quality local Lowland militia – and their inexperienced but politically reliable generals – who had been left in Scotland as the main army marched into England in January 1644. One by one they were to be defeated in their increasingly desperate attempts to deal with Montrose. Each royalist victory improved morale, inspired recruits to join up, and acquired extra plundered weaponry and ammunition. For the moment the campaign turned into a 'clan war' between Campbell and Macdonald, with the added usefulness for Montrose of personally humiliating his arch-enemy. In midwinter 1644–5 Argyll's own Campbell lands in Argyll were being ravaged in a swift assault that saw his family residence of Inverary sacked.[117] The threat thus arose that Leslie's army would have to return home to deal with Montrose in 1645 and Parliament would be fighting without its main ally.

Chapter Five

The New Model Army and the 1645 Campaign: Could Parliament Still have Failed to Win in 1645?

The outcome of the failures at 'Second Newbury': a more unified Parliamentary army and command for 1645. But what if Cromwell had not been excluded from the 'Self-Denying Ordinance'?

The logic of Manchester's dispirited attitude to Parliamentarians' chances in the war and its probable outcome, leaving the old constitution intact, was to be evident among the victors after 1646. Ultimately, it led to Cromwell's radical solution of the problem – to be rid of the King. But for the moment, the campaign had ended in stalemate as in 1643 and the Parliamentarian leadership was now to become engulfed in the dispute over the best means to conduct a decisive campaign in the following year. The resolution was to be made to create one army, as already suggested by Waller, and to enact the 'Self-Denying Ordinance' to remove all political personnel from the conduct of the war. Essex was to be replaced as commander-in-chief by Fairfax – in command of a more professional army, a unified body not beholden to the semi-autonomous regimental structure of 1643–4 (based on the local Associations in the counties).[1] Tate was the chairman of the Parliamentary committee who had been examining Cromwell's claims of 25 November 1644 that the Earl's incompetence had lost the chance of victory at Second Newbury. A 'Root and Branch' Presbyterian, he was hardly a 'stooge' of those Independents who Manchester claimed wanted him ruined to bring about religious anarchy led by Independents. Manchester tried to have Cromwell arrested for 'treason' to the Anglo–Scots alliance, by allegedly threatening to break the latter up via English military defiance of a 'dishonest' peace. The Lords voted to back him, but at the crucial meeting at Essex House on the evening of 3 December the Commons leadership accepted legal advice from Whitelocke and Sir John Maynard that relying on witnesses' account of Cromwell's alleged words alone was too shaky legal grounds on which to proceed.[2]

But it was only a mixture of luck, Commons support among the pro-Independent MPs, and his perseverance that enabled Cromwell, an MP, alone to evade being banned from military command by the Ordinance. Ironically, his new pre-eminence in the House – from which he had been absent on campaign for the previous two campaigning-seasons – and the level of his support was boosted by his quarrel with Manchester. The Earl's allegations that he had criticized the Scots for attempting to force an unwanted Presbyterian Church on England, and had spoken of an Independent-manned army as a weapon to resist this, made him seem prepared to stand up for religious freedom; thus the pro-Independent MPs, and all those fearing a strict Presbyterian from for the Church, found it in their interests to keep him in the Army as a valuable ally. Despite his abilities his outspoken leadership of the attack on the Earl of Manchester for incompetence and lack of zeal in the Second Newbury campaign added to his controversial reputation among the Presbyterian MPs as a major supporter of the Independent sects.

Cromwell and his cousin St John were already reckoned as being in the faction allied to Vane, which pursued outright victory rather than being willing to negotiate with the King on easy terms. Cromwell's verbal attack on Lord Willoughby (a Presbyterian ally) for insufficient military zeal the previous winter had 'marked his card' in the question of this basic division. There was also the clash that had occurred between Cromwell and another of Manchester's subordinates, the Scots Presbyterian Lieutenant-General Crawford, in March 1644 over religious liberty in the army – which would have reverberated around military circles and infuriated the Earl. Cromwell had been infuriated by Crawford, in command at Buckingham, arresting and proposing to cashier a Lieutenant William Packer, a Baptist, apparently on grounds of his religion, and then threatening similar measures against Colonel Warner; he had written an indignant letter to Crawford complaining incredulously at the idea of turning out 'godly' and militarily competent officers on account of religion and keeping on immoral blasphemers.[3] The incident referred to the criteria for belonging to the Army, but overlapped with the current debate over comprehending as many godly non-Anglican Protestants as possible in the new State Church. Cromwell dropped his efforts in the Commons to have Crawford sacked, but the matter would not be forgotten. More recently, a Commons debate on the form of ordination for the new State Church clergy on 13 September had seen alarm at the extent of Scots-style Church discipline to be imposed on congregations, which Cromwell exploited. Were all the laity to be examined for their theological 'soundness' and godly but Independent defaulters expelled? Cromwell prompted St John to propose what became known as the 'Accommodation Order', requiring that efforts be made to allow those with 'tender consciences' to remain within the Church and to create a new Church structure conformable with the 'word of God' (however that was defined). The motion was adopted without a vote, which argues for general agreement on it, with even some firm Presbyterians who disliked the Independent 'sectaries' (e.g. Sir Symonds D'Ewes) supporting it. However, the Assembly of Divines, being prodded by the Commons to hurry up with providing a new 'Directory of Worship' to replace the Anglican Prayer-Book, reminded the latter on 8 November that the new Church should be on a Presbyterian model.[4] The imposition of a Presbyterian model was also taking place at 'grass-roots' level within the Eastern Association, as shown by the current purge of all non-Presbyterian office-holders from Cambridge colleges by the University's new Chancellor – none other than Manchester. There was also the sustained campaign of iconoclasm of 'blasphemous' images in East Anglian churches (e.g. stained glass and statues) by the militant commissioner William Dowsing, 'Provost-Marshal' of the Associations – the worst such outbreak since the 1540s.

The numerically dominant part of the Commons at present favoured the retention of a disciplinarian 'established' Church, but in the Presbyterian rather than episcopal form; local bodies of 'godly' lay elders, self-appointed zealots and watchdogs of orthodoxy such as themselves, would appoint and control the clergy and crack down on heresy. The latter was particularly important to anxious MPs, with the lapse of licensing having led to an explosion of religious pamphleteering which had favoured 'Root and Branch' – the Presbyterian cause – in its initial anti-episcopal impetus in 1641–2 but now included less welcome demands for religious toleration. The new licensing ordinance of 1643 had not entirely put the genie back in the bottle. Prynne and the other Presbyterian pamphleteers, who had been the victims of Church discipline and persecution in the 1630s, now wanted to deny the freedom they had demanded to the non-Presbyterian sects who were mushrooming in Parliamentary-controlled areas (especially London). As shown by his writings of 1644, when not calling for the judicial murder of his old foe Laud – with success as the Archbishop was now put on trial – Prynne was demanding as strict a disciplinarian structure for the Presbyterian as for the Anglican Church – though controlled by 'democratic' lay leadership via the Commons, not by the clergy as in Scotland.[5] The irony was not lost on their intended victims, whose demands for religious freedom were backed up by a faction of MPs including Cromwell and Sir Henry Vane. (This was the atmosphere in which John

Milton emerged as the champion of religious toleration in his 'Areopagitica').

Manchester, Cromwell's enemy, was one of the leading Presbyterian supporters in the Lords. The dominant faction of Presbyterian MPs, led by Denzel Holles and Sir Philip Stapleton, were thus antagonistic to Cromwell on religious grounds as well as being natural allies for Manchester in his attack on him, and feared Cromwell's 'lax' attitude to controlling the radical sects. The current ecclesiastical Assembly of Divines at Westminster – with a pro-Presbyterian majority – now decided to recommend a Presbyterian form for the Church of England, with strict disciplinary control and prescription of belief, which Cromwell opposed, and in doing so were naturally backed by the Scots military leadership in England as well as the Scots divines in the Assembly. To both, carrying out a comparative 'godly' reconstruction of the English Church was the logical aim of the Anglo-Scots alliance of 1643, the religious equivalent of the defeat of the King, and completion of the holy work of Reformation begun in Scotland with the revolt of 1637. Having sought to force the Covenant on their allies in 1643, they now lent the politico-military weight given to them by their part in Marston Moor to the cause of a Presbyterian State Church. Using the Old Testament terminology within which they sought to define themselves, the original 'Covenant' of God with the 'Chosen People' of Moses in the wilderness had entailed a strict system of godly rules defining belief and conduct so it was doing God's work to see that the English Church followed the Scots example – and the Lord had punished waverers and backsliders with military defeat. On 13 January 1645 the Commons voted for the establishment of the full Presbyterian system in every parish in England.[6] But there remained a strong if minority group even in the Assembly that opposed such a disciplinarian Church, who preferred that objectors be allowed to create their own congregations outside the new Presbyterian parish-system. They were led by Jeremiah Burroughs, Philip Nye, and Thomas Goodwin, all of them former ministers to émigré English religious congregations in the Dutch United Provinces and so victims of Laudian Church discipline. To them, and to Cromwell, the Presbyterians were merely replacing one (religious) tyranny with another that was every bit as brutal – a common occurrence in revolutions.

Cromwell was clearly identified as the principal opponent of the Earl of Manchester, who needed to be silenced, and after his return to London at the end of the campaigning season he repeated his accusations in the Commons. On Monday 25 November he accused his senior commander of 'backwardness in all action, his averseness to engagement (battle) or what tends thereto, his neglecting of opportunities and declining to take or pursue advantages against the enemy'. If Manchester had joined Waller and Essex more quickly the King would have lost all the south except for Oxford, Winchester, and Wallingford. All this was a reference to the debacle at Newbury.[7] His attack on a senior pro-Presbyterian peer rallied Essex and other Lords to the latter's defence, in a far more drastic manner than the Earl's own public defence of his conduct in the Lords on 28 November.[8] On 1 December 1644 a meeting of their faction at Essex House in London considered impeaching Cromwell, but it seems that the latter's popularity in the Army and the Commons led to MPs Denzel Holles and Sir Philip Stapleton persuading the meeting against it. But Manchester persisted and duly made a list of accusations against Cromwell in the Lords on 2 December 1644. They included seeking to divide the English Parliamentarians from the Scots, an allegation that could be used to indict him for treason under the terms of the alliance as undermining the united 'war effort', and saying that he wanted an exclusively Independent-manned army, which could if necessary stand up to the Scots and resist a 'dishonest' peace if they backed one. (The allegation that Cromwell had also spoken disparagingly of the nobility and 'hoped to see never a lord in England' should have swung the Lords' opinion against him as a social leveller and threat to the established order – but was unprovable.) At best, it was a generalization of the complaints Cromwell had made over the treatment of men like Packer.

In the most politically serious charge, that relating to the Scots, the crucial question was whether Cromwell's criticism of the Scots amounted to being an 'incendiary' against the alliance, which was legally actionable – and whether the word meant the same in English legal terminology as it did in Scots. In the latter accusation, Cromwell could be alleged to be threatening a fatal breach between the two allies and among the religious 'wings' of the Parliamentary cause before the King was defeated, a spur to panic MPs into condemning him.

The Lords duly voted to endorse Manchester's complaints and send them to a mixed committee of peers and MPs, but at a crucial meeting of the 'Presbyterian' faction leadership at Essex House on the evening of 3 December the plan suffered a fatal blow. Called in to give their legal advice, Bulstrode Whitelocke and Sir John Maynard advised that the legal grounds – particularly over the definition of Cromwell's words as 'incendiary' – were not based on solid enough evidence to be sure of success in an impeachment. Most of the evidence was circumstantial and relied on the Earl's unsupported words.[9] The case was duly dropped, but it had brought Cromwell's antagonism towards a Presbyterian settlement of the religious issue to greater attention in the House and made him seem willing to use military force if necessary to stop it. As Manchester had intended, this added votes to the cause of excluding him from military command in any new army – but his sterling service to the 'cause' in the summer of 1644 meant that uncommitted MPs and peers would fear the military effect of removing him.

In reply to the attack on Cromwell, the advocates of a more 'professional' Army leadership for 1645 pressed on with the 'Self-Denying Ordinance', which would exclude all serving MPs and peers from military command (unless given special dispensation). The main effect would be to exclude Manchester and other militarily inadequate peers like Essex and Willoughby from command, as peers could not resign from the Lords in order to continue their military careers but an MP could always leave the Commons. With adequate numbers of votes, an MP like Cromwell could also be given a special dispensation to continue serving in the Army. Conveniently, the affected peers in command were all allied to the Presbyterian faction who supported a disciplinarian State Church. On 9 December Cromwell spoke in favour of the Ordinance as it was introduced in the Commons by Zouch Tate, warning that the cause of Parliament was in a 'bleeding, nay almost dying condition', and his ally Saye and Sele introduced it in the Lords.[10] It passed the Commons on the 19th after a move to exempt Essex from it was lost by seven votes.[11] The Lords seem to have refused to endorse it, and they faced a threat by the Commons 'hardliners' to reactivate the question of whether setting up a their committee on Cromwell's charges against Manchester had been a breach of privilege as the Commons had not been informed first.[12] The Ordinance was not passed by the Lords until 15 February, by which time the negotiations at Uxbridge (see below) could be seen to be failing so the idea of a drastically reformed Army was thus more acceptable. Northumberland and his allies also sought to insist that the Houses, not the new commander-in-chief, nominate the new army's officers and that all be required to take the Covenant – an attempt to exclude Cromwell and his allies.

A determined attempt was made to ensure that Cromwell was removed from the army, and as of Naseby in June 1645 the issue was still unresolved; the lieutenant-generalship (second-in-command) to commander-in-chief Fairfax was left vacant when the new command was proposed (by Cromwell and his ally Sir John Evelyn) on 19 January. When the Ordinance was finally passed on 3 April, Cromwell received a temporary, renewable forty-day exemption from it rather than the permanent exemption proposed by his allies. This carried his service up to 12 May, and was duly extended then until 18 June (which took in the Naseby campaign[13]). The question of appointing him as the sole MP or peer allowed military command to become entangled in the issue of Manchester's charges and his attitude towards

Presbyterianism. Indeed, to some MPs the 'Self-Denying Ordinance' offered an opportunity to be rid of Cromwell as a military commander – as a political threat – as well as the current lacklustre peer commanders such as Essex – as a military threat. In addition, the majority of the Lords rallied to the right of Essex – and Manchester – to continue in command, their removal being a threat to the social and political pre-eminence of the Parliamentary peers.

The 'what ifs…' of Cromwell's exemption from the Ordinance
The indecision of the majority of MPs over Cromwell's role in the Army is shown by the fact that his command as lieutenant-general to Fairfax was temporary and was extended piecemeal for short periods. If the attempt to force him to resign from the Army had been successful it would have neutralized his main source of support as a political actor in 1646–9 and made him as dependent on political allies as the other pro-Independent Commons leaders Vane and St John. Lacking the prestige of success in command in the 1645 campaign (and more so in 1648) and personal contact with his men, he would have been driven to rely on his son-in-law Henry Ireton as his main conduit to the Army and been unable to take part in the Army debates over the constitution at Putney in November 1647, putting Ireton in an even greater eminence.

Alternatively, he could have chosen to resign his seat and stay in the Army as being more useful to his concept of what God required of him, namely achieving victory for the forces of the saints against popery. But that would have lost him his unique role as both an Army and Commons figure, and although his military duties reduced his effectiveness in the House until autumn 1651, his role thereafter would have been reduced. He would still have been eligible for the Councils of State in 1649–53 – the selection of their members lay with the MPs and he was a leading figure in the Independent faction without the ultra-radical drawbacks that affected General Harrison's position – and so been a political leader while in London. But he would not have been in a position to take part in Parliamentary debates, or – legally – to enter the House and dissolve it on 20 April 1653.

What if Cromwell had chosen to continue serving in the House in spring 1645, or more likely have stayed in the Army until victory and then re-entered the Commons by a by-election after summer 1646? Fairfax, who was technically supreme commander throughout the period 1645—50 but had been politically eclipsed by his more active juniors since the end of the war, was unlikely to have been able to hold back the Army mutiny against the Presbyterian MPs' control of power in summer 1647 had Cromwell not been in the Army to support the rebels. He had no sympathy with the demands of political radicals or sectaries in the Army, and would have been bypassed anyway. The political leadership of the Army would simply have gone to the other principal 'Grandees', the political militant Ireton and the religious militant Thomas Harrison, who had an interest in framing the new constitution and/or religious settlement and took a major role in debates on them. In any case, it is unclear to what degree 'Grandees' such as Cromwell and Ireton were behind the Army mutiny against Parliament and the seizure of the King in summer 1647, as opposed to just taking advantage of 'grass-roots' action. Cromwell's absence in the Commons need not have made a major difference to the events of that summer and autumn, and he would have been a probable victim of Presbyterian MPs' attempts to expel him from the House and thus dependent on the Army to restore him. His family relationship would have kept him in close touch with his son-in-law Ireton, although he would not have been eligible to take part in the 'Putney Debates'.

It is possible that once the leading Presbyterians had been driven out of the Commons by armed force in summer 1647 Cromwell would have been able to arrange a vote to restore himself to military command as Fairfax's deputy. The Independents in the Commons, and their sectary allies, needed a reliable ally in a major position in the Army to counter Fairfax's Presbyterian sympathies. If not, he would have been unable to take charge of defeating the royalist revolt in 1648 and then to become commander-in-chief after Fairfax resigned – or to take control of coercing Ireland. Fairfax opposed the King's execution and was a moderate Presbyterian in his politico-religious sympathies; he had no ambition to lead (or even take part in) the Commonwealth and the Army after the 'revolution' of late 1648 and would still have ended his career then. The most likely commander-in-chief to succeed him would have been Ireton, assuming Cromwell had not forced his own recall. The possibility arises that a more 'civilian' Cromwell, used to working in the Rump with his fellow-MPs not away fighting in Ireland and Scotland in 1649–51, would still have been frustrated enough at his colleagues' behaviour to use his Army sectary allies to purge the Commons in the name of religious toleration and a less 'corrupt' political settlement. But he would have been seen as less of a military ruler as he was not the current 'lord general' at the time.

Could peace have been agreed before the New Model came into action?
The Ordinance and the creation of a 'professional' Parliamentary army now proceeded, but at the same time peace proposals had a new impetus. Indeed, the unusual energy that some MPs showed for the latter – in contrast with

the overtures of 1643 and 1644 – were connected to their fear of what an untrammelled Army of religious radicals could achieve, and of the social implications of the removal of the politically and religiously 'moderate' commanders such as Essex and Manchester. On the King's side, the north of England had been lost as a result of Marston Moor; the brilliant 'hit-and-run' guerrilla campaign that Montrose had opened in the Highlands was still 'low-key' and far from conquering the Lowlands, and there was no sign of early aid from Ireland or France.

The initial proposals sent by Parliament to the King in November – before the controversy over the Cromwell/Manchester feud had reached its height – were concurrent with the agreement of the Presbyterian-dominated Assembly of Divines at Westminster that the Church should take on a Presbyterian form, and were drawn up with Scots help or leadership. They duly required that Charles should concede that England must take the Covenant and establish a Presbyterian Church, as decided upon by Parliament and the Assembly but as near as possible to the Scots model.[14] This uncompromising attitude was a warning to the Independent MPs like Vane, who went along with it reluctantly, and thus boosted support for Cromwell against Manchester and his Scots allies that winter – adding to Cromwell's ability to stay in the Army. The Scots' overplaying their hand duly helped Cromwell and his allies in their political campaign for greater Church freedom in any final settlement, as well as enabling Cromwell to use his military position to work against the Presbyterians in 1646–7. Had the joint Anglo-Scots Presbyterian terms for settlement not been set out so definitively, Cromwell – as MP and as lieutenant-general – would have been at greater risk of eviction from the Army in spring 1645 and duly been weaker in subsequent years, with long-term consequences for politics as the form of government and Church was struggled over. But it was unrealistic to have expected either the dogmatic and triumphalist Scots, who believed in the Covenant as the necessary 'godly' solution to Church problems in both kingdoms, or 'Root and Branch' MPs like Holles and Stapleton to have been more cautious about their intended solution to the religious question. As shown by the hysterical tone of writers like Thomas Edwards, they feared the uncontrolled burgeoning of radical sects as both heretical and a sign of anarchy.

In political terms, the Parliamentary proposals of November 1644 entailed no amnesty for a list of fifty-seven leading royalists, headed by Princes Rupert and Maurice, or for royalist Catholics and participants in the Irish rebellion. Less important offenders were to be excluded from office, and the estates of those proscribed were to be sold to defray the costs of the war; the less important royalists were to have a third of their property sold off. Others were to pay a tenth of their estates. The militia and Navy were to be placed permanently under Parliamentary commissioners, and either the Houses or their nominees were to decide on all government appointments; Charles was thus to be king in name only. In religious matters, every citizen in both kingdoms – headed by the King – was to take the Covenant, and Parliament and the Assembly would direct the form the new Church was to take.[15]

The commissioners duly arrived at Oxford on 23 November, just as Charles returned from Donnington Castle, amidst public anger and contempt, and their announcement of the list of those to be proscribed met mocking laughter from the assembled courtiers. Charles asked if they had powers to treat, and was told that they were only empowered to receive his answer; he later called in privately on two moderate commissioners – Holles and Whitelocke – and asked for their opinions on how the war could best be ended. Whitelocke drew up some ideas, but prudently disguised his handwriting in case the paper was used by the royalists against him; the King was clearly trying to divide the Parliamentary leadership and dangled his openness to reason to the less fervent MPs. He returned his official, sealed reply to the delegation on the 27th; it was found when it was opened at Westminster on the 30th that it was a request for a safe-conduct for his envoys, the Duke of Richmond and the Earl of Southampton.[16] This was duly granted. In December the two peers brought Charles' request to Parliament that commissioners be named to meet his representatives for a negotiation. This was agreed, though the Commons (with its Presbyterian majority likely to support the uncompromising tone of the November proposals) blocked a Lords attempt to keep the nomination of the negotiators with the two Houses. Instead the 'Committee of Both Kingdoms', dominated by the 'war party', would select them.[17] In the meantime small but significant developments in the war as it wound down for the winter had been in Parliament's favour – the fall of Liverpool (a port that could be used to bring royalist Irish into England) on 1 December to Sir John Meldrum,[18] the relief of recently acquired Montgomery Castle in the upper Severn valley, and the relief of the isolated inland Parliamentarian West Country stronghold of Taunton by Waller's deputy Holborn on 14 December. In the north, Newcastle fell to the Scots in October. On 11 January a surprise attack over Culham Bridge on the Parliamentary garrison at Abingdon, threatening Oxford from the south, failed despite the inadequacies of its commander, General Browne. Known derisively as the 'faggot-monger' due to his sideline of shipping firewood down the Thames to London – to offset wartime dependence on Newcastle coal, now in Scots hands – Browne was afflicted by military mutinies but had the competence to beat Rupert's men off. Meanwhile, George Goring, new royalist commander for Hampshire, Sussex, and Kent, moved east on 9 January to attack Fareham but his offensive towards Portsmouth ground to a halt for want of troops.[19]

The Commons sought to make an example of Laud as swiftly as possible by executing him under the Act of Attainder, which required proof that he had committed treason and was duly resisted strongly in the Lords. Militant MP William Strode reminded the Lords of their duty to submit to the demand for 'justice' of the multitudes who had demonstrated in London demanding execution of the architect of Church repression and 'popish' innovations, and he and the zealous prosecuting counsel Prynne clearly fancied a role carrying out the will of the said masses against the symbol of tyranny (a precursor of the roles of Fouquier-Tinville in the French Revolution, Trotsky in the Russian Revolution, and Khalkali in the Iranian Revolution). But this argument could be turned against them and the other belligerent Presbyterian zealots, although in the short term the efforts of the Lords to save Laud from what amounted to 'lynch law' were unsuccessful.

The peers refused to renew the current ordinance legalizing courts of martial law, but their stubbornness over Laud's attainder on 2–3 January 1645 only caused browbeating by the Commons at a conference and threats to turn both Houses into a joint body where the peers would be easily outnumbered and outvoted. The legal argument that Laud's crimes were not covered by the current legal definition of treason met the response that Parliament could vote for any extra crimes to be treasonable, and they reluctantly voted for Laud's execution on the 4th. On 10 January the Archbishop was beheaded on Tower Hill – the same place where his controversial predecessor Archbishop Sudbury, another unpopular cleric appointed Treasurer, had been beheaded by the rebels during the Peasants' Revolt in 1381.[20] The execution of the captive Hothams, would-be betrayers of Hull in 1643, was less controversial. But there was concern that Parliamentary high-handedness was a rising threat to the principles of their own cause. Essex spoke for the cause of justice and moderation in retorting that:

> Shall posterity say that to save them from the yoke of the King we have placed them under that of the populace?[21]

All this added to the controversy between Cromwell and Manchester and the 'Self-Denying Ordinance' in presenting a warning to thoughtful and moderate peers and MPs that the sooner the war was brought to an end the better. Even senior figures in the Lords sympathetic to a Presbyterian Church settlement, like Essex and Warwick, had the threat of the Ordinance to consider if the war went on – and the danger of the Commons usurping their rights and defying them, as it did in its insistence on both Hothams being executed and Laud being sacrificed to his zealot enemies. These peers would be backed by moderate MPs worried at the current state of the nation and dubious over the uncompromising tone of the November demands on the King, most notably Whitelocke. The potential for a sympathetic hearing to Charles' commissioners was thus better than in the two previous winters – though much could still go wrong, with the Church settlement the main problem. On Charles' part, he wrote to the Queen (abroad in France) in December that he was very hopeful of success in 1645 as his enemies were weary of the war and were bitterly divided between Presbyterians and Independents. But as to the terms of any settlement, he would never abandon either the episcopal Church or his right to run the militia.[22] Were his opponents – or at least their negotiators – so desperate that they would be prepared to patch up a form of words to satisfy both sides sooner than see the evident problems of the Parliamentarian factions escalate disastrously in the next year? And – even less likely – would they ever have enough votes in both Houses to carry through acceptance of any agreement?

As the preparations for the negotiations at Uxbridge began, a form of compromise was reached within the Parliamentary leadership over the Scots army. The creation of the professional New Model would lead to men – and officers – being selected on grounds of talent and zeal, with the danger of an Independent majority. Cromwell, accused of intending to use the Army as a weapon against the Presbyterians and Scots by Manchester, was able to secure exclusion from the 'Self-Denying Ordinance' – though his superior, Fairfax, was doctrinally Presbyterian. But it was Cromwell, as representative of the 'Committee of Both Kingdoms', who asked the Commons on 30 January 1645 to allow the Scots army to move south to assist the New Model in the next campaign.[23] Apart from this being an olive branch to his critics for short-term tactical reasons, it showed that he put a unified command and victory above sectarian struggles – and in 1644 he had been arguing for a continued unified command after Marston Moor. Victory came first, and it is probable that he and his Independent allies in the Commons were hopeful that the Uxbridge negotiations would fail anyway due to the positions of King and Parliament being so far apart on religion and the militia.[24] If this was their calculation, it was aided by the nature of the men chosen to conduct the negotiations. In order to secure the triumph of a Presbyterian State Church and hopefully persuade the King of its desirability, the Scots theologian Alexander Henderson rather than an Englishman was chosen to be the delegates' religious assistant – a zealot leader of the Prayer-Book Rebellion in Edinburgh who would see that the religious terms were not ameliorated. The delegates included the Earls of Loudoun and Lauderdale, two senior Scots peers involved with the Covenanter cause from the start, and the Independent MPs Vane and St John – who notably took little role in the proceedings, probably privately disapproving of the uncompromising tone and expecting them to fail. In tactical terms, the Independents would gain if the Scots and their religious allies were shown up as unable to reach a settlement and as being too uncompromising to act effectively for peace.

Negotiations at Uxbridge, January – February 1644: a dialogue of the deaf?

The negotiations at Uxbridge were thus unlikely to succeed, except by a dramatic compromise – particularly on the Church – which was unavailable. Charles' mood had been stiffened by the execution of Laud, a reminder of the previous occasion when he had given way over the execution of a faithful minister and had reproached himself for it afterwards. The Earls of Loudoun and Lauderdale, two senior peers leading the four Scots negotiators, had made it clear to French ambassador Sabran that the Scots reasoning over abolishing episcopacy was neither political nor religious. Only an English monarchy shorn of its bishops was able to guarantee the future safety of the Scots Church from more meddling; their demand for full Presbyterianism as a 'sine qua non' was for their own security, not for religious reasons[25] (though Henderson no doubt saw it differently).

Numerically the sixteen English commissioners outnumbered these men. The senior English Parliamentarian peers present in the negotiating team, the Earls of Pembroke and Salisbury, were a spent force politically and so unable to carry any attempt to insist on ameliorating the terms offered – Hyde reckoned that they had lost all credit in both Houses and were too afraid of prosecution and personal ruin from vengeful militant colleagues to force their views on the latter. Pembroke told Hyde that the Commons was dominated by low-class rogues, and seemed helpless.[26] Due to the importance of the Scots alliance, whose worth had been proved at Marston Moor, the English leadership could or would not stand up to the Scots – and English Presbyterians in the negotiating team, like Holles, backed the strict religious demands as a way of forcing the political neutralization of bishops for the future. Nor would Vane and the Independents yet stand up to the Scots and the latter's Commons allies; their political 'nerve' would be greater once the King had been defeated (thus making the Scots Army less essential) and the New Model had proved its military worth. The considerable – and desperate? – hopes for success and peace among the populace had no effect in stimulating generosity on terms.

In deciding on negotiating policy, the Commons decided to treat under the three heads of religion, the militia, and Ireland; a day would be allocated to each subject in rotation, and if no agreement had been reached after the first nine days each subject was to have a clear 'run' of three days. If there was still no agreement at the end of these further nine days, plus another two, the talks were to end. On religion, the Parliamentary terms were that the King should take the Covenant, episcopacy and the Prayer Book of 1559 should be abolished, and a Presbyterian Church system and theology be introduced. The militia and the Navy should be placed under commissioners named by Parliament, plus others named by the Scots (not to exceed in number a third of the English total), and conversely the Scots militia was to be placed under a body of Scots Parliament nominees plus an English group (a maximum of a third of their number). The military co-operation of the 'Committee of Both Kingdoms' would thus continue. Charles was to accept a Parliamentary cancellation of his Irish negotiators' agreement of a truce with the Catholic rebels, and the resulting war was to be controlled by Parliament.[27] This would prevent any leniency towards Catholics.

Talks duly opened at Uxbridge on 31 January. As was to be expected, the King's representatives sought to drive a wedge between the rival religious factions and within the Presbyterian faction of his opponents. On the first day Hyde duly enquired about the precise nature of the intended Presbyterian system, intending to expose disagreements; given that the King would not consent to abolishing the bishops, breaking up the unified Parliamentary position was his negotiators' best hope. Hyde, unlike Charles, seems to have done his best to achieve success, not just 'talk out' the issues to gain time ahead of the next campaigning season; in his correspondence to his negotiators Charles indicated unrealistically that the best way to proceed was to scare the opposition into flexibility with talk of prosecution for treason and divine damnation for rebellion.

Could moderate royalist negotiators such as Hyde and Lord Hertford 'bounce' Charles into an agreement with the help of similar flexibility on the other side? Hyde was the crucial figure in this, given that his administrative skills made him the chief organizer and co-ordinator of the royalist negotiators; his main foe in terms of royalist court politics and demands to accommodate Catholicism (Ireland included) in any settlement, the Queen, was abroad. Hopefully, the convocation of royalist clergy in Oxford – sitting in tandem with Charles' Parliament – came up with their own ideas for a settlement on 10 February,[28] and it was put to the talks on the 13th. It required the bishops to be kept on, but shorn of disciplinary powers unless approved by presbyters chosen by the clergy; Parliament was to reform abuses, the Prayer Book to be altered as agreed, and freedom granted to all clergy to perform which kind of Church ceremonial they wished without prosecution.[29] Suspension of legal penalties would thus grant freedom of worship to the Presbyterians and Independents – a generous gesture and major concession, though not likely to be reciprocated as the two religious groupings concerned were not so sanguine about tolerating bishops and the 'popish' Anglican liturgy. The talks duly continued on the basis of the Parliamentary side keeping to their position; the moderate Earl of Pembroke honestly if embarrassingly declared that if Charles gave way on this issue now for form's sake he could always revoke it in a few years.[30] This kind of dissembling was to be difficult for the King even in straitened circumstances in 1646–8, though he was then to be driven to concede a three-year Presbyterian experiment. In 1645, not yet defeated, it was even more unrealistic to expect him to agree. Hyde claimed that one of the Scots commissioners, Lord Loudoun, asked him to urge Charles to give way on the Church so the Scots could then back him on secular matters; the other Scot, Lord Lauderdale (ironically later a minister to Charles II) was less helpful.

On the militia, Charles would only concede a temporary handover of control to a body consisting half of Parliamentary nominees and half of his own. Considering the balance of forces in the war, this was reasonable enough as an expression of military reality in a basis for a truce. He would allow some royal officials to be nominated by Parliament, but not senior ones. He was prepared to make concessions over Scotland without consulting Montrose, despite his early insistence on doing so. The question of dealing with the Irish rebels was more insoluble, given that the Parliamentarians would not accept that the royalist/Catholic truce was a political necessity to aid hard-pressed Protestant settlers rather than a godless royal acceptance of tolerating murderous Catholics. The resulting deadlock on these issues and the King's firm attitude towards Presbyterianism encouraged the pro-Presbyterian majority in the Lords – recently exercised against the attacks on the Earl of Manchester – to rally to the 'war party' in the Commons despite the two Houses' disagreements, and on the 15th the Lords finally accepted the 'Self-Denying Ordinance'. They secured their request that the Ordinance was acceptable only if each senior New Model appointment was individually approved by the two Houses, thus putting Cromwell and other contentious Independents at the mercy of a veto.[31]

The result was to make it a matter of timing if Cromwell could have his appointment to the New Model agreed before it entered battle, and in June he had to hasten to Naseby once Parliament had approved the officers' appeal for his appointment. Even so, he nearly missed the battle and his command was only extended for three months (and another four in October).

There were also some private, unofficial talks at Uxbridge chaired by Sabran. These brought together several of the senior negotiators, most notably Holles – whose stance on the terms of peace in 1646–7 shows that he was allied to the Scots on matters such as the need for a strict Presbyterian Church structure with disciplinary powers and neutralization of royal power over the militia and civil appointments. They do not seem to have been effective, and Holles was to be over-confident of the King's desire for a settlement now as later. But the 'pro-peace' intriguer Lord Savile (currently at Oxford as a royalist adherent but prepared to maintain contacts in London in the interests of working out a settlement at considerable personal risk), was to claim on his expulsion from the royalist camp that Holles claimed he would keep in touch with the King thereafter and inform him of moves for peace in London. When Savile revealed this to Parliament that summer this was used by Holles' enemies to undermine the latter, and a Commons committee investigated the charge. Holles denied it and claimed he had been 'set up' by the Independent leaders Vane and St John and the moderate Presbyterian Lord Saye and Sele, his rivals in the Parliamentary civilian leadership – and he claimed that they had their own contacts with the King. There had also been rumours of secret contacts between Holles, Loudoun, and none other than veteran court intriguer Lady Carlisle (as alleged ex-mistress of Pym presumably with links to the Commons Presbyterians).[32] Lady Carlisle, the 'original' of Alexandre Dumas' villainess 'Milady de Winter', had a habit of cropping up at the heart of political intrigue, as at the attempt to arrest the 'Five Members'. Holles was to reappear as in favour of a limited monarchy and a Presbyterian State Church but little religious toleration in 1647–8 and in 1660.

Nothing could be proved on either side. But it is quite possible that one or both groups of Parliamentary religious rivals represented at Uxbridge – Presbyterians and Independents – explored the chances of the King or his advisers being flexible on a settlement, and did so privately so as to avoid their enemies in the Commons charging them with treachery. Holles and his allies had no enthusiasm for the spectre of a New Model Army run by Independent officers, a danger that in the event was to overthrow Holles' party's control of the post-war Commons in summer 1647. Conversely, Vane's group was opposed to the harsh terms and religious intolerance that the Holles-Scots alliance proposed as the basis for a religious settlement. Such private contacts with Oxford during and after Uxbridge would have encouraged the King in his current belief that his enemies were breaking up into faction-fighting.

In the stalemate at Uxbridge, Charles resorted to a bold but futile proposal that both armies be disbanded and then he would go to

Westminster to meet Parliament (20 February).[33] The point was that the Parliament in question would include all Members expelled or who fled from the 'rebel' body in London since 1642 and would thus be more favourable to him. A popular desire for peace and the weight of moderate peers and MPs would thus aid him in the votes on a resolution of the problems in question. Naturally unwilling to throw away a strong position when they were undefeated, the Parliamentary commissioners refused. A royalist proposal to have the question of religion sorted out by a joint meeting of Parliament and a National Synod was also rejected on the 22nd, and the talks ended as the time-limit ran out.[34] The campaigns resumed. In any case, by 19 February the King had heard of Montrose's run of remarkable successes in the Highlands and this now opened the possibility that the Scots rebels, mainstay of the Presbyterian cause, would be overthrown by military force in the coming months.

Montrose shifts the military balance in the King's favour

The 'Presbyterian Cavalier' James Graham, with a mixed army of Protestant royalist Lowlanders, Highland Catholics based on the Macdonald clan, and Irish mercenaries brought in by his lieutenant Alistair 'Mac Colkitto' Macdonald, was evading the divided armies of the Covenant in an exhausting chase around eastern Scotland and making sporadic descents on the Lowlands to attack places such as Perth and Aberdeen. Wearing his militarily less skilled opponents out in unfamiliar territory and outsmarting their advantages of superior numbers and weaponry, his fit and ferocious Highlanders were defeating the Covenanter armies one by one. The senior Covenanter clan leader and political 'hardliner' of 1637–40, Argyll, had suffered the humiliation of having his home territory pillaged and his residence at Inverary Castle sacked,[35] and on 2 February 1645 Montrose wiped out his Campbell private army at Inverlochy after a daring march round the flanks of Ben Nevis – a thirty-six-hour trek, partly in the dark – to take his opponents by surprise. Having intended to trap Montrose at Kilcumein (the later Fort Augustus) between the Campbell army to the south and the advancing Earl of Seaforth's Caithness (Mackenzie) clansmen to the north, Argyll was caught by surprise to see the enemy descending on him from the hills. According to tradition, the later bard Iain 'Lom' Macdonald, a local clansman who lived until 1715, acted as Montrose's guide. The Campbell infantry (c. 2,000 Campbells and 1,500 of Baillie's men, with two cannons) was commanded by a military veteran, Sir Duncan Campbell of Auchinbreck, and was in a better shape than the townsmen of Perth at Tippermuir or the Aberdonians but it was still no match for the royalists at close quarters. While his men were butchered and Inverlochy sacked, 'Mac Cailean Mor' abandoned his clansmen and sailed off down Loch Linnhe in his galley.[36]

As yet most senior nobles in Lowland and Highlands alike stood aside from the mainly Catholic royal army under its ex-Covenanter leader, with even the King's loyal 'Lieutenant of the North' Huntly only furnishing a small contingent under his son Lord Aboyne. But Montrose seemed to be invincible, and the destruction of Campbell power removed a major element of the Covenanter military coalition. The possibility arose of a royalist victory in both England and Scotland in 1645 – or at least of the Scots having to abandon their allies to save the Lowlands and thus losing all that they had gained in northern England in 1644.

The King would have been in an even stronger position had Montrose been able to achieve this success earlier, as his campaign had only opened in early September 1644 with the battle of Tippermuir. Montrose indeed had requested his despatch north in 1643 and made one unsuccessful venture over the Border; the King had delayed granting him his authority and had offered him very few men. Montrose's plan was never seen as more than a 'side-show' to the command in Oxford. But his near-solitary journey north to 'safe' royalist areas without an encumbering large royalist escort had enabled him to travel fast and to avoid being intercepted by the Covenanters' Lowland armies, which were likely to have defeated him en route. In any case, Alistair Macdonald's Irishmen – sent by the Marquis of Antrim at Charles' request – did not arrive in the Highlands from Ulster until June 1644. Until then, Montrose would have been short of the backbone of his highly mobile army and dependant on the goodwill of Huntly as senior royalist clan-leader in north-east Scotland. As in 1638–9, a large portion of the blame for slow and sluggish royalist military action must lie with Huntly, who had fallen victim to a Covenanter attack in 1639 when he should have been leading his tenants to assist Charles and Hamilton in Edinburgh (or at least been on his guard against attack). Much was probably down to the Marquis' pride of social rank in his failure to back Montrose with his full military might in 1644 – the latter was socially his junior, a minor lord from the eastern lowlands in the Mearns, and had previously been fighting for the Covenant.

The campaign to Naseby, spring 1645

Was an early confrontation between Charles and the New Model inevitable or accidental? Did he misjudge the danger to Oxford? And what happened to his northern strategy?

The Catholic dimension as of winter 1644–5. European and Irish prospects for the King

In addition to military success in Scotland and the truce in Ireland, winter 1644–5 was seeing rising hopes of aid to the King from the Continent. Henrietta Maria was active in France, with the major French military successes of autumn 1644 leading to French occupation of the Rhineland and the cutting of the Spanish/Imperial military supply route from Italy and Austria to the Spanish Netherlands. Now that France had achieved its main military objective, the regency government for Louis XIV under Queen-Mother Anne of Austria (and Cardinal Mazarin) should be more ready to assist Louis' aunt and uncle to save their thrones. Mazarin duly offered Henrietta Maria the finance to assist if she could persuade a senior and experienced military commander in imperial service, the deposed – by France – Duke Charles of Lorraine, to abandon his threats to France and command her army.[37] The Queen was also negotiating with Stadtholder Frederick Henry in the United Provinces, requesting a Dutch mission to London to order Parliament to reach terms on pain of invasion and 3,000 Dutch troops if they held out. Prince Charles would now marry his sister Mary's sister-in-law, Frederick Henry's daughter. The Queen's envoy to Holland, Dr Goffe, was duly offered Dutch shipping to transport any army assembled by Duke Charles from his followers – who Mazarin would be glad to see removed from the Continent.[38]

Indeed, the semi-autonomous pride, manpower in tenantry, and military traditions of the great French nobles and hereditary princes on their eastern borders, such as Charles of Lorraine (a descendant of the House of Guise) acted in Charles' favour under the post-1643 regency for Louis XIV. These great nobles had been placed within political and military bounds by, and felt excluded from their traditional claims to influence by, Louis XIII's 'centralizing' minister Cardinal Richelieu in 1624–42, and Regent (Queen-Mother) Anne's chief minister Cardinal Mazarin was heir to that policy. In literary terms, aristocratic resentment at this centralization by 'jumped-up' royal ministers fed into the hostile myths of Richelieu and Mazarin used by the novelist Alexandre Dumas in his 'Three Musketeers' books. They did not take kindly to the monopoly of power and influence at the boy-King's court by Mazarin, a.k.a. Giulio Mazarini, an Italian 'interloper' protégé of

Richelieu who was suspiciously close to the Queen-Mother, and if not kept occupied fighting the Empire and Spain could easily turn on the government to overthrow him. It was thus to Mazarin and Anne's interest to send an expeditionary force to assist Charles once France had achieved its aim of forcing the Empire to the negotiating table over the weak eastern frontier, and this was to become an increasing threat to Parliament through the period 1644–7. Due to the 'Auld Alliance' policy of using Scotland against England, they could also assist the partly Catholic army of Montrose in Scotland against the Covenanters.

Charles also sought military aid from the Catholic Irish rebels' government at Kilkenny, via his agent the Earl of Glamorgan (a Catholic, son of the principal magnate in south-east Wales). According to the terms of the 'Cessation' agents from the Confederation had been at Oxford in March 1644, though sent packing in May as Charles veered back to treating with the rebels via Ormonde – whose hoped-for military successes could bring them to more acceptable terms. The prospect of their Catholic army coming to England to tackle the persecutory Protestant Parliament appealed to Glamorgan as saving his own Welsh Catholic tenantry from persecution. In Glamorgan's bold imagination it seemed that a large-scale international intervention by Irish and European Catholic powers could overturn the military balance against Parliament, and he accordingly worked to counter the efforts of pragmatic civilian – Protestant – royal advisers such as Colepeper and Hyde to keep a line of potential negotiation open to Parliament. In April 1644 Glamorgan had been given a commission to take command of the 10,000 Irish troops promised to Charles under the 'Cessation', a logical move given his experience of handling Catholic levies in South Wales, and had been granted the Dukedom of Somerset (held by his ancestors in the fifteenth century) plus the right to sell off wardships to raise cash. He had reputedly been offered the hand of Princess Elizabeth, Charles' second daughter, for his son,[39] though this was never carried through. The Irish invasion-plan was also linked to Charles' commission in November 1644 to a young Norfolk royalist, Roger l'Estange, to seize his local port of King's Lynn for an invasion-force to land; the plotter was arrested but reprieved.[40] Charles' plans did not lack for originality, but were becoming more desperate.

In the event, the distrust of the Scots army in Ireland for the allegedly pro-Catholic Ormonde led to their general Munro evicting the latter's garrison from Belfast (13 May),[41] and that summer's campaign between Munro and the Catholic rebels in the north saw Ormonde maintaining a strict neutrality. The possibility arose of the Confederates needing Charles' military assistance and so being willing to accept more tolerable terms –

provided the angry clerics did not veto them. Alarmed at the prospect of a royalist accommodation with the rebels leading to the King surrendering some disputed lands (including his own?) to the rebels, pro-royalist 'Old English' peer Lord Inchiquin, a leading armed magnate in Munster, even defected to Parliament that summer. At the renewed negotiations between the Catholic rebels and Ormonde in Dublin in September, the 'official' rebel line kept to the demands for the repeal of all (religious) penal legislation, plus that of the laws on appeals and praemunire (aimed at banning papal legal interference in the Irish Catholic Church). Unofficially some of the moderate peers, led by Lord Muskerry, assured that security for life and property to the rebels would be sufficient for his faction and they would trust the King to implement the formal legislation later. He only spoke for a minority, though; others, led by the rebel generals Owen Roe O'Neill and Preston who had the 'clout' to coerce the clergy if needed, would not trust Charles and had no thought for his difficult politico-religious position within England. Charles had to balance the need for an Irish peace against the outrage his English subjects would feel at a 'surrender to popery'; he thus talked of suspending rather than abolishing the anti-Catholic penal laws.

He was unlikely ever to hand back the centralizing powers of the English government over the Irish Parliament, based on Poynings' Law of 1494, which was another key issue – and without that the rebels would fear that a militantly Protestant English Parliament could easily cancel any ameliorating orders issued by the King. On 15 December 1644 Charles informed Ormonde that he would be prepared to suspend the penal laws but not move against the Acts on appeals or praemunire, and when Ormonde attempted to offer his resignation[42] Charles refused to take this possible opportunity to replace him with a new Lord Lieutenant who would go further in his concessions to the Catholics. Glamorgan was the obvious person, was a Catholic so appealed to his co-religionists, and was eager to become involved, but he had no military experience, Irish landed allies and armed tenants to back him up, or political 'clout' in Dublin. Glamorgan was therefore to be sent out to Ireland in 1645 to work with not replace Ormonde, and it seems from a later complaint of Charles' in February 1646 that the King made his new envoy promise to be guided by Ormonde's advice. Appointing Glamorgan thus did not mean going behind Ormonde's back, though the timing of Ormonde's offer to resign in December 1644 suggests that the later was unhappy about the prospect of accepting the sort of terms suggested by Lord Muskerry. Glamorgan's instructions on 2 January specifically said that he could negotiate with the rebels on any matter that Ormonde was 'not willing to be seen therein' or was 'not fit for us presently publicly to own'; however, Charles would support any terms that Ormonde accepted.[43]

The terms concerning Catholics that would be acceptable to the 'peace party' at Westminster, keen to bring their own radicals under strict control in a disciplinarian Church, were bound to be far different from anything encompassing Catholic toleration – as seen at Uxbridge. The attitude of Parliament to the Irish Catholics remained inflexible, and delineated in terms of the atrocities of 1641; the captured 1641 plotters Lord Maguire and Hugh Macmahon's escape from the Tower of London (August 1644) led to their being brought back to official attention on their recapture. Both were executed as traitors, Macmahon in November and Maguire in February 1645, and the arguments of the latter that he was an Irish peer so entitled to trial by his fellow-peers were ignored.[44] Equally bloody vengeance on the other rebel leaders and their followers could be expected when the opportunity arose, egged on by Parliament's new Scots Presbyterian allies, and the Uxbridge terms spoke of allowing Parliament not the King to control the intended war of reconquest in Ireland. Glamorgan's imaginative schemes thus presented a temptation to Charles – who was appreciative of the loyalty and sacrifices of his Catholic subjects – to hold out until he had enough foreign Catholic aid to improve his military position and secure better terms (or until he did not have to negotiate at all). At the same time, the successes of Montrose were an argument for holding out until the latter could come to his aid or force the Scots army to leave northern England; after Inverlochy the Earl wrote excitedly to his sovereign in anticipation of being able to reduce Scotland to its due obedience to Charles and then come to his aid.[45]

On 12 March 1645 Glamorgan was empowered in his formal royal negotiating commission to treat independently of Charles' Lord Lieutenant Ormonde on any matter that the latter did not wish to be involved in. Ormonde, vociferously opposed to treating with the rebels on even Muskerry's terms, was to be excused from the murky business of negotiating concessions he found unacceptable in the 'greater good' of sending aid to the King, but he was still expected to give his approval afterwards. Charles promised to accept any terms that Glamorgan should induce Ormonde to agree to, showing that the Lord Lieutenant's – no doubt reluctant – agreement was still required.[46] Unfortunately, Glamorgan was shipwrecked en route to Ireland from Caernarfon at the end of May and was left stranded in Lancashire for a few weeks. Instead, Charles told Ormonde to offer the Irish legislative independence by abolishing Poynings' Law, one of their key demands.

The English campaigns open

The campaigns of 1645 now opened, with hopeful signs for Charles of mutinies by disorderly Parliamentary soldiers (e.g. at Henley in February) who were abusing their right to free quarter. Elements of their cavalry refused to take orders from Waller, their new commander, rather than from Essex.[47] Cromwell had to be sent to take command of his men from the Eastern Association before they would obey orders to march west to link up with Waller's army in the southern Home Counties.[48] Charles now sought to set up his own rival to the Eastern Association, a 'Western Association' of Dorset, Devon, Somerset, and Cornwall, to centralize recruitment and command, and in March Prince Charles (Duke of Cornwall) was sent to Bristol as nominal head of a new Council based there.[49] The finance needed to pay for his household and advisers could have been better spent. His councillors notably included royalist 'moderates' such as Hyde and Colepeper, men opposed to Charles' plan to use Catholic Irish troops, and thus removed them and their cautious counsels from the King's entourage. Possibly they, like Ormonde, were being sidelined from a position where they knew what was going on in his Irish negotiations and could intervene. Hyde had doubts over how the civilians like himself could work with the prickly local generals Goring and Berkeley, and tried in vain to be excused from going. The King failed to make it clear in writing who had seniority, making mutual defiance by rival generals more likely. The King also failed to remove two problematic senior officials in the new command, the Prince's elderly 'Governor' (the Earl of Berkshire) and dithering Chamberlain Lord Ruthven, who were no use at making decisions. The Oxford parliament, a sign of political moderation and a rallying-point for constitutionalism backed by their faction, was adjourned until October in March.[50] One major royalist drawback was now worsening – though in itself it would not have been decisive. The personal discipline and soldierly professionalism of Charles' commanders was poorer than that of Parliament's, although both sides had personal and ideological feuds – as seen by the enmity between Cromwell and Manchester. The sober conduct, honesty, and careful personal relationships of men such as Essex and Waller – and Fairfax and Cromwell – was in sharp contrast to the drunkenness, prickly natures, and readiness to resort to grudges and/or violence of a significant number of royalist commanders. Outright defiance of orders was only committed by the most senior Parliamentarians, pre-1645 – Essex and Manchester. Manchester's grudge against Cromwell was not the norm for senior inter-Parliamentarian relationships – and Cromwell despised the Earl and Lord Willoughby for professional incompetence, which was more a professional than a personal dispute. The conduct of the men on both sides was not noticeably different, however, as illustrated by the trouble in Waller's and Manchester's armies in later 1644 and the attack on the Parliamentarian General Browne by mutinous troops. Early in 1645 there were Parliamentary mutinies by troops worried at what would happen to them once the 'New Model' was set up, especially at Henley-on-Thames.

Given the emergence of many of Charles' senior generals from the aristocratic culture and feuds of court, a 'hangover' of court feuds was inevitable – as was the fondness of certain officers for settling differences with duels. A small royalist court still existed at Christ Church, Oxford, where bored officers could indulge in excess and quarrel with one another when not on active service. Charles had always sought to impose rules of seemly conduct on his courtiers, but this was necessarily relaxed in wartime at Christ Church compared with the earlier situation of regulation at Whitehall. Aristocratic courtiers bred to horseback activity and fighting had an advantage in seeking out appointments of command, quite apart from regarding it as their natural 'right' – and when she was in England in 1643–4 the Queen was assiduous in promoting her favourite courtiers' claims on her husband. Disorderly conduct by bored, undisciplined, or unpaid troops – and the resulting alienation of the affected populace – occurred on both sides. But this was shortly to change – the rigid discipline and orderly conduct of the New Model was to be in sharp contrast to this earlier picture, and in 1645 the problems of poor conduct by quarrelling generals and plundering troops were to appear far worse for the King's side. It was more symptomatic of a lack of professionalism than decisive, though Hyde – no friend of the roistering 'Cavalier' officers anyway – was to accuse the King's officers of losing the war from drunkenness. His main target appears to have been his habitual foe Goring, who was particularly criticized for allowing his troops to live off 'free quarter' (i.e. plunder from) the locals in his area of command. Modern military writers have concurred, calling Goring talented but a ruffian.[51] Arguably the poor disciplinary record of the south-western royalists aided the emergence of the belligerently neutral 'Clubmen' in the area in 1645 – though the latter were opposed to both armies equally as 'brigands'. But Goring, unlike commanders such as Newcastle, was not a rich aristocrat who could pay his men out of his own pocket if no funds arrived, and he had no local estates to call upon for supplies. (His lands were in occupied West Sussex.) He did attempt to secure pay for his men to avoid the necessity for looting, by imposing a 'tax' of 6d per day for the use of each of his cavalrymen from the counties, which he commanded on 23 March. But after over two years of war any extra burden was bound to be resisted, and his lack of tact towards other commanders (e.g. Sir Richard Grenville) was a more serious military problem. Nor did the King issue unequivocal orders about the 'chain of command' – who was to obey who, the Prince's Council to defer to Goring or vice versa?

Goring opened his command with an impressive but inconclusive move across the south on Waller's headquarters at Farnham in January 1645, which was enough of a threat to persuade Parliament to ask Cromwell to bring the Eastern Association cavalry there. But thereafter Goring was not as swift to implement strategy or respond to a potential danger as the previous south-western commander Hopton, and his command against Waller and Cromwell suffered a poor opening as a sudden royalist attack secured Weymouth in February but he did not bring any help. The attackers could not evict the Parliamentarians across the harbour in Melcombe Regis, although Colonel Herbert Morley's Parliamentarian reinforcements from Sussex were held up by adverse winds at Portsmouth. Goring failed to send support, and the lost positions were soon recovered as local Parliamentary reinforcements under Colonel William Batten arrived.[52]

Goring decided to open his campaign with an attack on Taunton, the main urban Parliamentarian base in Somerset and usefully isolated from potential rescue. (If Lyme Regis, their nearest town and port, had fallen in 1644 it would have been in a hopeless position.) Robert Blake, the doughty defender of Lyme Regis so he had both local status and experience of risky defences, led the defence as Goring arrived on 11 March; Goring ordered both Sir John Berkeley, commander at Exeter, and Sir Richard Grenville (besieging Plymouth) to bring most of their troops to aid him but only Berkeley turned up. Possibly Goring's abruptness led to Grenville refusing to leave the siege of Plymouth to aid him at Taunton, though the latter was notoriously independent-minded and his interests as a semi-autonomous Cornish commander were centred on reducing Plymouth, a potential threat to his locality.[53] The attack on Taunton had to be postponed, as Waller and Cromwell had joined forces in Sussex and were now marching into the west, reaching Andover on the 8th. They intercepted a royalist cavalry party of 400 men under Colonel James Long, Sheriff of Wiltshire, en route back from Oxford after escorting the Prince to Bristol at Devizes on the 11th and cornered them in separate groups as they headed for safety at Bath; Long and all but thirty-odd men were captured. Goring had to respond to this threat, and was aided by Waller's temporary diversion from his intended rendezvous with cavalry refugees from Taunton (to be at Cerne Abbas on the 19th) to an unsuccessful attempt on Bristol. While Goring was advancing from Taunton Waller was absent in the aborted move on Bristol, where a plot failed to open the gates,[54] but Colonel Holborne's Taunton horse met up with Cromwell (advancing west from Ringwood) at Dorchester successfully on the 31st and Waller arrived a few days later. Now backed up by Grenville who had been following the Taunton Parliamentarians, Goring confronted the three Parliamentarians' forces around Bruton in Wiltshire but as he had better infantry they moved back to the villages around Salisbury, where a series of swift cavalry raids by the royalists kept their opponents on the defensive through April but no battle followed. The expiry of Waller's command under the 'Self-Denying Ordinance' ended the Parliamentarian campaign, and Goring was able to move back to tackle Taunton.[55]

Goring had failed to press his advantage during Waller's absence, though he was a vigorous enough commander in the skirmishes around southern Wiltshire in April. His habit of plundering the local countryside was more problematic, given the outcome that summer – increasing resistance to the predominant army (or both armies) in Dorset and Somerset by armed locals. In fact, the first outbreak of such militant defiance of both armies by villagers infuriated at the long war, 'free quarter', and arbitrary impressments, looting, and taxation came not in Goring's area but in Herefordshire in March, where several thousand locals converged on Hereford – a movement aimed at Colonel Massey, the Parliamentarian commander at Gloucester.[56] Using Goring may not have been a decisive factor in the failure to take Taunton or the growth of anti-royalist feeling in the south-west, which led to the outbreak of militant neutrality by 'Clubmen' sick of pillaging that summer. But the King was becoming as careless of his subjects' welfare as of securing his generals' co-operation or keeping the Irish Catholics at arms' length, and the quarrelsomeness and lack of united leadership of the Prince's Council was symptomatic of the weakness of central command in Oxford. All this reduced morale, and was to aid the Parliamentary onslaught on the area after Naseby. The declining state of royalist effectiveness was symbolized by the successful night-time Parliamentary assault on Shrewsbury on 22 February, which caught the defence unawares. The attackers paddled boats across the Severn unobserved and dealt with the sentries, and fierce fighting in the streets saw commander Sir Michael Ernle, leading the defence in his nightshirt, cut down and his men rounded up.[57]

Inception of the New Model

The creation of the New Model now proceeded slowly, with last-minute struggles by the 'peace party' and 'hard-line' Presbyterians to resist some of its new officers. Only six of the twenty-four regimental commanders on the first list that the Commons sent to the Lords and about a quarter of the other officers were approved quickly. Ian Gentles has analysed the list of fifty-seven men whom the Lords wanted omitted and identifies about thirty-five of these men as Independents;[58] only one was a Presbyterian. The Commons insisted on the original list being accepted and the Lords had to give in.[59] But the Lords now attempted to insist that the commander of the New Model should only have authority over garrisons 'adjacent' to his field of operations, not over all garrisons in the country – and the new commander's instructions left out the requirement given to his predecessor Essex to preserve the King's person.[60] The commander of the Navy, Warwick, was also replaced – by his 'professional' seaman deputy, William Batten.

The revised 'Self-Denying Ordinance' was passed in the Houses on 3 April with the peers and MPs commanding armies duly resigning their offices. Essex's army at Reading was now disbanded and the new Army established, and some 7,226 infantry and 6,600 cavalry were transferred to this from the three defunct armies of Essex, Manchester and Waller. This left 7,174 infantry and a new regiment of 1,000 dragoons to be raised, by impressments from London and the south-east; the new army stood at between 19,000 and 20,000 at the muster on 27 April.[61] The mixture of a lack of men and lack of money prevented any early royalist attack while their enemies were inert; Rupert was raising men in the south-west Midlands ahead of a new campaign and the King was at Oxford. Later in April, Cromwell opened the season's activities with a raid around Oxfordshire to round up all the heavy horses available and thus deny the King's forces the ability to use them in transporting the royalist artillery to Rupert at Hereford for his campaign. This duly delayed the artillery-train's departure. He also intercepted a small force under the Earl of Northampton at Islip, and unnerved the inexperienced young commander of nearby Bletchingdon House into surrendering without a fight. The King promptly had the latter, the son of ex-Secretary of State Windebank, shot for cowardice[62] – attitudes were hardening on both sides. (This incident was used in the Channel Four TV drama 'The Devil's Whore').

It would appear from the probable contents of a letter that Charles sent to Montrose that he was intending to march north to link up with the Scots royalists,[63] logically in the Lowlands, which was a 'high-risk' strategy but if successful would provide him with major reinforcements. Presumably the King intended Rupert to keep the enemy in England at bay and was confident that his main strongholds there, led by Oxford, could hold out in the meantime if the New Model did not chase after him into Scotland. The Scots Army could be expected to follow the King home to endeavour to save their regime, and if Charles was able to outpace or slip past them and link up with his Scots and Irish troops he could expect the strategically brilliant Montrose to defeat the enemy.

Attention now moved to northern England, as the Scots government ordered Leslie to despatch part of his army under Baillie and Hurry home to deal with Montrose[64] – thus weakening the Scots grip on northern England. Rupert wrote to Charles on 24 April to join him quickly for the march north,[65] but the King could not set out from Oxford without enough horses to drag his artillery; he therefore required Rupert to bring enough horses to him and Goring to abandon the plan for a second siege of Taunton and come too. Goring arrived at Faringdon on 3 May and Rupert at Oxford on the 4th; the Prince of Wales and his entourage had meanwhile held a rally of loyalists at Bridgewater where the raising of a new south-western army of 8,000 men was promised.[66] This would take some time to assemble. The siege of Taunton was delegated to Grenville, who was wounded en route at the siege of Wellington House and had to withdraw from the action, and then to Sir John Berkeley from Exeter.[67] In the meantime the New Model (11,000 men) under its new commander Fairfax set out from Windsor on 30 April with Parliamentary orders to relieve Taunton, an aim that could only be countermanded by his civilian 'controllers', not on his own initiative. Like a Russian Civil War Soviet general, he had an accompanying group of 'commissars' to keep an eye on his activities and see that the central government was obeyed – perhaps understandable given the disaster that had followed Essex's ignoring orders in June 1644. On 2 May he met Cromwell (now detached from the defunct Waller army in the south-west) at Newbury, their successful conjunction being disrupted by an ambush on a party of Cromwell's troopers by Goring.

Like Essex and Waller in 1644, Fairfax was not at liberty to be flexible as circumstances changed – Essex, relying on social rank, had defied orders in heading into Cornwall – and thus missed the chance to change direction from Taunton and follow the departing Goring towards Oxfordshire. Changes of strategy had to be cleared with Parliament, leading to vital delays. He was not ordered to move after Goring by Parliament until 3 May, being sent firm orders on the 5th and receiving them on the 7th at Blandford Forum.[68] An opportunity to catch the armies of either Goring or the King alone was missed. Part of Fairfax's army under Colonels Weldon and Graves duly marched on to rescue Taunton, while he took the main body back up to the Oxford area but was too late to catch Goring. Luckily for Parliament, a general assault by the attackers on Taunton was driven back on the 8th as the fires they lit to burn defenders out of the houses close to their breach in the walls were blown back in their faces by the wind. On the 11th the siege was broken up as the relief-force approached; the fall of the town would have been swiftly reversed in any case as its walls were too damaged to hold the New Model troops back but Blake's success in holding out rallied his and Parliament's reputation.[69] As the successful leader of two West Country defences during 1644–5, an inspiring leader, and a skilled strategist, Blake was in an excellent position to press his claims to a naval command (which would include West Country sailors mindful of his heroic reputation) in coming years. His naval successes and heroic national reputation in 1652–7 would have been more difficult without his Civil War triumphs.

On 11 May, before Fairfax's arrival in the area with his large army, Charles left Oxford with around 11,000 men for the summer campaign.[70] The King's success in avoiding a potentially disastrous attack by the New Model while he was delayed in Oxford in late April to early May was due to a mixture of the renewed royalist attack on Taunton (which distracted Fairfax from heading direct to the upper Thames region) and the Parliamentary refusal to learn from their mistakes in 1644 and give full authority in strategic decision-making to Fairfax. The 1645 campaign would be decided on the battlefield by relatively equal forces. But the King made one major mistake now, by giving full military authority in the south-west to the abrasive Goring.[71] Unified command was one advantage, but Goring was unfit to receive this power as far as his ability to co-operate with rather than offend people went. The new command would undermine the chances of military success through co-operation among the local royalist leadership. Rupert was equally contemptuous of civilians and social inferiors, but he was a better general and was not in command of any geographical area; his strength lay on the battlefield. Hyde and the civilians in the Prince's Council were now effectively sidelined.

The royalist council-of-war at Stow-on-the-Wold on 6 May was faced with a dilemma. Was the army to head north to regain territory and link up with Montrose, the argument of Rupert and his ally Sir Marmaduke Langdale (commander at his local Carlisle)? Or was it to concentrate on dealing with Fairfax in the south, in a repeat of the 1644 campaign against Essex? (Fairfax was still believed to be headed for Taunton.) It was decided to split up the army, with Goring to deal with Fairfax while the King and Rupert marched north. Charles informed Ormonde that he would relieve Chester, and then either attack East Anglia – presumably via tackling Leslie's Scots army in Yorkshire – or move back south again to join Goring and deal with Fairfax.[72] The chance for a quick confrontation with Fairfax by a united army in the south was lost; the alternative of taking all the army north was rightly judged too risky, though in any case Rupert wanted to remove his rival Goring from the King's counsels. As it happened, the timing of the council-of-war meant that Goring was too late back in Somerset to have halted the relief of Taunton; he only arrived at Bristol on the 12th, a day after the relief.

In the meantime, the 'Committee of Both Kingdoms' made a similar mistake, by deciding (10 May) to send Fairfax to besiege Oxford while it was left to the Scots to deal with the King;[73] as in 1644 after Marston Moor, the Parliamentary army was split. It would seem that the Committee was swayed by Lord Saye and Sele, thanks to his confidence in the allegation by Lord Savile (recently arrived to offer his services after banishment from the court in Oxford) that the King's governor of Oxford, William Legge, was prepared to open the gates – and Goring to switch sides too – provided that assurances were given about the survival of the monarchy in a peace-settlement. Saye acted on behalf of a Committee sub-committee set up to consider the surrender of royal fortresses in encouraging Savile to work with the latter's supposed ally within Oxford, Lord Newport,[74] and on 22 May Fairfax duly arrived at Marston outside Oxford to link up with the forces already present under Cromwell and Browne. The siege of Oxford followed, without success in the expected betrayal, and as the King advanced north from Worcestershire the Cheshire Parliamentarian commander, Sir William Brereton, had to abandon the sieges of Chester and Hawarden (18 May).[75] Nor did Leslie hasten to answer an appeal from the Parliamentarian commander in Yorkshire, Lord Fairfax (the New Model commander's father), for aid[76] – he was too distracted by the latest news of Montrose's successes. The New Model was tied down uselessly at Oxford, and the opportunity arose for the King to restore his position in the north – and defeat Leslie.

The King was at Market Drayton in Staffordshire on 22 May, and decided to avoid the poorer roads of Lancashire in his northwards march and move east instead. This would also keep him in touch with Oxford if he needed to return south to save it from the New Model. Goring was summoned from Somerset and Lord Gerard from South Wales to join him in Leicestershire, a solidly enemy county that could be looted for supplies and where his presence would serve to draw the New Model away from too prolonged an investment of Oxford.[77] The choice of course was prudent, as Charles was soon warned that Oxford was running out of supplies. His cause was also prospering in south-west Wales, a pro-Parliamentarian enclave surrounded by solidly royalist lands, where Sir Charles Gerard defeated Rowland Laugharne and retook Haverfordwest to close in on the Parliamentarian heartland of Milford Haven and Tenby.

In any case, a royal northwards dash in May 1645 would not have been able to link up quickly with Montrose, who had moved north from the Great Glen into the Moray region in February–March to collect more reinforcements from the locals around Elgin, better-armed than his Highlanders (and Protestants, to repair his reputation with the Lowlanders he needed to win over) and proceeded to sack the mansions of resisting pro-Covenanter lairds to warn them of the fate in store for 'rebels'. Lord

Gordon, eldest son of the temporizing Huntly, came over from the Covenanter army (perhaps annoyed at not being given a command) with some of his Gordons, and Seaforth and other northern clan chiefs abandoned the declining Covenanter cause to save their lands from plunder. However, Montrose's march south-eastwards into the Aberdeen area was met by a well-armed force under Baillie, arrived from Leven's army in northern England, and with Hurry advancing to back him up Montrose's path southwards was blocked. His skilful and lengthy 'fencing' with Baillie's army to avoid a dangerous head-on clash preserved his army but bored his impatient and loot-hungry Highlanders, who preferred more direct tactics and drifted away from his army back to their glens in defiance of any concept of military discipline. Short of men and with around 200 cavalry and 600 infantry left, Montrose had to move back to safety from Dunkeld in early April, sacking Dundee en route on the 4th and being caught during the action by Baillie who missed a chance to destroy the royalists in the confusion in the burning town.[78] He evaded Baillie's pursuit by hours to regain the safety of the hills, retreated across country west to Balquhidder (above Loch Lomond) to be joined by Huntly's younger son Lord Aboyne from Carlisle, and with Alistair Macdonald's return had enough men to tackle Hurry. Rather than joining up with Baillie to hunt Montrose down in western Atholl, Hurry had been sent north to tackle the Gordons and this divide of the Covenanter army gave Montrose his chance. A better general than Baillie, Hurry managed to evade battle in the Spey valley until he had forced his enemy to advance into hostile territory around Elgin, sacked by the royalists earlier in the campaign, but was outsmarted on the battlefield. Montrose lured Hurry's army into a trap at the village of Auldearn near Elgin (9 May), placing his standard by Macdonald's men within the difficult-to-attack enclosures in the settlement so Hurry would assume he was there and advance. The royalist cavalry then took Hurry on the flanks with a direct charge in the manner of Rupert, with a lucky downpour wetting the matches of Hurry's musketeers and the Covenanters' initially successful assault on the village driven back by the Highlanders and Ulstermen. Once again Montrose's smaller numbers proved the better army in close combat, with his Gordon cavalry (driven to avenge recent Covenanter executions) driving Hurry's from the field and Montrose then smashing the Covenanter right wing. Their exposed left and centre, tied down fighting Macdonald over the village, were then rolled up and fled the field.[79]

The rout of Hurry at Auldearn left the road south to the Lowlands open to Montrose, but he was far from any area of Scotland reachable by Charles. To make sure he would not attempt it, Leven moved the main Covenanter army in England across westwards from Yorkshire into Westmorland. Given that Goring had further to march to reach Charles in Leicestershire than Fairfax would do, the King's concentration on the north opened up the possibility that the New Model would be able to attack Charles before Goring arrived. This was what happened in the event, and in retrospect it appears that Charles was willing to risk this and thus placed himself in danger. In the meantime, Goring (a poor strategist) had shown more interest in his local predominance in Somerset than in any haste to join the King, mustering 11,000 men on Sedgemoor on 11 May and boasting in his letters about how he could either attack Weldon's forces inside Taunton successfully or force them out to be routed in open country. Obsessed with the vision of his own local glory, he blandly supposed that he would have plenty of time to defeat the enemy in Somerset and then hurry to the King's aid; the cautious Parliamentarians in Taunton did not oblige by falling into his trap so he had to give up and leave for the Midlands. It would have made more sense for him to head direct from the Sedgemoor rally to the upper Thames to support under-provisioned Oxford, but thanks to the King giving him supreme authority the Prince's Council in Bristol could not order him to do so. The only positive result of Goring's Somerset manoeuvres was that Parliament ordered Massey south from Gloucester to deal with him; en route Massey proceeded to take Evesham on 26 May to cut the King's supply route from South Wales through the Severn and Avon valleys to Oxford. But the fault was not only Goring's; when Digby wrote his first of two missives to him from the King ordering him to move up to the Midlands (sent off 19 May) the Prince's Council decided to ask for a delay in this and just send those troops that had come from the area back there, not the whole army. This would protect Somerset better. They gave in when a second order from Digby arrived.[80]

The situation of Oxford now became the centre of attention, and Goring was ordered to turn aside from the direct route to Leicestershire to head for Newbury. He was either to relieve Oxford alone or, if not practicable, to harass the New Model's siege.[81] As described by the King's aide George Digby in a letter to Secretary Nicholas at Oxford on 26 May, if the city could hold out for four to six weeks the King would be enabled to pursue his course in the north Midlands and set his army in the best position they had been for years. Also, as Digby wrote to Goring that day, if Oxford could hold out for six to eight weeks the King would be able to restore his position in the north-east – starting by recapturing Pontefract – and either defeat the Scots or force them into retreat.[82] Leven was now without part of his army under Hurry, who Montrose had just defeated, and the people of Yorkshire were fed up with his army's depredations; he was in a weaker position than he had been in summer 1644. But the perilous state of Oxford at the end of

May postponed any royal attack on Leven's diminished army, enabling him to evade battle until he could meet up with his English colleagues. If Charles and Rupert were aiming to catch him alone, and to defeat him while Hurry was away in Moray chasing Montrose, they should have set out from Oxford earlier. In that critical issue of timing, Cromwell's cavalry raid to strip the Oxford vicinity of horses who could pull the King's artillery in April had given the Scots in Yorkshire valuable time.

Digby evidently expected much from the King's presence in the north Midlands, though the fact that this diversion from the march north aided Oxford could not avoid the truth – Charles was no nearer linking up with Montrose. Digby's basic strategy was to keep Charles from moving out of reach of Oxford into Yorkshire, so that Goring (advancing from Somerset) and Gerard (in South Wales) could link up with him and the three could then tackle the New Model; Rupert's ideas centred on the King confronting Leven and/or linking up with Montrose. Why had Oxford not been better provisioned for a long blockade, seeing as when the King had left he was bound to be absent for a long period? Digby wanted Charles to link up with Goring and Gerard to deal with the New Model, not head north at all. If Rupert's advice was to be followed and the King concentrate on the north, why had he not called Goring and/or Gerard up to the Cotswolds to defend Oxford before he set out? Muddled strategy helped to make both Digby's and Rupert's plans void in May–June 1645. In the meantime Charles achieved the morale-boosting storming of Leicester on 31 May, and the threat he posed duly made the Committee order Fairfax to abandon the siege of Oxford and march north on 2 June. Fairfax moved off on the 4th, joining up en route with that part of his army sent north earlier to reinforce Leven, and thanks to a demand from the New Model officers at their council-of-war on the 8th Parliament agreed to send Cromwell (now back with the Eastern Association pending resolution of the issue of his command) to join them as lieutenant-general.[83] Vermuyden's troops also rejoined Fairfax, on the 7th near Newport Pagnell.

The King stayed immobile at Daventry as the New Model advanced, with the evidence suggesting that he and his senior officers considerably underestimated its effectiveness and its greater coherence and fighting spirit than Essex's army in 1644. Rupert and the Yorkshire officers still preferred his departure to Yorkshire to resume the attack on Leven now that Oxford was safe, and Digby's group preferred staying in the south and linking up with Goring and Gerard – neither of whom had arrived yet. They also advocated a raid on the Eastern Association heartland, without considering the likelihood that any such attack would be speedily caught by the advancing New Model. The King's Council of State in Oxford also favoured this course, which had the advantage of keeping the King's army closer at hand if Oxford was attacked again.[84] Charles' only reply to them was a complaint to Secretary Nicholas on 11 June that the civilian Councillors had been presuming on their importance by accusing Prince Rupert of insubordination towards them.[85] If Rupert had won the debate there would have been no battle in Leicestershire, and every chance that Charles could force the under-strength Leven into battle on less favourable terms than when he had fought in July 1644; unless the New Model could reach Leven in time he was at serious risk. But this strategy depended on Charles being far enough ahead of Fairfax to have time to take on Leven in Yorkshire before the New Model caught them up.

In the event, Charles was apparently unaware of how close the New Model was to Daventry, and was out hunting when he first heard of the enemy's approach. Where were his scouts? The royalists moved off to Market Harborough, where a council-of-war met and Rupert advised against fighting. According to the King's secretary Walker, Charles preferred the belligerent advice of Digby and John Ashburnham.[86] When Fairfax established himself around eight miles away at Kislingbury on the 12th the sight of some Parliamentary cavalry that evening came as a surprise to the royalists. The scattered royalist regiments were recalled to their 'command centre' on Borough Hill. The intention was to carry on their intended march towards Yorkshire not to offer battle, but they were never likely to outmatch their pursuers. Battle was joined at Naseby on the 14th, with Goring having sent a last-minute message from Somerset that he was still unable to march to the King's aid and advised a delay in fighting for some weeks. His absence reduced the King's numbers, which have been estimated at around 7–8,000 compared with around 14,000 in the New Model. The latter would have been around 14,400 men if fully up to strength, but was slightly lower; it also had the 600 men brought at the last minute by Cromwell. Only Fairfax's chaplain Joshua Sprigge claims the numbers of the two armies were nearly equal, and most sources place the royalists as significantly smaller; the King claimed he had 4,000 infantry and 3,500 cavalry on 4 June, and Lord Belasyse said the number was under 12,000. Brigadier Peter Young estimated them as around 9,500.

The royalists were too confident as the New Model approached, and their scouts on the 12th inadequate. Granted that once Fairfax had been allowed to approach the King's inferior force so closely a battle was unavoidable, it would have been much wiser to move away from Daventry as soon as Oxford was known to be safe – either north towards Leven or west to await Goring and Gerard. The ultimate responsibility for the delay in making a choice of action – and being willing to risk meeting the advancing New Model in battle without Goring's presence – lay with the King.

Naseby: a battle inevitably lost?

The advantage of numbers lay with the Parliamentarians at Naseby, and the King and Rupert clearly under-estimated the difference between the New Model and the armies of 1644. The new army had more coherence, and a more skilled commander than Essex in the form of Fairfax who had shown his strategic ability and resolve in the face of superior enemy numbers in Yorkshire in 1643–4. His deputy Cromwell was the best commander of cavalry available and could exploit opportunities on the field quickly and effectively, as shown by the officers' determination in petitioning Parliament to send him to the battlefield in time. Unlike the King with his body of proud and quarrelsome aristocratic cavalry officers, he had the will to enforce strict discipline – his men would not go charging off the battlefield to loot the enemy baggage-train, Rupert's fatal mistake at Edgehill, and he had been able to despatch them quickly to wherever they were next needed at Marston Moor. (The royalists were supposed to have guessed that he had arrived at Naseby from the greater discipline shown in the New Model cavalry's camp.) The New Model had a body of disciplined officers under one central command, chosen for their ability not their Parliamentary or local prominence (or their financial ability to raise troops). It was more than the uneasy alliance of local armies who were not used to fighting together that Charles had confronted at Marston Moor. All this added to its numerical superiority and recent training in making it a formidable threat to the King's forces, but the latter still had the psychological advantage of proven success at their last encounter with the main Parliamentary army (Lostwithiel) and Rupert's expertise and cavalry force. The royalist pikemen under Astley had the advantage of experience on the field, however well-trained or religiously motivated their opponents were, and seem to have had the better of the initial clash. Some of the royalist cavalry regiments, such as Rupert's 'Bluecoats' and the King's own Lifeguards, were as disciplined as the New Model's cavalry, and Sir Marmaduke Langdale's tough northern regiment was experienced at fighting together and determined though inferior to Cromwell's men.

As the two armies faced each other on 14 June, the usual seventeenth century battle-tactics used in the Thirty Years' War were adopted. The Parliamentary foot under Philip Skippon (Thirty Years' War veteran and commander of the Trained Bands of London in 1642) was in their centre, facing north and opposed by the royalist foot under his fellow-veteran Sir Jacob Astley. Ireton's New Model cavalry was on the Parliamentary left wing, facing Rupert; Cromwell was on their right wing, facing Sir Marmaduke Langdale. The initial uncertainty over a muddle over whether and where to fight in the early hours of 14 June favoured the

Parliamentarians, as their enemies were uncertain if the New Model was going to fight and abandoned a favourable position near Great Oxendon. The initial encounter between the senior commanders early that morning was near Clipston, where Rupert interrupted the Parliamentarian army's manoeuvres – Cromwell had successfully advised Fairfax to move from his original battle-line to one further up the ridge above Naseby, to force the royalists to charge up a steeper hill. Seeing Fairfax and his officers riding off after an initial reconnoitre of the site, Rupert (who had originally argued that the King should wait for Goring) thought this was a sign that the New Model would withdraw and march off. The royalists accordingly moved from their original rallying-point, and succeeded in taking over the eminence of Dust Hill – which meant that they did not have to cross boggy ground to attack and that Fairfax had to wheel his army round to meet them.

The battle opened with a royalist charge by both cavalry and infantry; the first contact was between Rupert's men and Ireton's, with some of the latter's regiments hanging back to await the charge and others pressing forward. The royalist charge was not uniformly successful, with Prince Maurice's regiment and one on the royalist cavalry's 'left' both being driven back in the initial clash. Despite Ireton's numerical superiority the different elements of his wing met the enemy attack with different ability at resisting – a sign of their lack of experience in the field – and his cavalry, successful against their immediate opponents, had to come to the rescue of some hard-pressed infantry. He was wounded and temporarily fell into enemy hands in the resulting fierce struggle, and Rupert exploited the opportunity to drive the Parliamentary cavalry back in disorder. As at Edgehill, Rupert should have turned 'inwards' to attack the enemy infantry in the centre but charged on towards the enemy baggage-train in the rear at Naseby village. This time he was driven off by a determined resistance and had the sense to order his men to return to the battlefield; the distraction to his cavalry was only short term but meant they missed a crucial stage of the battle. The Parliamentary baggage-train was closer to the field than at Edgehill, but still about two miles distant; while Rupert was riding up to the train demanding their surrender and being shot at his absence reduced royalist numbers further.

An injury to Skippon in the centre disheartened the numerically superior New Model infantry, which had the advantage of numbers (c.4,000 to 3,000) but was already exposed to the royalist cavalry on its flank thanks to Ireton's problems. The front ranks fell back in disorder, thus breaking up their solid 'squares' of pikemen, which were the best defence against a charge by infantry or cavalry; their officers had to take refuge with the infantry behind to stiffen their resistance. As with the Scottish 'schiltrons' in the Wars of Independence with their spears or the British 'squares' with their muskets at

Waterloo, a solid mass of disciplined men bristling with weapons and/or firepower would present a 'hedgehog' effect to attackers and break up an enemy charge. But in a clash of two bodies of infantry men using similar tactics without major interference by cavalry, the possession of ground and victory depended to a major extent on sheer 'push and shove' tactics – in which numbers and discipline usually decided the victor, and a cavalry intervention on the enemy's flanks could easily cause panic or a fatal diversion of force to fight them off.

Rupert was not available to back up his colleagues in the centre, albeit temporarily this time. Meanwhile on the Parliamentary right wing, Cromwell – aided by a reinforcement of several hundred Lincolnshire cavalry that had arrived just in time for the battle – had around 3,600 men to face around 2,000 attackers under Langdale. The royalists had to attack uphill, which put them at a disadvantage, though broken ground on the extreme 'right' impeded a charge down that flank onto the royalists. After Whalley's New Model horse had routed the less-trained northern royalist cavalry regiment commanded by Langdale, the royalist infantry was opened to attack. Cromwell duly charged, but concentrated his main force on moving inwards onto the royalist centre; three regiments could be spared to advance towards the royalist reserves behind them where the King was in command. The King proposed to stand and fight, but was advised by one of his escort to retire rather than put himself at risk. His turning his horse's head was taken by an unknown officer as a general signal to retire, a command was issued, and the reserve infantry accompanied him about a quarter of a mile back from the battlefield and so lost touch with events (and lost morale too as they seemed to be fleeing). Had the King led the reserves in advance, the sight of them might have added to potential for panic in the Parliamentary infantry where even the centre had been disheartened by Skippon being wounded. The practical impact of the reserves would have been limited unless this panic had occurred quickly; Cromwell was likely to have fallen upon them with his full force of cavalry.

Cromwell now attacked the royalist centre, the latter being without cavalry support either from Rupert or from the reserve, and Colonel Okey mounted his dragoons (a flexible force protecting the extremity of the Parliamentary left wing) to join in the attack. Those regiments of Ireton's that had earlier broken up in the initial onslaught now rallied and advanced, adding further pressure to the struggling royalist infantry, and the latter had broken up and fled by the time that Rupert returned to the field. He was met by the returning element of Ireton's cavalry, which had retreated earlier but had minimal losses and were thus fresher for a combat than his men. Sir Edward Walker testified that Rupert's men were now too tired from the chase to

Naseby village to act – and this was entirely the experienced Prince's fault. He rode off to join the King's retreated cavalry reserve, thus preserving a substantial but militarily ineffective body of royalist cavalry for another day; Fairfax cautiously forbore to attempt any interception. Two of the royalist regiments put up a fierce struggle as the Parliamentarian tide swept over them, resisting the initial impetus of attack; what more could they have done had Rupert and the King used fresh cavalry to defend them? The cavalry and the King escaped safely to Ashby-de-la-Zouch, abandoning their headquarters at Leicester; the Parliamentarians celebrated their triumph by putting all the Irishwomen that they captured among the King's camp-followers to the sword.

The result of the battle saw the royalist infantry virtually destroyed, with fewer severe cavalry losses but a major blow to morale. Around 700 royalists were killed in the battle and around 300 in the 'hot pursuit' that followed. Around 5,000 royalists seem to have been captured, crucially including 500 or so officers who were thus unavailable to train future royalist troops even if Charles could obtain the latter from Ireland or Scotland. The effect on morale from the battle was probably worse than the physical losses, and the boost to the New Model – as the instrument of divine will to its more fervent Independent soldiers and officers – correspondingly great. (The way that Ireton's men had broken up in the first onslaught indicated that the recently trained infantry were far from perfect.) The King lost his entire artillery train and most of his ammunition, together with his baggage-train, which embarrassingly contained his private correspondence. The capture of the latter enabled Parliament to broadcast the written evidence of his treacherous and ungodly willingness to bring in 'papist' Irish troops, Continental mercenaries, and anyone possible to turn on his subjects – a major blow to his reputation.[87] The long-term effects of the resultant propaganda offensive in 'The King's Cabinet Opened' thus gave increased backing to those 'hard-line' officers and MPs who argued that Charles could not be trusted, though the dominant faction in Parliament was to press on doggedly with talks with him in 1647. Arguably this was the start of the process of disillusion with Charles among men like Cromwell and Ireton – who had had no direct experience of dealing with Charles in person as of 1645 – that led ultimately to regicide. The concept of the King fighting for his subjects' liberties or for Protestantism could now be countered by evidence that he was prepared to use a bloodthirsty army of Catholics – including Irishmen responsible for the massacres of 1641 – in the cause of restoring his personal authority. He would promise anything to anyone and negotiate with rival sources of troops simultaneously, illustrating his untrustworthiness and lack of patriotism. This disgust with the King seems to have affected some important politico–military 'players' of the next stage of the conflict more than others – most crucially Cromwell.

In military terms, the advantage of numbers had lain with the New Model. But their infantry had held together in a crisis less well than their cavalry, although Rupert's presence to press home the initial royalist advantage over Ireton might still not have been decisive. Skippon was able to keep the Parliamentary centre in a better condition under pressure, albeit hampered from offensive action by his wounds; if Rupert had turned straight to the attack and been able to drive the entire Parliamentary left wing back the latter's right wing cavalry under Cromwell had the numbers to spare men for a rescue once Langdale was defeated. At best, the battle could have been a draw if enough of the Parliamentary infantry had fled in time to make Cromwell's intervention too late to save them. Rupert would have lost proportionately more of his cavalry (in attacking the Parliamentary left wing and then the centre) than the New Model had done, and the weight of numbers would have still been to the latter's advantage in a second encounter. As events turned out, the disaster at Naseby would prove to English provincial observers – moderate royalists in particular – that Charles was very unlikely to win the war and thus they had better come to terms with the imminent victors. In propaganda terms, its aftermath showed his untrustworthiness and his ability to ally himself to hated foreign Catholics in the interests of personal gain – though this did not end efforts to come to terms with him as for all his failings he was still monarch and thus essential to a stable political and religious settlement.

After Naseby – was the war irretrievably lost? Or could Charles have used Montrose and the moderate Scots Presbyterians against the New Model?

Langport and the south-west
The King now had very few infantry and minimal ammunition, besides the inevitable effect of a major defeat in discouraging any more assistance from the British Isles or abroad. He still had the undefeated Montrose in the Highlands to rely on, and his best hope was to delay a Parliamentary victory by defensive tactics until either Montrose or a Protestant royalist/ Catholic ex-rebel coalition of Irish put together by Ormonde could send troops to England. The resolute attitude of Parliament to a military conquest of Ireland and the destruction of its Catholic community added to Charles' hopes of major military support from there – it was in the latter's interests to keep him in power. The threat of a bloody Protestant revenge for the 1641 massacres and a new 'plantation' already hung over Ireland, and in Scotland

the Covenanters were equally uncompromising in their hatred for the royalists. Bringing Irish troops across the Irish Sea to Gwynedd and/or Chester and Montrose overrunning the Lowlands and luring Leven's Scots Covenanter army home to fight them were viable options, and Montrose's greatest successes were yet to come. However, Charles does not seem to have appreciated that the quality of training, discipline, and weaponry available to both these potential 'rescuers' were much inferior to the New Model – which was to make short work of the Irish Catholics in 1649 though it never faced Montrose. Even if the Irish royalists and the ex-rebels arrived in large numbers they lacked the skill and adaptability to prevail on an English battlefield, quite apart from Protestant English royalists being uneasy at fighting in the company of 'papists' implicated in the 1641 massacres (which Parliamentarian propaganda would have played up). It was also a large assumption that Montrose could defeat Leven's large and well-armed Covenanter army and clear the way to invade northern England, as even in his most impressive victories against the better Covenanter troops on a relatively open battlefield (e.g. Kilsyth) he faced inferior enemy generals not Leven or David Leslie. Most of Montrose's defeated foes were hampered by being 'amateur' urban or rural levies, being exhausted from long marches to intercept him, being caught out by a master-tactician on a problematic battlefield, being charged at close quarters by expert Highland swordsmen, or having second-rate generals (e.g. Argyll and Baillie). Montrose's list of victories was impressive, but he never faced Leven or David Leslie and their full army across an open battlefield in a 'set-piece' combat – that would have had to precede any royalist invasion of northern England and the result of this clash was uncertain. As events would show, Montrose could not even keep his victorious army together for long enough to meet Leslie's troops on equal terms on their hasty return home late in summer 1645. His best hope would have been for some mischance to delay Leslie in England until those Highland royalists who had returned home in August 1645 'joined up' again for the next campaign, which would probably have depended on a strong royalist showing in northern England or the north Midlands in August–September. The real-life rout of Montrose's small 'core' army at Philiphaugh was avoidable, but his victory over Leslie and securing of all Scotland in autumn 1645 was always a 'tall order'. The best chance of this would have been had it been Leslie who was delayed – in England – and if Montrose had been the one to take his foe by surprise, probably in an ambush while 'on the march' in the Borders (Ettrick Forest?) around October 1645.

The optimistic promises made to and by the Queen of foreign assistance, now published by a gloating Parliament in 'The King's Cabinet Opened', were less useful to Charles though their troops would be better quality. A Protestant state like the Dutch United Provinces was unlikely to lend aid to him against a Parliament that seemed to be winning, and Cardinal Mazarin and Queen-Mother Anne in Catholic France were equally cautious of committing themselves to a course of belligerence that would lead to war with Parliament and its fleet. Even if a seasoned Catholic general like the Duke of Lorraine could be brought into play with Continental troops to add to the Catholic Irish, could this be done soon enough to save the royalist military cause? The Queen's current encouragement to the Vatican to co-ordinate support, revealed in the captured correspondence taken at Naseby, was a propaganda boon to Parliament. Hyde had been warning for years against the King relying on the mirage of international Catholic support that his Queen urged; his counsels were thus totally sidelined. In London, the victory brought a sense of relief but also reopened the question of what form a settlement would take. The 'peace-party' (led by the Presbyterian peers) in the Lords voted for a speedy re-opening of negotiations on 20 June, assuming naively that the King would see sense and respond – and their allies the Covenanter Commissioners added a request that this settlement would duly settle the religious issue quickly (i.e. for a Presbyterian State Church[88]).

The King now retired to Hereford, belatedly reinforced by 2,000 Welshmen under Lord Gerard and still reasonably optimistic. He now had around 3,000 infantry and 4,000 cavalry and was anticipating that reinforcement from Goring which had failed to reach him in the Midlands. Indeed, on 18 June he wrote to Ormonde that if the latter could send him some reinforcements within a couple of months his cause would be in a better position by winter than it had been since the war began.[89] This was clearly losing touch with reality, and shows that the King's hope of Irish aid (see above) neglected the likely quality of these troops. Even if he had the men to fight another major battle by winter 1645–6 due to Welsh, Cornish, and Irish volunteers he would not have the expertise – or the ammunition – to face the New Model with any real hope of success. The only general he had capable of matching greater numbers, training, and artillery with sheer skill at using any advantage of ground was Montrose, who was cut off from him by several undefeated Scots armies – and would have to face Leslie's solid blocs of infantry and cavalry with a mixed army of Highland and Irish irregulars before he could reach Charles. Now David Leslie finally secured the surrender of Carlisle (28 June),[90] cutting off the Scots royalist route southwards, and marched south to the Midlands, while the Committee of Both Kingdoms wisely gave Fairfax the freedom to act as he thought best in his new south-western campaign.[91] Freeing him from having to wait for new orders before each change of target improved his ability to act quickly, and he was able to advance into Somerset to halt Goring's third investment of Taunton. The temporary exemptions of the three best MP generals still in service – Cromwell, Middleton on the Welsh Borders, and Brereton in Cheshire – from the Self-Denying Ordinance was extended.

The military focus now returned to the south-west, as the Committee of Both Kingdoms was advised by Fairfax. Unfortunately, Massey had proved unequal to holding Goring back. In order to make sure that the King and his Welsh armies did not fall on Fairfax's rear, Leven with the main Scots army at Mansfield were to be sent to besiege Hereford; they marched south-west via Alcester (8 July) to open the siege on the 30th. Behind them, Scarborough and Pontefract surrendered to the Parliamentarians in Yorkshire; the King was held up at Abergavenny recruiting and was unable either to confront Leven or reinforce Goring before Fairfax arrived.[92] The south-western royalists were, however, still fatally divided, with Sir Richard Grenville's small army still tied down blockading Plymouth and Grenville himself disliked by royalist and Parliamentarian gentry alike for his rack-renting, plundering, and extortion. The outbreak of angry and armed neutralism by local initiative, across the region but centred in Dorset, by the 'Clubmen' in June–July[93] indicated that there would be no more local enthusiasm for the King's cause – which unlike the New Model still depended on local volunteers. Their large and menacing array compelled Fairfax to meet a delegation at Dorchester on 3 July; they demanded a cessation of hostilities, freedom for any soldier who wished to leave the armies to do so, and the handover of all garrisons in Dorset to them. All he could do was to assure that he favoured peace as much as any man but that the King did not and was proposing to bring in armies of Catholic Irish and Frenchmen so he had to be confronted.[94] A similar delegation by Somerset 'Clubmen' was meanwhile presenting their demands to the Prince of Wales on 2 July,[95] and Fairfax could show that his army was better-disciplined than the royalists by executing looters.

Provided that the New Model defeated Goring, the 'Clubmen' could be contained by force as well as by showing goodwill; one party of them had been routed by troops from Lyme Regis. But whichever army lost the coming confrontation was at risk of attack during their – weakened – retreat by infuriated countrymen. The undisciplined and lawless Grenville outside Plymouth was the main royalist liability and luckily resigned his command at this point after more clashes with his colleagues, and Goring did his best to reassure the Somerset 'Clubmen' around his positions on the River Parret that provided the locals paid up their contributions to his troops they would not plunder. His promises were not always effective, not least where he was slow in paying or supplying his garrisons like at Langport. Fairfax advanced north-west to Beaminster, and Goring fell back from the latest failure at Taunton to defend the line of the Parret. He had a strong position in marshy country (useless for cavalry attacks by the New Model) with possession of all the bridges on the Yeo, which cut from east to west across the Parliamentary line of march north to Langport, as far east as Ilminster. But as Fairfax moved to the west of this position to cross the Yeo at Yeovil, where the bridge had been damaged but there were no royalist troops to prevent repairs, Goring failed to respond. The usual problem of such a defence, namely failure to guard all possible fords or to keep in close touch with the enemy, defeated him as Fairfax occupied under-manned Yeovil on 7 July and repaired the bridge.

Instead of replying in force with all his men or choosing an easily defensible position (Bridgewater?) Goring led an under-sized expedition in a final attempt on Taunton, but was surprised en route while resting (by Massey) and driven back in disarray. He moved back to Langport without defending the Yeo bridges at Long Suttton and Ilminster behind him. This left Fairfax free to cross the Yeo onto the north bank at Ilchester and advance on his positions, and to make matters worse Goring sent most of his artillery away to Bridgewater before the clash as if showing that this was only intended as a delaying action and so weakening his men's morale. He still held a strong position on the hillside up from a deep ford outside Langport, with access to his defences being up a narrow lane 'covered' by his musketeers, but in the battle of Langport on the 10th Fairfax's men forced this potential trap by a courageous head-on charge. The credit mostly belonged to around 350 cavalry under their officers, Slingsby Bethel in charge of the advance-party and Cromwell's brother-in-law John Desborough behind him; they faced a force three times their number but prevailed. Goring showed no ability to respond determinedly. The rest of the cavalry under Cromwell then made short work of the retreating royalists, whose infantry surrendered, and Goring had to flee to Barnstaple.[96] His infantry had been destroyed as surely as had Charles' at Naseby, and the remaining royalist troops surrounded in Bridgewater were tackled in a ferocious two-day assault on 22-3 July, which ended with the town's fall.[97] Given that no rescue was likely, the royalists in the western part of Bridgewater would have been advised to surrender once the eastern part of the town fell on the 22nd instead of stubbornly fighting on until the place was burnt down round their ears. They had their vital artillery to protect, but no hope of holding out long. Their desperate stubbornness and disregard of civilian casualties reflected the bitterness of the final stages of the war, with atrocities rising on both sides. The Somerset 'Clubmen' now sensibly came to terms with the victors, professing them satisfied that Fairfax was fulfilling his promises to cease all plundering. The end of the King's cause in the south-west was now only a matter of time, and even in South Wales his disheartened levies were starting to desert. A royal recruiting- rally at Cardiff in early July proved an embarrassing failure.

Bristol now lay open to attack by the New Model. In an ironic pointer to future conflicts among the victors, the news of Langport was carried to London by the firebrand democrat 'Freeborn John' Lilburne, future leader of the 'Levellers' and currently in dispute with the Presbyterian Church enthusiast Prynne over the necessity to pay tithes. Lilburne, a former Army officer and victim of 'Star Chamber' judicial barbarism under Charles' 'Personal Rule', had been as famous a victim of the King as Prynne, being flogged through the streets of London for libellous sedition. He was now active in controversial pamphleteering in London after being forced to resign from the Army for refusing on principle to take the Covenant (which even Cromwell had done). He had not received arrears of pay, and Cromwell sent a note with the news of victory asking Parliament to pay Lilburne his dues. The deliberately provocative Lilburne now proceeded to rake up a damaging allegation against Speaker Lenthall of the Commons, alleging that he had been equivocating at the height of Parliament's misfortunes in 1643 by sending a sum of money to Oxford. As was to be expected from a body and a Speaker touchy of their dignity and anxious to forget about such past embarrassments, the Commons proceeded to imprison Lilburne for libel. He took the opportunity to compose 'England's Birthright' – a forthright attack on the prospect of an oppressive Presbyterian State Church as no different from the Laudian one, and a defence of freedom of conscience (i.e. the right to allow the Independent sects to operate within a new Church) as an inalienable right of trueborn Englishmen. This right to (Protestant) freedom to worship as they pleased, after all, was what the zealous soldiers of the New Model had been fighting for. The right to a more democratic government of London than that by the current pro-Presbyterian City merchant oligarchy was also asserted. Published in October, this heightened the tension between the social and/or religious conservatives in the Commons and their rivals – and met a wide readership on the streets and in the Army. Lilburne was becoming the main spokesmen for the cause of combined religious and political liberty, with his mixture of concise logic, passion, fluency, and a respectable military record making him appealing to the more idealistic Army personnel. Given the proliferation of enthusiastically autonomous and theologically experimental Independent congregations in London since the fall of Laud in 1640–41, his arguments against any new form of Church discipline or secular oligarchy fell on fertile ears.

Montrose and the north: success, but too late to save the King?
Faced with Leven advancing west from the Midlands with the main Scots army and a Parliamentary reinforcement, Charles turned back to his cause in the north – where Montrose now destroyed another of the Covenanter armies, this time led by Baillie, at Alford. The latter, joined by Hurry's remnants, initially had the advantage of numbers (c. 2,000) and equipment over Montrose and was too cautious to risk being tempted into combat on the royalist general's chosen grounds. But as Montrose gave up their careful circling and pulled back into the difficult terrain of the central Highlands Baillie, more cautious than Hurry, had to move down the Spey for supplies and Hurry left him. He was further weakened by orders from the Edinburgh regime to hand part of his force over to his colleague Lord Lindsay, who they trusted more but who stayed clear of Montrose down in Atholl, though Montrose was weakened too by the withdrawal in June of Alistair Macdonald (temporarily to collect more clan troops) and most of the Gordons (on Huntly's orders). Eventually Montrose, rejoined by Lord Gordon who was defying his father Huntly, managed to tempt Baillie out of a strong defensive position near Keith with a move towards the defenceless eastern Lowlands, forcing his enemy to hasten after him. On the banks of the River Don at Alford on 2 July Montrose lured Baillie into an attack over the river and up a hill, positioning most of his men out of sight behind the ridge so that the over-confident Covenanters attacked and could be intercepted by his cavalry. Apparently it was Lord Balcarres rather than Baillie who insisted on an attack and fell into the trap, but the result in any case was a complete rout of the Lowlander infantry. The only setback was the death in battle of Lord Gordon, his principal ally amongst that clan and able to defy his father's temporising.[98]

Once again Montrose's success had shown that superior skill and élan could outwit the greater numbers and superior regular training of the Lowland Covenanters, and each success reduced his foes' morale. If his run of success continued, he might be able to win over the war-weary majority of the Scots leadership and their restive subjects to his side – provided that he could either do so before Leven returned, thus gaining the numbers and Lowland infantry to meet him on equal terms. The main problem remained the fissiparous nature of his undisciplined army, where the Gordon contingent supplied reluctantly by Huntly had temporarily deserted before Alford and some angry officers recommended Montrose to make an example of them after the battle. The Earl avoided doing this and giving the Gordons an excuse to defect permanently, but the death at Alford of Lord Gordon, one of Montrose's closest and ablest officers, added to his potential problem with that clan. The enthusiastic courtier George Digby claimed (28 July) that Alford meant that Montrose now had no major obstacle left in Scotland, though this was an exaggeration.[99]

While the New Model was carrying all before it in the south, the Scots wing of the Parliamentary coalition seemed to be collapsing. Parliament was complaining to the dilatory Leven – now heading for Hereford – about the list of depredations and extortions by his army in the north drawn up by aggrieved locals.[100] Leven's men's plundering around Hereford was to become notorious too. Some disaffected peers in Leven's army opened up a secret channel of communications to the King, a sign that the triumph of the Independent-led New Model might alarm sufficient numbers of Presbyterian peers in Scotland (as in England) to induce them to easier terms for a settlement. The block to this was likely to remain the King's obstinacy about a Presbyterian Church settlement, as it had been to Holles' hopes of the talks at Uxbridge. But in 1648 a sufficient number of senior Scots loyal to their Church were to enter into the 'Engagement' with the King, via Hamilton, in order to save the monarchy and confound Argyll's militants at home and the Independents in England. The dissidents' leader Lord Callander met with his royalist courtier nephew Fleming on 5 August without Leven finding out,[101] though Charles offered nothing definite. As Digby complained that day, the King had refused his suggestion that he make some vague promises to discuss the abandonment of episcopacy in order to lure in English and Scots Presbyterians[102] – Digby might be militarily unrealistic but his political skill was superior to his master's. If Charles had moved significantly on Church matters he could yet have cut the ground from under the New Model's feet, as he was to attempt to do – slowly and too late – with the Commons Presbyterian negotiators at Newport in 1648. Crucially, a gesture at this juncture could have persuaded war-weary Scots peers who faced the seemingly unstoppable momentum of Montrose in the Highlands – and thus broken up the greatest threat to Montrose's army, the better-equipped force that Leslie commanded. Nor was Charles able to fall back on the hope of help from Ireland; the initiative by Glamorgan had stalled and he was currently telling Ormonde to come over to England with whatever pro-royalist troops he could find.[103]

Now Rupert also backed up the idea of negotiating in a letter to the Duke of Richmond on 28 July:

> His Majesty hath now no way left to preserve his posterity, kingdom, and nobility but by treaty. I believe it a more prudent way to retain something than to lose all.[104]

Charles' revealing reply when shown this letter was to assert that as a soldier or statesman Rupert was correct and 'there is no probability but of my ruin'. But the King had to consider his position as a Christian too and save the Church – and God would not permit rebels and traitors to succeed.[105] This shows clearly the disastrous sense of priorities that was to frustrate attempt after attempt to secure a lasting settlement in 1646–8, and to lead ultimately to his execution. He showed no conviction that his duty as a Christian might also be to stop the unnecessary effusion of his subjects' blood and strike a tactical, short-term deal that sacrificed some religious principles. It also showed that even his nephew Rupert, who had the rank and the reputation to be listed to with respect, could not change his mind. For the moment, the struggle for his military survival was thrust into a matter of timing with the rising power of Montrose in Scotland balanced against the steeply declining graph of his fortunes in England. He pursued his earlier intention of reviving his fortunes in the north, where the occupation of the Scots army was deeply unpopular but they faced no military challenge, after having to dismiss his unsuccessful and extortionate South Wales commander Lord Gerard by noisy popular demand.[106] He left Cardiff on 5 August and headed north-east, avoiding Leven's army and entering Yorkshire via Doncaster (18 August) with a small force of 2,200 cavalry and 400 infantry. The local Parliamentarian army under Major-General Poyntze, who had just taken Scarborough Castle to prevent any reinforcement from the Continent, were reinforced by the swift despatch of Leven's deputy David Leslie with the Scots cavalry from Herefordshire to pursue the King and the latter was forced to move away.[107] On 20 August he left Doncaster. He headed into the Fens on a raid into the Eastern Association lands, and there heard the heartening news of Montrose's greatest victory yet.

Baillie's army having been destroyed by Montrose on 2 July, the Scots Parliament now had only a small force under Lindsay left to oppose the royalists until Leslie returned home. They duly ordered the raising of a new, and thus untested, army of volunteers to meet the threat, and moved themselves to Perth to join the levies and halt Montrose's advance south. But Montrose slipped past them and headed towards Glasgow, forcing Baillie to march after him; by dint of his usual skill and some Covenanter blunders he drew the latter's army into combat at Kilsyth on 15 July before Lord Lanark and his Clydesdale levies could join them and make their numerical advantage overwhelming. Even so the Covenanters had around 6,000 infantry and 800 cavalry to his, poorer-armed 4,400 infantry and 500 cavalry, but his mainly Highland troops had greater fighting-skill at hand-to-hand combat. The committee of Scots Parliament figures assisting – and ultimately controlling – Baillie, a Covenanter equivalent of Soviet

Commissars, had the authority to countermand his orders and duly voted to move their position in order to seize a strategic hill and cut off Montrose's line of retreat.

They ignored Baillie's warnings that Montrose might attack the army as it marched, and their army lost its one chance – of escaping Montrose's notice behind the brow of a hill – when some troops broke ranks to attack a royalist outpost and drew the Macdonalds on them. Montrose was alerted, and when a horde of ferocious Highlanders intercepted the marching Covenanter infantry the latter were cut to pieces. Most of the 6,000 Covenanter infantry were slaughtered, and the cavalry had to flee.[108] The result left the Lowlands unprotected against Montrose, and on 16 August he entered Glasgow. Edinburgh unprotected with Leslie still in England, surrendered and he was able to summon a Parliament for October. But his military success was deceptive – due to the need to conciliate the Lowlanders and the moderate Covenanter opinion he could not extort funds to pay his clan-based army, and the Highlanders were inclined to regard his success as the conclusion of their campaign. Their usual method of fighting was to go home with their loot after victory, and he had no means of compelling them to stay. Alistair Macdonald and his clansmen departed to attack the unprotected Campbells, their ancient foes, in Argyll, and Lord Aboyne took most of the Gordons home to Buchan.[109] Montrose was left without more than 1,000 men at most, mainly Irish from Antrim and so disliked by the Lowlanders, and the extent of losses his army had inflicted on the successive Lowland armies over the past year was a cause of resentment among the people from whom he would need to recruit a new force to meet Leven. Despite some support from the southern Scots peers, led by Charles' ex-minister Traquair, his position in August 1645 was more perilous than it looked. The fact that the Lowlanders would not pay for his Highland troops gave the latter no incentive to stay in his service, though the loyal Alistair Macdonald and some other clan commanders could be expected to return as promised in a few months. The question arose of whether Montrose could run a successful army without the ferocious and indomitable Highlanders, particularly with David Leslie and his trained troops hastening back north to deal with him.

Collapse in the south, late summer 1645. The 'Clubmen' and Bristol
Charles heard of the success at Kilsyth when he was in Cromwell's home town of Huntingdon on 24 August, but his position there was as illusory as Montrose's was to be in Glasgow. Cut off by advancing foes and without a strong army to meet them, he was forced to abandon his badly thought-out venture into the Fens and head back to Oxford. There (24 August) he found

that the New Model was continuing to mop up resistance in the south-west as it closed in on Bristol.[110] Badly defended Bath fell to Fairfax in person on 30 July during his march on Sherborne Castle, home of the long-serving and not always trusted royal minister the Earl of Bristol and now held by his stepson Sir Lewis Dyve. As at Shrewsbury, the royalists were taken by surprise – some enterprising attackers sneaked up to the main gate unnoticed and seized the ends of muskets that were poking through the barrier, shouting a demand for surrender, which was obeyed.[111] As Fairfax moved south the Parliamentarian forces suffered the attentions of the Dorset 'Clubmen', more militant than the Somerset group – possibly due to having suffered less from the exactions of careless royalist commanders like Goring, and in a mostly royalist area. Most of inland Dorset's gentry had been solidly for the King, with exceptions including the royalist-turned-Parliamentarian Sir Anthony Ashley Cooper of Wimborne St Giles (later the Earl of Shaftesbury, bugbear of Charles II). They were now prepared to resist even the inevitable winner of the conflict in their irritation over the continued exactions (legal and illegal) of passing troops, and promises of disciplined conduct by the New Model were inadequate to quell their mutinous assemblies. Cromwell's friend Colonel Charles Fleetwood seized a party of rioters at Shaftesbury on 3 August on Fairfax's orders, and next day a large assembly of around 2,000 'Clubmen' who had seized nearby Hambledon Hill were forcibly dispersed in an attack by Cromwell. About a dozen were killed as the ill-armed peasantry used the earthworks of the steep hillfort to defend themselves against the heavily armed New Model troopers, and several hundred were rounded up.[112] The show of force ended the worst of the 'Clubmen' threat, and Fairfax could proceed to storm Sherborne Castle on 15 August. Dyve and his garrison surrendered and were spared, and confiscated papers showed that the local royalists had been encouraging the 'Clubmen' in order to hold up the enemy advance.[113]

The New Model commanders now decided on 18 August to move northwards to besiege the only major port in the region in royalist hands, Bristol, despite the threat of catching the plague that was raging there. Fairfax replied to that argument that God would protect them in the city as surely as on the battlefield. The conquest of Devon was left for the moment, giving the troops of Goring and Sir Ralph Hopton a temporary reprieve from a hopeless defence. The siege began on 23 August. The news of Kilsyth compelled Leven to abandon the siege of Hereford on 2 September and march home to save Scotland from Montrose, having sent David Leslie on ahead via Nottingham but as a result having a reduced army to meet any attack by the King. Charles' arrival at Worcester on 1 September seems to have been the deciding factor in his calling off his Herefordshire venture.

This meant that the King was saved from having to deal with both the Scots and the New Model when he attempted to relieve Bristol.[114] The result of such a clash would have been disastrous for him, given that he was already outnumbered and his camp was filled with despondency as testified to by Digby. On 31 August Fairfax's forces outside Bristol intercepted a letter from Goring to the King saying that he would not arrive there to help Charles relieve it for another three weeks, thus enabling the New Model's commander to assess the practicality of taking Bristol before this threat would arise. An immediate attack was agreed on the failure of a summons to the city to surrender on 4 September, and its commander Rupert tried to haggle over terms to prolong the defence but was ignored. He had somewhere under 2,500 men, and his difficulties were compounded by the length of the fortifications he had to hold along the ridge of hills north of the city, a barrier constructed for a larger defending army by Fiennes in 1643. Abandoning any of them would only enable Fairfax to aim his cannons directly into the city, demoralizing resistance. On the morning of 10 September the southern and eastern defences were attacked, and the latter were breached. After a two-hour fight the crucial Priors' Hill Fort, on the hills above the city and controlling the junction of the northern and eastern defences, was stormed and its garrison mostly put to the sword by their frustrated opponents. The city was now open to bombardment and a street-by-street invasion and Rupert wisely surrendered in return for free passage to Oxford (11 September).[115] For his pains the King dismissed him from all his offices and ordered him to leave the country in an angry letter on the 14th,[116] removing his best commander – and a forceful advocate of seeking a settlement who had the necessary high rank to argue with him. The double loss of Bristol and of Rupert was a sign that the King could not expect to hold out much longer and was in a state of 'denial', looking for scapegoats.

The Prince opened negotiations with Parliament for a passport to leave the country, but they looked a gift horse in the mouth by insisting that he swear never to fight for the King again before he would receive one. Quite apart from the necessity of removing the King's best cavalry commander from the country at the earliest opportunity, there was the point that he was not an English subject but from the Palatinate – but he was subjected to the normal requirements for a royalist officer. There was a further complication in the matter of his removal, as his elder brother, the Elector Palatine, was currently staying in London and was on notoriously good terms with Parliament. He was at this time voted a Parliamentary pension of £8,000 per annum, and there were rumours that he was offering himself as an alternative candidate to be king should Parliament wish to depose his uncle. Rupert was whispered to be in league with him, ready to assist in arranging a compromise peace in return for a crown for his elder brother, and the simultaneous dismissal of Rupert's friend William Legge from the governorship of Oxford was accompanied by stories that he intended to surrender it to Parliament.[117] There had been unpleasant stories spread about Rupert' s intentions at Oxford during 1644–5, and hints that his concern for appointing personal allies to important military posts (e.g. Legge as governor of Oxford and the foreign Bernard de Gomme as quartermaster-general there) were about building up a faction with sinister intent. His critics included the Marquis of Newcastle, now in exile in Paris with the Queen and able to influence her letters to her husband, and Rupert's friend Henry Percy's sister Lady Carlisle, that inveterate intriguer, was active in London. The brother and sister were supposed to have been involved in a plot to have Prince Charles kidnapped and handed over to Parliament as a negotiating counter in winter 1644–5. In this light the King's anger at the suddenness of Rupert's surrender of Bristol does not seem so paranoid, though he was probably making too much of several unlucky coincidences.

After the fall of Bristol – the French factor in efforts to negotiate. Useless without the King facing reality and making major concessions?

The loss of Bristol meant that the royalists now lacked a major port within easy reach of the Continent, although Irish troops could still land in North Wales or at Chester. The recent French military triumph over the Habsburg armies at Nordlingen opened the possibility that Mazarin might be willing to send military aid, having achieved his war-aims in Germany, and forced the Emperor to the negotiating-table, and the Treaty of Bromsebro removed Charles' uncle King Christian IV of Denmark from the war and thus allowed him to intervene too. Henrietta Maria, still in France, was sanguine about these hopes and in August a more vigorous new French ambassador, Montreuil, arrived in London. His mission was, however, to negotiate a settlement if possible, thus preserving Charles as a potential ally and blocking the untrammelled triumph of a militarily aggressive Parliament and its army with the help of the Scots. Misreading Charles, he assumed that the King would sooner save his crown than insist on the survival of the bishops, the evident main obstacle to agreement.[118] The Scots commissioners in London were keen to avoid a takeover of their country by the resurgent Montrose – and were without part of Leven's army at hand for an immediate trial of strength in England, as it had to be sent home after the disaster to the Covenanters at Kilsyth. Their request to Parliament for military aid under the terms of the 1643 alliance was met with a counter-demand that they hand over Berwick, Newcastle, and Carlisle first.[119]

The discomfited Commissioners duly gave a favourable audience to Montreuil's efforts to arrange negotiations in September. Lord Loudoun assured him that the Scots were as eager for peace as the English, and Charles' ex-courtier Lord Holland (brother of the senior Presbyterian peer and ex-Lord Admiral Warwick), now withdrawn from politics and available in London, offered his services. It was agreed that Franco-Scots draft terms be sent to Henrietta Maria in France, and that if she could win her husband over France would then pressurize Parliament to accept them. Lord Balmerino even reminded Montreuil that France would thereby win Scots backing under the 'Auld Alliance' in case of a breach with Parliament-run England.[120] But this assumed greater willingness by Charles to abandon the Church to secure peace than in fact was the case.

Despite the loss of Bristol Charles remained hopeful of military success if he linked up with Montrose. Colepeper now proposed that the King summon Goring with his small army from Devon to join him at Oxford or Newark, bring Montrose south, and then launch an attack on London; France or the Irish could send troops to take over Goring's abandoned garrisons in the south-west. One battle should brush the New Model aside, and if the royalists emulated the discipline and orderliness of the New Model (a tall order for commanders such as the drunkard Goring) they should achieve its success in battle.[121] This left Leven out of the equation. Goring remained boastful (and drunken) but militarily inactive at Exeter, and was such a trial to his officers that they asked for the presence of Prince Charles as the only person with adequate authority in the south-west to overawe him. The Prince's Council had withdrawn to Launceston as the New Model moved on Bristol, and he now made an appearance at Exeter without effect on Goring but to be asked by the anxious local gentry to negotiate with Parliament for a truce independently of his father. To avoid such an embarrassing project but not offend the Devon gentry with a refusal, it was agreed just to send to Fairfax for permission from his Councillors Hyde and Colepeper to travel across country to the King to discuss the idea. Fairfax sent the letter on to Parliament,[122] and the matter was dropped as Charles returned to Launceston and unsuccessfully tried to use his prestige as Duke of Cornwall to rally recruits.

The final straws? Rowton Heath and Philiphaugh

The King pursued the mirage of a northern victory and headed north along the Welsh Marches, leaving Raglan Castle (Lord Glamorgan's family seat) on 18 September as Parliamentary General Poyntz closed in on him. Given the sullen refusal of the South Wales tenantry to make up his losses after Naseby, he had little choice but to move on and he was probably aiming towards Montrose's army. On 23 September he arrived at Chester with 340 cavalry, just in time to drive back Colonel Michael Jones whose besiegers had stormed its eastern outworks. His Life Guards and Sir Marmaduke Langdale's northern cavalry now tackled Jones' army and that of General Poyntz, which arrived in time to reinforce the former, but were defeated on Rowton Heath outside Chester on 24 September. Ultimately, a close-fought cavalry engagement was decided by the arrival of Jones' musketeers to relieve pressure on Poyntz's troopers by firing on the royalists, and Langdale's men broke and fled as they had done at Naseby; a sally from Chester by the gallant royal relative Lord Bernard Stuart bought time but left its commander dead. Charles, having watched the battle from the city walls, left next day for Denbigh with what was left of his cavalry.[123]

The route north was blocked by the Scots Covenanters, and even if Charles had been able to catch and defeat Jones' force on its own the royalists were too small an army to make much of an impact on the war-weary region. Once the King left the area it was only a matter of time before Sir John Byron's garrison in Chester would be starved out, and on 1 November Sir William Vaughan's intended relief-force was intercepted en route by Brereton and defeated at Denbigh. Byron sent his beautiful young wife to Oxford in an emotional appeal for support, but none was available. The locals in North Wales had lost any remaining appetite for the war, and the surviving garrison-commanders proceeded to bicker among themselves as they awaited the inevitable invasion by Parliament. Archbishop John Williams, the civilian in command at Conwy, was unable to impose any authority on the military officers.[124]

In the south, Poyntz's army closed in on Raglan though its strong walls held them back for months, apparently aided by ingenious mechanical contrivances designed by the inventor Marquis of Worcester (Lord Glamorgan's father). Charles had replaced Lord Gerard with Sir Jacob Astley as the local commander-in-chief after the disturbances during his stay at Raglan in late July, but he had already lost Cardiff to an angry assemblage of local gentry complaining about royalist military exactions (and military appointments of Catholics) on 18 September.[125] This 'Peace Army' was more socially elevated than the south-western English 'Clubmen', and also religiously 'Puritan' in a broadly anti-Laudian Church manner. Their sympathies were for the local Parliamentarian leadership, commanded by Rowland Laugharne, and the 'Puritan' Sir Richard Bassett of Beaupre Castle, Cowbridge, now took over Cardiff. The resultant purge of Anglican clergy was to enable the loyalist Sir Edward Carne of Ewenny to lead a royalist force on and seize Cardiff in February 1646, but this temporary revival was quickly broken in an armed clash by Laugharne's troops (18 February) and Carne and his ally Sir Charles Kemeys were imprisoned.[126]

In Scotland, Montrose was also hopelessly outnumbered; he arrived in Kelso to confront the returning Covenanter forces from England with at most 500 Irish infantry and around 1,200 cavalry, the latter mostly southern Scottish gentry. The latter were not used to fighting in his army, and Macdonald's Ulstermen were absent. Lord Aboyne had left with the Gordons, losing Montrose the most experienced of his remaining cavalry commanders, and the inexperienced Earl of Crawford had insisted on being given command of the cavalry. A socially important victim of Argyll, he could not be denied. David Leslie, arriving back from England ahead of Leven with the Covenanter advance-force on 6 September, had around 4,000 experienced cavalry used to combat at professionally fought encounters like Marston Moor. The Earls of Home and Roxburgh, intending to defect to Montrose, were lured to Leslie's camp and arrested; they would have done better to hurry to the royalists with local scouts to help Montrose to evade attack. Initially heading along the main road towards Edinburgh to await Montrose's expected retreat to the Highlands, Leslie was told that the royalists were encamped nearby outside Selkirk and launched a surprise attack on their rendezvous at Philiphaugh on the morning of 13 September. (One story blamed Charles' ex-minister Traquair for betraying Montrose's location to save himself from punishment in a Covenanter victory, which he saw as inevitable.) The royalist cavalry and recent recruits were cut to pieces in their camp, and in any case lacked the well-armed infantry or superior position that might have negated an overwhelming cavalry attack. The attackers were aided by fog, so Montrose could not work out where the main attack came from – but a Highland fighter like him should have anticipated that.[127] The disaster was avoidable had Montrose sent out adequate scouts – a rare lapse on his part. But had he been warned and had had time to flee he would have had to either fight for Glasgow against a far larger army or, more likely, pull back into the Atholl hills to await clan reinforcements.

Montrose fought his best with 150 horsemen to save his army at Philiphaugh until they were overwhelmed and he and a dozen or so survivors had to flee the battlefield. He had to flee to the Highlands while the Covenanter army slaughtered his captured Irish Catholic followers in cold blood, and the King's cause was lost. Exemplary executions at Glasgow included his lieutenants Nathaniel Gordon and Magnus O'Cahan, with all treated like barbarous Irishmen. But in any case the comparative numbers, training, and equipment of his small army – without his best Highland clansmen – after August 1645 meant that the disaster at Philiphaugh only anticipated an inevitable retreat in the face of the two Leslies and their large and well-armed forces. Even if the royalists had managed to retire intact to the Highlands – as would have been possible had David Leslie missed his chance and marched on to Edinburgh – Montrose would have been back where he was in spring 1645, evading and attempting to wear out Leslie as he had done to Baillie. The Scots Covenanters would have been back in full control of the Lowlands, and the King would have been unable to call on Montrose for support for the rest of the 1645 campaign. The royalist cause would have collapsed in England as it did in real life, if not yet in Scotland.

The close of the English campaigns – indicators for the future. From now on, Charles' victory depends on breaking up his opponents by political manoeuvres. The dealings of the King with Presbyterians, Independents, and Scots – and with potential foreign aid

The campaigning season of 1645 closed with the King holding onto a diminishing part of the south-west, which the New Model was slowly overrunning, most of Wales, and the area around Oxford. Despite his bold plans in the late summer, he had had no realistic hope of being able to defend this area against any concerted attack by superior numbers since Naseby. His plan of campaign in the north-west, crushed at Rowton Heath, had been wildly optimistic. Though his assessment that the populace was sick of extortionate Scots military occupation was correct, as petitions to the Commons showed, local resistance to the unprecedented burden of military occupation (and to the excise taxes across England) was only to turn to active royalism in 1647. At best he had been able to hope for a holding operation until Montrose could draw off and defeat the two Leslies, and Philiphaugh ended that prospect. Indeed, the royalist camp had had no clear idea how weak Montrose was in the aftermath of Kilsyth as his best troops returned to the Highlands – a factor that had meant Montrose was very unlikely to be able to defeat the superior and well-armed Covenanter army now in England. For the moment the King still had a substantial bloc of territory, if only small armies to defend it – Goring, already defeated at Langport, and Grenville were no match for Fairfax and the Welsh levies poorly armed and led.

The end of the war was clearly approaching, and royalist realists turned to how Charles could salvage a workable and bearable resolution from the wreckage. The fact that neither Scots Covenanters nor English Presbyterians were talking of deposing the King was one advantage; Charles was essential to both as the guarantor of their planned settlements. As seen in contemporary notions of society, the monarch was the keystone of the arch of government – and the figure who ensured legality for a settlement. Now Lord Holland proposed to Montreuil in London in October that Charles should leave doomed Oxford to join the Scots army, and duly put this to the Scots commissioner Lord Balmerino who agreed.[128] There had probably already been contacts between Oxford and Leslie. The logic of the plan, which Charles was to adopt the following spring, was that if the King could come to an arrangement with the Scots this would enable him to use their army to pressurize Parliament to be reasonable with the English peace terms. He would do this by sacrificing the already lost cause of the Scots Church and backing some form of Presbyterianism in England. Hopefully for Charles' plans, the Scots army was continuing to demand the payment of its overdue arrears of pay from Parliament, which the latter was unable to raise – and unwilling to do so unless the army co-operated more and ceased harassing the protesting northern civilians. The army was offered £30,000 on 1 November provided that it proceeded to besiege Newark as per Parliamentary orders, but the Commons also voted on the 13th that it must withdraw its garrisons from all northern towns.[129] The rising tension between Commons and Scots army acted to Charles' benefit. Leven sent a direct request for talks from Charles to Parliament and would not deal with the King himself,[130] but in London the Scots Commissioners now delivered their terms for an agreement to Montreuil as mediator on 17 October. These centred on a Church settlement as agreed by the Parliaments and ecclesiastical assemblies of both kingdoms. Assuming that the latter for England meant the current Assembly of Divines, dominated by Presbyterians, the religious allegiances of personnel in both implied a Presbyterian majority. Once the King had given satisfaction and this had been done, the Scots would then help him achieve his requests on other matters as far as practicable.[131]

The new commander of the Scots Guard at the French court, Sir Robert Moray, was deputed to take the terms from Montreuil to Paris to seek Henrietta Maria's response. The London Presbyterian MPs in favour of using this French conduit to the Queen to win over the King for a quick peace were backed up by the veteran courtier Lord Holland, seeking both to save his master's throne and frustrate the Independents, and by the ever-intriguing Lady Carlisle (now encouraging Montreuil). In the meantime, the capture of Digby's correspondence at the fall of Sherborne Castle – now examined by Parliament – showed that Charles was anticipating his Queen's success in arranging for Prince Charles to marry the Stadtholder's daughter in return for Dutch shipping blockading England, and the state of royal plans to involve France and Denmark in the war.[132] Nor had Charles given up hope of Irish Catholic troops. This evidence stiffened the resolve of the 'pro-war' faction in Parliament to tie the untrustworthy King strictly to its terms in a settlement. The 'Recruiter' elections for vacant or 'vacated'(i.e.

royalist) seats in the Commons in early autumn 1645 had given this group an important boost in numbers, in that those elected included a number of experienced and 'hard-line' military commanders – including Cromwell's son-in-law Henry Ireton, future co-leader of the Army 'Grandees' against the Presbyterian MPs in 1647–8, and the increasingly radical sectary Thomas Harrison. (However, other seats had gone to Presbyterian military men, such as Edward Massey of Gloucester.)

In religious terms, the Independents and others who favoured wide toleration in a Church settlement seem to have accepted – for the moment – that the need for Scots agreement and the numerical majority of Presbyterian MPs in the Commons meant that the new English Church would be Presbyterian. Their efforts were concentrated on reducing the disciplinary powers of the new bodies of 'elders' who were to exercise local power in this Church; the choices of who were to become Elders and their right of determining offences deserving excommunication were now under consideration. Crucially, the initial experiment for a Presbyterian Church system in London was to involve a body of nine 'triers' – three ministers and six laymen to elect the Elders in each of the sub-divisions into which the area was to be divided, with these nine electors to be appointed by Parliament.[133] The legislature, not the clergy, was thus to be in overall control of the scheme unlike in Scotland, and this should give latitude for the widest possible comprehension of Church members and toleration for diverse religious opinions in it. It might even be acceptable to a majority of Independents. It was duly opposed by the 'hard-line' Presbyterians in both kingdoms, and the Scots zealot Robert Baillie appealed to the Presbyterians in the City of London for support in freeing the projected Church from Parliamentary supervision. (The City Presbyterian congregations were strongly against toleration of sects within the Church as leading to anarchy and blasphemy by self-appointed local religious groups, as seen by their petition to Parliament on 15 January.[134]) In another sign of the irreconcilable ecclesiastical spilt, the pro-Independent minority in the Assembly of Divines now declared on 22 October 1645 that they could not and would not produce their requested proposals for the form of Church government – a form of 'minority report' dissenting from that of the strict Presbyterian majority – as it was impossible to expect a fair hearing from the majority on it. The Lords came to their rescue and revived Cromwell's earlier idea for an 'Accommodation Order' for a committee to consider a compromise between the two hostile religious factions.[135]

With Montrose defeated and in flight to the Highlands, the entire force of the Scots army could be brought to bear on the surviving royalist enclaves in the Midlands and in late November they moved to besiege Newark, obeying

Parliamentary orders.[136] In the complex world of the inter-relationship of English and Scots campaigning in 1645, this showed that the luck that David Leslie had had in catching Montrose at Philiphaugh impacted on Anglo-Scots politics in winter 1645–6. Had the Earl been able to slip away with most of his new army to the Highlands in September 1645 and meet up with Alistair 'Mac Colkitto's Macdonalds again, the Leslies would have had no option but to trail after him round the region as their predecessors had done the previous winter – there was no other Scots army available. Given Montrose's ability to defeat vastly superior numbers when the ground could be turned to his advantage, Leslie could not have dared to leave more than a small force in England. The Scots military factor would have been reduced in English politics, and with no Scots army at Newark Charles could not have used them as a 'bargaining chip' against Parliament and in due course thrown himself into their control. Ironically, Philiphaugh reduced the chances of Charles being forced to come to an agreement with his English foes in spring 1646 by lack of a Scots alternative.

The King and the Independents versus the Presbyterians?

On 24 November the Scots commissioners requested that Parliament met their need for supplies for their army and arrange to settle religion and reach terms quickly with the King. The Commons now started to draw up a formal list of terms, though this was a slow process, and it showed a suspiciously materialistic eagerness to define the extent of high-ranking peerages and annual grants to be made to the victors' leadership.[137] Meanwhile the Queen had given a cool reception to the Scots proposals brought to her in Paris by Moray, particularly over accepting a Presbyterian Church in England, as might have been expected by anyone with knowledge of her character and sense of priorities. She was hoping for overseas Catholic aid co-ordinated by the vigorous new pope elected in September 1644, Innocent X, who had hopefully sent a nuncio (Rinuccini) via France to assist the cause of the Catholic rebel confederation at Kilkenny. Rinuccini, a Florentine with no knowledge of England or Ireland, was in Paris in July–August 1645 though the Queen could not meet him due to the propaganda use Charles' enemies in England would make of this; in return the Queen's emissary Sir Kenelm Digby visited Rome for aid but could only obtain a warrant for 20,000 crowns. The lack of firm financial, let alone military aid, and Mazarin's preference for negotiating to fighting reduced the Queen's hopes of Catholic support and duly made it more logical for her husband – still promising his more pacific peers that he intended to hold out in October – to at least pretend to negotiate. Arguably the papal choice of Rinuccini was a major blow to Charles' hopes, as the inexperienced and dogmatic Italian used all his power and the prestige of his office to demand more 'hardline' terms of predominance for the Irish Catholic Church in any rebel-royal alliance. Having shunned the 'moderate' secretary of the Confederate government's Kilkenny Council, Richard Bellings, when they met in France, once he landed in Ireland he opposed any accommodation with Ormonde on Charles' favoured terms. His papal backing meant that the Earl of Glamorgan, a devout Catholic, was likely to be won over to his point of view as that of the Holy Father, not argue with him. Indeed, Glamorgan foolishly showed the legate his unofficial letter from Charles, which promised to accept whatever terms he regarded as necessary – without telling Rinuccini that Charles had also meant him to be guided by the Marquis. As a result, the Earl secretly agreed to new terms for a papal-Irish-royalist alliance that would require future lords lieutenant of Ireland to be Catholic plus the return of all confiscated Catholic Church lands and open toleration of their faith.[138]

In Irish Catholic Church terms, it was a necessary guarantee that no later English-appointed administration in Dublin would go back on its promises. In terms of finely balanced English politics, it was political dynamite that could be used to accuse the King of being a Catholic 'fifth-columnist' and it showed Glamorgan's extreme naivety. At best, Glamorgan was gambling on firm papal aid being more useful to Charles than risking papal wrath to assuage English opinion. Worse, a copy of the 'Secret Treaty' was among the papers of the Archbishop of Tuam, a Rinuccini ally, when he was killed near Sligo by Scots forces in October – and the document was duly sent to London. By Christmas Ormonde, in Dublin, was also aware from the document's capture of what Glamorgan had been doing behind his back. As will be shown later, the news arrived just as the King's adviser Digby turned up in Dublin desperate for Irish aid.

During his stay from 4 October to 3 November at his main surviving Midlands garrison at Newark, before the Scots army arrived, Charles authorized Sir William Vavasour to surrender to Parliamentary forces in order to travel though the rebel-held area to London and contact the Independent leadership. The evident intention was to build on their mutual antipathy to a Presbyterian State Church, which Charles regarded as incompatible with his Anglican beliefs. According to what Montreuil heard of the secret talks which resulted, the Independents (Vane? St John?) were prepared to guarantee that the New Model would declare for the King and put half its garrisons in England at his disposal if he would grant them a free hand to take over Ireland, set up freedom of worship for their resulting colony there, and enforce toleration on the new English Church. The Army would coerce Parliament to agree if necessary. If this idea was serious, whoever raised it – presumably a senior civilian MPs like Vane – was evidently despairing of the sort of Church to be expected in a Presbyterian England and was already prepared to use the Army – backed up by the legal authority of the King – to compel the Parliamentary majority (and the Scots) to abandon the form of disciplinarian Presbyterian Church that they were insisting upon for England. This was the nucleus of the potential settlement that the Army's 'Grandees' were to consider with the King in winter 1647–8.

Apparently some of Charles' senior remaining peers at Oxford, such as Southampton, Lindsey, and Hertford, urged him to agree to this; he refused, and they were so angry that they contemplated seizing him and handing him over to Parliament to end the bloodshed. When he heard of this threat, via Vavasour in London, Charles hastily sent a letter to the Speaker of the Lords asking for talks to commence and proposing that he come to Westminster in person once Parliament had named its negotiators.[139] The offer was not taken up, probably wisely as royalist sources indicate that it was only another attempt by Charles to buy time while he waited for foreign aid to be mustered by his wife.

The different fates of Tiverton and Basing House: signs for the future split in the Army leadership?

In the meantime, the war was winding down. Devizes surrendered to Cromwell on 23 September and Berkeley Castle to a local siege on the 26th. The New Model split up on the 28th with Fairfax marching the main part of it into Devon while Cromwell took a force to Hampshire to reduce the remaining garrisons there, although the delay in the Army's pay from London caused Fairfax to have to halt at Chard as his unpaid men threatened mutiny. On 11 October the convoy of pay duly arrived and the offensive could resume,[140] with Goring inactive in Exeter and Grenville down in Cornwall; on 19 October Fairfax easily took Tiverton Castle. Notably, the commander (Sir Gilbert Talbot) had refused to surrender on demand so under the laws of war the garrison could be put to the sword. However, when the drawbridge suddenly collapsed and the attackers stormed inside the castle before they had expected to do this, Fairfax sent orders for clemency – even for the Catholics who the militant soldiers hated – and these were obeyed.[141]

Cromwell now marched to Winchester, where the overwhelming power of the main New Model artillery-train under John Dalbier and the lack of any royalist army in the field made success inevitable. The town was overrun and the castle on its hill to the west (one-time principal stronghold of the Anglo-Norman kings in England) was subjected to intense shelling. The castle held out for a week but surrendered after a brief bombardment on 5 October.[142]

The final siege of Basing House followed, with the complex earthworks that had withstood sieges from less well-equipped forces in 1643 and 1644 now pounded intensively to open breaches. The ultra-loyalist Catholic resident and commander, the Marquis of Winchester, had called his home 'Loyalty House'; this grand aristocratic courtier despised rebels and was clearly determined to try to hold out as long as he could on principle rather than to admit it was hopeless. His garrison and the refugees sheltering within the fortifications included many local and some Irish Catholics, and no doubt feared for their safety at the hands of the radical Protestant 'sectaries' among the attackers. The precedents for Parliamentary treatment of captured Catholics were not encouraging, and since the massacres in Ireland in October 1641 Parliamentary propaganda had been making the most of the bloodthirsty crimes committed by Catholics (cited in 'revenge' killings during the war).

Relief was impossible, and the garrison were in a difficult position with regards to their rights as combatants in that they were a mixed body of 'professional' soldiers and volunteers, many of them Catholics, rather than a recognizably coherent regimental force from one of the royalist armies – the sort of men to whom the New Model usually gave quarter. They unwisely refused the summons to surrender sent on the 11th, thus giving the attackers an excuse to justify any killings, and breaches were swiftly opened in the walls by the New Model cannons. As might have been expected, Cromwell's attitude in his eve-of-assault prayers on the night of the 13th–14th showed that he regarded Basing as a nest of idolaters, which it was his holy duty to extirpate. The breaches were stormed and the mansion was taken by assault in the early morning of 14 October, with its grandiose luxuries and signs of Catholic worship inflaming the soldiery to looting and destruction. Chaos and the anticipated massacre followed in the aftermath of the assault, with Winchester making no effort to offer a white flag and attempt to save lives but fighting on until he was overpowered. The 'idolatrous papist' Catholic furnishings were duly vandalized by the troopers of the New Model, and around 100 people (mostly Irish, as was often the case) were slaughtered – possibly a quarter of the garrison and their 'camp-followers'. The Marquis was spared, unlike many of his soldiers and civilians, and was harangued by Cromwell's radical Independent regimental chaplain Hugh Peters about the destruction showing God's punishment on his idolatrous co-religionists. He coolly replied as he surveyed the ruination that if the King had no other territory in England but Basing House he would willingly have given it all up to this fate out of loyalty. The septuagenarian former court architect Inigo Jones, who had been advising his fellow-Catholic Winchester on the defence, was notoriously robbed of his clothes by Parliamentary soldiers and carried out of the ruins in a blanket. In a sense, Basing House was a 'dry run' for Cromwell's most infamous military action – Drogheda in 1649. With Basing lost Cromwell's campaign to secure Hampshire concluded, and the royalist survival in western Devon over Christmas was due to the New Model going into winter quarters around Exeter rather than to any military strength.[143]

The south was irrecoverably lost, and the week that Basing House fell the King left Newark for the north in a vain effort to get to Montrose who was still rumoured to be successful. In doing so he ignored the advice of Newark's governor, Sir Richard Willis, who preferred him to collect all his surviving Midlands garrisons and attempt to break through south-westwards to Goring. Once Charles was put right about Montrose's prospects, at the Marquis of Newcastle's Welbeck on 14 October, he turned south again to double back to Newark and go on to Oxford.[144] Lord Digby was sent with Langdale and the latter's 1,500 cavalry to Lancashire in an endeavour to get through to Montrose, and after an unexpected and nearly successful clash with Poyntz's cavalry at Sherburne (15 October) he managed to get to Galloway but found the royalist cause in the Lowlands lost. He ended up taking refuge on the Isle of Man.[145] Charles, returning to Newark, had an unexpected final meeting with Prince Rupert, who had been lurking at Belvoir Castle and seemed more concerned with his own honour than the precarious military position. The Prince turned up at Newark and demanded a formal court-martial into the charges that he had shown cowardice in surrendering at Bristol. He had the backing of Willis and other officers at Newark, who had been at odds with Rupert's recent critic Digby as a civilian and after the disaster at Sherburne had proof of the folly of his Montrose plan. On 19–21 October Rupert appeared before a council of the King and his senior officers and was absolved of any blame over Bristol by his uncle.[146] Poyntz was now moving south on Newark, and with an attack probable Charles and his advisers had to leave to avoid a showdown with superior Parliamentary forces. Rupert left for the Continent after a bitter scene at dinner with his uncle, where he backed up his friend Willis' complaints at the latter's replacement as governor of Newark and Gerard weighed in too concerning his removal as commander in South Wales. The King was accused – to his face, by Gerard – of listening to bad advice, with Rupert apportioning blame to Digby and the King saying peevishly that they thought him a child who Digby ordered around. After this unedifying scene Rupert left for Belvoir, having called his troopers together for an armed parade, which may have been intended to intimidate Charles but if so failed to move him. On 3 November Charles returned to Oxford, arriving on the 5th. Sir John Belasyse replaced Willis at Newark, and, Sir Thomas Glemham, formerly governor of York in the 1644 siege, now took over as governor of Oxford. The latter's outlying garrisons, including Woodstock Palace, were mostly to be abandoned that winter to strengthen the city's garrison. In South Wales, the fall of Chepstow Castle and Monmouth Castle to siege-expert Sir Thomas Morgan[147] left the King with Raglan Castle.

Goring, apparently in poor health but ignored by his officers too, left Exeter for France in late November. The New Model, in winter quarters around the city, did not press a siege yet but it was only a matter of time, and the 'army' that the Prince of Wales summoned to gather at Tavistock on 26 December was under-strength and poorly armed and motivated. The locals in Cornwall, alienated by Grenville's careless depredations, were in no mood to fight. In the New Year the Parliamentarians moved forward west of Exeter to confront the King's south-western cavalry commander Lord Wentworth, whose quarters at Bovey Tracey were raided by Cromwell in an overnight attack on 9 January. Wentworth and those others who managed to escape fled back to Tavistock, where the news of the disaster caused the Prince's army to retreat on Launceston.[148] Grenville urged the appointment of a new commander who would have the confidence of the officers, but when Hopton – the most successful choice available, and one with a high reputation locally from his 1643 campaign – was appointed by the Prince on 15 January Grenville refused to serve as his infantry commander. He preferred to stay in Cornwall at the head of the local levies, but was arrested for insubordination instead.[149] Even Hopton could not save the situation, and the New Model's next offensive was as much about conciliatory propaganda to sap the enemy's will to resist in a hopeless cause as about military strategy.

Fairfax moved south to take Dartmouth on the 18th and gave the Cornish garrison free passage home with money, assuring them that his men were not robbers unlike Grenville's; this duly undermined the latter. He then proceeded to surround Exeter, reducing Powderham Castle to its south en route on the 26th and opening the siege on 8 February. Hopton could bring around 5,000 troops, mostly cavalry (undisciplined veterans of Goring's chaotic command), to the relief, and due to a mixture of his poor-quality soldiers and the heavy rain decided not to attack the superior New Model troops head-on but to construct a strong defensive position and trust that the enemy would waste their manpower and morale trying to take it in bad weather. He set up his position at Torrington, with the town strongly defended by earthworks and the royalist cavalry standing ready on a nearby common to harass the attackers, and on the 18th the assault began. Initial attacks were driven back, but after dark a Parliamentary reconnaissance party secured a poorly defended barricade and the news emboldened their colleagues to move in. Poor royalist discipline undermined the initially successful defence, as a party of cavalry in the town turned tail too soon. Hopton collected his main cavalry from the common to find that the infantry would not make a stand, and as they were slowly driven back his ammunition-depot in the church blew up. The town had to be abandoned, most of his army melted away leaving him at Stratton with a small force of around 1,200 infantry, and the Prince retired to Truro. Hopton retired to Bodmin.[150]

The royalists' only hope was reinforcement from overseas, but a messenger sent by the Queen from France promising an imminent expeditionary-force had landed at Dartmouth thinking it was still in royalist hands to find his mistake too late. His letter fell into Fairfax's hands, so the latter was able to act before any expedition could materialize and he pressed on into Cornwall to take Launceston on 25 February and Bodmin on 2 March. No opposition materialized in the war-weary county as it had to tackle the last Parliamentary incursion, under Stamford in 1643. Another letter promising foreign Catholic help for the royalists, this time from Digby and Glamorgan in Ireland, fell into the New Model's hands as a royalist ship landed unawares at Padstow. It was duly milked for its propaganda value, with the New Model chaplain Hugh Peters (a local, born at Fowey of Huguenot parents) reading it out to the populace at Torrington and explaining self-righteously how it showed that the King intended to hand them over to murdering papists. The Prince and his advisers, at Pendennis Castle (protecting the entrance to the Fal estuary adjacent to Falmouth) heard that no help could be expected from France until the end of March, and there was no prospect of holding out that long. On 2 March they sailed for the Scilly Islands. The same day Hopton held a council-of-war of his officers at his intended rendezvous at Castle Dinas hill fort, only to find all but one of them voting to open surrender-negotiations. The Cornish royalist gentry had decided that the only course was to secure the best terms possible, and Hopton had no prospect of fighting.

Messengers were duly sent to Fairfax in reply to his envoy demanding surrender on the 6th, and negotiations opened at Tresilian Bridge on the 9th. In the meantime the New Model continued to advance to drive the message home, assisted by the wholesale desertion of many of Hopton's officers. On 10 March Fairfax entered Truro, and the surrender was eventually agreed on the 14th. All soldiers and all officers not exempted from pardon by Parliament could either stay in England, provided that they swore never to fight against Parliament again, or go abroad; those excluded from pardon could either leave or ask Parliament for a pardon. On these terms the King's Cornish army disbanded itself on 20 March. That left only the question of securing the surrender of those isolated garrisons still defying the New

Model, of which the island of St Michael's Mount was the most notable. Bravely, John Arundell at Pendennis Castle defied Fairfax's summons and had the distinction of being the last castellan to hold out on the mainland. In Devon, Berkeley was holding out at Exeter, kept safe for the moment by the strength of its walls but in a hopeless position as soon as the main New Model force returned from Cornwall; Barnstaple and Dunster Castle held out in North Devon and Fort Charles at Salcombe in the south. These all surrendered during the next few weeks, Exeter (with the King's infant daughter Princess Henrietta Maria, left behind by the Queen in July 1644 and not removed by her father later) on 13 April. Raglan Castle, Glamorgan's residence and headquarters in South Wales, was now reduced by Rowland Laugharne to end resistance there; Corfe Castle in Dorset, last stronghold in central southern England, had been surprised by a sudden descent by local magnate Sir Walter Erle in February – allegedly assisted by agents within the garrison who left the main gate open as a cavalry posse galloped up. All the King had left in central England were the Oxford area, Sir Jacob Astley's dwindling South Wales army at Worcester, and isolated garrisons such as Newark. That left the Scilly Islands to be reduced once Parliamentary ships were available; luckily some royalist privateers were on hand to protect the Prince of Wales and his Council and evacuate them to Jersey.[151]

Montreuil and the potential royal-Scots agreement: how France was responsible for the King entrusting himself to the Scots army not to the New Model

The French ambassador decided to intervene in person and went to Oxford, arriving on 2 January 1646, to urge Charles to go to Newark and negotiate with the Scots there – accepting the terms of Uxbridge at once as a sign of his goodwill. Once the Scots were assured of his support for their terms on the Church, and his reliability on their main demand, the rest could follow. In return, Charles refused again to accept a Presbyterian Church system for England and claimed that the Scots did not want it for religious motives but in order to use confiscated episcopal lands to pay off their army and to prevent the re-establishment of episcopacy in Scotland. Charles proposed to offer the Scots the Church's lands in Ireland to pay off their army instead so that they would not need English Church lands, and to get France to act as guarantor that he would not re-establish episcopacy in Scotland. The English Church would remain Anglican, but would tolerate Presbyterians.[152] This was a major concession on his part, but only out of necessity and nowhere near meeting the united demands of Presbyterian political and religious leaders in either country. Montreuil took the King's ideas back to Westminster for a hostile reception, and on 10 January Charles' next communication to him conceded an English synod to draw up the form of the new Church in England but would only admit some Scots to it.[153]

No doubt the majority would be Anglican or at any rate pro-toleration. Crucially, Charles' requests to Parliament to be invited to come to London under safe-conduct were not given a favourable reception; he was told on 23 December to wait for their own terms to be delivered to him first. On 3 January a further Parliamentary message told him, as the cause of the war, to give satisfaction to their terms before they would invite him to come to London.[154] Did this push him into taking the Scots army as a serious option instead – and so bringing about the political stalemate between King, Scots, and Parliament of summer–autumn 1646?

Ireland and France: could either have saved the King's fortunes in time, or did his agents' talks only infuriate Parliament and show up his untrustworthiness?

In Ireland, the desperate state of the King's military position combined with the strong position of the Irish Confederate Catholic rebel government, based at Kilkenny, to make aid available only on rebel terms. To be fair to the latter, they had had experience of the harshness, acquisitory tendencies, and anti-Catholic legislative behaviour of Charles' trusted officials in Ireland in the 1630s – especially of Strafford. Loathed by Parliament in 1640–41 as an alleged agent of Catholic revanchism and as prepared to use Irish Catholic troops on the English and Scots, Strafford had not had Catholic support either, as he enforced centralized government on the indigant 'Old English' landowners – Catholic but royalist – as well as on the 'native' Catholic Irish and sought land from both for plantation, antagonizing major lords like Inchiquin as well as Gaelic tribal magnates in Connacht. The Confederate government duly required Charles to restore full political autonomy and religious freedom to Catholics, not trusting him and negotiating from a position of strength as his English fortunes declined.

Charles' Irish royalist forces under Ormonde lacked the strength to coerce them, and the arrival of the papal legate Rinuccini in autumn 1645 as the harbinger of serious Continental support emboldened them. To add to Charles' weakness, his selected agent in the talks at Kilkenny was himself a Catholic enthusiast, the South Wales magnate Lord Glamorgan (heir to the Marquis of Worcester, head of the Beaufort family and leading magnate of Monmouthshire). The heir to Raglan Castle, royalist bastion in South Wales, was a 'feudal' magnate used to chivalrous loyalty to his King and deference from his tenants, like the Marquis of Winchester and Earl of Derby in England, not a realistic and experienced political actor – and he was a Catholic aware of his co-religionists' sufferings from the harsh but politically necessary penal laws. Any royal envoy would have had little chance of talking the Catholic rebel leadership into different terms unless the King had been in a stronger position in England and the Kilkenny government had had little prospect of foreign aid. As mentioned above, Rinuccini was even more determined than the lords and clerics on the rebel Council at Kilkenny on harsh terms that would restore the full powers of the Catholic Church and guarantee its control for the future. Glamorgan gave way to him on all matters, agreeing on 25 August 1645 not only to the free exercise of the Catholic religion – essential given the rebels' experience of the 1630s – but guaranteeing all Catholic churches regained since 1641 (i.e. at the expense of local Protestants) and exempting the Catholic clergy from any legal interference by the Protestant Church. This went beyond what Charles was prepared to grant and showed a willingness – by a Catholic negotiator – to abandon local Protestants who had been evicted since 1641, although Charles told Ormonde he could concede free Catholic worship where they were the majority community.[155] It was a major gift to Parliamentary propaganda, if ever implemented; the 10,000 men that Charles would receive in return would be militarily inferior to the New Model. Also, as mentioned earlier, a copy of Glamorgan's private agreement with Rinuccini on the terms to be guaranteed to the Church was captured by Scots pro-Parliamentary troops in Sligo in October and found its way to London.

Glamorgan could not even arrange in return for the treaty for Ormonde, as royalist commander in Ireland, to join his troops with those of the Confederates for an attack on pro-Parliamentary Presbyterian Ulster. The alliance was not implemented, and after more talks in November the rebel 'Supreme Council' agreed to keep the religious terms of an alliance secret until Charles gave his approval – thus meaning that joint military action or a rebel armed expedition to England could precede the announcement. Ormonde and the English royalists could thus look the other way and pretend that they had no knowledge of the offensive terms, and Glamorgan promised that if Charles refused his consent he would personally see that the rebel force returned home without being forced to fight for the King.[156] Glamorgan, returning to Dublin to consult with Ormonde and organize aid for Chester in December, was arrested over his secret activities at Kilkenny as news of the Rinuccini treaty reached Ormonde. He was seized by order of the King's visiting adviser Digby, who had just arrived via the Isle of Man after his failed attempt to get through to Montrose in the Highlands and knew that his master desperately needed military assistance at Oxford. Meanwhile, a captured copy of the secret treaty was passed on by the royalist Ulster Scots to Ormonde and by Parliamentarian agents to London. Glamorgan – and the King – could thus be vilified in London in January for surrendering to Catholic demands and abandoning the Irish Protestants.[157] Indeed, according to a despatch by Montreuil on 22 January some Independent leaders at Westminster were so angry at the King's alleged anti-Protestant behaviour that they proposed deposing him, excluding the semi-adult Prince Charles who had technically been in arms against Parliament as commander-in-chief in the south-west, and making either Prince James or Prince Henry a puppet-king.[158] This notion for a solution was to persist until 1649. Had Charles fatally miscalculated by using Glamorgan as his envoy or by not denouncing his concessions swiftly, and did he really think that 10,000 poorly armed, inexperienced Irish Catholic troops would survive an encounter with the New Model?

An equally politically dangerous but slightly more useful pro-Catholic treaty was made on the King's behalf that winter by another enthusiastic Catholic royalist. The veteran courtier Sir Kenelm Digby, a political ally of the Queen acting as her agent and sent by her from Paris, reached an agreement with Pope Innocent in Rome. Charles would suspend the penal laws in England and Ireland, granting freedom of Catholic worship, and in return for this when Digby arrived back in Paris in January the current assembly of the French clergy voted him one-and-a-half million francs. This was supposed to pay for an army of around 5,000 infantry and 2,000 cavalry, probably commanded by the Duc de Bouillon[159] – and a more formidable force than the Irish army due to French Catholic troops and commanders' participation in the Thirty Years' War. The alliance between the King and France now involved the Queen's idea of Prince Charles marrying his cousin, the 'Grand Mademoiselle', daughter of her brother the Duc d'Orleans (a veteran intriguer and enemy of Richelieu). To the embarrassment of the Scots Commissioners in London, these revelations of a papal-French-royalist alliance concurred with leaks that their envoys were also dealing with Charles – though these talks, via the Scots royalist courtier Will Murray, were on the basis of Charles granting a Presbyterian Church in the two Protestant-run kingdoms, England and Scotland. The French proposals were not even militarily useful, as a letter from the Queen promising this help was intercepted en route to the Prince of Wales in Cornwall by Fairfax's men at Dartmouth. Long before any French troops could be mustered the New Model had overrun all of Cornwall.

Charles was clearly ready to guarantee seemingly contradictory promises to the rival parties, and the outcome was for none of them to trust him. But as he was the King and supreme legal authority for any lasting settlement, the parties had to negotiate even if they could not trust him – only those Independents who were considering his deposition had drawn the logical conclusion from his unreliability. For the moment, Charles publicly assured the Houses on 29 January 1646 that Glamorgan had exceeded his instructions.[160] But now the precise terms that Sir Kenelm Digby had reached in Rome were received in Ireland – and they showed that that Catholic had gone beyond even what Glamorgan had promised, as he guaranteed that the King would place all his current Irish royalist fortresses in the hands of either Irish or English Catholics in return for the royalist and rebel armies combining to evict the small Parliamentarian army in Ireland and the Scots-aided Ulster Presbyterians. The Irish Catholics would have equal religious freedom with the Protestants, and the Irish parliament regain its legislative independence; all anti-Catholic legislation in England was to be revoked by the King and confirmed by the next English Parliament. In return 12,000 rebel troops would sail to England to assist the royalists – provided that the latter encompassed a small English Catholic army.[161]

This virtually placed the King and his party as the agents of Catholicism in both countries and was a gift to Parliamentary propaganda – and to Rinuccini, who was able to induce both the Confederate rebel council, whose religious and political safety was improved by these generous terms, and Glamorgan – a loyal Catholic not likely to defy the Pope's wishes – to agree to it. Only Ormonde refused. In return for this agreement, now concluded by Glamorgan with Rinuccini and the Confederates in February 1646 without reference to the King, 3,000 or even 6,000 troops would be sent to Charles in England. Glamorgan duly proceeded to Waterford to await the expedition, but the fall of Chester to Parliament on 3 February held up matters.[162] In reality, even had the expedition sailed before blockaded Chester surrendered a few thousand inexperienced Irish troops would hardly have made much impact against the Parliamentary forces, and would probably have ended up eating the Chester garrison out of their remaining supplies quicker. The besieging commander, Brereton, was an experienced and well-equipped officer and not likely to panic, even if he faced superior numbers of Irish. Only a swift Continental expedition could have achieved anything, and by now Exeter – their likely port of arrival – had been besieged by the New Model under Fairfax and the alternative, Dartmouth, been taken (18 January).

So far the New Model's concentration on the south-west had saved Charles and the increasingly isolated royalist headquarters at Oxford, but the final crisis could not be long delayed. The Queen's optimistic plans for a French expedition could not achieve fruition before the end of resistance in the area, thus blocking the route to Oxford where the 'hard-liners' from surrendered or captured royalist garrisons were concentrating. Nor could the few thousand Irish who Glamorgan expected to bring over pose a realistic challenge to the New Model. This did not halt Charles' multi-natured negotiations with all potential sources of aid, be they the Scots army (Presbyterian), the civilian Independents in London, or Catholics overseas. His private determination, as seen in a letter to the Queen on 5 March, remained not to accept any Presbyterian Church in England as it would mean surrendering any control over ecclesiastical matters, becoming no more than one voice among many in running the devolved Church, and reducing himself to a cipher.[163] This placed a major obstacle over any agreement with the Scots due to their desire for an English Presbyterian Church – as laid down in the terms of the 1643 alliance with Parliament. But it did not prevent him from negotiating throughout 1646–7 in the hope of a compromise, such as retaining bishops as nominal superiors of Presbyterian-style elected Elders – a settlement was presumably to be forced on the militant party among the Scots by loyal peers in the interest of saving the monarchy and restoring political stability in both kingdoms. Crucially, Montreuil continued to negotiate between King and Scots and urge Charles to trust himself to the Scots army. The best terms he could achieve from the Commissioners in London were that Charles should agree to the proposals over the Church, the militia, and Ireland made at Uxbridge, and send his confirmation in writing to the English Parliament, the Scots Commissioners in London, and the Estates in Edinburgh.[164] Once he had done that, the Scots would help achieve an amnesty for all the royalists – or at best temporary banishment for their leadership.

The divisions among MPs in London continued to hold out hope for Charles of dividing them, and were shown up by the controversy over the fourteenth clause of the Ordinance for a Presbyterian Church, which the Houses adopted in March. This dealt with the vital matters of Church discipline, and laid down that in the case of a churchgoer committing some infraction of this, which was not proclaimed worthy of excommunication by Parliament, the Church holders should merely suspend them and leave it to Parliament to decide on the verdict.[165] The supremacy of laity over clergy in discipline – the line on Parliamentary supremacy over jurisdiction taken by such English Presbyterian leaders as Prynne – was thus asserted, to the annoyance of the Scots clerics at the Assembly of Divines. This had potential for an English vs Scottish Presbyterian split, which was hopeful for the King in his agenda of using the Scots army to coerce Parliament. Royal strategy also conversely meant encouraging the Independents, who were even more opposed to the Scots line than the majority of English Presbyterian MPs were. Dangling the prospect of royal help for achieving toleration to the Independents, Charles' aide John Ashburnham wrote to Vane on 2 March asking for help to have Charles invited to London so that he could work for toleration in the settlement. If peace was unobtainable without a

Presbyterian Church so be it, but Vane could be assured that Charles would then work with him to alleviate the result and if necessary overthrow the religious settlement, so as to achieve toleration.[166] To the Queen, Charles wrote that he would grant toleration to the Catholics if they would work at home and abroad to restore him and the Anglican Church – which was not compatible with the aims of either Presbyterians (in both countries) or Independents.[167]

On 14 March the main royalist force in Cornwall under Sir Ralph Hopton agreed to the proposed terms of surrender, leaving only a few fortresses in Cornwall holding out. The governor of Oxford and former commander of the infantry at Naseby, Sir Jacob Astley, had been gathering royalist troops from the disintegrating cause in the south-west Midlands and set out for Oxford with around 3,000 men to be trapped at Stow-on-the-Wold by the three converging small Parliamentary armies of Morgan, Birch, and Brereton. Numbers were about equal, but morale was not; the outcome showed that the royalists lacked the will to fight even though loyalty had brought them this far. A demonstration of their loyalty to their King to save their honour was more in their minds than serious chances of victory. Attacked in the early hours of 21 March, the royalists started to surrender as soon as it was clear that they were having the worst of the fight and the King's last English army collapsed. Handing himself over to the victors, Astley made the famous jibe that they had done their work and could now go and play unless they fell out among themselves.[168] That was the King's best hope, and Charles was to do his best to avoid coming to a settlement with any one of the contending parties in the expectation that delay would enable something better to turn up. At risk of capture as the Parliamentary armies closed in on Oxford, he left the city in disguise for an uncertain destination on 27 April.[169]

The 'what ifs' of 1644–5. Saving the royalist cause: when was it lost and how could it have been saved?

It is noticeable, as has been illustrated during the foregoing narrative, how the 'arc' of plausible 'what if' questions alters from 1643 in 1644–5. In 1643 the most plausible alternative outcomes to events all feature a royalist victory, with the crucial issues being: (a) the extent and timing of the 'three-pronged' advance towards London; (b) the Gloucester and Newbury campaign. As was seen in the coverage of the 1642 campaign, once a quick victory by one or other side (probably the King's army) at Edgehill and / or a royalist occupation of London had been avoided in October–November 1642 the war was 'decentralized' into smaller local regional conflicts. This development in early 1643 did not produce fairly stable 'battle-lines' that were difficult to breach, which was difficult in England anyway owing to the nature of the geography. The maps that can be drawn of the 'battle-lines' are complex and fluid through 1643–4, though with some constants such as Parliamentary control of the south-east of England and royalist control of the west and of Wales (with a few exceptions). But the regional conflicts meant that even a crushing victory by one party in one region – e.g. the royalist overrunning of the south-west in early summer 1643 – was reversible, and subject to exceptions (mostly isolated enemy garrisons protected by geography or strong walls holding out). Success by the main 'field armies' in the summer 1643 campaign did not guarantee an easy or quick victory across the country, though this would have produced a probably unstoppable momentum in the long term.

Given the inexperience and disorganized nature of the lumbering main royalist and Parliamentarian armies in the crucial Gloucester/Newbury campaign, an outright and crushing victory by either side then was unlikely except by luck. Essex, the Parliamentarian commander, was experienced but cautious, and the King was inexperienced and lacked military flair; Rupert had the latter but was prone to misjudgements or losing control of his men. An advantage of geography or numbers/ firepower on the battlefield (absent at Newbury) could have tipped the balance at a battle between the two main armies in 1643, perhaps with the royalists having the advantage over an exhausted Essex on the Cotswold ridge after his march to Gloucester and/ or having stormed the town before he arrived. The victory would then produce a 'snowball' effect as the King marched on London and the surviving Parliamentarian commanders had to negotiate their surrender against overwhelming odds or flee. But is this feasible – would the visibly inferior side have risked a battle at all unless trapped? Would one side have risked all on a hunch that the enemy was in a dangerous position and would crumble quickly if attacked with vigour at a weak point? This was the sort of gamble taken by Montrose, with a small and desperate army short of weapons and ammunition (e.g. at Tippermuir), not by any English commanders who had less need to take risks. Heavy losses in a frontal assault tended to unnerve the most senior English commanders into not repeating this – e.g. Charles after Edgehill and after probing the enemy positions at Gloucester. The exceptions, the men with 'élan' who gambled with their men, were mostly royalist and tended to end up killed leading from the front – e.g. Sir Bevil Grenville. The more methodical Cromwell shared their ability to judge a battlefield and inspiration to win devotion from his men, but only pressed forward at the right moment when he had the necessary resources (which he lacked as a minor commander in 1643). Notably, in a similar situation to Rupert of a successful cavalry charge on one 'wing' of an enemy – at Winceby in 1643 – Cromwell could stop his men and turn them inwards on the remaining enemy forces. What if Rupert had done this at Edgehill? Or the King had had a more experienced cavalry commander there (necessarily a man of high social rank)? To a lesser extent, Waller (who at this date had more troops and a more senior rank) in 1643–4 was the same type of 'steady' and cool-headed commander as Cromwell, with devotion from his men. The royalists had fewer of these, though Hopton was as methodical (but lacking a 'spark' of quick thinking in a crisis, and accused by Hyde of being a better second-in-command than supreme commander). History is traditionally kinder to the winners than to the losers, and the royalist commanders were the latter so more open to criticism – and some of them survived battle only to be 'rubbished' by their foes in writing for their personal failings (e.g. Goring's fate at Hyde's hands). The modern verdicts of historians such as Peter Young and John Barrett largely concur with Hyde, though giving more credit to Goring and to Lord Byron. Had Sir Bevil Grenville not been killed 'leading from the front' in 1643, would he and his disciplined Cornishmen have been a more valuable asset to the King in 1644–5 than the wayward Goring ? What if Charles had totally trusted Rupert, rather than had courtiers whispering about the latter's brother Charles Louis' designs on the King's throne which Rupert might aid? Could Rupert have saved the day at Naseby had he trained his cavalry to rein in their enthusiasm and think of the 'big picture' on the whole battlefield? Could he have mauled Essex's army on the march en route to Newbury and so made victory there easier, had he been brought into the 'chase' quicker and so caught Essex up? But the choice of war-winning strategy lay with Charles, not with the more talented Rupert – and the King was never one to seize the moment competently, from his slackness after Edgehill in 1642 to his failure to escape from Newport, Isle of Wight, in time to avoid arrest in November 1648. Notably, Charles did not unleash Montrose on the Scots Covenanters until summer 1644, when his cause was collapsing in the north – what if he had sent him (and Antrim had sent Alistair Macdonald) to the Highlands in summer 1643 to prevent Leven's army having the leisure to invade England?

A similar question lies over the issue of a royalist victory in 1644, which was in any case less likely now that thousands of experienced and well-armed Scots were in the field to aid Parliament. Leven and David Leslie, leading an army of principled Covenanters fighting for a self-declared 'godly' cause like the New Model was to do in England in 1645–6, were less likely than an outnumbered and not particularly zealous local English Parliamentarian general of 1643–4 (e.g. Manchester) to seek to negotiate after their side had lost a vital battle and seemed to be facing annihilation. They did not quail in

1650 after the disaster at Cromwell's hands at Dunbar, but fought on – and would probably have done so against an even more 'ungodly' royalist foe in summer 1644 had they lost at Marston Moor. A victory by Rupert and the Marquis of Newcastle at Marston Moor in July 1644 was unlikely unless by luck – the death of a senior enemy general in the battle causing panic? – due to their being outnumbered by an increasingly 'professional' Eastern Association/ Scots army. Rupert, outnumbered and having accomplished the relief of York as the enemy pulled back, might not even have fought without the 'push' of a letter from the King urging it on him. In that case the three enemy forces would have split again, and Rupert and/or Newcastle would have had to reconquer the north-east and tackle the Scots again later. Even had Rupert won decisively and pushed the Parliamentarians' eastern army back into Lincolnshire and wiped out their smaller northern army at Marston Moor, any failure to destroy the compact, well-armed, and disciplined Scots would have left the latter at large ready to save the northern Parliamentarians from complete disaster. With 'backs to the wall' and facing the danger of a third royalist invasion of Scotland, the Scots' heavy infantry had the will and the firepower to defend the Fairfaxes' West Riding towns and/or the town of Newcastle against assault from Rupert's force of mainly cavalry and lightly armed Welsh/ north-western tenant infantry. Could the King risk losing ground in the south to bring up his main force to break this impasse, while Waller's army was still in one piece albeit demoralized by losses at Cropredy Bridge? Notably the King did not have a substantial navy (unlike Parliament) so he could not easily move artillery or troops by sea, whereas Parliament was able to send its ships to intervene as far afield as Devon/ Cornwall (1644) or Hull/ Bridlington (1643).

Royalist victory at Marston Moor could thus have produced a stalemate rather than a national victory, unless the Scots had been so badly mauled that Rupert or the King could then reconquer the north-east successfully and back up Montrose's emerging campaign in Scotland in autumn 1644. Lacking much artillery, had the King's forces won at Marston Moor they were still unlikely to have retaken walled Hull or Newcastle; success would have occurred in the open countryside and so been reversible by a new enemy force sent from London or Edinburgh. Diverting major royalist manpower to the north in July–August 1644 would, however, throw away a chance of success in the south, and it is more likely that had success at Marston Moor been followed quickly by the King's success in Cornwall (as in real life) Charles would regard the north as a 'side-show'. Nor would local southern commanders have been amenable to marching north – Goring and Sir Richard Grenville, Charles' best if flawed local commanders there, were notoriously insubordinate. The deadlock would more likely have been broken in spring or early 1645 than in 1644, as Montrose's crushing successes forced the weakened Scots Covenanter army back into the Lowlands to deal with him and the latter abandoned northern England. Had Leven suffered serious losses of men and munitions at Marston Moor, Montrose could then have routed David Leslie (or him) at Philiphaugh rather than the other way round – provided that he had had warning of the Covenanters' approach in time and had been able to mount one of his brilliant ambushes with the southern Scottish royalist peers' levies. This would have left Montrose in control of all Scotland except Edinburgh Castle, and secured the King's northern flank at a time when he was confronting the surviving Parliamentary forces in southern England. Assuming that he had defeated Essex's main army in Cornwall in August 1644 as in reality, he would have had control of all the north as well as the south-west and would have faced the Parliamentarians at 'Second Newbury' in October–November from a better position. Victory at the latter would then have driven more moderate Parliamentarian generals and MPs to negotiate and the others to face having to flee the country. But this outcome is still a less than likely scenario, unless the King had been helped at 'Second Newbury' by even worse Parliamentarian command confusion than reality and had caused major casualties and secured most of the enemy artillery. Taking a major Thames Valley town such as Reading in the 'follow-up' would have unnerved the resistance too. Regarding Parliament's reaction, a conciliatory approach by the King's 'tame' Parliament at Oxford concerning possible peace-terms would have helped – but royalist civilian advisers such as Hyde would have had to combat bloodthirsty demands by generals such as Goring for outright military victory plus lots of executions. The legal argument that the Parliament at Westminster was 'illegitimate' as it was constrained by militant London fanatics (seen in winter 1641–2) could have encouraged some MPs to defect to Oxford.

The most plausible 'what ifs' of 1644 are for a Parliamentarian rather than royalist victory, however. As we have seen, the main 'field army' of Essex narrowly missed a chance to capture the King at Woodstock in June 1644 as it moved around Oxford, and proper co-ordination between Essex and Waller (who unfortunately hated each other) could easily have led to a siege of Oxford. The King would then have had to fight to save his 'capital' at a time when Rupert and the northern armies were preoccupied with the Marston Moor campaign, abandon the latter to save Oxford and so lose all the north, or abandon Oxford and be driven back into the Severn valley. The crucial reasons for the summer 1644 Parliamentarian campaign turning into muddle, a strategically risky march all the way to Cornwall, and defeat at Lostwithiel were Essex's personal choices. He defied Parliament's orders in the process – would a less confident but still aristocratic commander who had replaced him for the 1644 campaign (a surviving Lord Brooke?) have done this? The choice to march into the west at all was due to the royalist siege of Lyme Regis, the Parliamentarian equivalent of Stalingrad in the Second World War as it held up a locally dominant 'invader' at a symbolic strongpoint for vital weeks. The Parliamentarian relief-force's decision to march on into Cornwall, which made less strategic sense, was probably due to over-confidence by Essex about local Lord Robartes' claims of support there, though Essex had the option of advancing less far and extricating himself quicker once the King advanced on him. (Unlike in 1643, he showed little appreciation of the need to be flexible and mobile.) But for the Lyme Regis/Cornish campaign, Parliament might have won in 1644 – or at least captured Oxford and forced the King back into Wales ahead of a decisive advance over the River Severn in 1645.

In that case, one cannot see any overwhelming Commons support in winter 1644 for the plan to create a new army in spring 1645; if Parliament was winning already there would have been less frustration with Essex and the badly co-ordinated local armies. Would Cromwell and his allies have been unable to muster the votes to replace the latter, and would his principal foe Manchester have retained his command plus more political 'clout' at Westminster? Without the New Model favouring religious toleration, would the socially conservative Presbyterian majority of MPs, allied to Manchester's faction on the Lords, have been able to insist on a 'hardline' Presbyterian State Church being set up in 1645–7 without the military intervening to stop them? The Parliamentarian victory of 1645 would thus have probably led to a settlement on the lines of the 'Nineteen Propositions' of 1642, with the King constrained by a bloc of oligarchic Presbyterian aristocrats headed by Essex (until he died in 1646), Warwick, and Manchester and by that Presbyterian majority of MPs who were to be stymied by the New Model in real-life 1647 and 1648. This has one 'caveat' in that the King was an unreliable negotiating partner, and even if the destruction or return to Scotland of Leven's Covenanter army in 1644/5 meant that he could not hand himself over to them (as in real life) he could have fled the country. Logically driven back from Oxford to Worcester and into Wales in summer–autumn 1644, he would have had the options of heading to Ireland (to join Ormonde's royalists) or to France (to join his wife).

The defeat of David Leslie or Leven (already badly mauled at Marston Moor) by Montrose in late summer 1645 presents another possibility. What if Charles had lost all of England but been able to rely on a royalist-occupied Scotland? Montrose, of course, was not a 'hard-line' royal loyalist but an ex-

Covenanter, a Presbyterian who had backed the 'rebels' in 1638–40 and was partly driven into supporting the King from 1641 by rivalry with the implacable Argyll, 'King Campbell'. Despite his poor reputation in the Protestant Lowlands for employing an army of 'murdering papists' and slaughtering thousands of 'godly' Lowlanders in battle and at Aberdeen, he was capable of reaching out to moderate Covenanters and was endeavouring to attract their peers to his side in summer 1645 when this was aborted by Leslie's attack. Indeed, his shortage of men when his unreliable (often Catholic Highlander) clan allies were absent at home meant that he needed Protestant Lowlander troops, plus southern Uplands/Lothian aristocrats' tenants, to fight for him if he was to have a viable army in autumn 1645. His victory over the last co-ordinated local Covenanter army at Kilsyth left the Lowlands at his mercy as of July–August 1645, but this did not mean that he was capable of invading England to assist the King even had he then routed Leslie or Leven. A few hundred Irish mercenaries under Magnus O'Cahan (the nucleus of Montrose' army as of August 1645) plus the 'part-time' Highlanders mustered by swashbuckling Alistair 'Mac Colkitto' Macdonald and the clan levies of the Gordons would not defeat the Parliamentarian 'field army' as it existed in 1644, let alone the New Model. To create a viable force, Montrose would have had to rely on the combination of 'moderate Covenanter' peers and their tenants who were to form Hamilton's real-life 'Engager' invasion-army of 1648. This coalition could have been created given time, and the personal presence of the (defeated?) King plus his (insincere) promises to retain the Covenanter Church would have boosted recruitment. Had the Parliamentarians won in southern and northern England in 1644 and then moved on to the west and Wales in spring 1645, they would not have had a need to create the New Model – which was to defeat the real-life Scots royalist invasion in 1648. The Parliamentarians who faced Charles and Montrose would have continued to be led by an aristocrat as there would be no 'Self-Denying Ordinance' to ban peers from command, unless the exhausted Essex and the timid Manchester had both 'retired' (voluntarily or not) and the more capable Waller or Fairfax replaced them. Cromwell would have been at best the second-in-command, commander of the heavy cavalry as the indispensable 'star' of the cavalry actions in 1644 and the 'godly' creator of the best Eastern Association regiment.

The resultant clash between King/ royalist Scots and Parliament would possibly have occurred in spring 1646 in the north-west, around Preston as in the real-life 1648 invasion. But there is also the chance that if the papacy had not sought to meddle in Irish Catholic 'rebel' politics in 1645–6 there would have been a successful move by Ormonde to build on the shared antipathy of '1641–2 royalist' Irish (mainly Protestant, some Catholic) and

'1641–2 rebel' Irish (Catholic) to the threat of destruction by the English Parliament and lure some 'rebel' Catholic commanders to ally with him on Charles' behalf. There were many personal and family links between Ormonde and senior 'rebel' Catholic peers at Kilkenny – as suspicious 'hard-line' legate Rinuccini noted. There was a potential for all these senior landowners to combine in 1643–5, had the Catholics been prepared to stand up to their clerics and not had the lure of papal money and weapons if they followed Rinuccini; and a different pope than the ambitious and autocratic Innocent X would have sent a different legate (if any). Worse, the 'hard-line' Catholics had a military leader of reputation and competence to hand, in Owen Roe O'Neill – whose genealogy gave him a claim on the loyalty of a substantial 'bloc' as being of the ancient Ulster royal blood and nephew of the great rebel leader Tyrone. What if Charles' English position had collapsed quicker? Both the royalists and the Catholic 'rebels' would have been facing annihilation and the seizure of their lands from the victorious Parliamentarians as of late 1644 or 1645, with an invasion of Ireland a probability. With no papal mission to take 'hard-line' control of the 'rebel' Catholics for a new Catholic state running all Ireland and limit the King's powers, and papally directed priests adding their support, could the less fanatical Catholic generals have been prepared to fight for Charles if he arrived in Ireland as a refugee in spring 1645? He would have had to guarantee full toleration for the Catholic Church and a return of confiscated lands, but this was not as objectionable to him as was signing up to the Covenant. Instead of a defeated Charles trying to cozen one victorious anti-Anglican 'national autonomist movement' (the Scots Covenanters) into supplying him with troops, would he have done the same to another – their Catholic equivalents in Ireland? Would he and Ormonde have been able to put together a royalist-'rebel' coalition and army to intervene in England later in 1645, or have taken this to Scotland to support Montrose when he secured the Lowlands plus Glasgow/ Dumbarton in July 1645? But would this spectacle of a large-scale 'papist' invasion have lost Montrose any chance of moderate Covenanter support, and made him and Charles dangerously dependent on Irish troops who were no match for the better-armed English Parliamentarians?

Notes

Chapter One

1. S. Gardiner, *History of England 1603–42*, vol x, p. 136.
2. Wing Mss. C 2600.
3. Archives du Ministère des Affaires Etrangères, Paris: Correspondence Politique: Angleterre, no. 46, letter from Marquis de la Ferté-Imbauld, 16/26 December 1641.
4. *Commons Journal*, vol ii, p. 339.
5. Coates, D'Ewes Diary, p. 216 n; Clarendon, *History of the Great Rebellion* (ed. W. D. Macray, Oxford 1888) , vol I, p. 84.
6. *Diary of Sir Simonds D'Ewes* (ed. Wallace Notestein, New Haven, US, 1925), p. 330.
7. See John Adamson, *The Noble Revolt*, pp. 474–6 on the Lunsford appointment crisis.
8. Clarendon, vol I, pp. 454 and 471; National Archive State Papers 16/486/110; *Lords Journal*, vol iv, p. 493.
9. The threat by the Commons to impeach her servant Daniel O'Neill (*Commons Journal*, vol ii, p. 366) is the likeliest occasion for this fear to have crystallized.
10. National Archives: L C 5/135, entry for 28 December 1641.
11. *Lords Journal*, vol iv, p. 495.
12. *Commons Journal*, vol ii, p. 366.
13. Gardiner, *History*, vol x, p. 138; National Archives SP 31/3/73, f.10r–v; *Commons Journal*, vol ii, pp. 368–9.
14. *Lords Journal*, vol v, pp. 414, 416.
15. Sir Philip Warwick, *Memoirs* (1702) p. 225.
16. John Adamson, *The Noble Revolt: the Overthrow of Charles I* (Weidenfeld and Nicolson 2007) p. 496.
17. William Lilly, *Life of Charles I (1774)* , pp. 232–4; CSPD 1641–2, pp. 238, 242, 249.
18. D'Ewes Diary, p. 232; *Commons Journal*, vol ii, pp. 368–9; Lord Mayor's Archives: Common Council Journal, vol 40 f. 15.
19. British Library Mss.: E 131/14: A Great Conspiracy of the Papists, Against Worthy Members of Both Houses of Parliament (1642). Also R. Clifton, 'Popular Fear of Catholicism' in *Past and Present*, vol 152 (1971).

Chapter Two

1. Clarendon, vol ii, p. 293.
2. For example, see the defiance of the townsmen of Manchester: British Library: Thomason Tracts E 141 (45). Also Gardiner, vol I, p. 34.

3. Gardiner, p. 112. See also *Lords Journal*, vol v, p. 576 for the King's speech.
4. Thomas Carte, *Life of Ormonde*, vol v, p. 352.
5. See aslo C. Carlton, *Charles I: the Personal Monarch* (Routledge 1983), pp. 239–40.
6. See Barbara Donaghan, 'Casuistry and Allegiance in the English Civil War' in Derek Hirst and Richard Strier (eds), *Writing and Engagement in Seventeenth Century England* (Cambridge UP 2000) pp. 89–111.
7. Thomason Tracts E 112 (8): A True Report of the Occurrences at the Taking of Portsmouth; E 116 (15): A Relation From Portsmouth, wherein is declared how the castle was taken; also J Vicars, Jehovah-Jireh: The God in the Mount (1643), pp. 158–61.
8. But see also Gardiner, *History of the Great Civil War*, vol I, pp. 16–17 on Rupert's naked extortion from local communities.
9. British Library Additional Mss. 18992: Charles' letter to Littleton, August 1642.
10. Anthony Fletcher, Outbreak of the English Civil War, pp. 298–300; Thomason Tracts: E 116 (40): A True Relation of How the Isle of Wight Was Taken.
11. See Keith Lindsey, *Fenland Riots and the English Civil War* (London 1982).
12. British Library: Additional Mss. 18992.
13. Trevor Royle, *Civil War: the Wars of Three Kingdoms*, p. 164.
14. Thomason Tracts: E 115 (4): A True Relation of... His Majesty's Setting Up His Standard; Clarendon, vol v, pp. 447–9.
15. Gardiner, *History of the Great Civil War*, vol I, pp. 21–6.
16. Whitelocke, *Memorials*, p. 65.
17. G. Davies, 'The Parliamentary Army Under the Earl of Essex 1642–5' in *EHR*, vol 49 (1934), pp. 34–54.
18. See Charles reply to this mission: HMC Argyll Mss., 6th Report, p. 612.
19. See *Commons Journal*, vol ii, p. 369 on Commons control of the Tower as of 6 January.
20. Gardiner, vol I, pp. 13–14 and 16–17.
21. See Russell, *Fall of the British Monarchies*, pp. 503–506 for desertions from London.
22. Richard Baxter, *Reliquae Baxterianae*, p. 42; Edmund Ludlow, *Memoirs*, p. 19; Whitelocke, *Memorials*, pp. 73–4; Gardiner, vol I, pp. 29–31.
23. See Chapter 3 n. 25.
24. *Lords Journal*, vol v, p. 411.
25. Gardiner, vol I, p. 37.
26. *Lords Journal*, vol v, p. 412.
27. Rushworth, *Collections*, vol vi, p. 65; Ellis, *Original Letters*, series 1, vol 3, p. 291.
28. *Lords Journal*, vol v, pp. 414, 416.
29. Warburton, *Memoirs of Prince Rupert and the Cavaliers*, vol ii, p. 12; also Thomason Tracts: E 124 (26): Denzel Holles, An Exact and True Relation of the Fight Near Kineton.
30. As above; also Thomason Tracts: E 126 (15): Edward Kightley, A True and Full Relation; E 126 (24), and E 124 (32), Lord Wharton's 'Eight Speeches Spoken in Guildhall' for the Parliamentary version of events; E 126 (24), Relation of the Battaile Fought... Between Kineton and Edgehill, and Clarendon, vol 6, p. 88 for the royalist version. For commentary and analysis, P. Young and R. Holmes, *The English Civil War: A Military History of the Three Civil Wars* (2000) pp. 73–81.

31. See the official royalist account in Thomason Tracts: E 126 (24).
32. Gardiner, vol I, p. 51.
33. Clarendon, book ii, pp. 388–98.
34. *Lords Journal*, vol v, p. 324; Gardiner, pp. 53–6.
35. Bodleian Library: Tanner Mss lxiv, f. 87.
36. Gardiner, pp. 56–7; Warwick, pp. 254–5.

Chapter Three
1. As Chapter 2, note 19.
2. BL Harleian Mss. 164, f. 220b.
3. Gardiner, vol i, p. 80.
4. See Clarendon, *History of the Rebellion*, vol iii, pp. 144,192; *Dictionary of National Biography* article on Bedford by CH Firth (vol 49); and John Adamson, *The Noble Revolt*, pp. 160–61, 321.
5. Whitelocke, p. 65.
6. *Commons Journal*, vol iii, p.98; Rushworth, vol v, p. 156; Gardiner, pp. 94–5, 135,164–6.
7. *Lords Journal*, vol v, p. 299.
8. Thomason Tracts E 99; BL additional Mss. 18980 ff. 38–52.
9. Warburton, vol ii, p. 151.
10. Ibid.
11. Thomason Tracts E 93 (3): A Brief Relation of a Plot Against Bristol.
12. Sir Ralph Hopton, *Bellum Civile*, p. 30 ff; HMC Portland Mss. vol I p. 92; Gardiner, vol I, pp. 86, 131; *Commons Journal*, vol iii, p. 41; Clarendon, *History of the Rebellion*, vol vii pp. 88–9.
13. Hopton, pp. 43–4; Bodleian Library: Clarendon Mss no. 1738, part 1; Clarendon, History…, vol vii, p. 89.
14. Thomason Tracts: E 94 (12): A letter from Sir William Waller to the Earl of Essex against a Great Victory he obtained at Malmesbury; E 97 (2): The Victorious and Fortunate Proceedings of Sir William Waller and his forces in Wales and other places since they left Malmesbury; E 99 (2) , E 100 (18) and E 247 (26) Mercurius Aulicus newsletters; E 247 (28): Mercurius Bellicus… wherein is the relation of the taking of Hereford by Sir William Waller. Also Jehovah-Jireh, pp. 292–3.
15. HMC Portland Manuscripts, vol I, pp. 710, 712; also, John Adair, *Roundhead General*, chapter 9.
16. Thomason Tracts E 99 (18): The battaile of Hopton Heath; E 267 (11), A new discovery of hidden secrets. Also Peter Young, 'The battle of Hopton Heath' in *Journal of the Society for Army Historical Research*, vol 32.
17. Thomason Tracts 116 (20): Dagon Destroyed. Also Gardiner, vol I, pp. 146–8.
18. Rushworth, vol v, p. 325.
19. Ibid.
20. Gardiner, pp. 126–7.
21. Thomason Tracts E 101 (2): Certain Information…
22. Hopton, Bellum Civile (1902 edition), pp. 48–50; Adair, *Roundhead General* p. 74.
23. Thomason Tracts E 60 (8): The Parliamentary Scout, 6–13 July 1643; also in E 60, see A Weekly Account, 3–10 July; Jehovah-Jireh, pp. 376–80.

24. 'The Vindication of Richard Atkyns', edited by Peter Young, in *Journal of the Society for Army Historical Research*, vol 55 (1957), p. 65. For Roundway Down see Atkyns, pp. 36–8; Thomason Tracts: E 61 (6): A true relation of the late fight between Sir William Waller and those sent from Oxford; Bodleian Library: Tanner Mss. 62, f. 54; British Library Mss. 1103, f. 77/5: Sir John Byron's relation to the Secretary of the Last Western Action; Peter Young, 'The Royalist Army at the Battle of Roundway Down' in *Journal of the Society for Army Historical Research*, vol 49 (1953).

25. Thomason Tracts E 61 (6): A True Relation of the Late Fight; E 64 (12): A Relation by Colonel Nathaniel Fiennes concerning the Surrender of Bristol; E 64 (12): Fiennes' defence of his actions. Also Warburton, vol ii, pp. 236–44; Bodleian Library: Clarendon Mss. 1738 (3): Slingsby's Narrative.

26. Rushworth, vol v p. 64; Thomason Tracts : E 97 (3): Certain Letters from Sir John Hotham.

27. Rushworth, vol v, p. 275; British Library: Harleian Mss. 164, f. 234; *Commons Journal*, vol iii, p. 138.

28. Gardiner, pp. 161–3; Geoffrey Trease, Portrait of a Cavalier: William Cavendish, First Duke of Newcastle (Macmilan 1979) p. 116.

29. Gardiner, pp. 142–3.

30. Trevor Royle, *The Great Civil War*, p. 259. See also T. Bevis 'The Siege of Crowland Abbey' in *Lincolnshire Life*, vol xxxvi (1997) and Young and Holmes, pp. 106–8, on Cromwell's role in spring 1643.

31. Thomas Carlyle, *Letters of Cromwell*, vol I, p. 141.

32. Thomason Tracts: E 62 (8): Special Passages. Also Bodleian Library: Tanner Mss. lxii, f. 194 and J. West, *Oliver Cromwell and the Battle of Gainsborough* (1992).

33. See Thomason Tracts: E 67 (3): Certain Information, September 1643. This is an account of the royalists' missed opportunity to gain Plymouth, when the governor (Alexander Carew) tried to hand it over but was arrested by his officers.

34. BL: Harleian Mss. 164, f. 233: Bodleian Library Mss: His Highness Prince Rupert's Late Beating Up of the Rebels' Quarters.

35. Clarendon vol vii, p. 192; for Dorchester, Bodleian Library: Tanner Mss. 62, f. 218.

36. Ibid, f. 197; Warburton vol ii p. 280.

37. Bodleian Library: Tanner Ms. 62, f. 97.

38. British Library: Harleian Mss. 164, f. 100b.

39. Sir Philip Warwick, *Memoirs of the Reign of Charles I* (1702).

40. Clarendon, vol iii (1888 edition), p. 144.

41. BL Harleian Mss. 164, f. 100b.

42. *Lords Journal*, vol vi, p. 127.

43. BL Harleian Mss. 164, f. 123; Bodleian Library Tanner Mss. lxxi, f. 168.

44. Adair, *Roundhead General*, p. 103.

45. Thomason Tracts: E 63 (10): A Declaration of the proceedings of the Honourable Committee of the House of Commons at Merchant Taylors' Hall for Raising the People of the Land as One Man under the Command of Sir William Waller; BL Additional Mss. 31,116 f. 66; *Commons Journal*, vol iii, p. 183; *Lords Journal*, vol vi, p. 187.

46. Thomason Tracts E 669 (19), f. 8: A True Relation of the Taking of Bristol; E 255 (16): A True Relation of Colonel Fiennes His Trial, f.6; Warburton, vol ii, pp. 236–54; Publications of the Somerset Record Society, vol xviii, pp. 58, 92–3.

47. *Lords Journal*, vol vi, p. 171; BL Harleian Mss. 165, f. 145.

48. H. Atkin and W. Laughlin, *Gloucester in the Civil War* (Tempus 1992); also BL Additional Mss. 18778 ff. 11–13 on the women's demonstration.

49. Trease, *Portrait of a Cavalier*, pp. 117–18.

50. Thomason Tracts: E 69 (15): A True and Exact Relation of the Marching of the Two Regiments of the Trained Bands of the City of London, by H. Foster.

51. Clarendon, *History of the Rebellion* (1888 edition), vol iii, pp. 195, 222–4.

52. As n. 50; also 'Journal of Prince Rupert's Night Marches' in *EHR*, vol xiii (1898) and 'Prince Rupert's Diary', Wiltshire Record Office: Ms. 413/444; J. Dorney, *A Brief and Exact Relation of the Most Remarkable Passages that happened in the Late Well-Formed (and as valiantly Defended) Siege Laid Before the City of Gloucester*, pub. London 1643.

53. 'Journal of Prince Rupert's Night Marches' and Dorney, op. cit.

54. Gardiner, vol I, p. 204; W. Money, *The First and Second Battles of Newbury and the Siege of Donnington Castle* (1881), passim.

55. George, Lord Digby, *A True and Impartial Relation of the Battle between His Majesty's Army and that of the Rebels near Newbury in Berkshire*, pub. Oxford 1643.

56. Warburton, vol ii, p. 288; 'Rupert's Diary' in Wiltshire Record Office: Ms. 413/444.

57. Digby, *True and Impartial Relation…*; also Thomason Tracts: E 69 (2): A letter from our Headquarters at Reading (Parliamentarian); E 69 (15): Foster, A True Relation… (ditto); E 70)10): A True relation of the late expedition (official Parliamentarian account); Byron's account (Royalist) in Oxford: Clarendon Mss. 1738 and Clarendon's account (ditto) in his History of the Rebellion, book vii, pp. 231–4. Analysis in: W Money, *The First and Second Battles of Newbury and the Siege of Donnington Castle* (1883); Keith Roberts, *First Newbury: The Turning-Point* (London 2007).

58. Gardiner, pp. 224–5.

59. Gardiner, vol iii, p. 40.

60. Bodleian Library: Carte Mss., vol iv, p. 434.

61. See article by Padriag Lenihan on Preston in the *New Dictionary of National Biography* (OUP 2001).

62. Gardiner, vol I, pp. 117–18.

63. Ibid., p. 120.

64. Ibid., p. 122.

65. As n. 63.

66. Ibid., pp. 224–5

Chapter Four

1. *Lords Journal*, vol vi, pp. 242, 294–6; *Commons Journal*, vol iii, p. 269; Thomason Tracts: E 252 (2): Perfect Diurnall, 9–16 October 1643.

2. Adair, pp. 140–41.

3. HMC Reports, Portland Mss., vol I, pp. 163–4; also British Library: Thomason Tracts E 77 (14) A Great Overthrow given to Sir Ralph Hopton's whole Army by Sir William Waller near Farnham; E 77 (15) Mercurius Civicus, 23–30 November 1643.

4. Adair, p. 141.

5. BL Additional Mss. 101, b.64, E. Archer 'A True Relation' p.8; Thomason Tracts E 78 (22): A Narrative; *The Military Memoirs of Colonel John Birch, written by Roe, His Secretary*, ed. J. Webb (Camden Society 1873) p. 4.

6. Thomason Tracts: E 81 (12): John Travers, An Exact and True Relation of the Taking of Arundel Castle by Sir William Waller; E 81 (21): Certain Propositions Made by Sir William Waller at the Surrender of Arundel Castle; E 81 (22): Mercurius Civicus, 4–11 January 1644 and Mercurius Bellicus, 4–1 January 1644; E 252 (10): Perfect Diurnal, 27 November – 4 December 1643; Hopton, *Bellum Civile*, pp,.73–4.

7. British Library Mss. 101, p. 64: E. Archer, A True Relation of the Trained-Bands of Westminster, the Green Auxiliaries of London, and the Yellow Auxiliaries of the Tower Hamlets, under the Command of Sir William Waller, from Monday the 16 of October to Wednesday the 20 of December, 1643; Thomason Tracts E 76 (5): The Soldiers Report concerning Sir William Wallers fight against Basing House; E 77: *Mercurius Aulicus*, 12–19 November and *Mercurius Britannicus*, 20 October – 7 November and 12–19 November; Gardiner, pp. 229–31.

8. Manchester alleged in late 1644 that Cromwell was hostile to the nobility 'per se' and looked forward to them losing their titles. See also *Reliquiae Baxterianae* for confirmation from a sympathetic observer that Cromwell favoured idealistically motivated men from lower social class in his promotions.

9. Thomason Tracts: E 69 (13): A True Relation from Hull; E 51 (11): Hull's Mismanaging of the Kingdoms Cause; E 70 (7): Certain Information.

10. *Lords Journal*, vol vi, pp. 255–6; British Library: Thomason Tracts: E 74 (1): The True Informer. HMC Rawdon Manuscripts, vol vi, p. 105; Young and Holmes, pp. 155–7; R Brammer, Winceby and the Battle (Boston 1994).

11. Thomason Tracts: E 51 (11): Hull's Mismanaging the Kingdom's Cause; E 74 (1): The True Informer.

12. Thomason Tracts: E 71 (22): A True Relation of the Victories; Gardiner, p. 242.

13. BL Harleian Mss. 165, f. 280b; *Lords Journal*, vol vi, p. 404.

14. Harleian Mss. 165, f. 233b; BL Additional Mss. 18779, f. 21.

15. Thomason Tracts: E 79 (27): A Narrative of the Disease and Death of John Pym.

16. Thomason Tracts: E 79 (16): Certain Considerations to dissuade men from the further Gathering of Churches.

17. Baillie, vol ii, p. 111.

18. Thomason Tracts: E 31 (17): Certain Considerations; Baillie, vol ii, p. 135.

19. *Commons Journal*, vol iii, pp. 384, 392, 504; *Lords Journal*, vol v, p. 405; BL Harleian Mss. 166, f. 64; BL Additional Mss. 18779, f.59 and 31,116, f. 113 (Whitacre's Diary); Harleian Mss. 166, ff. 9, 14.

20. *Commons Journal*, vol iii, p. 392.

21. As n. 16.

22. Thomason Tracts : E 80 (7): The Apologetical Narration.

23. Gardiner, pp. 268–9 and 275.

24. Gardiner, pp. 290–2.

25. 'R.W.', Bloody Tenet of Persecution, printed in Haller, *Tracts on Liberty*, vol iii, pp. 105–73.

26 Thomason Tracts: E 30 (6): His Majesty's Speech delivered at Oxford; HMC Rawdon Manuscripts, pp. 117–19.

27. Warburton, vol I, pp. 368, 370; Thomason Tracts: E 32 (12): The Scottish Dove.

28. Gardiner, pp. 273–4.

29. Ibid., pp. 272–3.

30. Burnet, pp. 251–69.

31. Thomason Tracts: E 31 (10): The True Informer; C. S. Terry, *The Life and Campaigns of Alexander Leslie*, Earl of Leven (London 1899), pp. 181–211. Also Trease, p. 126.

32. Ibid., pp. 126–8.

33. Thomason Tracts: E 79 (23): The Parliament Scout.

34. Thomason Tracts: E 30 (7): Mercurius Civicus; E 141 (13): Magnalia Dei; Rushworth, vol v, p. 303.

35. Gardiner, p. 316.

36. Rushworth, vol v, p. 566.

37. Bodleian Library: Clarendon State Papers, vol ii, p. 165.

38. *Lords Journal*, vol vi, p. 411.

39. Gardiner, p. 316.

40. Thomason Tracts: E 38 (10): His Highness Prince Rupert's Raising of the Siege of Newark.

41. BL Harleian Mss. 166, f. 33; Additional Mss. 17677R, f. 246; *Commons Journal*, vol iii, p. 428; *Lords Journal*, vol vi, p. 419.

42. *Commons Journal*, iii, p. 39.

43. Gardiner, pp. 319–20.

44. British Library: Thomason Tracts: E 39 (24): The True Informer.

45. Hopton, *Bellum Civile*, pp. 100–103; Thomason Tracts: E 40 (1): A Fuller Relation of the Victory Obtained at Alsford, 28 March, by the Parliaments Forces (Parliamentarian); E 43 (24): The True Informer, 23–30 March; Hopton, *Bellum Civile*, pp. 100–103 (Royalist); HMC Portland Mss. no.3, pp. 106–10; analysis in Adair, *Roundhead General*, chapter 20.

46. *Lords Journal*, vol vi, p. 25.

47. Ibid.

48. BL Harleian Mss. 166, f. 56; *Commons Journal*, vol iii, p. 455.

49. Thomason Tracts: E 42 (19): A true relation of the proceedings of Captain Laugharne; E 46 (4): The Kingdoms Weekly Intelligencer.

50. Trease, pp. 127–8.

51. BL Thomason Tracts: E 252 (32): Perfect Diurnall, 6–13 May 1644.

52. Ibid., E 47 (8): A Particular Relation; E 47 (19): The Kingdoms Weekly Intelligencer.

53. Gardiner, p. 344.

54. Ibid.

55. Clarendon, *History of the Great Rebellion*, book viii p. 26.

56. C. V. Wedgwood, *The King's War, 1641–7*, p. 310.

57. BL Harleian Mss. 378, f.6; 166, ff.63, 65, 66 (letters by Waller to Speaker Lenthall).

58. Thomason Tracts: E 39 (2): Mercurius Aulicus, mid-April 1644; Napier, Memorials of Montrose, vol ii, p. 389.

59. BL Additional Mss. 18,981 f. 185.

60. Thomason Tracts: E 2 (20): An exact Diarie, by R. Coe; BL Harleian Mss. 166, f. 84.

61. BL Additional Mss. 17,677R f. 321.

62. BL Harleian Mss. 166, f. 84.

63. Ibid f. 86; *Lords Journal*, vol vi, p. 16.

64. *Commons Journal*, vol iii, p. 528.
65. *Commons Journal*, vol iii, p. 328; National Archives: Committee of Both Kingdoms: Letter Book, 12 June 1644.
66. Ibid., 14 June 1644 (Essex to the Committee of Both Kingdoms).
67. Commons Journal, vol iii, p. 542.
68. Thomason Tracts: E 51 (15): A full relation of the siege of Lyme.
69. Rushworth, vol v, p. 684.
70. Thomason Tracts: E 51 (15): A full relation of the siege of Lyme; E 51 (9): A Letter from the Earl of Warwick; Bayly, The Civil War in Dorset, pp. 147 ff: print of Edward Drake's 'Diary' of the siege.
71. Warburton, vol ii, pp. 418–19.
72. HMC Ninth Report, vol ii, p. 436.
73. As n. 71.
74. National Archives: Committee of Both Kingdoms, Day Book, entries for 23 and 24 June 1644; Committee of Both Kingdoms Letter Book, 23 June 1644 (Committee to the county committee, Hertfordshire).
75. National Archives: Committee of Both Kingdoms: Letter Book, letters of 25, 27 and 28 June 1644 by General Browne to the Committee.
76. Thomason Tracts: E 2 (6): Mercurius Aulicus, 23–9 June 1644 (Parliamentary account); E 53 (18): An Exact and Full Relation of the Last Fight between the Kings Forces and Sir William Waller on 29 June; E 252 (51): Perfect Occurrences, 28 June – 5 July 1644; Warburton, vol ii, p. 472; analysis in Peter Young and M. Toynbee, Cropredy Bridge 1644 (1970), and in Young and Holmes, pp. 185–8.
77. Calendar of State Papers Domestic 1644 pp. 301, 307–57.
78. Gardiner, pp. 365–6.
79. Ibid., p. 326.
80. Thomason Tracts: E 51 (10): The Kingdoms Weekly Intelligencer.
81. Gardiner, pp. 370–71.
82. Ibid., pp. 372–8.
83. Warburton, vol ii, p. 238.
84. Margaret, Duchess of Newcastle, *The Life of the first Duke of Newcastle and Other Writings* (J. M. Dent, 1916), quoted in Trease, pp. 132–3.
85. Gardiner, p. 368.
86. Thomason Tracts: E 2 (1), Ash's 'Intelligence'; E 2 (14): Watson's 'Relation'; E 341 (1), Manifest Truths; E 54 (19): Eglinton's 'Full Relation of the Battle of Marston Moor'; P. C. Newman, The Battle of Marston Moor 2 July 1644: the sources and the site (Chichester, 1981); Peter Young, Marston Moor 1644: The Campaign and the Battle (1967).
87. Trease, pp. 141–2.
88. National Archives: State Papers Domestc, no. diii, p. 56.
89. Gardiner, *History of the Great Civil War*, vol ii, p. 21; Trease, p. 143.
90. Gardiner, pp. 24–5.
91. National Archives: Committee of Both Kingdoms, Letter-Book: 2 July 1644.
92. CSPD 1644–5, pp. 453–69, 476–7.

93. National Archives: Committee of Both Kingdoms, Letter Book, 2 July 1644 letter by Waller to Committee.
94. *Lords Journal*, vol vi, p. 629.
95. BL Additional Mss. 31,116 f. 135.
96. Thomason Tracts: E 4 (120): The Kingdoms Weekly Intelligencer.
97. Gardiner, p. 11.
98. Warburton, vol iii, pp. 9, 16.
99. Rushworth, vol v, p. 701; Thomason Tracts: E 10 (19): Mercurius Aulicus, August 1644; Clarendon, *History of the Great Rebellion*, book vii, pp. 109, 115–16; for analysis, Young and Holmes, pp. 207-11.
100. BL Additional Mss. 5460, f. 325b.
101. CSPD 1644, pp. 501–502.
102. BL Harleian Mss. 126, f. 128; Additional Mss. 31,116 f. 165.
103. Gardiner, pp. 39–40.
104. Ibid.
105. CSPD 1644–5, p. 157.
106. *The Autobiography of Lord Herbert of Chirbury*, ed. Sidney Lee (London 1886) pp. 279–85.
107. Gardiner, pp. 43–5.
108. Thomason Tracts: E 22 (10): Simon Ash, A True Relation of the most chief occurrences at and since the Battell at Newbury until the disjunction of the three armies; *The Quarrel Between the Earl of Manchester and Cromwell*, ed. J. Bruce, Camden Society (1875) pp. 63–4: 'Narrative of the Earl of Manchester's Campaign'. For analysis of the battle, Young and Holmes, pp. 216–21.
109. *Quarrel of Manchester and Cromwell*, pp. 87-9; Thomason Tracts: E 22 (10): Ash, True Relation; National Archives: State Papers Domestic no. diii.56, pp. 4,19, 20, 24–5.
110. National Archives: State Papers Domestic, d iii, 56, p. ix.
111. *Commons Journal*, vol iii, p. 704; BL Additional Mss. 116, f. 175.
112. Wishart, chapters 4 and 5.
113. A Short Abridgement of Britaine's Distemper (Spalding Club, Aberdeen 184) vol ii, pp. 73–4; Wishart, pp. 55–7.
114. Napier, Memorials of Montrose, vol ii, p. 163.
115. Gardiner, p. 142.
116. Wishart, chapter 6; Napier, vol ii pp. 160-70.
117. Wishart, chapter 7; Britaine's Distemper, pp. 91–3.

Chapter Five
1. Gardiner, p. 117.
2. Whitelocke, p. 116.
3. W. C. Abbott, *Letters and Speeches of Oliver Cromwell*, vol I, p. 277.
4. Rushworth, vol v, p.780; BL Harleian Mss. 166, f. 113b; *Commons Journal*, vol iii, pp. 626, 691; *Lords Journal*, vol vii, p. 61.
5. Gardiner, pp. 76–7; and for the iconoclasm by William Dowsing in East Anglia, see John Morrill 'William Dowsing and the administration of iconoclasm in the Puritan Revolution' in Trevor Cooper (ed.), *The Journal of William Dowsing: Iconoclasm in East Anglia during the Civil War* (Woodbridge 2001) pp. 817–19.

6. BL Additional Mss. 31,116 ff. 181b and 186b; *Commons Journal*, vol iii, p. 733, vol iv, p. 12.
7. *The Quarrel of Manchester and Cromwell*, p. 78.
8. *Lords Journal*, vol vii, pp. 73, 76, 79, 80.
9. As note 2.
10. Rushworth, vol vi, p. 4.
11. *Commons Journal*, vol iii, p. 726.
12. *Commons Journal*, vol iv, p. 25.
13. Ludlow, *Memoirs*, p. 116; BL additional Mss. 27962K f. 425b; *Lords Journal*, vol vii, pp. 289–98, 302, 433; *Commons Journal*, vol iv, pp. 169–70, 176; Ian Gentles, *The New Model Army*, p. 11.
14. *Lords Journal*, vol vii, p. 54.
15. Ibid.
16. *Commons Journal*, vl iii, pp. 710, 712.
17. Gentles, p. 99.
18. Rushworth, vol v, p. 747.
19. Ibid., p. 808.
20. *Commons Journal*, vol iv, pp. 12, 13; *Lords Journal*, vol vii, pp. 127–8.
21. Agostini to Doge, 6/16 December 1644: CSPV 1643–7, ed. Allen Hinds.
22. Quoted in Gardiner, pp. 114–15.
23. *Commons Journal*, vol iv, p. 37.
24. By contrast, the civilian 'hard-line' war-party seems to have hoped that the creation of the new army would shock Charles into giving way at Uxbridge. See British Library: Thomason Tracts, E 258/9: 'Perfect Occurrences', 27 December 1644 – 3 January 1645.
25. BL Additional Mss. 5461, f. 65b.
26. Clarendon, *History of the Great Rebellion*, vol viii, p. 245.
27. Rushworth, vol v, pp. 865, 879, 887.
28. Bodleian Library: Clarendon Mss. 1824; see also *English Historical Review*, 1887, p. 341.
29. Rushworth, vol v, pp. 872–3.
30. Clarendon, *History of the Great Rebellion*, book viii, p. 243.
31. *Lords Journal*, vol vii, pp. 191, 222–4, 230–31.
32. C. V. Wedgwood, *The King's War 1641–7*, pp. 410–11.
33. Rushworth, vol v, p. 920.
34. Ibid., p. 922.
35. Wishart, chapter 7.
36. Ibid.; *Britaine's Distemper*, pp. 101–102; Napier, vol ii, pp. 460–88.
37. Gardiner, pp. 171–2.
38. Ibid.
39. Ibid., pp. 158–9.
40. Rushworth, vol v, p. 804.
41. Gardiner, p. 161.
42. Ibid., pp. 162–4.
43. Ibid., p. 166.
44. Ibid., pp. 156–7.

45. Napier, vol ii, p. 484.
46. Gardiner, p. 175.
47. BL Additional Mss. 31,116 f. 196b.
48. National Archives: Committee of Both Kingdoms, Letter Book: Committee to Cromwell, 3 March 1645.
49. Clarendon, *History of the Great Rebellion*, vol ix, pp. 6–7.
50. Ibid.
51. Ibid.
52. Clarendon, vol viii, p. 169; see also Young and Holmes, p. 337.
53. Gardiner, p. 181.
54. Bodleian Library: Clarendon Mss. nos. 1833, 1834, 1842.
55. CSPD 1644–5, p. 229.
56. Thomason Tracts: E 260 (15): The Weekly Postmaster, 8–15 April 1645; E 260 (22): Perfect Passages, 16–23 April 1645.
57. Thomason Tracts: E 276 (3): The Kingdom's Weekly Intelligencer, mid-March 1645; E 277 (8): The Moderate Intelligencer.
58. Thomason Tracts: E 270 (26): Shrewsbury Taken; *Lords Journal*, vol vii, p. 329; analysis in Young and Holmes, pp. 228–9.
59. Gentles, p. 18.
60. BL Harleian Mss. 165, f. 193; Mss. 546, f. 151b; *Lords Journal*, vol vii, pp. 268, 272–7.
61. BL Additional Mss. 25465, f. 33; *Lords Journal*, vol vii, pp. 297–9.
62. Thomason Tracts: E 279 (11): The Kingdoms Weekly Intelligencer, 22–9 April 1645; E 281 (3): An Exact Journal, 24 April – 3 May 1645; E 281 (4): Mercurius Civicus, 24 April–1 May 1645.
63. Gardiner, pp. 200–201.
64. Ibid., p. 203.
65. Ibid., p. 204.
66. BL Additional Mss. 18,982 f. 46.
67. Warburton ii, p. 80.
68. Clarendon, *History of the Great Rebellion*, vol ix, p. 15.
69. Gardiner, pp. 206–207.
70. Thomason Tracts: E 284 (9): Two Letters, the One from Fairfax, the Other from Colonel Ralph Weldon; E 284 (11): A great victory at the raising of the siege from before Taunton; E 285 (10): A Narrative of the Expedition to Taunton.
71. Gardiner, p. 208.
72. Clarendon, vol ix, p. 31.
73. Gardiner, pp. 209–10.
74. *Lords Journal*, vol vii, p. 390; R. Bell (ed.), *Memorials of the Civil War* (London 1849) p. 228.
75. BL Additional Mss. 32,093 f.211.
76. BL Additional Mss. 11,331 ff. 119b and 138.
77. Gardiner p. 214.
78. HMC Reports, vol I, p. 9.
79. Wishart, chapter 9.
80. Wishart, pp. 98–103 and 389–91; *Britaine's Distemper*, pp. 122–6.

81. BL Additional Mss. 18,982 f.61.
82. Gardiner, p. 230.
83. Bodleian Library: Clarendon Mss. 1889.
84. BL Harleian Mss. 166, f.216; *Commons Journal*, vol iv, pp. 163, 169; *Lords Journal*, vol vii, p.411.
85. BL Additional Mss. 18,082 f.64.
86. Quoted in Gardiner, pp. 139–40.
87. Ibid.
88. Thomason Tracts: E 262 (10): Perfect Occurrences; E 288 (21): A Glorious Victory; E 288 (27): Three Letters; E 288 (32): A true relation of a great victory; E 288 (38): A more exact and perfect relation of the great victory in Naseby Field. Also Joshua Sprigg, *Anglia Rediviva*, pp. 32–7 (Parliamentarian); Sir Edward Walker, *Historical Discourses upon Several Occasions* (1702, royalist), p. 130; analysis in Peter Young, *Naseby 1645* (1985) especially chapter 15; Barry Denton, *Naseby Fight* (Partizan Press 1985). For the capture of the King's papers, see R. E. Madicott, 'The King's Cabinet Opened: a case study in pamphlet history' in *Notes and Queries* (1966) nos. 2142–9.
89. *Lords Journal*, vol vii, pp. 441–2.
90. Carte, *Life of Ormonde*, vol v, p. 14.
91. Rushworth, vol vi, p. 118.
92. BL Harleian Mss. 166, f. 220b; *Commons Journal*, vol iv, p. 182.
93. Gardiner, p. 223.
94. Thomason Tracts: E 262 (20): Perfect Occurrences; E 292 (24): The desires and resolutions of the Clubmen.
95. Sprigg, *Anglia Rediviva*, pp. 61–6.
96. Bodleian Library: Clarendon Mss. 1894.
97. Thomason Tracts: E 261 (4): The copie of a letter concerning the Great Battle at Langport; E 292 (28): An exact and perfect relation of the proceedings of the army, and Proceedings of the Army 6–11 July 1645; E 292 (30): A true relation of a victory; E 293 (8): Captain Blackwell: A more exact relation of the great defeat given to Goring's Army in the West; Sprigg, p. 71.
98. Thomason Tracts: E 293 (27): Sir Thomas Fairfax entering Bridgewater; E 293 (32): Three great victories; E 293 (33): The continuation of the proceedings of the army; E 293 (34): A fuller relation from Bridgewater; Sprigg, pp. 68–74.
99. *Britaine's Distemper*, pp. 138–40, 133; Wishart, chapter 9; Baillie's *Letters and Journals*, vol ii, p. 409.
100. BL Additional Mss. 18,982 f. 74.
101. Gardiner, vol ii, pp. 308–309. 102.
102. Gardiner, p. 285.
103. Ibid., p. 286.
104. Carte, *Life of Ormonde*, vol vi, p. 305.
105. Warburton, vol iii, p. 149.
106. Rushworth, vol vi, p. 132.
107. Walker, p. 117.
108. Walker, p. 135; Baillie, vol ii, p. 309.
109. Baillie, vol ii, pp. 420–3; Wishart, pp. 122–5, 402–403.

110. Wishart, chapter xv.

111. Walker, p. 136.

112. Thomason Tracts: E 294 (30): A Fuller Relation of the Taking of Bath.

113. Thomason Tracts: E 296 96): Two great victories; E 296 (7): Two Letters; E 296 (14): The proceedings of the army. Also Sprigg, p. 86.

114. Thomason Tracts: E 297 (3): Sir Thomas Fairfaxe's Letter concerning the Taking of Sherborne Castle.

115. Gardiner, p. 309.

116. Thomason Tracts: E 300)19): Mercurius Civicus, 4–11 September 1645; E 308 (22): Rupert's Declaration; Sprigg, pp. 97–110.

117. Clarendon, *History of the Great Rebellion*, book ix, p. 90.

118. Gardiner, pp. 317–18.

119. Bodleian Library: Carte Mss. lxxxiii, f. 94.

120. *Commons Journal*, vol iv, p. 273.

121. Bodleian Library: Carte Mss. lxxxiii, f.109.

122. Clarendon State Papers, vol ii, p. 188.

123. Clarendon, *History of the Rebellion*, book ix, pp. 74, 81.

124. Thomason Tracts: E 303 (18): The King's forces totally routed; E 303 (24): A Letter from Poyntz.

125. Thomason Tracts: E 308 (14): A True Relation of a Great Victory.

126. Geraint Jenkins, *The Foundations of Modern Wales, 1642–1780* (Oxford UP 1993) p. 18.

127. Jenkins, pp. 18–19.

128. Wishart, chapter xv; *Britaine's Distemper*, p. 150.

129. Bodleian Library: Carte Mss. lxxxiii, f. 101.

130. Commons Journal, vol iv, p. 305.

131. *Lords Journal*, vol vii, p. 638.

132. Gardiner, *History of the Great Civil War*, vol iii, pp. 3–4.

133. Thomason Tracts: E 329 (15): The Lord George Digby's Cabinet.

134. Gardiner, vol iii, p. 7.

135. *Lords Journal*, vol vii, p. 104.

136. Thomason Tracts: E 309 (4): A copy of a Remonstrance.

137. *Commons Journal*, vol iv, p. 362.

138. Ibid., p. 359.

139. Gardiner, vol iii, pp. 13–14, 30–40.

140. Ibid., pp. 16–17.

141. Sprigg, p. 145.

142. Thomason Tracts: E 306 (1): The Taking of Tiverton.

143. Thomason Tracts: E 304 (13): A Diary; Sprigg p. 144.

144. Thomason Tracts: E 305 (3): The Moderate Intelligencer; E 305 (8): The full and last relation; E 305 (10): Mercurius Veridicus; Sprig, pp. 148-9.

145. Gardiner, vol ii, pp. 368–9, 372–3.

146. Thomason Tracts: E 305 (14): A Great Victory; Calendar of the Clarendon State Papers vol I pp. 283–4; Bodleian Library: Clarendon Mss. 1992.

147. Warburton, vol iii, p. 201.

148. Ibid., p. 207; Walker, p. 147; Thomason Tracts: E 307 (14 and 15): Two letters of Colonel Morgan relating the taking of Monmouth.

149. Sprigg, p. 176.

150. Clarendon, *History of the Great Rebellion*, vol ix, p. 141.

151. Sprigg, pp. 179 and 182–96; Thomason Tracts: E 323 (8): A true relation concerning the late fight at Torrington; E 324 (6): A fuller Relation of Sir Thomas Fairfax's routing all the King's Armies in the West... at Torrington; E 325 (2): A more full relation.

152. Thomason Tracts: E 327 (7): A letter sent ... to William Lenthall... concerning Sir Thomas Fairfax's Gallant Proceeding in Cornwall; E 327 (12): The Late Victorious Proceedings of Sir Thomas Fairfax against the Enemy in the West; E 328 (15): A More Full and Exact Relation... of the Several Treaties between Sir Thomas Fairfax and Sir Ralph Hopton; Sprigg, pp. 207–13.

153. *The Diplomatic Correspondence of Jean de Montreuil and the brothers de Bellievre, 1645–8*, ed. J. G. Fotheringham (Edinburgh 1898-9) vol I, pp. 66, 71, 94–9.

154. Clarendon State Papers, vol ii, p. 209.

155. *Lords Journal*, vol vii, pp. 31, 46, 72; Thomason Tracts: E 11 (23): The Diary, 11 December 1645.

156. Carte, *Life of Ormonde*, vol vi, p. 305; Gardiner, vol iii, pp. 33–4.

157. Ibid., pp. 37–8.

158. *Commons Journal*, vol iv, p. 408.

159. Montreuil Correspondence, vol I, pp. 115–16.

160. Gardiner, p. 44.

161. *Lords Journal* vol viii p. 132.

162. Gardiner p. 50.

163. Bodleian Library: Carte Mss. vol xv, ff. 546, 617.

164. Gardiner p. 72.

165. Ibid p. 73.

166. *Commons Journal* vol iv p. 464; *Lords Journal* vol viii pp. 208–9.

167. Clarendon State Papers vol ii p. 226.

168. Gardiner p. 72.

169. Rushworth vol vi, p. 140. Carte, Life of Ormonde vol vi pp. 362–3; Napier, vol ii pp. 274–5; Gardiner p. 97.

Bibliography

Primary sources

Bodleian Library Oxford: Carte Mss.

Clarendon Mss. no. 24.

Tanner Mss. no 60.

British Library: Additional Mss. 18981, 18982, 24465, 25465, 31116.

Harleian Mss.

Sloane Mss.

Thomason Tracts.

Historical Manuscripts Commission: Portland Mss.

House of Commons: Commons Journals, vols 2–5.

House of Lords: Lords Journal, vols 4–6.

National Archives: Committee of Both Kingdoms: Day Book.

National Archives: Committee of Both Kingdoms: Letter Book.

National Archives: Committee of Both Kingdoms: State Papers, vol 16.

Paris: Archives du Ministère des Affaires Etrangères: Correspondence Politique: Angleterre.

Calendar of State Papers Domestic: 1641–3, ed. W Douglas Hamilton (Longmans 1887).

Calendar of State Papers Domestic: 1644, ed. Hamilton (Longmans 1888).

Calendar of State Papers Domestic: 1644–5, ed. Hamilton (Longmans 1890).

Calendar of State Papers Domestic: 1645–7, ed. Hamilton (Longmans 1891).

Calendar of State Papers Venetian: 1640–2, ed. Allen Hinds (HMSO 1924).

Calendar of State Papers Venetian: 1642–3, ed. Allen Hinds (HMSO 1925).

Calendar of State Papers Venetian: 1643–7, ed. Allen Hinds (HMSO 1926).

The English Revolution, vol I: Fast Sermons to Parliament (Cornmarket Press, Oxford 1970).

The English Revolution: Newsbooks, ed. Robin Jeffs (Cornmarket Press Oxford 1971).

The English Revolution: Newsbooks Vol 1: Oxford Royalist vol 1: Mercurius Aulicus, January – August 1643 (1971).

The English Revolution: Newsbooks Vol 2: Oxford Royalist vol 2: Mercurius Aulicus, September – March 1644 (1971).

The English Revolution: Newsbooks Vol 3: Oxford Royalist vol 3: Mercurius Aulicus, April 1644 – March 1645 (1971).

The English Revolution: Newsbooks Vol 4: Oxford Royalist vol 4: Mercurius Aulicus, April – September 1645 (1971); Mercurius Rusticus, May 1643 – March 1644; Mercurius Anti-Britannicus, August 1645; Mercurius Academicus, December 1645 – March 1646.

Letters and Papers of Robert Baillie, ed. D. Laing, 3 vols (Edinburgh 1841–2).

Baxter, Richard *Reliquiae Baxterianae*.

Bruce, J., ed, *The Verney Papers: Notes of Proceedings in the Long Parliament, temp Charles I, from memoranda by Sir Ralph Verney* (Camden Society 1845).

Carte, Thomas, ed., *Collection of Original Papers* (London 1839).

Earl of Clarendon (Edward Hyde), *History of the Great Rebellion*, ed. W. D. Macray (Oxford 1888).

State Papers Collected by the Earl of Clarendon, ed. R. Scope and T. Monkhouse, 3 vols (Oxford 1767–86).

The Writings and Speeches of Oliver Cromwell, ed. W. C. Abbott, vol 1 (Cambridge Massachusetts 1937).

Cooper, Trevor, ed., *The Journal of William Dowsing: Iconoclasm in East Anglia During the English Civil War* (Woodbridge 2001).

The Diary of Sir Simonds D'Ewes, ed. Willson Coates (1942).

The Diary of Sir Simonds D'Ewes, ed. Wallace Notestein (New Haven, US, 1925).

Memorials of the English Civil War: Correspondence of the Fairfax Family, ed. R. Bell, 2 vols (1849).

Gardiner, S. G., ed., *Constitutional Documents of the Puritan Revolution*.

Gilbert, J. N., ed., *History of the Confederate War in Ireland by Richard Bellings*, 7 vols (Paris 1882–91).

P. Gordon of Ruthven, *Short Abridgement of England's Distemper* (Spalding Club, Aberdeen 1842).

Haller, W., ed., *Tracts on Liberty in the Puritan Revolution, 1638–47*, 3 vols (New York 1934).

The Autobiography of Lord Herbert of Cherbury, ed. S. Lee (London 1886).

Hopton, Sir Ralph, *Bellum Civile* (1902 edition).

Memoirs of the Life of Colonel Hutchinson (London 1806).

The English Levellers, ed. Andrew Sharp (Cambridge Texts in the History of Political Thought: Cambridge UP, 1998).

The Memoirs of Major-General Ludlow 1625–1672, ed. C. Firth (Clarendon Press 1894).

The Journal of Sir Samuel Luke, ed. I. G. Philip, 3 vols (Oxfordshire Record Society, 1950–53).

Margaret Cavendish, Duchess of Newcastle, *Memoirs of William, Duke of Newcastle and his Wife Margaret*, ed. Sir C. Firth (London 1907; also the 1913 edition pub. by J. M. Dent).

The Oglander Memoirs: Extracts from the Manuscripts of Sir John Oglander, Knight, ed. W. Long (1888).

Petrie, Sir Charles, ed., *The Letters, Speeches and Proclamations of Charles I* (Cassell 1935).

Memoirs of Prince Rupert and the Cavaliers, ed. Eliot Warburton , 3 vols (London 1849).

Rushworth, J., *Historical Collections*, 8 vols (London 1659–1700).

Spalding Memorialls of the Troubles in Scotland, ed. J. Stuart, 2 vols (Spalding Club Aberdeen 1831–2).

Sprigge, Joshua, *Anglia rediviva… being the history of the … army under Sir Thomas Fairfax, 1647* (reprint Oxford 1849).

Vicars, J., *England's Parliamentary Chronicle*, 3 vols (1643–6): vol 1, *Jehovah-Jireh. God in the Mount*; vol 2, *God's Ark overtopping the World's Waves*; vol 3, *The Burning Bush not consum'd*.

Walker, Sir Edward, *Historical Discourses upon several occasions*, ed. H. Clopton (1705).

Warwick, Sir Philip, *Memoirs of the Reign of Charles I* (1702, reprint Edinburgh 1813).
Webb, J., *Memorials of the civil war... as it affected Herefordshire and the adjacent counties*, ed. T. N. Webb, 2 vols (1879).
Whitelocke, Bulstrode, *Memorials* (Oxford 1853).
Wiltshire Record Office: Mss. 413/444.
Wishart, George, *Memoirs of Montrose* (London 1893).

Secondary sources
Abell, H., *Kent and the Great Civil War* (Ashford 1901).
Adair, John, *Cheriton 1644: The Campaign and the Battle* (Kineton 1973).
Adair, John, *Roundhead General: the Campaigns of Sir William Waller* (Sutton 1997).
Adamson, John, *The Noble Revolt: the Overthrow of Charles I* (Phoenix 2007).
Atkin, H. and W. Loughlin, *Gloucester in the Civil War* (Tempus 1992).
Barrett, John, *Cavalier Generals: King Charles I and his Commanders in the English Civil War 1642–6* (Pen and Sword 2004).
Bayley, A. R., *The Great Civil War in Dorset 1642–1660* (Taunton 1910).
Braddick, M., *God's Fury, England's Fire: A New History of the English Civil Wars* (Allen Lane 2008).
Brailsford, H. N. and C. Hill, *The Levellers and the English Revolution* (Cresset 1961).
Brammer, R., *Winceby and the Battle* (Boston, Lincs, 1994).
Bruce, J. and D. Masson, eds, *The Quarrel between the Earl of Manchester and Oliver Cromwell; An Episode of the English Civil War* (Camden Society, new series, vol 12, 1875).
Broxap, E., *The Great Civil War in Lancashire* (Manchester 1910).
Carpenter, S. D., *Military Leadership in the English Civil War 1642–51* (London 2005).
Carte, Thomas, *The Life of James, Duke of Ormonde* (University of Ireland Press 1851).
Carlton, Charles, *Charles I: The Personal Monarch* (Routledge 1983).
Coate, M., *Cornwall in the Great Civil War and Interregnum 1642–1660* (Truro 1963 edition).
Cressy, David, *England On Edge: Crisis and Revolution, 1640–2* (Oxford 2006).
Cust, Richard, *Charles I: A Political Life* (Longmans 2005).
Cust, Richard and Ann Hughes, *The English Civil War* (London 1997).
Edgar, F. T. R., *Sir Ralph Hopton: The King's Man in the West 1642–53* (Oxford UP 1968).
Farr, D. N., *Major John Lambert 1619–1684* (2003).
Farrow, W., *The Great Civil War in Shropshire* (Shrewsbury 1926).
Firth, C. H., *Cromwell's Army: A History of the English Soldier during the Civil Wars, the Commonwealth and the Protectorate* (Greenhill Books reprint 1992).
Firth C. H., and G. Davies, *The Regimental History of Cromwell's Army*, 2 vols (Oxford 1940).
Fissel, Mark, *The Bishops' Wars: Charles I's Campaigns Against Scotland 1638–40* (Cambridge UP 1994).
Fletcher, Anthony, *The Outbreak of the English Civil War* (Edward Arnold 1981).
Gardiner, S. R., *History of England 1603–42*, 10 vols (1883-4).
Gardiner, S. R., *History of the The Great Civil War* (Windrush Press, 1988 reprint).
Gaunt, Peter, ed., *The English Civil War* (Oxford 2000).
Jenkins, Geraint, *The Foundations of Modern Wales 1642–1780* (Oxford UP 1993).

Gentles, Ian, *The New Model Army in England, Scotland and Ireland 1645–51* (Blackwells 1991).

Gibb, M. A., *The Lord General: A Life of Sir Thomas Fairfax* (Drummond and Co. 1938).

Godwin, G. N., *The Civil War in Hampshire* (Southampton 1882; reprinted by Oxley and co, New Alresford 1951).

Hexter, J., *The Reign of King Pym* (Cambridge, Massachusetts 1941).

Hirst, Derek and Richard Strier, eds, *Writing and Political Engagement in Seventeenth Century England* (Cambridge UP 2000).

Holmes, Clive, *The Eastern Association and the English Civil War* (Cambridge University Press 1974).

Hutton, Ronald, *The Royalist War Effort 1642–6* (Taylor and Francis 1982).

Kishlansky, Mark, *The Rise of the New Model Army* (Cambridge University Press 1979).

Lilly, William, *Life of Charles I* (London 1772).

Lindley, Keith, *Fenland Riots and the English Civil War* (London 1982).

Keith Lindley, *Popular Politics and Religion in Civil War London* (Aldershot 1997).

Malbon, Thomas, *Memorials of the Civil War in Cheshire and the Adjacent Counties*, ed. E. J. Hall (Record Society of Lancashire and Cheshire vol 19, 1887).

McLachlan, Tony, *The Civil War in Wiltshire* (Salisbury 1997).

Memegalo, Florence, *George Goring (1608–57): Caroline Courtier and Royalist General* (Ashgate 2003).

Money, W., *The First and Second Battles of Newbury and the Siege of Donnington Castle, 1643–6* (London 1881).

Morrill, John, *The Revolt of the Provinces* (Allen and Unwin 1976).

Morrill, John, *Reactions to the English Civil War 1642–9* (Macmillan 1982).

Morrill, John, Blair Worden, and Ian Gentles (eds), John Morrill, Soldiers, Writers and Statesmen of the English Civil War John Morrill, (Cambridge UP, 1998).

The New Dictionary of National Biography, ed. C. Mathew (Oxford UP 2001).

Newman, P. C., *The Battle of Marston Moor 2 July 1644: the Sources and the Site* (Chichester 1981).

Pearl, Valerie, *London and the Outbreak of the Puritan Revolution: City Government and National Politics 1625–43* (Oxford 1961).

Reid, Stuart, *Crown, Covenant and Cromwell: The Civil Wars in Scotland, 1639–51* (Pen and Sword 2012).

Richardson, Richard, *The English Civil War: Local Aspects* (Sutton, 1997).

Royle, Trevor, *Civil War; The Wars of Three Kingdoms 1638–60* (2005).

Russell, Conrad, *Unrevolutionary England, 1603–42* (Hambledon Press 1990).

Russell, Conrad, *The Fall of the British Monarchies, 1637–42* (Clarendon Press 1991).

Thomas-Sandford, C., *Sussex in the Great Civil War and the Interregnum 1642–1660* (Chiswick Press 1910).

Snow, W. F., *Essex the Rebel* (Lincoln, Nebraska 1970).

David Stevenson, *The Scottish Revolution 1637–44* (Newton Abbot 1973).

Terry, C. S., *The Life and Campaigns of Alexander Leslie, Earl of Leven* (London 1899).

Trease, Geoffrey, *Portrait of a Cavalier: William Cavendish, First Duke of Newcastle* (Macmillan 1979).

Underdown, David, *Somerset in the Civil War and Interregnum* (David and Charles 1973).

Wanklyn, Malcolm and Frank Jones, *A Military History of the English Civil War, 1642–6: Strategy and Tactics* (Longmans, Harlow 2005).

Wedgwood, C. V., *The King's War, 1641-7* (Collins 1958).

Willis-Bund, J. N., *The Civil War in Worcestershire (1642–6) and the Scottish Invasion of 1651* (Birmingham 1905).

Wood, A. C., *Nottinghamshire in the Civil War* (Oxford 1937).

Young, Peter, *Edgehill 1642: The Campaign and the Battle* (Kineton 1967).

Young, Peter, *Marston Moor 1644: The Campaign and the Battle* (Kineton 1967).

Young, Peter, *Naseby 1645* (Century 1985).

Young, Peter and Richard Holmes, *The English Civil War: A Military History of the Three Civil Wars* (Ware, Herts 2000).

Articles

Bevis, T., 'The Siege of Crowland Abbey' in *Lincolnshire Life*, vol 36 (1997).

Davies, G., 'The Army of the Eastern Association 1644–5' in *EHR*, vol 46 (1931).

Davies, G., 'The Parliamentary Army under the Earl of Essex'. *EHR*, vol 49 (1934) pp. 32–54.

Firth, C. H., 'Two Accounts of the Battle of Marston Moor', *EHR*, vol 18 (1890) pp. 345–52.

Firth, C. H., 'A Memoir of Major-General Thomas Harrison' in *Proceedings of the American Antiquarian Society*, new series vol 8 (1893) pp. 390–464.

Firth, C. H., 'The Siege and Capture of Bristol by the Royalist Forces in 1643' in *Journal of the Army Society for Historical Research*, vol 4 (1925).

Green, E., 'The Siege and Defence of Taunton 1644–5' in *Proceedings of the Somerset Archaeological and Natural History Society*, vol 25 (1879).

Hardacre, P., 'The end of the civil war in Devon: a royalist letter of 1646', *Transactions of the Devon Association*, vol 85 (1953) pp. 95–104.

Malcolm, Joyce, 'A King in Search of Soldiers: Charles I in 1642' in *Historical Journal*, vol 21 (1978) pp. 251–73.

Newman, P. R., 'The Royalist Officer Corps' in *Historical Journal*, 1990.

Notestein, W., 'The Establishment of the Committee of Both Kingdoms' in *American Historical Review*, vol 17 (1911–12).

Prest, J. M., 'The Campaign of Roundway Down' in *The Wiltshire Archaeological and Natural History Magazine*, vol 53 (1949–50).

Young, Peter, 'The battle of Hopton Heath' in *Journal of the Army Society for Historical Research*, vol 32 (1936).

Young, Peter, 'The Royalist Army at the Battle of Roundway Down' in *Journal of the Army Society for Historical Research*, vol 49 (1953).

Young, Peter, ed, 'The Vindicaiton of Richard Atkyns' in ibid, vol 55 (1957).

Index